Prologue

Gibraltar turns his Fire Captain's SUV into the church driveway, pulling beneath the giant United States of America flag hanging from the ladders of two fire trucks. He drives through the crowded parking lot looking for an empty space to park.

After making one slow pass down one row he turns back up the next row and gazed up at the church as he slowly passed by it to the next row. He read Ocean Breeze Apostolic Church.

Gibraltar finally finds a place to park, beyond the lot in the grassy field. He looked down at the piece of paper with the eulogy that Pastor Ross had given him to read off, then stares up at himself in the rearview mirror. ***Why am I doing this? I can't do this!*** He argued in this mind as he opens his vehicle door and steps out.

He slowly makes his way through the parking lot, looking at every car taking it all in, noticing each one of them, what color they are, the type, which ones are older, which ones haven't had a bath in a while. ***Just breath.*** His thoughts continue as he takes a deep breath coming up to the front and walking under the awning where crowds of people all dressed in black talked quietly amongst themselves.

He walks through the front doors into the foyer. "Gibraltar!" He heard his name called out and searches around to find where it came from.

"Oh, McKenzie!" He said back excitedly walking towards the beautiful young woman who had just called him out.

"I'm so sorry for the loss of your colleague." She said timidly giving her condolences as they embrace in a warm hand shake.

"Thank you." He simply nods and continues past her.

Walking into the sanctuary the first thing Gibraltar see's is the casket open up front. He takes off walking down one of the aisles towards it, a surreal, almost out of body feeling as though he was not actually in there.

Several people acknowledge him as he blankly makes his way past them to the casket.

Stepping up to the casket he begins to sob. “I’m so sorry.” He spoke gently reaching into the casket. “It is my fault you are here, I should have never let this happen…please forgive me.” He whispers down to his crew member as though they could still hear him.

Gibraltar after making his apologies quietly went and took his seat, awaiting for them to call him up for the eulogy. After what felt like an eternity he finally hears the pastor call his name to come up to the platform.

He walked up onto the platform and took the mic from the pastor and set the piece of paper on the podium. “Hell…hell…hello everybody.” He stutters out nervously and begins to cry. “I…ah…I’m sorry.” He paused again at the thought that he doesn’t deserve to be the one doing this and starts uncontrollably crying. “I CAN”T DO THIS!” He cries out, sets the mic down and all but runs back out of the sanctuary.

One

Several months earlier;

"Hello Misses Ross. How are you doing?" The young girl said as she walked up to her ex-teacher in the hallway.

"Hi Suzie, I am doing just fine." McKenzie replied as she looks down on her with a big smile showing her excitement of being back in school.

"It's Suzanne now!" She quickly corrected her with a defensive tone.

"I know it's Suzanne, I was your teacher all last year, remember? We always called you Suzie." McKenzie casually stated.

"Well…Suzie is a kid name and I'm in the fifth grade now, so its Suzanne now."

McKenzie gives her a bewildered look. "Yesss Ma'am!" She replied in a strong but polite tone. "I will be sure to let Ms. Jackson know this. She is going to be your teacher this year."

Little Suzie looks up to McKenzie with a (duh look) and a tilt of her head. "I know this, we met her last week at the pre-school year meeting."

"Very good, Misses Jackson is super cool and very nice. You are really going to enjoy her class. Did you have a good Summer?" McKenzie questioned her as she looks down the hallway towards the front doors where the flow of students had seemed to slow.

"Oh…ah…yeah! We had lots of fun, I rode my bike a lot…like everyday a lot, we got to go to the beach several times and went swimming, 'cept when the sharks was in the water, we didn't want to get eaten by them. We…"

Suzie continued to ramble about her Summer as McKenzie stopped listening and noticed the students slowly starting to drift back out of the front doors. "That's really nice Suzie." McKenzie cut her off flatly. "I really need to see what's going on out front. How about we catch up a little later." She said as she looks down on Suzie who is already heading another direction.

McKenzie curiously begins to walk towards the front doors. At the end of the hallway the crowd of students are gathered just outside the doors. She pushes one open and heard the many gasps and surprised sounds from them all. Looking out to the left she saw what has them all in a frenzy.

At the end of the driveway in the drop off zone one of the school buses had crashed into another one of the school buses in the drop off zone. Seeing this McKenzie reacted instantly and started pushing her way through all of the stationary students. After she made her way through the crowd she takes off running to the scene.

At the driveway end on the sidewalk there stood one of the schools hired security officers. The officer was standing there in a frozen panic state, unsure of what she should be doing. “Hey you!!! Go to the back of that bus and help the Students get off!” McKenzie demanded her.

The officer slowly begins to nod her head. “Ok…yea…I think I can do that.” She spoke as though McKenzie’s demand barely snapped her out of her trance.

McKenzie quickly ran to the front doors of the bus that had been hit. She held up her hands to the glass to remove the glare so that she could see inside. The bus driver appeared to be unharmed, being that the other bus crashed more towards the center of the bus, several rows behind the him.

“Open these doors!” McKenzie beats on the windows.

The bus driver shakes his head. “I can’t its jammed.” She read his lips as he attempted the handle again showing her that it would not budge.

"Ugh!" Frustrated she glanced back into the windows trying to see behind the bus driver to further asses the situation, and noticed the students all frantically trying to scurry out of the back of the bus.

McKenzie quickly ran to the back of the bus to help them all off. When she made it to the back of the school bus the security officer has already almost helped them all off.

There was only a few left when one stopped to say. "Help! There is a girl stuck in there. She's trapped in her seat and can't get out!"

In a panic McKenzie rushed the final few students off the bus and scrambled to jump up into the back of the bus. As she was awkwardly crawling into the back of the bus she finally heard the sirens getting closer.

She rushed down the center aisle to the middle of the bus and about five rows behind the driver in the seat closest to the window she see's a young girl. "I heard your stuck?" McKenzie questioned as she gazed down and saw her left leg pinned with the sheet metal siding caved in on it.

The young student with glass all over her from the broken windows started to cry. "Yesss…I cant move my leg at all…and it hurts really badly!"

"What do we do?" The bus driver panicking asked McKenzie as he stepped back to them.

"Well she is really stuck in here, and I believe their going to have to move the other school bus back to get her out. It appears to be wedged against the side still. You may need to stay up in the seat in case the firefighters will need you to try to open the doors again." McKenzie directed the frenzied bus driver. He nods and agreed with her making his way shakily back to the front.

"Hey sweetheart." McKenzie spoke in a calm comforting voice, taking a hold of her right hand. "It's going to be ok. The firefighters should be here any moment and they will get you out of here to get your leg looked at. What's your name honey?"

"Its..." The young girl sniffled and looked up to her with big sad brown eyes. "Its Phathom." She whipped the tears from her face. "Can you tell Misses Ross that I am going to be late for my first day of her fourth grade class."

McKenzie brushes Phathom's coal black hair back out of her face trying to keep from crying herself. "It's quite ok Phathom. I am Miss Ross and I am pleased to meet you. I am truly sorry...it's...it's not in the classroom." She struggles to hold her composure.

"Really!" Phathom's eyes brightened up and she smiled looking up at her teacher. "Your Miss Ross? Your not at all what I imagined you to look like."

Puzzled with half a smirk on her face McKenzie gazed back down on her. "Oh...no really? Why is that? What were you expecting me to look like?" Phathom contorted her face remembering that her leg is still pinned and hurting. McKenzie squeezed her hand a little tighter. "So what did you expect me to look like?"

Phathom looks up to her with a twist of her head showing she is pondering the thought. "Well…really I thought you would be old, but you not and you are really pretty. I've never had a teacher really pretty like you before."

McKenzie's eyes begin to tear up. "Awe…" She started to sob again, catching herself trying to hold it together for Phathom. "Well thank you very much Phathom, that is really sweet of you to say. Do you hear that? The fire trucks just shut off their sirens, which means they should be in here any moment now and we will get you out of here."

Phathom nods. "Okay!" She painfully let out.

There was a loud bang at the front of the bus. "It wont open, it's stuck!" The bus driver yelled again.

McKenzie turns her gaze to the back of the bus staring down the aisle. A guy fully dressed in the fire fighters uniform jumped into the back of the bus, he done so, so gracefully it was as though he glided into the back of the bus. Then without hesitation she watched him walk purposely straight towards them.

McKenzie watched him as he studied and assessed the situation, looking at the whole problem trying to determine the solution. The fire fighter then reached for his radio on his shoulder. “Hey Samuel…got a copy?”

“Here Doc” A voice came back over the radio.

“You all need to get that front door to the bus that has been hit open. Then send Barry in with the Jaw’s of Life. We’re going to need to do some re-arranging in here. Then you and DeAndre need to hook the engine up to the back of the other bus, we are going to need to back it up.” He spoke quickly and efficiently into his radio.

“10-4”

“Ok I’m Captain Crichton.” He returns his focus back to McKenzie and Phathom. “With Miami Dade Fire Department. We are going to get you out of here and to the hospital. So ma’am, if you could go ahead and exit the bus so that we have room to work in here.” The Captain attempted to give his demand politely.

“No!!!” Phathom shouted. “Don’t leave me!”

“Well Captain.” McKenzie spoke with some authority. “This here is Phathom, and she is very scared. Phathom would you be ok with me getting out of this gentleman’s way if I promise to hold your hand from the seat behind you?" Phathom' sniffled and nods in agreement. "So Mr. Fireman I am going to be in the seat behind her out of your way."

Captain Crichton shrugs his shoulder to her and catches a fiery spark in her emerald green eyes. "Ok Phathom, I know it is hurting right now, but your going to have to be a little patient and brave. Which I know wont be a problem from you, you I know are a very brave young lady." He spoke confidence into her.

Phathom gives him a confused look. "How do you know that? You don't know me."

As he dug supplies out of his bag he gazed her in the eyes in attempt to give her some extra bravery. "Because, I can see it in your eyes. You are a very strong willed person. Now we are going to have to get that bus that has decided to park on your left leg moved back out of the way. However there are several things that must be done before hand."

Captain Crichton heard a commotion at the front of the bus so he stood and saw the bus driver struggling with the door handle in attempt to get the front doors open. "I'll be right back Phathom."

"What the heck is the hold up?" He cussed towards the bus driver.

"It's...it's the door...it's jammed." The nervous bus driver stuttered out.

The captain took a step down towards the doors and with one swift kick of his right foot the door swung open. “Barry, there you are. Are you ready to take out a couple of seats?” Barry gave him a smirky grin holding up the Jaw’s of Life.

On his way back down the aisle he called back into his radio. “Hey LT. How is it going on your end? You about to get hooked up?” He asked hopefully so.

“10-4 We almost have it thirty seconds.”

“Ok good deal, its going to take me a little longer. Wait on my mark before you start pulling. Beatrice, Felipe I am going to need you two out front with a gurney and a splint as soon as he starts moving the other bus.” He spoke into his radio as he pulled a tourniquet out of his bag.

“No problem Doc, be there and ready.” Felipe responded over the radio.

“Doc?” Phathom questioned. “I thought you said you was a Captain?”

Doc chuckled at Phathom’s perceptiveness. “Yes, I am Captain Gibraltar. However my crew calls me Doc because of my medical training. Really though it’s a much longer story than that actually, but another time. Right now you are about to feel a lot of pressure on your leg as I tighten this belt, and it is likely to hurt a bit.”

Phathom looks over her shoulder with fear in her eyes at McKenzie. "So" Gibraltar attempts to distract. "Who is the nice lady who decided to stick it out with you Phathom?" He quizzed as he gazed at McKenzie with a slight glimmer in his eyes. Instantly embarrassed at his question he quickly lowered his gaze back on Phathom.

"She's my fourth grade teacher Misses Ross." Phathom claimed enthusiastically. "And she is really pretty!" She added making McKenzie blush.

Gibraltar glanced back towards McKenzie noticing her bashfully keeping her eyes on Phathom. "Yea I noticed." He mentioned without thought.

"Ok Doc." Barry cut in. "I have the front three legs cut. Your going to have to step back for me to get the last one. Gibraltar steps back out of the way allowing Barry to get in with the Jaw's of Life. He quickly clamps down on the final holding leg and shears it off. "Ok she's loose, should move out of the way easily now." Barry claimed as he stepped back out of the way with the large tool in his hands.

Captain Crichton took and lifted the seat up, pushing it over the ones in front of it then knelt down in front of Phathom further assessing the situation. "Ok Phathom, it looks as though your leg should be freed as soon as they moved the other bus back. Its probably going to hurt, but as soon as you are free I am going to get you out of here. It is all going to happen really fast. Now I am going to tighten up the tourniquet."

As he tightened up the belt Phathom's face begin to grimace with pain. "Ok Samuel we're ready here back that bus up." He spoke into his radio.

"10-4"

The bus slowly starts to back off the wall that was holding Phathom's leg captive. As the pressure was raised off her leg she began to scream in agony. "No!!!No!!! Stop it your hurting her." McKenzie demanded.

"We have to get her out of here. Its hurting more now because below her knee has been crushed and all her blood is now trying to flow back into it." About the time he explained this Phathom's leg flopped free.

Gibraltar immediately picks Phathom up and rushed her out of the front of the bus, McKenzie hot on their tail. They step off the bus just as the medics had arrived with the gurney. Gibraltar laid her down on the bed and looked into her pain struck eyes. "Ok now Phathom, you are in good hands. Beatrice and Felipe are the best medic team you could ask for." He looked over to his medic. "Her lower left leg is completely crushed it definitely need a splint."

Phathom begins to panic and looking around. "Miss Ross! Miss Ross!" She cried out.

McKenzie pushed up in between the medics. “I’m right here Phathom. I think you can trust them.” She attempted comforting her.

“Will you go with me?” Phathom cried.

McKenzie placed a hand on Phathom trying to not be in the way of them starting the IV. “Oh honey, I cant I have a class to…”

“That’s bull!” Gibraltar cut her off. “This student here needs you right now way more than any of those others at this moment. You can ride to the hospital with her. I’ll let the principal know this. I am sure they have a substitute around here somewhere for this specific reason.”

McKenzie looks up at him with teary eyes and gives a weak nod. “Your right, Ok Phathom I’ll ride with you to the hospital.” She gave in as they all walked down the sidewalk to the ambulance.

Two

“Apollo! Get your tail over here!” Gibraltar cursed at his four year old Dalmatian fire dog. “You know better than to get too far away from me in these situations.”

Apollo yelped and turns back towards his best friend just as a large beam broke and crashed down in between them, completely engulfed in flames. Gibraltar quickly steps up to the beam trying to determine his next plan of action to get Apollo out.

“Argh! You dumb mut.” He kicked at the beam. “Look at what you have gone and done now, you’ve done went and got yourself trapped.” Apollo gives him a loud whimper.

Gibraltar kicked at the beam several more times to no avail, then looks across the flames to Apollo who is sadly looking back at him, through the same flames. “I’ll be right back.”

“Ruff, ruff.” Apollo barks as Gibraltar runs back out of the door way headed back out to the fire truck. He quickly gets back out to the truck and starts looking through the side compartment for his axe, but does not find it where it was suppose to be, so he begins checking other compartments.

As Gibraltar is looking in the back side of the truck he noticed Alex (the rookie) struggling with the fire hose connections, unable to get it connected to the truck. “Hey rookie! Have you seen my axe?” He yelled out at Alex.

“No I haven’t. Have you checked the front side compart…”

“No you idiot.” Gibraltar cut him off. “I would never have thought about checking where it is suppose to be.” He rudely responds. “That’s exactly why I am asking you.”

Frustrated Gibraltar ran past the back of the truck grabbing a shovel out of its mount as he flew past the rear end of the fire engine headed back into the smoldering apartment complex.

He returned back to the beam that had his dog trapped on the other side of it. “Apollo... whrrrit” He whistles. “Hey boy can you hear me?” Stepping up and gazing around the beam (unable to stay close for long) he hears Apollo give a weakened whine.

Apollo attempted to run up to the beam, but quickly had to back off due to the extreme heat. Gibraltar then caught a glimpse of him through the ever thickening smoke. He pokes at the beam with the shovel, testing it to see if it may move, however it was solidly stuck in place. He took the shovel and wedged it underneath the end of the beam and begins to attempt to pry it loose. He pries a moment , has to back off a moment, and repeats the process several more times each attempt leaving the shovel in the same place. Finally he decides to give it one final go, stepping up he widens his stance gains his balance and pulls with all his might.

“SSSnnaappp!” The shovel broke with not nearly as much force as Gibraltar thought it should have had.

“Arghh!” He cusses himself for being cheap and getting the budget shovel.

He steps back up to the beam gazing into the room searching for Apollo, unable to see anything through the thick smoke.
“Apollo…Apollo…Hey boy can you hear me?” No bark, no whine, no whimper.

Gibraltar steps back up to the beam for one more last survey and noticed that the flames were all to the right side of the room and the wall to the far left side appeared to be untouched, which he thought to be only a simple Sheetrock wall.

With a new idea and plan, Gibraltar takes off, back down the hallway to the next room over. “Kawham!” He kicks the door open easily and runs back through the empty apartment to the adjoining wall of the room that has his best friend trapped.

On the wall there stood a dresser drawer in his way, with an unknown source of power he seems to throw the full and heavy dresser halfway across the room out of his way. With the dresser out of the way Gibraltar begins checking for studs by kicking softly at the Sheetrock wall.

Once Gibraltar had determined where the studs were he begins kicking the wall as fast and as hard as he can with his size eleven and a half boot. Smoke starts billowing out of the hole immediately as he continued to kick until he had a hole that he feels is wide enough for him to fit his broad shoulders through.

Satisfied finally that he will fit through the hole Gibraltar starts shimmying his way through. “Apollo!” He calls out as he gets to his feet. “Apollo, you crazy mut where are you?” He called some more as he shuffles his feet around the room trying to feel for his dog unable to see a thing.

When he finally checked the furthest corner from the flames he felt Apollo laying there (Not moving or conscious). He reaches down and takes his dog in his arms, then heads towards his newly made passage way, first he places Apollo through, then he shimmies himself back through.

As Gibraltar wedged himself back through the hole he knocked his helmet off on the other side of the wall. The helmet being the last thing on his mind he scooped up Apollo and ran them both back out of the complex as fast as he could.

When they reached the back of the fire engine Gibraltar checked Apollo’s pulse and found a weakened one. He takes off a mask from the oxygen bottle and awkwardly held it over his dogs face then turns the bottle all the way up to flush out the carbon monoxide. He knelt down and gently laid Apollo to the ground holding the mask to his face (being made for humans it wou stay otherwise).

"Apollo…hey buddy…" He patted him on his cheek. "Come on you have to be ok…please…wake up." About the time he said this Apollo slowly started to open his eyes. "Ahh…ok." Gibraltar sighs with relief. "Your going to be alright Apollo, man you really did give me a good scare this time."

"Hey Doc." A voice statics over his radio. "I really could use a hand over on the west side of the complex. We have a very frantic lady over here claiming her mother is trapped inside the complex. I couldn't understand much else before she fainted on me. Also I need you to check on our water situation, what's taking so long to get our hoses on. Over!"

"10-4 Barry." He leans over the back corner of the truck looking down the side and noticed Alex in the same position struggling to get the hose connected.

Gibraltar rushed down the side of the truck, grabbing the hose and almost knocking over Alex in the process. Almost as quick as Gibraltar took the hose he had it slid into place with ease.

As soon as the rookie see's him connect it he reached for the valve. "Whoa!!!Whoa!!!Whoa…What the heck are you doing rookie!" He yelled out stopping Alex from pulling the lever. "We have told you this over and over, never turn the water on without clearance. DeAndre you have a grasp on the hose? We have water about to head your way." Gibraltar spoke urgently into his radio.

"10-4 give it to me. About dang time!" DeAndre ungratefully replied.

Gibraltar looked over to Alex and nods for him to go ahead and turn the water on. He quickly turns the lever releasing the flow of water bringing the hose to life. "Ok now rookie! Watch Apollo for me and make sure he don't follow me." He demanded Alex as he takes off running around the complex.

Gibraltar rounds the corner of the building and turns his gaze to DeAndre who has the hose spraying towards the flaming complex. DeAndre catches a glimpse of him and points over to a small crowd. He gives his colleague a thumbs up and slightly shifts his direction.

Gibraltar gets over to the crowd just as Barry breaks an inhalant to run under the fainted ladies nose bringing her back to consciousness. "Ma'am, you say you know someone in the building?" Barry blurted out as he sits her up.

"Uhh…umm…" She shakes her head and blinks a couple of times, trying to remember where she was. "Ugh…" She muttered again. "Oh no, my mother!" She cries out.

"Ok ma'am, your going to have to take a breath. Which apartment does your mother stay in?" He attempts to calm her down.

"Umm…she's in…" She sniffles a little more. "She's in two-eleven." She claimed as she lifts her arm pointing towards a second floor window next to where the flames seem to be primarily located.

"Ok two eleven? You sure?" Gibraltar urges her on, then takes off before she is able to completely nod her head.

He runs over to DeAndre. "DeAndre! Hey we have confirmation on someone in that second floor apartment, focus your spray on the apartment next to it. Hey Samuel." Gibraltar calls on his radio. "Hey LT! Come in!" He attempts to call his lieutenant once more, with no response. "Hey Barbie." He now attempts to call his 911 dispatch.

"Hey baby, I really thought you was going to go through this whole event without speaking to me. What can I do for you?" She questions him in a playful way.

"Yea…real quick. Do you have the blue prints of this place pulled up?" Gibraltar Speaks to her looking at the side of the apartment complex contemplating his next step to take.

"Of course I do. You should know me better than that by now." Barbara claimed with great confidence.

"Ok good, I'm on the Westside of the complex and the entrance is completely engulfed in flames and I need to get to an apartment on this side." He quickly explained the situation to dispatch.

"Ok doll, go back to the front entrance and I will guide you back through to that side. The whole building is connected." She tells him and he does not hesitate in the least bit.

As Gibraltar is running back towards the front he calls back to his Sergeant. "Barry, I did not make it to the final three apartments over here on the first floor. If you could, would you get a check on them when you are done over here?"

"Ok Doc, take your next left." Barbie guides him through his radio as he runs through the first floor hallway.

Running full speed down the hallway Gibraltar slows down barely enough to make a fast turn around the corner. "Kawhaam!" He collides with Samuel. "Clank." His axe and Samuel both fall to the floor as though he ran into a brick wall.

"Hey I've been looking for this." Gibraltar complained as he picked up his axe. "You really are going to have to get your own axe. Where the heck have you been? Why aren't you answering your radio?" He quizzed as he continues to move down the hallway.

"Sorry my radio is dead. I was..."

“Whatever!” Gibraltar cuts his off. “I really don’t care, tell your excuses to someone who really gives a rats. Come on.” He says waving his hand for Samuel to pick up the pace. “We have an elderly possibly trapped near the flames!” He yells back as he now is running in front of his Lieutenant.

“There is a stairwell to the end of this hallway. It will take you just three doors down from the apartment you are looking for.” Barbie gives him some more guidance.

“10-4 Barbie, you’re a doll.” Gibraltar replied back as he pulls his mask up over his face so that he can breath easier in the thickening smoke.

At the door to the stairwell he quickly shoots it with his infrared thermometer. “Eighty-eight degree’s” He claims. “It’s clear come on Samuel.” They both get to the second floor door together and he again shoots the door. “Three hundred twenty degree’s.” He calls out the temp. “We cant go through this one.” He curses at the thought.

“Hey!” Samuel doesn’t hesitate. “Ask Barbie if there is an apartment above two-eleven we can go into?”

Gibraltar (Johnny-on-the-spot) asked the question. “Yea honey there is. It’s three-eleven.” The dispatch responds to the question.

“Yea.” Gibraltar nods his head and followed Samuel quickly up to the next floor.

Samuel reaches this door first and shoots it with his thermometer. “Eighty-four degree’s, ok its clear lets go.” He pushes his way through the door.

“Hey LT. What’s the plan?” Gibraltar questioned as they stroll down the hallway.

“That’s simple, we go out the window of this one and in the one below us.” Samuel replied as though he thought his Captain should have known the answer.

“Heh…yea simple.” Gibraltar whispers to himself.

“Ok here we are three-eleven, eighty-two degree’s” He tempted the door. “Ok its clear lets go.” Gibraltar says as he takes his axe and swings it upside down hitting the door in between the door handle and the door jam, the door fly’s open.

Captain Crichton and his Lieutenant rush through the doorway where the tenants to the apartment are both sitting on the couch with headsets over their ears and video game controllers in their hands, simultaneously they looked at the fire fighters with a bewildered gaze.

“Miami Dade Fire Department!” Gibraltar said loudly as they pushed their headsets off their ears. “You two really need to get out of here.”

They both jump up frantically and the woman attempts to run back into the apartment when Samuel holds out an arm and cuts her off. “Did you not hear him? You need to leave now, the building is going up in flames and in mere moments all the exits will be blocked off."

"But I need to get…" She starts in.

"Ma'am, are there any pets or other people in the apartment?" He quickly asked.

"Well…ugh…no but." He turns her towards the front door. "Well but, no buts, leave now!" Samuel dutifully demands as her male companion grabs her arm and guides her out the door.

Gibraltar and Samuel both get back on track and go over to the window. Samuel slides it open and shoves the screen out. "Oh goody, drain pipes." He states as he looks out to the side of the window and without hesitation jumps out onto them. He slides his way down to the next apartment as Gibraltar watches him glide down n the pipes with ease.

Gibraltar stares down at his LT as he rips the screen off and smashes the window to the second floor apartment. "Ohha…come on Samuel! Do you always have to make this monkey business look so easy?" He started off yelling then lowered his tone realizing Samuel could no longer hear him.

Gibraltar eases his way to standing in the window seal and placed his left boot on the drain pipe slides it up and down realizing that he wont have any traction on it. "Great I'm going to have to leverage my weight to counter balance my way down." He speaks to himself out loud.

He takes a hold of the pipe with his left hand and simply puts trust into his training and steps out balancing himself onto the pipes and awkwardly makes his way down to the next floor window.

Once outside the window to room two-eleven he found himself very thankful he had Samuel to go first and bust it out before he made it there. He reached over, grabbed the window frame and stepped over into the window in a much easier fashion than he had envisioned.

“Hey Doc.” Samuel started talking to him as he picked himself up to his feet and gathered his wits from the climb down. “Mrs. Wilkens does not walk well, so you can forget her playing Spiderwoman and scaling down the drain pipe and the fire is right outside her only exit.” Samuel explained the situation as he had assessed it waiting on Gibraltar to climb down.

Gibraltar turns his gaze over to the elderly lady, seeing her frightened eyes and noticed how frail she looked. He turns around and looks out the window, at nothing in deep thought. “Ok.” He said turning around reaching for his radio. “Barry you got a copy?” He calls into it.

“I’m here Doc. Just finished clearing out the first floor. Watcha need?” Barry calls back to him.

“Ok perfect, Barry go get the catch blanket, Alex and come over to the West side of the building. Felipe, Beatrice, DeAndre you all getting this? We need all hands on deck I don’t think Sarg. and the rookie can catch us by themselves" Gibraltar calls for his whole team into his radio and quickly gets a response from them all.

"Ok Mrs. Wilkens, I'm Captain Crichton with Miami Dade Fire Department." He knelt down beside her sitting in her chair. "We are going to get you out of here, it will however be in kind of an un-orthodox manor. So I am going to need you to put a little faith and trust in us. Can you do that?" He softly speaks to her and she reluctantly nods her head.

He gets back to his feet and goes over to the window and looks down at his whole team gathering underneath them with the catch blanket. "Ok ma'am" He takes her by the hand and guides her over to the window. "Samuel, I am going to fall with her in my lap. I need you to make sure our feet clear so that we don't get thrown into an unwarranted flip.

"Ok Station Thirteen." He looks down at his crew already exactly where they needed to be. He gives them a thumbs up and turns to Samuel handing him his axe. "On the count of three. "He sits in the window seal and takes Mrs. Wilkens in his arms. "Are you ready?" She gives him a nervous nod. "Ok" He knows she is really not nor never will be, but they have to get through this. "Here we go, one…" He starts the countdown. "Two…three…" They both fall smoothly out of the window and onto the blanket.

Three

Phathom's face brightens up as she sees her teacher walk through the door to her hospital room, both arms full of things. "Hi Phathom, How are you?"

The excitement in her eyes quickly diminished as McKenzie asked the question. "They cut my foot off!" She cried out sadly as she pulls her blanket back revealing a bandaged numb just below her left knee.

"I know." Tears begin to wail up in McKenzie's eyes. "But hey! I have been talking with some of the Nurse's and Doctor's, they promise me that you have one of the best amputee specialist in the world. They say he is going to build you a new state of the arc foot that he promises will be better than your other one." She attempts to cheer them both up.

"Yea but…I want my foot back." Phathom pouts.

"So…have your parents been able to see you much?" McKenzie changes the subject.

“My mom…ugh…she has been calling me all the time. I keep telling her that I am ok, but you know moms, they worry too much. She keeps telling me that’s her job. Their suppose to come see me when Dad gets off work this evening. Its hard on her always having to watch my four younger brother and sisters by herself, ya know.”

“Wow.” McKenzie relieved talking about her family has shifted her mood, slightly. “You have four siblings?” She remarks with a shocked look on her face.

Phathom giggles at her surprised look. “Yea, three sisters and one brother, Duncan he’s the youngest…Well Denise and him are twins, they just turned one last month. Then there is Kelly, she’s four years old and Savannah, she’s seven.”

The shocked look in McKenzie’s eyes becomes very real and vibrant as Phathom explained all of this to her. “Oh my…you all are a big, I bet very fun family.”

Phathom gave her a bewildered gaze as she shrugged her shoulders. “Yea I guess…well some of the times, when Kelly and Savannah don’t be getting on my nerves, that is.”

“Yea.” McKenzie laughs at her. “I understand, I have a younger brother and sister. They used to get on my nerves all the time also.”

This put a smile on Phathom's face. "Really? You have younger…siblings. (Is that how you say it?)" McKenzie smiles and nods back. "You said they used to get on your nerves. They don't anymore? How did you get them to stop?" She curiously questioned.

"Well." McKenzie stands. "We grew up to be friends that help one another out." She walked over to the counter where she had placed all the stuff she had brought in. "Arthur and Chloe, boy were they annoying when we were kids. I always stayed mad at them." She grabs a bag with books and turns back around.

"So they don't make you mad anymore?" Phathom asked her as she started placing the books on a rolling table.

When McKenzie was placing them on the table she noticed a bright pink tablet of sorts. "Well Phathom, we all still upset each other from time to time, for sure because we are all human and make mistakes. However we have all learned to love and support each other instead of annoying one another. What is this?" McKenzie picks up the tablet.

"Oh, that's a tablet with a book and a game on it. Captain Gibraltar brought it to me. He said I get to be the first guinea pig for this idea he has."

She looks to Phathom puzzled. "That's the fire captain who rescued you off the bus? He came by to see you?" She nods her head with a big grin. “Well I hope he was nicer to you than he was when he got you off the bus. He was kind of a jerk then.”

“Ugh…” Phathom drops her jaw. “No he’s not! He is really nice, in fact he told me he was going to bring his Dalmatian, Apollo to see me…he’s a fire fighting dog!”

McKenzie walks back to the counter placing the tablet behind the things she had brought thinking to herself. ***Ugh, a dog! I cant believe he’s going to distract her with his dog.***

“Ok Phathom.” McKenzie takes a deep breath and turns back around with her school laptop in her hand sitting it on the rolling table next to her books, then pushes the table over to her. “I have been talking with all the Nurse’s and staff here, like I said I have it all set up to where it will be like you wont miss another day of class, plus I will be coming by after school every day to see you and work with you on the days lessons.”

McKenzie turned back around and grabbed another box with more school supplies. She takes it over and pulls all the contents out, placing them on the table then opens the laptop. “I have set up several cameras in our classroom, plus you will be logged into the rest of the classes laptops. You will be able to watch the whole classroom from many different angles.” Phathom sincerely attempted to share her teacher’s enthusiasm, but then her expression saddens. “What’s the matter Phathom?” She questions with empathy.

“Well Miss Ross…it’s really just not the same. I want to be there, with my classmates and friends in the classroom.” Phathom pouted.

McKenzie places her hand on her shoulder giving her a half grin. “I know Phathom.” She speaks softly. “And I promise…as soon as you can be, you will be. The doctors want to make sure that you get the best results from the prosthesis, so that’s why they want to keep you here for several more weeks. It will all be over with before you know it and you will be in the classroom. And I will be with you every step of the way. Actually I have it set up to where if you need me or just someone to talk to (day or night) anytime you can just hit this button on your laptop, and video chat with me.”

McKenzie spends the next hour or so showing Phathom how to work the laptop, all her different subjects, and textbooks. They was disturbed three times in total, twice by a nurse and once by a case worker, who was very helpful and eager to get her started in classes. “Ok Phathom…”

Ms. Ross is interrupted by a knock at the door. When the door flew open Apollo runs through the door followed by Gibraltar who suspiciously shuts the door behind himself.

Apollo runs straight for Phathom’s bed, placing his front paws up on the bed and begins to lick her face. She begins flailing and giggling at the same time petting Apollo. “Apollo!” She squeals excitedly. “Its so nice to finally meet you.” She claims pushing him back down off of her face.

Gibraltar looked over at McKenzie. “Hello Misses school teacher. How are you?”

She sighs and continues to pack her things. “It’s Miss Mac…I mean Miss Ross.” She corrected herself dryly, glancing back at Captain Crichton noticing he is now wearing a T-shirt and skinny jeans instead of the fireman’s outfit she seen him in the first time. The shirt and ball cap both have the badge MDFD tagged on them.

“Sir!” A custodian from the front desk pushes his way through the door and walks into the room. “I know you heard me calling you, and you seen me trying to signal you to hold the elevator. Dogs are not allowed in here. You can not have your dog in here.” The custodian points over at Apollo who is oblivious to everything around him except Phathom.

“Ok then…what about firefighters?” Gibraltar argues forcing a puzzled look from the custodian. “Fire fighters, are they allowed in here?” He asked the question a bit more sternly.

“Just because you are a fire fighter it does not make you above the rules sir. You can not have a dog in here.” The custodian held his ground.

“I’m not talking about me, I am talking about my dog, Apollo! He is also a firefighter, badge and all…Besides look at how happy that little girl is seeing him. She just lost her leg in the war." Phathom shoots Gibraltar a surprised look while he winks at her. "Show the man Phathom." He asked playfully. Phathom raises her blanket bank revealing the bandaged stub on her left leg.

"Ok…" The custodian gives him a somber stare. "Fine then, just keep your dog on a leash when you are leaving and don't tell anyone I said so." Said the custodian on his way back out of the door closing it behind him.

"See there Phathom, if you ever have any trouble, or if someone is giving you heck, you just tell em you lost your leg in the war. It'll work every time."

"Ughh!!!" McKenzie steps forward. "No Phathom… you cant do that…that is lying…you cant do that it will only cause trouble."

Phathom gives her a slight frown from her hospital bed while petting Apollo. "But it got Apollo able to stay and visit." She complained.

Oh yeah Phathom." Gibraltar steps up in between them. "Look at what I found for you." He hands her a stuffed pirates doll. "Arghh ye der matey, shiver me timbers." He made an attempt to mimic a pirate. "His peg leg is on the right foot though."

Phathom wails out in laughter at him about this. "You remembered me telling you that my uncle who works on a boat and always acts like a pirate. My uncle does a much better, RRR dere cap'n." Phathom took her shot at mimicking a pirates voice.

McKenzie crosses her arms and shifts an angry gaze over to Gibraltar. He raises and tilts both hands and begins moving his lips (what?) without the sound actually coming out of his mouth. "Phathom do you have any more questions about your…"

"Hey." Gibraltar cuts her off. "What's this doing hidden way over here?" He holds up the bright pink tablet.

"Ugh…argh!!!Captain…Doc…" McKenzie says flustered. "Fireman…sir whoever you are, can we speak outside for a moment?"

He shrugs and looks over to Phathom raising his eyebrows giving her an (I'm-in-trouble-now) look. "I guess…so if Phathom thinks she can watch Apollo a minute for me." Phathom nods and Gibraltar follows McKenzie out the door. "Its just Gibraltar…You can call me Gibraltar." He said solemnly as he followed her out the door.

McKenzie turns towards him, directing him behind the door keeping herself in view of Phathom and Apollo. With the door cracked and Phathom's attention focused on Apollo she gazed straight on Gibraltar with a seriously stern eye. "Now Captain Crichton!" She starts in. "I do not know what kind of games you are used to playing down at the fire house, but this is a very real matter here. Phathom has just lost her foot and is going to have to learn how to live with that."

He nods. "Um…yeah I know this, I kinda was the one who pulled her off the bus remember? And I'm only trying to cheer her up."

"With a pirate doll!" McKenzie snaps back. "That's like making fun of her only having one leg. This is no joking matter Ger…I mean Captain Crichton. What are you doing here anyways? It cant be common practice for the Fire Captain to visit people in the hospital.

Non-chalantly he shrugs his shoulders again. "Well it might be more common than you think. I definitely didn't intend on seeing you here though. It is quite the added bonus." He gazed strongly into her eyes as she rolls them, growling and growning, more and more frustrated with him. "But its definitely not often I get to save a fourth grader from a crash and then help with the recovery also."

"Ugh! Your not helping her recovery, your playing games with her. Distracting her from the real world." She glanced back to Phathom making sure she isn't paying attention to her frustration.

"We all need a break from the real world every now and then." Gibraltar makes an argument. "Especially you." He mumbled instantly regretting so.

"Ugh!" McKenzie flails her arms to her sides, then turns around then back to face him with a hard stare. "Ok, well I have her set now where she will be able to start her classes, and she does not need any distractions. She needs to focus on her school work and learning about her prosthesis. So you need to take your gaming tablet thingy with you, she has what she needs to do all her school work and I think it would probably be best if you and Apollo limited your visits." She speaks at him with a demanding tone. "Or maybe go find a burning house to run into instead of visiting at all." She added resentfully.

"Ok." Gibraltar simply nods un-phased by anything she has really just griped about.

He really didn't just hear a word I just said, did he? She asked herself, then gives him a frustrated nod with her head.

"So Miss Ross…is it? What are you doing Friday evening?" He asked optimistically and he notices her hesitate and ponder this question.

"That is none…"

He cuts her back off. "Would you like to go have a drink maybe?"

"I don't drink!" She states without thinking.

"Ok, how about a coffee then. Surely you like some sort of coffee, or tea maybe?" He persistently pushes.

"Captain Crichton I will…Ugh!" She said as she flailed her arms again and storms back into Phathom's hospital room.

He follows her in closely. "I guess that's a no?" He mentions as she gathers her things without responding to him.

"Phathom." McKenzie turns her focus back to her student. "Did you have anymore questions for me?" She asked throwing her purse over her shoulder.

"Nope." Phathom looks up from Apollo and shakes her head. "Not that I can think of."

"Ok, well remember if you need me you can call. I will be calling you before class in the morning and we'll get you set up to be in class with us."

"Okie dokie." Phathom nods as McKenzie leaves her room.

Gibraltar walks over and plops down in the chair beside Phathom's bed. "You know she thinks you're a jerk?" Phathom says naturally.

He leans back in the chair and stares up at the ceiling in a daze. "Yea I know, but I think she likes me anyways." He looks over to Phathom who just smiles and shrugs.

Four

The lunch bell sounds. “Ok Chil…” McKenzie catches herself, she had made a promise to herself that this year she would call her children students, instead of children. “Ok students lunch time, we’ll go over chapter three in your Social Studies book when we return.”

The whole classroom stood simultaneously and flooded out of the room. “Ok Phathom.” She looks into her laptop monitor. We’ll see you after lunch, don’t eat too much Jell-O now!”

“Ugh…” Phathom rolls her eyes on the screen. “When I get out of here, I’m never going to eat Jell-O again.”

McKenzie laughs at her comment. “Ok, we shall see about that!” She stands up from her desk and walks toward the door and props it open.

Standing in the doorway watching the mass of students trickle down the hall, she looks across and saw her friend and colleague Jemma standing in the doorway of her classroom. “JJ!” She calls over the students in a loud but not yelling tone. “I am so glad we made it to lunch, I am starved.”

The majority of the flow of students has passed when they both step out the same and start walking side by side down the hallway in the opposite direction of the students.

"For once I am actually not." JJ responds with a glimmer in her eyes. "In fact I believe my Lean Cuisine might actually fill me up today." She claims cheerfully.

"Mr. Laudermann, Mr. O'connell." McKenzie greets the other teachers with a nod of her head passing by them in the hallway.

"I'm really glad they took the later lunch this year." McKenzie speaks in a lower tone as they get out of ear shot. "I'm always so hungry by lunch time. So what has you all chipper today? Did you see Mark this morning?"

"No." Jemma shakes her head. "Actually I had a date with Jonas last night."

"Jonas?" McKenzie said sternly stopping her stride in the middle of the hall. "JJ, who is that?"

Her friend stops a couple steps ahead of her and turned back around to face her. "He's a mechanic at the dealership where I bought my car. I was getting my oil changed last week when he asked me out."

McKenzie starts back walking towards their break room. "Oh." She said solemnly.

"Yea I know, seems kinda dirty and gross, a greasy mechanic...but really he cleaned up very nicely." They walked into the break room together.

In the break room there are several teachers already sitting around a big table in the middle. To one side there are three different vending machines, and the other side has a couple of refrigerators, countertops, cabinets, and several microwaves. At the very end of the room there is two tables one in each corner.

McKenzie and JJ both walk over to the fridge and retrieve their lunches. McKenzie takes hers straight to their corner table, while JJ stops by the microwave plopping her lunch into it pressing the number two for two minutes.

JJ doesn't wait on her meal before she walks over and stands at their table. "Cold Mickey D's French fries!" She picks one up off the flattened fast food bag where McKenzie had just dumped them. "Ughh…gross." She gags as she chews it up.

"You really need to dip them in mustard." McKenzie claims as she squirts a glob of mustard on the bag.

"Umm…no thank you." JJ tremors at the sound of the mustard bottle. "I'm good, so what super sized meal are you eating today?" She cautiously questions. "A Big Smack?" JJ screws up her face and gives her friend a curt shake of her head. "That is so gross, I don't know how you eat a cold super sized meal everyday and stay looking like that. When I have ate these diet T.V. dinners everyday for two years and can't loose a pound.

Especially with that huge sugary soda, does your soda not get all watered down?" She asked as she takes a drink.

"Nah, I get it without the ice. It does get kinda flat though."

"Kinda!" Jemma smacks her lips. "That is totally flat, why don't you just get a bottle?"

"Bottles don't come with the meals." McKenzie explains, as JJ walks off to retrieve her meal from the microwave.

She returns to their table with a steaming tray. "Ugh…" She shakes her head. "I still can't believe you and your cold fast food."

McKenzie shrugs non-chalantly as she dips her burger into the mustard. "Ou ete old issa or akfest?" She mumbles out holding her hand up not realizing how full her mouth was.

"Huh?" Jemma crunches her brow.

McKenzie takes a drink of her soda holding a finger up as she washes the bite down. "You eat cold pizza for breakfast, right?"

"No." She shakes her head with a shrewed face. "I have tried it, and I often hear of people doing so, but I prefer my pizza hot and melty."

McKenzie shrugs her shoulders. "So…this Jonas? Does Mark know you was going on a date with him?"

“Ow…ouch.” Jemma fingers off the plastic film from her steaming T.V. dinner. “You know that Mark and I are just friends…”

McKenzie stops her friend there. “So that’s a no.”

JJ tilts her head with an empathetic look in her eyes. “McKenzie come on, your not being fair. You know how I feel about Mark.” She says as she takes a bite of her meal, having to suck in extra air to cool it off.

“Your right, I do know how you feel, and I don’t think its fair to Mark you keep doing this. You do this too often and he always gets hurt. And you always end up feeling bad.”

JJ nods in agreement with her bestie. “But you know Mark can’t do it for me…I mean he’s a good friend and he has always been there for me, but I still just don’t feel fulfilled with him. Now I’m getting old enough I am ready to find the one to settle down with the rest of my life. And Jonas…well I don’t know he just really feels right. He was so nice and polite and the perfect gentleman. After our date we went to my apartment…”

“What!!!” McKenzie said in a louder tone than she meant, checking over to make sure other teachers aren’t paying any attention. “You don’t even know him.” She leaned over the table and whispered with shock written all over her face.

"He was really sweet and we seem to talk so well and understand each other perfectly. I'd say you should understand, but your misses uptight and I think you enjoy living life alone and frustrated. Besides Jonas is a good man, I can feel it. He may actually be the one. He is Cuban though, so convincing my moms Puerto Rican side of the family may take a bit of work, but other than that I am sure he is the perfect one. Any who that's enough badgering about my love life. What about yours? I mean when was the last time you even went on a date? What was it six months ago? And then God knows how long before that." Jemma takes a long pull from her water bottle.

"Well first of all, I am not uptight!"

Jemma swallows her water bobbing her head back and forth at McKenzie's defensive statement. "Sure your not." She claims.

"And you know there just isn't anyone right at the church right now, and I have faith that God will bring along the right one at the right time. I just have to be patient."

"See." Jemma sigh's. "Not just uptight, but also way too busy living in your family's shadow to actually get out and enjoy yourself." She somberly stated.

"Hey! Its not my family's shadow. Its my Holy Spirits shadow I follow in. The spirit filled journey is way more than just following a family tree, its about following God's path for my life." McKenzie explains as she dips the last bit of her Big Smack into the mustard. "And besides for your information." She takes the topic away from another religious argument. "I had a guy ask me out on a date yesterday."

JJ perks up with a shocked look all over her face, staring straight at McKenzie shoving the last bite into her mouth which was slightly larger than a bite. "Ohh! Really!" She was curious. "So I'm guessing you said no…or well at least that you'll have to think about it, or you would have said that you had a date coming up. So who was it? Anybody I know?"

McKenzie shrugs taking a little extra time to chew up the huge bite before taking a drink to wash it down. "Do you remember the Fire Captain that helped rescue Phathom from the crashed bus the first day of school?"

"No." JJ shakes her head. "There was a lot going on that day, it was quite frantic."

"Yea." McKenzie agreed. "It was, but anyways he brought his dog to visit Phathom at the hospital yesterday and he asked me what I was doing Friday."

Jemma pushed her half ate diet dinner slightly forward indicating she was finished. "So…a Fire Captain…ouah! That sounds hott, well maybe unless he's old. Which I am guessing, most of them are. He's not old is he?" Her friend has her full attention.

“No he’s not that old…well I mean he’s a few years older than us, but he’s far from an older man. However it doesn’t matter he’s an idiot anyways. He had the audacity to ask me out while I was griping at him because he brought a stuffed pirates doll with a peg leg…I mean what kind of moron brings a doll with a peg leg to a young girl who just lost a foot?”

Jemma burst out into laughter getting the attention of several other teachers in the room. “See (uptight).” She leaned over and whispered. “I think that’s kinda cute, and even more so that you got to show him that you are uptight right out of the gate, so there won’t be any surprises later on. So is he cute?”

A dazed look comes across McKenzie’s face as she stares past her friend. “He is! You think he’s cute, and you told him no. To do what on Friday eat a tub of ice cream and watch Big Bang Theory re-runs on T.V.” She calls her out.

“Hey! I didn’t say I thought he is cute, and besides Phathom just lost a foot, its not some game to play around about. Are you done?” She points to Jemma’s lunch.

“So he’s ugly then?”

McKenzie takes her friends forks and takes a bite. “Ugh.” She gags. “That’s awful, I don’t know how you can eat those everyday.” She claims as she struggled to swallow the bite.

“Yea the Alfredo isn’t as good as the others, the red sauce seems to microwave better…So he’s ugly then?” She reiterates drawling out the last word.

“No!” McKenzie snaps back. “He’s definitely not ugly, besides it don’t matter. I’ll probably never see him again anyways, I kinda told him that it would probably be best that he didn’t come around distracting Phathom anymore from her school work.” McKenzie caught herself wondering if she wasn’t really more worried about him distracting her now.

“Well maybe he wont listen to you, and he will try again. I really think you should take him up on the offer next time, if there is a next time.” Jemma challenges her. “I mean he’s a Fire Captain over a fire station, he cant be that bad of a guy. At least go out with him once and see where it might go. Heck who knows maybe he is that really great guy who just lives on the outside of the box that you have always lived in, and he is just waiting on the right one to slightly step outside the box to bring him back into the box.”

McKenzie’s gaze shot past Jemma again, really contemplating the revelation her friend just gave her. “No! There is now way. Not even a remote chance, he seemed way to stubborn to not even be childish, and I know there probably isn’t even a slight chance he would probably be caught in the church, so it’s still a double no!”

"Yea…yea…Misses uptight." JJ said with a quirky tilt of her head as she stands up putting her trash onto McKenzie's flattened fast food bag, crumbling it all together.

"Argh!" McKenzie grumbles under her breath as JJ walks off with their trash. "I'm not uptight!"

Five

"KaWham!" Gibraltar slammed the drivers side door to his SUV. "Can you believe that moron Marshall Spector has the audacity to make us Captains do his capacity checks!" He complains as his Lieutenant gets into the passenger side of his vehicle.

"Well…he is the Fire Marshall, isn't that kind of their job? To tell us fire fighters what to do?" Samuel responds wryly, to his friends whining.

"No!" Gibraltar looked over at his friend with a bewildered gaze. "Not hardly Samuel, its their job to make sure the community and public follow fire codes, to make our job easier and safer. Not to pawn his work off on us. That dirt bag, like I don't have anything better to do…ahh!!!" He pounds on his steering wheel a couple of times before pushing the ignition starting the SUV.

"Ok so, you have to do a few capacity checks, or counts, or whatever it is. No big deal, not like it's the end of the world." Samuel partially defends the Marshall's decision.

Gibraltar slams the SUV into reverse and backed out of the parking space. "So What! Now your going to take his side? Its at least an extra three to four hours a week (maybe way more) just driving around to different places. Then who knows how much time the paper work is going to take each week. Arhh!!! That sorry son of a 'Hooonkkk!!!'" He blew his horn at a little elderly lady who backs out in front of him, causing him to have to slam on his brakes. "If he is having trouble finding time to do his own job then he should hire an assistant, not expect us to do it for him."

Samuel reaches over and turns the radio up. "Ok, so your mad someone in a higher position than yourself is delegating you some of his work. Isn't that what you do to me all the time? Do you think I should be mad at you?"

Gibraltar glanced over at his LT as he waits on traffic to pull out onto the road, rolls his eyes reaching and turning the radio back off. "You should probably be mad at me, but not for delegating my work to you. Your my Lieutenant that's what I am suppose to do." They pull out onto the highway. "Sure he does rank higher than me in a sense, but he isn't suppose to be able to make me do his job for him." Gibraltar continues to whine as he is loosing ground.

Samuel turns the radio back on. "If it bothers you that much, you should just file a complaint on it."

Static comes over the radio. "Station Thirteen this is Barbie at dispatch. We have a chest pain complaint at one-fifteen West Patterson, requesting immediate medical assistance, over."

"10-4" Gibraltar reached for his radio as he looked at his map on the dash showing him he is only five minutes away from the address. "Ok doll, this is Doc, LT and I was just on our way back from our town meeting. We are actually only a few blocks out. Anything else to go with the chest pains?" He makes a quick right hand turn at the same time turning on his lights and siren.

"No sweetie, that was all I got. She said she was going to call their daughter and hung up on me."

"10-4. Beatrice, Felipe, you two get all that? Meet us there with the wagon."

A short moment of silence before Felipe came over the radio. “10-4 Doc, on our way fifteen minutes out, see you there.”

Gibraltar glanced over at his LIeutenant. “You know what? Your right I am just going to have you do the capacity checks.” He said in defiance.

“Yea whatever.” Samuel yawns. “Hey Doc, so I’m thinking I am just going to sit this one out. I’m beat Sam kept me up till midnight on the phone last night. Every since I put that ring on her finger last week she has been driving me insane with all these questions and pictures of dresses, venues, cakes, hors d’oeuvres. Do you know how many different ways they can turn shrimp into a snack?”

“Yea, yea.” Gibraltar cuts him off. “Spare me all the shrimpy details, and no of course you cant sit this one out.” He demands politely.

“Come on Doc! You have this one, besides Beatrice and Felipe will be here shortly. Did I tell you after keeping me up all night? She sent me over a hundred pictures of different table cloths, then calls me not thirty seconds after she sent them at three a.m. this morning to ask me if I had a chance to look at them all.” Samuel continued building his argument to take a nap in the truck.

“Oh! Boo hoo, isn’t that how you say it? I’m sorry about your bad…”

“Come on bro.” Samuel stops him short. “I need to talk to someone, I mean I don’t know what I am going to do. I’m keeping up now…barely, but if she keeps me going like this before we are married and living together, I'm not sure I will be able to keep up after the fact."

Gibraltar turns the SUV down West Patterson. "Ooahh! I'm sure you will figure it out. However I am sorry, I cant let you sit this one out. You know that if something was to happen you would never forgive yourself for sitting out. We both know and understand this will most likely be a routine check up, but you can never be 100% on something going South."

Samuel nods his head and sighs in agreement with this thought in mind. "Whoa…whoa…right there." He points as his Captain fly's past the house. "One-fifteen West Patterson."

Gibraltar slams on his brakes, once stopped fully he puts the vehicle into reverse and using his review mirror and back up camera drives in reverse back to the house. He pulled his SUV up over the curb half in the yard and half in the street leaving the driveway for the ambulance. At almost exactly the same time he puts the vehicle in park and hits the button opening the back lift gate, then kills the engine.

Together Gibraltar and Samuel jump out fluently and effectively. Gibraltar runs around the back, grabs his medical bag and takes off running passing Samuel, and getting to the front door just before his lieutenant does.

“Miami Dade Fire Department!” Gibraltar raps on the door. “We received a 911 call, someone is experiencing chest pains at this address.” He knocks loudly again.

“Oh good.” The door swings open wide. “Your here, hurry its my Lenny he’s having a heart attack and he’s going to die. I don’t want him to die.” The barely five foot tall lady, that doesn’t weigh a hundred pounds, with short curly blue hair claims as she grabs Gibraltar by the arm. “Follow me.” She’s guides him through the small living room, that has the T.V. playing mid-day soap operas.

They step into the hallway. “Honey, who’s that at the door.” A voice called back from in the house.

“Lenny, it’s the medics.” She yelled as she looked back at Gibraltar. “You are the medics, right?” She added the question, realizing she had just assumed so before.

“Beaula!” Lenny grumbled as they walk into the bedroom, where he was sitting on the edge of the bed. “I told you not to call them. My leg just fell asleep, I am so sorry gentlemen she has made y’all waste a trip on me, but everything is fine here.” He stated non-chalantly in attempt to show them off.

“So your not having chest pains?” Samuel asked.

“Chest pains! Oh Lord no, is that what my Beaula told you. She really gets into a frenzy from time to time. My right leg was asleep, I fell and had a difficult time getting back up onto the bed. Which from the floor at my age of seventy-five is difficult enough with both legs wide awake.” Lenny explains the whole situation as he views it.

Gibraltar nods understandingly so, looking at the older gentleman sitting on the edge of his bed. “So you never said anything about chest pains?” He questioned

Beaula stepped up to the other side of Lenny. “He has been complaining of being weak, and he’s always short of breath now when he mows the lawn, and I always know’d when your right leg is numb that means your having a heart attack. That’s why I told the nice lady on the phone he was having chest pains.” She states with the utmost concern.

“Beaula, honey! Uhh!” Lenny sighed. “I’ve told you this before, its your left arm. Your left arm goes numb when your having a heart attack! Gentlemen I assure you two, other than getting old and unable to do as quickly and efficiently as I used to be able to do, I am quite healthy. Sorry to be a bother.”

Beaula steps in between her husband and Gibraltar looking up to him in the eyes. “He’s no Doctor, but neither am I. So what is it, your right leg or your left arm goes numb when your having a heart attack?”

Gibraltar sits his bag on the edge of the bed easing past her. "Since I am here anyways, would you mind if I at least check your vitals? Just to be sure…Mr. Lenny…umm sorry I didn't get your last name."

Lenny crunches his eyebrows giving Gibraltar and Samuel stern looks. "If I tell you my last name are you going to charge me for coming by here?"

Gibraltar sits on the edge of the bed next to Lenny. "Ok, so it is fairly common that a person experiencing a heart attack will have numbness in their left arm." Lenny shoots Beaula an I-told-you-so look. "However when we are talking about the heart messing up, a person can experience any number of pains or numbness anywhere in the body, or nothing at all. But at a glance here Lenny I am sure you are ok and that you have had a sleeping leg once or twice to know that's what it was. I am here however and I am sure they will be charging you whether I check your vitals or not, simply because your wife dialed 911. Your insurance company should cover the cost if you don't need to go to the hospital. So for everyone's sake can I please check your vitals? It wont take but a couple of minutes."

Lenny gives him a slight very reluctant nod of the head. "Its Hotchkins." He grumbles.

"Well its good to meet you Mr. Hotchkins. Sorry its under these circumstances." Gibraltar attempted to empathize with him.

He pulls out the blood pressure cuff and a pulse ox device, placing one on the finger and the other on his upper arm. “Five minutes out.” They hear over their radios.

“I’ll go meet them at the door and show them where we’re at.” Samuel responds eagerly already tired of being there.

Gibraltar holds his hand up halting him. “Lets hold off.” He calls back on his radio. “10-4, you two can hold in the driveway. Transport may not be necessary…over.”

Gibraltar places the stethoscope into his ears and continues to check Lenny’s vitals signs. “Ok one thirty-four over seventy-six, with a pulse of eighty-four, and oxygen is ninety-six. Well I’d say your blood pressure is way better than mine after having to ride around with Samuel for a while.” He jabs at his friend, earnestly. “And you have the vitals of a very healthy person. Is your leg still asleep?”

“No.” Lenny shakes his head. “That went away before y’all got here.”

“Ok, so you can stand?”

Lenny nods and slowly rises to his feet.

“Ok, you say you feel fine. I’m not seeing anything that concerns me or that says otherwise. Would you like us to take you to the hospital in the ambulance?” Gibraltar questioned knowing the answer.

Lenny looks at him angrily. “What! No way, so you can charge me thousands of dollars for nothing. You just said I was fine and healthy.”

Gibraltar smiles at him. “Your right, I just have to ask. I don’t see a need for you to go to the hospital and rack up a bunch of medical bills…”

“Ughh!” Beaula interrupts them. “What about his weakness and shortness of breath?”

Gibraltar turns to look at her. “Well Mrs. Hotchkins, at his age I do suggest normal check ups with your primary care doctor.”

“But I cant get him to go to the Doctor.” She snaps back.

“Ok Lenny, You definitely should make sure to keep your routine check ups. They are cheaper than the hospital bills if something was to happen. A lot of times the Doctors can catch and keep things from happening. And ma’am, he is right, these are a couple of very unfortunate side effects to getting older.” Gibraltar gives them both a lecture explaining things they should do.

“Lenny you are definitely not having a heart attack right this moment, but as I was saying a little bit of blood work from your Doctor may prevent you from having one next week. So…go see your…Doctor.” He tells Lenny sternly as though the demand was him telling a teenager to do something. Gibraltar returns the items from his bag back into it and removes his latex gloves.

“Thank you gentlemen and like I’ve already said I’m sorry to make y’all come out for no reason.” He apologizes again.

“Non-sense Mr. Hotchkins.” Samuel chimes in. “You was no bother at all. You was able to learn something, and we were just talking about how bored we was, with too much time on our hands, needing something to do.” He looks over to Gibraltar. “Right Doc?” He adds slapping his friend on the shoulders as they turn to exit.

Six

“Phathom!” McKenzie knocks and enters into the hospital room. “I have come baring gifts.”

“Aha!” The balding man (a couple inches shorter than McKenzie’s five foot seven inch stature) wearing a lab coat spoke spunky. “You must be Phathom’s mother?”

McKenzie sits her bags on the counter. “No, I’m Her teacher Miss Ross. I brought her, her homework.”

The Doctor looks at the tray in her hand with puzzlement. “Oh! That looks more like an ice cream sundae to me. I wish some of my homework would have looked that tasty. I am Dr. Tolbert and I was really hoping you was her mother. We were just discussing some of our next steps and it’s usually a bit better with an adult present.”

McKenzie sets the ice cream sundae on Phathom’s table and wheels it over to her. “Her you go Phathom a change from that Jell-O.” Phathom smiles appreciatively with big eyes. “That’s good…Dr. Tolbert you said?” He nods. “Well her parents did sign a release of information and put me on the list to be disclosed information. Since I have been with her so much they thought it might be helpful. It should be in her chart, McKenzie Ross is my name.”

Doctor Tolbert makes a couple quick swipes on his tablet. “Aha! Very good, yep there you are, very good. So as I was just explaining to Phathom here, I am Doctor Tolbert. I am an amputee and prosthetic specialist, with added doctorates in robotics.”

“Look at this.” Phathom hands her a single page brochure with a picture on it. “This is what my new foot is going to look like.” She claims. “Well, sort of…the underneath the skin part of it.” She adds.

“Wow!” McKenzie remarked with big eyes staring at the brochure. “It looks like a robotic human skeleton.” She made this comment, legitimately surprised.

“O yes! This is amazing!” The Doctor speaks highly of his work.

“Doctor Tolbert says I’m going to be able to run faster, and jump higher than all the boys with my new foot he is building for me.” Phathom attempts to shove a big spoonful of the sundae into her mouth leaning over the cup so the excess doesn’t fall onto her shirt.

“Oh yeah, that’s great.” McKenzie said wryly placing a hand on her shoulder thinking. ***What is it with these men and their making this a game.***

“Well.” The good Doctor gives a chuckle. “Lets not get ahead of ourselves now Phathom. We are going to have to start off walking first, and it’s a long ways from there to running, much less running a marathon.”

Ok good, maybe he is realistic after all.

“But, however you are right.” Doctor Tolbert walks to the opposing side of the bed where he can better face McKenzie without leaving Phathom out. “I am very excited and optimistic with your situation. For one the schools insurance company has already said they want you to get the best treatment possible, not only now but for the years to come.”

Oh! Now I see he’s excited about the blank check. McKenzie’s negative thoughts return.

"This means every couple of years we will not only be growing the size with you, but be giving you a more updated version. So one good thing I feel has helped us most, is the fact that I was the one able to do the amputation. I was able to take my time and ensure that we kept some very critical parts. Most often being that amputations are emergency situations, the acting surgeon ends up butchering valuable connections by just millimeters with his scalpel. But being that I was the one here and was the one able to do the amputation I was able to save some very valuable parts, tendons, muscles, and nerves to give us optimum success with the prosthesis."

McKenzie held up her hand pausing the Doctor. "I have a question, kinda a silly one maybe."

He gives her a curious look. "Ok, go on." He urges her, with a wave of his hand.

"So…most leg prosthetics I have ever seen, which I cant say has been more than a couple, then one or two on T.V. but they are usually just a shock in a shoe or in some cases I see runners are running with a curved flat metal bar. Why is it that your attempting to make the whole skeleton?"

Doctor Tolbert's face lights up with an ear to ear smile. "Definitely not a silly question at all." He answers in the most inspiring tone. "So there is a lot of beauty in our skeletal design, or well in God's design of life in general. It is really astonishing, but bones and limbs are my specialty so I choose to speak on them. So every bone, joint, tendon, and muscle God gave us serves a good purpose and in the feet especially so. Since God designed us to be nomadic and our feet and legs are the primary source of movement from one place to another. I truly don't believe that God has this part of our skeletal system wrong. Down to the last bone on our pinky toes, every piece there is built for movement and stability in all directions. Most people don't recognize this or never stop and take time to think this through but our skeletal foot is a remarkable design. It is designed to take the brunt of our weight in straight forward movements heel to toe rocking back and forth perfectly. Now very few people actually walk straight. Most people walk naturally with their feet pointed outward, (well its really not natural, just to them). Now this percentage of people could be higher than seventy-five percent, it may even be as high or higher than ninety percent. Anyways that's not the relevant part to me, just think about it sometimes when you are walking. Are you really walking straight? Or are your feet pointed outward or inward while you walk?"

I've never thought too much about this. McKenzie questions herself.

"So is my robots foot going to make me walk straight?" Phathom asked quizzically, getting a laugh out of the overtly happy Doctor.

"Well with any luck Phathom, it will teach you (unconsciously) how to properly walk (fingers crossed). That's my hope."

“Whoah…whoah…wait a minute.” McKenzie interrupts him. “You don’t know what your doing? Your testing things on her? What if her parents do not want you using their daughter as your guinea pig.”

“No, no, no…” He quickly shakes his head and puts up a calming hand. “I am truly sorry. I did not mean it as though she is going to be some sort of test subject, with any risk. Here the risk are as minimum if not less so than any other normal prosthesis. Her prosthesis will naturally stay in the normal position and spring in all the right places a normal foot would move without the Artificial Intelligence part feeding it directions. The robotics and AI part of it are the new and very exciting part of this prosthesis that several colleagues from all around the world and myself have been working really hard on. And its only new because none of us have had a nine year old patient yet and the results have varied greatly on other patients depending on certain parts that was left on their limbs. Which is why I was glad to do the amputation, I really do feel that we can be extremely optimistic here. If the AI doesn’t perform properly, it wont be the end of the world. We just reprogram it without the AI. And I promise it will work better than any other normal prosthetics. This I feel one hundred percent confident about. However if the AI does do its job like I believe it will, it is going to start out learning her normal walk, just as though she never lost her foot. So if she walked with her foot pointed outward it will allow her to continue doing so. Then the program will teach itself the proper adjustments it needs to make to adjust her walk making such slight adjustments she will not notice them at all. This goes with all her steps, jumps, runs, and any kinds of movements at all, teaching her how to move more fluidly and efficiently. This is a really beautiful opportunity for her and she truly has landed in the right place at the right time."

McKenzie gives the Doctor an almost approving look. "So your telling me her foot is going to have intelligence of its own? What is to keep it from trying to…I don't know…jump ship so-to-speak?"

"Well." The Doctor nods. "That in simple terms is that the AI will be programed to make only very slight adjustments to her movements at a time. It is honestly so much more complicated than it sounds. But most of which would bore you to death."

McKenzie nods her head understanding and thinking about all the long and intricate math he must have done to get to this point, trying to solve all these issues. "Yes I am sure it is. It definitely sounds very interesting and you really seem to know what you are talking about." She turns her gaze to Phathom. "What do you think Phathom?"

She looks up to her teacher swallowing another spoonful of ice cream. "Hmp." She shrugs her shoulders. "He told me he would take pictures of my other foot and reverse and put this…umm…umm…well it's a big long word I cant say, but its suppose to feel like real skin to wrap around the outside of my robots foot. I think that's way cooler than Mr. Peg leg here." She holds up shaking the pirates doll, sending extra emotions through McKenzie's already feeble thoughts.

"Haha." She said none hysterically. "I suppose so, it has to be better then just having a wooden peg for a leg. Huh?"

Doctor Tolbert steps back around the end of the bed. "Here is my card, can you please get this to Phathom's parents and let them know I will be needing to meet with them first thing Monday to get some different consent forms signed. Ok Phathom I will see you soon, and if I had a teacher like Miss Ross here I would keep her around to keep bringing me homework." The chipper Doctor said before walking out of the hospital room. McKenzie half expected to see him jump and click his heels on his way out with his extra zealous personality.

McKenzie looks at Phathom, who now has chocolate and carmel all over her face from the sundae, so she goes over to the sink and turns on the hot water just before grabbing a wash cloth. "So Phathom?" She starts running the wash cloth under the water. "I was thinking since its Friday evening and its no fun spending Friday evenings alone." As she is talking about this she thinks about how its actually the worst feeling in the world spending Friday evenings alone. Then she thinks back to the countless Friday evenings she has spent by herself. "Maybe we can order a pizza and watch a movie? I figured it would give you something different then hospital food." She rings the rag out and turns back around.

"Yea that's what my parents thought to. They're 'posed to bring pizza with all my…siblins and they was 'posed to see if my bestie, Tiffany can come with them." Phathom spoke cheerfully.

McKenzie brings the wash cloth over to Phathom. "That's sweet." McKenzie attempted to hold back her tears and not speak so jealous. "Phathom here, you have stuff all over your face." She hands her the cloth and dries her hands mostly on her skirt and pulls out her phone.

She pulls up her message screen and scrolls down to Jemma's name, then types a new message. {Pizza and a movie 2nite? Send.} "So your family, your bestie, and pizza, sounds like a really fun evening." McKenzie attempts to share her enthusiasm and not sound envious.

"Yea it will be! There 'posed to bring a board game also."

McKenzie gives her a none intentional dry smile, then noticed the bright pink tablet on the table, instantly thinking about what she would have been doing tonight if she hadn't blew Gibraltar off. ***Probably dinner and a movie, no maybe a simple coffee and a walk (no…no way he's that sweet). Knowing his immatureness it'd probably be an arcade with pizza, lots of beer, and video games. BLAH!!!***

“I told him to take his gaming tablet thingy back with him, you have plenty to do.” She gripes as she picks up the tablet.

“Oh no Misses Ross, that’s not a gaming tablet. It’s a book…well it has a game on it to…I guess, but you have to read the book first, or at least some of it. The game you can only play once you’ve read so much of it first. Anyways I am done with it there is only one book on it.” Phathom explains the tablet in attempt to defend Gibraltar.

McKenzie’s phone chimes and she quickly glanced at it. {Can’t…Date with Jonas 2nite…Sorry Raincheck?} More depressed now she roughly shoves her phone back into her skirt pocket.

“So…just one book? And you can’t play the game until you read it? Hmm. What book is it?” She quizzes as she becomes more intrigued.

“Oh!” Phathom brightens up. “It’s a really good book, called The Hatchet by Gary Paulsen. Its about a boy who has to survive in the wilderness when his plane crashes. The game is kinda boring though, its really more like a test with a bunch of questions about the book.” She solemnly adds this last detail.

“OK.” McKenzie placed the tablet in her purse. “When he comes back for it you can tell him I have it and he can text me to get it back.” ***God am I now playing with fire?*** She prays to herself as Phathom nods oblivious to the games going on in McKenzie’s mind.

"I heard the sadness in your voice when I said we couldn't hang out tonight. I'm really sorry Misses Ross." Phathom shows her sympathy to her teacher.

McKenzie places her right palm on Phathom's face holding back her tears. "Don't at all be sorry. I am really happy you are going to be able to spend time with your family and friend. Besides you and I will have plenty of time to spend together." She attempts to give her an authentic grin.

Phathom nods with a smile.

"Ok Phathom, do you have any more questions for me today?"

"No." Phathom shakes her head.

"Ok, don't forget to give Doctor Tolbert's card to your parents and have them call him ASAP. Have fun this evening and I'll talk to you soon." McKenzie gives her a big farewell grabbing her purse and bag heading towards the door.

"Bye Miss Ross, Have a good weekend!"

McKenzie knocks and turns her key, opening the door to her childhood home that also serves as the parsonage for Ocean Breeze Apostolic Church. "Mom…Dad…its McKenzie!" She calls into the house shutting the door behind her. “Are you home?” She steps into the quiet living room.

“Yes I’m here!” She hears her mother call back. “Your dad hasn’t made it back yet, but I’m in the kitchen.”

McKenzie started to walk straight back for the kitchen then decides to take a detour. She walks around the couch and over by the fireplace in the front left corner of the living room. She slowly walks by looking up on the mantle. First there is a picture of her brother Arthur standing at a convention with his fiancé.

Her brother and fiancé have been together for a year and a half, being engaged almost a full year with no wedding date in sight. ***Hmph, typical Arthur never in a hurry for anything.***

Then onto the next picture she looks at her younger sister and her family, who is happily married with two small children. She smiles at how happy they look on the church platform last Christmas.

She then walks down to the last photo, being one of herself standing there all alone. ***God please help me to be happy for my family and not jealous of them.*** She prays her saddened prayer and makes her way back to the kitchen.

“Hey mom, How are you?” McKenzie greets her mother who is unloading the dishwasher.

“Hey McKenzie, is everything ok?” She questioned her daughter somberly.

“Yea, just fine. Why?” She remarks with a puzzled expression, in attempt to act.

“Just asking, I’m not used to seeing any of my children anymore. If its not Sunday, Wednesday, or weekly prayer meeting none of you are ever around.” She scolds her child for not showing up more often.

McKenzie walked over to the coffee maker and pulls out the drawer with small cups of different flavored coffee’s and cappuccinos. “Ohh mommm!!! I’m sorry, I keep telling myself that I am going to start stopping by more often.” She decides on the French vanilla.

“Yea well, at least your not keeping my grand babies away from me like Chloe.”

McKenzie’s spine slightly jerks at this comment as she started the single cup of coffee. “So I was thinking I would have dinner with you and Dad this evening. If that’s ok with you two?” She asked hopefully.

“Oh…McKenzie, you know normally that would be ok. However your father and I have a date with the Duffy’s. Their missionary’s from Israel, they’ve asked us to help coordinate their fundraising efforts and with everything going on over there with Gaza and Iran right now they are in big need.” Her mother explains why she has to give her, her third rejection for this Friday evening. ***God should I just have went out with Gibraltar? What do I do!!!AHHHH!!!!*** Her thoughts scream in her head.

"Oh." McKenzie said selfishly only thinking about how she is going to end up alone, yet again this Friday evening after all. "No big deal." She attempts to snap out of her trance. "That's very interesting, yea they do need all the help and prayers they can get right now." She tries to sound interested.

"I do have some extra tuna salad from lunch today. Its pretty good, you can take it with you."

McKenzie takes her coffee over to the table and has a seat. "Nah, that's ok, I can stop and pick something up."

Her mom goes over to the sink rinsing out a rag before she starts to wipe the counter tops down. "McKenzie I have told you and told you, you really needed to get something more nutritious in your diet. You may feel like your able to get away with it now…but all that fast food isn't good for you. I know I taught you how to cook. Having it your way at your place is much healthier than having it your way their way."

McKenzie chuckled at her moms slogan. "You know mom? If I didn't understand you, that would not have made sense at all."

Her mom chuckles back at her. "Isn't that what not understanding means?"

McKenzie takes a sip of her hot coffee staring right past her cup. “I guess so.” She states in a haze of thought. “You know…” She stops to think about this. “Well actually you don’t know, but it is really difficult making and cooking meals for just myself.”

Her mom stops what she was doing, turned around and leaned against the counter. “What do you mean I don’t know? I have cooked for just myself plenty and still often do for lunch.”

McKenzie sits her cup on the table. “No you don’t understand…I mean you and Dad married straight out of high school.” Her true reason for being frustrated comes out. “You never had to fix dinner for yourself, over and over, day after day, year after year. You went straight from your childhood family, straight to your grown one.” She made that complaint as though it was one long breath.

Her mom sit there leaning against the counter staring at her daughter making sure she was finished before she spoke. “Your right McKenzie.” She starts with that comforting motherly voice. “I don’t know what its like to be a twenty-six year old single having to make dinner for myself every evening. But I do know what it feels like to be alone. Every year when your father goes to Men’s Conference or the occasional trip he makes by himself. That loneliness is a very miserable feeling and I did only teach you how to cook for at least five all the time. But sitting around eating Big Smacks all the time sulking about it just makes it more miserable. Do the math McKenzie its one fifth. Go to the grocery store and try cooking something for yourself. Think of it as therapeutic or at least it will take a few minutes of your time where you don't feel alone."

McKenzie takes another sip of her coffee gaining strength from her moms lecture. "Your right mom…sorry I almost lost it on you." She walks over and they embrace in an affectionate hug.

"You don't have to be sorry. That's what I am here for, you can come by more often if your lonely." They separate and look each other in the eyes for a long moment.

Mom I wish that would help but my loneliness goes way beyond just being around you. She thinks to herself, which her mom knew this but the do not further discuss the situation.

"Highya ladies, wow what did I miss." Her dad walks in, in his blue jeans and boots. He walks over to McKenzie. "Hey McKenzie, its good to see you. Everything ok?" He questions the same as he gives her a hug.

"Yep just fine, I was just on my way to the grocery store." She claimed smiling at her mother.

"Ugh!!!Why cant you take your boots off outside!" Her mother gripes at her father. "I literally just swept and mopped." She shakes her head looking at the trail of dirt he had just made on her clean floor.

Seven

Gibraltar pulled into Station Thirteen's drive. The two large garage bay doors were both open with both main fire engines parked in they're perspective spots. The smaller door where the ambulance is kept remained closed.

Samuel and DeAndre are both in the parking lot shooting hoops on a basketball goal they have mounted in between the two large bay doors.

He pulled over and parks in front of the door that was closed. Samuel runs over to greet him. "The Captain on a mid Saturday morning? Since when did you decide to start joining us like this?" His LT questions him as he climbs out of his SUV, (More a statement than a question).

"Well…I have a little extra paperwork to catch up on this week, plus I made a brunch soup and I thought I would let you all try my strange concoction." He explains to his friend as he is stepping to his back door to remove a large tub from his back seat.

“Did you say Brunch soup?” DeAndre curiously walked over.

“Yea I did.” Gibraltar states turning around looking at his colleague as Samuel shuts the door. “I have been trying to figure out a way to incorporate more pumpkin into my diet, (I feel it is a highly underrated source of nutrition) and as much as I would love to eat pumpkin pie all day long its probably not the best thing for you.”

“Oh…pumpkin pie…I love pumpkin pie.” DeAndre’s mouth waters.

“Anything exciting happen last night?” Gibraltar quizzed as they all head toward the door.

“Nah…really it was a quiet Friday night. We had one fender bender where someone ran a red light. But no injuries…or well at least not until the lawyers get a hold of it, but we didn’t even put a Band-Aid on anyone.” Samuel tells of their big night.

The three of them walk into Station Thirteen through the middle garage door, between engine two and the ambulance. They walk behind the ambulance around further into the spacious garage.

The bottom floor of the station is compiled of a workout room (with an array of equipment), locker rooms, and showers. Upstairs is the living quarters and a couple of offices. In the living quarters there is a kitchen, dining area, and two bunk rooms (one for the ladies with four beds, and the other for the men has eight beds).

The normal live in crew they attempt to run is six, however this crew only has five at the time being. Their normal protocol is a four man crew on the big ladder truck and the two medics for the ambulance. The second smaller engine is only run by an on call crew.

Once they all walk behind the Ambulance sitting quietly in its bay, Gibraltar sticks his head in the gym area and seen Barry on the stair master climbing away. “Hey Barry! I brought you all a brunch soup.” He held the tub up for his Sargent to see.

“Ok sounds good.” He glanced back and gives a thumbs up. “I’m going to be really hungry in…” He looked down to the display screen. “Twenty minutes thirty-two seconds.” He stated as the three of them walk off headed upstairs.

“Man I really don’t know how he does it, or why he runs up those steps for a hour or more straight. He takes upwards to two hundred-fifty to three hundred flights of stairs. There isn’t a skyscraper in the world that tall.” DeAndre said with exhaust in his tone.

“We’ve been playing basketball that long and often play for hours on end. What’s the difference?” Samuel makes an argument as they emerge upstairs.

“Well there is a huge difference.” DeAndre starts his comment off as he imitates a basketball juke around the two of them, taking an imaginary shot in front of the kitchen counter. “We do lots of smack talking in between shots giving us lots of breaks. Sarg. don’t take breaks, pauses, or stop for anything, heck I sometimes wonder if he’s even breathing. He just steps…steps…then steps some more. Then when he finally gets off, he seems to have been starved, going straight for the carbs and skipping all the proteins that most of us go for when we get done working out.”

Gibraltar begins pulling the contents out of the tub placing them on the counter. “I guess he’s more into endurance training than muscle building. Hey why don’t one of you go get Beatrice and Felipe.”

“Get us for what?” Beatrice walks through the kitchen door as he said this.

“Oh…hey Bea, I brought brunch, thought you all might appreciate the extra nutrients today.”

She nods and steps back out the door to go get her partner.

“You know I really wish you would hire another fire fighter for our shift. Do you know how much of a pain it is for just us three to run that huge ladder truck is?” Samuel makes a complaint about having to carry the extra weight.

“Yea…yea…LT I know this and have known this. As I have told you I have been searching, I just haven’t had any good candidates applications come through." Gibraltar checks Samuel, making sure he knows he understands him.

"Que Pasa Doc." Felipe greets his Captain as he walked through the kitchen doors.

"What's up Felipe. How's it going?"

"I'm good." Felipe gave Gibraltar a curt nod. "I guess…well not really…a bit frustrated with this A&P studying. Do you know how difficult it is to memorize every bone, tendon, organ, vein, and artery in the human body? There is so much more to our body's than people might think." Gibraltar gives Felipe an understanding grin as he explains his frustration.

"Of course he does. Why else would we call him Doc?" Samuel gives his two cents sarcastically as his normal self.

"You know I have often wondered this myself. You all calling me Doc makes me feel like I am impersonating a Doctor." He attempts to defend himself from Samuels punch line.

"How many other Fire Captains do you know who took two years of Medical School at Johns Hopkins University?" Barry takes Samuel's side as he walks into the kitchen wiping his face with a hand towel.

"So what is this that you have brought us for brunch." DeAndre said looking over at the stuff on the counter getting impatient with all this talk.

“I have here a pumpkin with beat soup.” Gibraltar removes the lid from the crock pot releasing the steam in a dramatic manner. “I tried a little experiment with beats. Beats are awful, they smell bad and they taste worse, however they are an amazing super food.”

All their faces cringe up, except for Barry’s. “Well I think it sounds amazing.” He comments almost drooling over the food as much, as he was sweating over it.

“That’s a really pretty color.” Beatrice looked in the pot with a sparkle in her eyes. “Remarkable…” She adds dreamy.

“Yea I thought so also.” Gibraltar agreed with her amazement. “I actually feel like it turned out pretty well overall. I also made some cinnamon raisin bread to go with it.”

“I’m sold!” Barry grabs a bowl and steps up between Gibraltar and the pot.

“EWW!!!” Beatrice crunched up her face at the thought of eating Barry’s sweat with her soup. “Your going to get sweat in the pot.”

Barry pauses long enough to whip his brow again before he scoops some of the porridge into his bowl. He grabs a chunk of the bread then goes to walk away, but before he took too many steps he turns around and grabs another chunk of the bread.

“Hey! Save some for me.” DeAndre’s worried he’s going to starve.

“There is plenty. I have two more loaves of the bread in the container.” Gibraltar said as he started to fill bowls and pass around.

“Wow! This is really good.” Barry gives his compliments to the chef shoving the bread into his mouth.

“Yea but you’ll literally eat anything…Sarg…” Samuel remarks at Barry’s huge appetite getting a laugh from the whole crew.

They all spend a few minutes trying the strange concoction out.

“Mmm…” Beatrice’s eyes shine with delight. “This taste really amazing. It’s perfectly creamy and soothing, not too sweet, yet not to savory, but the raisin bread truly sets the dish off…Compliments to the chef…Doc.” She made her remark holding her bowl up in the air as everyone else nod in agreement with their mouths full.

“Yea…yea…everyone, its just Captain to you all. Thank you all and I’m glad you like it, plus it actually has a ton of health benefits in it, so eat up.” He appreciates all their compliments while trying to encourage them to eat healthier. “I’m going to leave it here for you all to work on the next day or two.” They all show him extra appreciation. “Ok now I am going to be in my office the next couple hours trying to sort through all this new paperwork I have been thrown into. If anyone needs me for any reason that’s where I’ll be.” He lets his crew know he is there for them as he walked out of the kitchen area, followed closely by Samuel.

“So does this you having to do capacity checks mean you are going to be bringing us food more often?” Samuel questions rhetorically, following him down the hallway hitting a sore spot.

Gibraltar stops and turns to look at his friend strangely and chuckles while he shakes his head before turning back around to walk through his office door.

Gibraltar’s office is modestly spacious with the back wall being a floor to ceiling window that his large desk is centered off of. The glass wall behind his chair looks out over the garage portion of the station, looking down on both fire engines and the ambulance.

One of the front corners of the office has a love seat, two chairs set around a coffee table, and an end table in the corner with a lamp. The opposing corner has a floor to ceiling bookshelf, so full of books that several stacks of books lay in front of the others without a slot to be placed into.

Gibraltar walks in behind his desk looking down on the fire engines and takes notice of something he hasn’t seen yet. “Hey!!!There’s a big scrape and dent on engine number two. How long has that been there?” He turns around giving his Lieutenant an angry glare.

“Ohh…ahh…umm…yea about that.” Samuel stutters.

“Oh…yea about that. You knew about it? And I didn’t? Its not recent?” Gibraltar begins to raise his voice with anger.

“Well…it hasn’t been there too long…a week and a half…maybe two. When I was filling it with fuel the corner awning at the station caught it. They had just resurfaced there lot.” Samuel gives his reasoning.

“I don’t care about your excuses. Why the heck am I just now hearing about this? Not to mention I had to notice the damage myself.” Gibraltar cusses at his Lieutenant thinking about the money the insurance company is going to want.

“Hey its just cosmetics!” Samuel attempts to defend himself.

“Really!!!” Gibraltar sits in his chair behind his desk. “Really…just cosmetics. What about the station?”

Samuel takes a seat in front of the desk. “Its no problem, barely bent the tin back a little. The owner really appreciates us and what we do, he said not to worry about it.”

Gibraltar leans back in his chair shaking his head. “What!” He said hastily. “Don’t worry about it, since when have I ever insinuated that we don’t worry about damaging property? That’s not who we are. Which gas station was it? Hopefully its something simple you and I can fix ourselves. Otherwise if we have to claim it on insurance I may have to exclude you as a driver.”

“What!” Samuel now worried about his job. “One little scratch and it’ll make our insurance go up? Surely not.”

“We are a fire department, you can’t even sneeze around here without the insurance company wanting to raise our rates. Just please next time…” He takes a deep breath. “If there is (I hope not) but if there is whether their worried or not, know that I am, so…please let me know immediately. Which gas station was it? I will get a hold of them on Monday and at least invite them to the station for a barb-a-que to deter any complaints they may have about our incompetent drivers.”

Samuel see’s no point in further arguing and tells his Captain which station it was so that he could scribble it down on a sticky note.

Gibraltar stood and went over to the filing cabinet retrieving some folders. “Has Samantha been taking it easier on the wedding planning?” ***Did I really just ask him that? Why did I really just ask him that? I really don’t want to here him complain about his love life anymore.*** He thought to himself after he asked the question.

“Oh no…if anything its worse. I was so glad this was our work weekend, I am actually able to get some rest here. Last night was the first full nights sleep I have had all week. Even if we would have had more calls I probably would have slept more.” Samuel gladly gives his friend some of his frustration.

Gibraltar returns to his seat as he listened to his friend start his complaining. “Why don’t you just talk to her about it?”

“Pwcha!” Samuel snorts out. “Then I would never hear the end of it. You know how Samantha is. Do you really think that’s an option?”

Gibraltar looks over at him thinking about the couple of times he has met her. “Yea.” He opens one of the files he had pulled out. “Your right, your screwed.”

“Yea duhh! I’m just going to keep listening and saying yes honey, ok honey, whatever you think honey. That’s what guys do, well…what normal guys do. I don’t know what your issue is.”

Gibraltar raises his eyes from his work leaving his head in the down position. “Hey I’m sorry, I just think that the relationship should be a little more…well a little more even. You both should be able to agree on things, not just one of you pushing the other one around.”

Samuel gets up and walks over to a mini fridge in the corner, that is stocked with bottled water and takes one out. “See I don’t get you. You are a Fire Captain in really great shape and you are rich. You could literally have your choice of any woman yet you choose to live alone.” He said with a slight bit of envy in his voice, sitting back down in his chair.

“I’m not alone right now, I have you.” He claims in a less than historical tone. “And besides that’s exactly it, all those women want the hunk Fire Captain or the rich guy and that's not who I am, or well that's not my main purpose in life." He paused thinking through what he had just said. "In fact I really don't know what my main purpose is yet, maybe I should find myself first." He said out loud meaning for it to be more a thought than a statement. "But I need someone real…someone who don't care about those things, or well at least don't care about those things first. They should care first about me and who I really am, not the titles the world has placed on me. My personality should come first…and besides I did ask someone out the other day for your information."

"What!" Samuel stops the bottle mid air just before he took a drink. "You did? Who???Do I know her?"

Gibraltar stops writing, sits back in his chair, and crosses his fingers together over his stomach. "You remember that little girl who got her foot hung up on that bus crash the first day of school?"

"Umm…Yea…" Samuel nods with a slightly worried look on his face. "She's like nine years old."

"Yea that's her…Phathom. Her teacher."

"Ooahh…the teacher, now that makes more sense."

"Yes the teacher, now may I continue?"

"Please, by all means." Samuel nods for him to go on.

“So Miss Ross, as she told me to call her.” ***I really need to get her first name.*** “She was at the hospital the other day when I took Apollo by to visit Phathom.” As he speaks his gaze moves past Samuel turning into a dazed dreamy look.

“Ok…so this Miss Ross is there at the hospital. A teacher and a Firefighter hot combo. So you asked her out? When’s the first date?” Samuel questioned assuming he wasn’t rejected.

Gibraltar blinks and seems to come back to Earth. “Well…I’m not exactly sure yet. She was kinda griping at me when I asked her out and she kinda said no…well more like heck no, without the heck, no pun intended.” He goes back to shuffling through his paperwork.

“So your telling me she doesn’t like you and that is why you are stuck on her?” Samuel said with animosity.

“Oh no I am sure she likes me, she just doesn’t know it yet, and I am not exactly sure what makes me like her so much. Maybe its her seriousness, if she is ever going to enjoy life then she needs someone to force her to relax a little. And I…well it probably wouldn’t hurt if I had someone to help me live a bit more soberly.”

“But!” Samuel puts his water bottle on the edge of the desk. “Doc, you’re the most serious guy I know. You just totally jumped my rear over a scratch…barely more than a scratch…” He corrected himself.

“Yea that’s here at work though, but everywhere else I so often find myself treating everything like it’s a game of sorts. I know there has to be something more to life.”

“So your going to chase the one who told you no and clearly didn’t act as though she had any interest in you at all?” Samuel is trying to understand his friend.

Gibraltar shrugs his shoulders. “I wouldn’t say she didn’t have any interest. She just clearly had a lot on her mind with trying to get Phathom set up with classes and all. Really she was just stressed out and needs a bit of time to relax. I’m sure it will be different next time I run into her.”

“Next time you run into her?” Samuel is now confused. “What are you going to do? Are you going to stock her at school? Follow her to the grocery store?” He chuckled at his question that was more of a comment.

“No way! She brings Phathom her school work everyday after school, and Phathom has already asked me to bring Apollo back.”

Samuel looks past him shaking his head. “So your going to use your position being a Fire Captain, your Fire Dog, and a nine year old little girl who just lost a foot, to stock her.” He says smiling still shaking his head at him. “Very clever Doc! Very clever!”

Eight

McKenzie turns into the drive-in fast food diner to get a banana split for Phathom. She parked her car in the stall and rolled down her window. ***I might as well get my lunch for tomorrow while I'm here.*** The thought occurred.

She briefly glanced at the menu as though she didn't already know what she was going to get before pushing the red button. Within a few moments a young lady came over the speaker. "I hope you are having a great day." The voice sounds robotic. "Would you care to try one of our dollar ninety-nine milk shakes?"

McKenzie momentarily hesitated at the sales pitch, and almost went with it. "No thank you. I just need to get a banana split and a foot long chili cheese hot dog with mustard, onion, and pickles. The meal deal please with fries and a coke with no ice." She orders this as though she has made the order a thousand times.

"Ok ma'am, I got a banana split, a foot long chili cheese hot dog with mustard, pickles, onions, and a order of fries with a coke no ice. Would you care to make your combo a double XX size." The attendant threw out the next sales pitch just as robotic as the first.

"Yes absolutely." McKenzie answered, as though there was not even a reason she should have asked her.

The attendant gives her the total and lets her know that her order would be out shortly. McKenzie pays with her card and quickly rolls up her window, thinking of how hot and humid the day was feeling.

Waiting on her order she pulls the bright pink tablet out of her purse, immediately she recognized that it is way lighter than most tablets. Thinking, ***my cell phone most likely weighs more than this does.***

She was only a few pages from finishing the book and when she turned the last page the game popped up. She had previously played the game at several other intervals and thought it to be clever in the thought of making her think back on what she has read, inducing her memory. She also thought the game to be quite boring, which was the only thing she would tell Gibraltar.

The car hop then comes with her order taking her drink she puts it in her cup holder with the food and banana split going into her passenger seat, then heads for the hospital.

❖

“Hi Miss Ross!” Phathom spoke jovially with a glimmer in her eyes as McKenzie walks through her hospital room door.

“Well now you seem to be in a chipper mood today.” She feeds off of Phathom’s excitement.

“Yep…I am. Check this out.” Phathom pulled back her blanket revealing her new foot.

“Oh…my gosh…” McKenzie’s jaw dropped. “You have a new foot. Wow, that was really fast. I figured it was going to take a couple of weeks after your parents ok’d it, not a couple of days.” She blinks really fast making sure her eyes was seeing right. “Wow, it looks so real. May I feel it?”

Phathom nods with a big smile across her face. McKenzie reluctantly reaches her index finger out to the prosthesis as though it might shock her to touch it. “It wont bite you Misses Rosssss!” Phathom draws out her teachers name and giggled at her timidness.

McKenzie relaxes a bit with her cheer and rubs her hand over the prosthesis. “It feels like real skin.” She is amazed by the realness of the robotic foot.

“I cant wiggle my toes yet though.” Phathom is depressed by this fact.

McKenzie screws up her face giving Phathom a strange expression. “Your going to be able to wiggle your toes?” McKenzie asked as she put the cover back over her feet.

“I dunno.” Phathom shrugs. “Doctor Tolbert says he is very hopeful that once he gets it all connected right I will be able to. But he told me not to worry if I cant, that it will still work like a normal foot and hopefully I get to start walking on it next week.”

McKenzie goes back over to the counter where she had set her things when she came in, and grabbed Phathom’s banana split. “That is so awesome Phathom. Sounds like you will be running before you know it. Oh yeah, I almost forgot with all the excitement. I brought you a banana split.” She turned back around and Phathom’s eyes showed big as saucers. As she licks her lips McKenzie wheeled the tasty treat over to her. “So your in extra luck today. I didn’t assign any homework either, but do you have any questions or issues with the classwork today?” As she asked the question Phathom shoved the whole blob of whip cream into her mouth at once. ***Maybe I should have asked her that, before I distracted her with the ice cream.***

Phathom nods attempting to gulp down the delightfully light whip cream. “I baah blahh…” She attempts to speak with her mouth still half full then gulps down the last bit. “I do have one question. You was talking today about sin…sinomims?” She makes an attempt at the word.

"Synonyms." McKenzie corrected.

"Yea that, you said they was words that mean the same thing. Wouldn't be easier if there was just one word? Why do we need two words that mean the same thing?"

"Ooahh!" McKenzie makes an O with her mouth, giving Phathom an impressive look. "That Phathom is an excellent question my dear, and I really don't know that there is a simple or a complete answer to it, but I'll do my best to explain. So just because two words mean the same thing does not mean they always mean the same thing. Are you following?" She asked Phathom who confusingly nods anyways, taking another bite of the banana split.

"Ok so...lets take March for instance, it can be a month which can't have a synonym or you can use it as...lets say the school band marches down the field. We could also say they walked down the field. So March and Walk in these two instances are synonyms to one another." ***Wow this is a really poor example I must be confusing her big time.*** She thinks to herself that they may not even really be synonyms to one another. "Does that makes sense?" Tired she decided to just go with it anyways and Phathom gives her a knowingly nod of her head while she continued to really only worry about the ice cream in front of her.

“So just cause they can mean the same thing they can also mean something else when you are talking about something different, or sometimes putting different words in front of or behind it?” Phathom’s answer felt more like a philosophy.

“Yea sort of.” ***Yea but not really at all wow what kind of teacher am I. I cant even teach a simple synonym.*** She thinks to herself but she is really too tired to argue the point right now. “I’ll tell you what Phathom, I’ll get us some print outs on synonyms and we will get a better lesson on them next week.” Phathom nods contently digging back into her ice cream.

“Apolloooo!!!” Phathom yelled as the knock at the door brought the Dalmatian running into the room. He ran straight over to Phathom jumping his front paws onto her hospital bed and begins licking the sweet ice cream off her face making her giggle. “Apollo, silly dog quit it.” She pushes Apollo away from her face into her lap where he relaxes a bit as she pets him.

Gibraltar strolled in behind Apollo, getting a quick sigh with the rolling of her eyes from McKenzie before turning her gaze back on Phathom. Gibraltar walked in carrying a tablet identical to the other one, the only difference being this one was a neon green instead of pink. “Hi Phathom.” He turns and looks at McKenzie. “Miss Ross.” He nods his head with a way over the top smile on his face. “How are you two doing today?”

“We’re doing really good Captain Gibraltar and Apollo. How are y’all doing today?” Phathom with her left hand on Apollo’s head and a spoon for her ice cream in her right hand answers.

Gibraltar takes a couple steps forward, closer to the bed and more in sight of McKenzie who slightly shifts her stance away. “We are also good, but not nearly as good as you I can see.” He claims staring at her half eaten, mostly melted banana split on the table in front of her. “That looks yummy.” He places the tablet on the table beside the ice cream.

“It is.” Phathom nods quickly. “Its really good Misses Ross brings me ice cream every day!” Phathom lies on her teacher.

“Ugh!!! I do not.”

Gibraltar gives McKenzie a bewildered look, thinking he might actually have some ground to stand on now. “So you can feed her globes of straight sugar everyday, but I cant bring her a simple doll.” He complains.

“I do not bring her ice cream everyday. This is in fact only the second time and…”

“So your saying Phathom is lying?” He interrupted her not caring that she finished her argument. “I don’t believe a girl in a hospital bed is capable of such.” He shifted his gaze over to Phathom who cowardly lowers her head in defeat, admitting her guilt, without admitting her guilt. Then he gives her a disappointed look.

"As I was saying Captain Gibraltar."

"Just Gibraltar." He corrects her forcing her to give him another annoyed look.

"She deserves a treat, not something making fun of her leg."

With McKenzie's words a light came across Phathom's face and she pushes her table to the side. "Guess what Captain Gibraltar?"

"What is it Phathom'?"

"No you have to guess" She pushes Apollo back.

"Hmm..." Gibraltar pauses. "Hmm...Tua Tagovailoa is going to take the Dolphins to the Super Bowl this year?" He makes a quirky prediction, Phathom looks to him with a puzzled face. "Well???" He tilts his head.

"It has to do with me, not some dolphin with a super ball...silly goose."

Gibraltar puts a finger to his chin in deep contemplation, gazing at the ceiling. He held this pose for a long second before snapping his fingers and looking at her surprised. "I bet you got your wooden peg leg in and you are now ready to start your pirate training."

Phathom smiles really big with her mouth open. McKenzie see's the joy written all over this and can't help but smile herself, that is until Gibraltar glanced over in her direction, she quickly turned it into a frown.

"Nooahh!!!" Phathom laughs. "Its not a peg leg goof ball, its my real robots foot." She claims excitedly as she Yanks back her blanket revealing her feet.

"Uhh!!!" Gibraltar gasped. "It looks…" He walks over to the bed with his gaze stuck in shock on her feet. "It looks so…real." He picks up her right foot and tickles the bottom of it. She kicks and flails her foot back laughing. "Oh my gosh they even made it ticklish, that's amazing!"

McKenzie can't hold back her chuckle completely but by all means it did take everything she had to suppress the full laugh she had in her. She quickly puts her hand over her mouth hoping he didn't hear her. But then she catches a glimpse of Gibraltar's soft deep blue eyes staring straight through her, quickly she snaps herself out of his trance and crunches her brows in attempt to still look mad at him. Gibraltar just smiles and returns his gaze back down on Phathom.

"No way hosae. That's my real foot."

He blinks a couple of times looking back and forth between the two feet. "Oh wow, they really fooled me. So when are we going to race?"

“Ahem…” McKenzie butts in. “She’s a long ways from being able to run a race Doctor Crichton…” She answers for her. “I mean Captain Crichton.” She made the correction.

“Yea I cant even walk on it until next week.” Phathom sadly claims. “But then I promise, I’ll be playing fetch with you soon Apollo.” She said as she looks Apollo in the face smooching her lips rubbing under both of his ears, flopping them back and forth, making them both excited with the dream. “When I start walking I get to finally go home and start going back to class with all my friends.” Her hope continues to grow.

“That’s really cool Phathom. I am so proud of you, and as soon as you are ready Apollo has a whole bunch of tennis balls he is ready to chase.” Gibraltar shares their excitement.

McKenzie walks over to the table and takes the neon green tablet off of it. “I really hope you didn’t plan on leaving her another gaming tablet. She has lots of homework she needs to focus on.”

Phathom drops her jaw, McKenzie notices the shock and immediately remembers that she didn’t have any homework today. “Uh! Miss Ross you said I didn’t have any homework today.” Phathom whimpers as Gibraltar gives her a surprised look and a big grin on his face.

“I in fact did really bring this one to trade with her and their not really gaming tablets, they are books.”

“Yea the game was actually boring.” McKenzie remarks giving Gibraltar whole new life.

“Ohah…So Miss Ross you actually read the other one? Phathom did you enjoy The Hatchet?” He adds shifting his gaze back to her.

“Yes I did.” She claimed while she still sit there petting Apollo. “It was very interesting and I hope my plane wont crash in a scary wilderness like that.” McKenzie notices a twinkle in her eyes as she explains her jovial reading experience, she however stubbornly does not respond.

“That one in your hand Miss Ross is Amazonia by: James Rollins. So The Hatchet was the first book I remember reading when I was around Phathom’s age. Amazonia is the first adventure/Sci-Fi full size novel I remember reading when I was a young adult. I would have never been able to read a book this size when I was her age, but I think she is way smarter and a much better reader than I was at her age.” Gibraltar explains his early start with books.

McKenzie gives him a look of slight interest, he takes notice but attempts not to acknowledge so. “Ok so, why don’t you put more than one book on here?” She legitimately questioned.

“That is a very…very…good question.” Gibraltar goes over to a seat in the corner and sits. “It is by design, it is part of a Non-Profit I plan on starting (Save-the-Books Foundation).” He paused after naming his idea, proud of himself trying to get McKenzie to share his excitement, but she fails to do so. “So…have you ever handed someone a book or has someone ever handed you a book?”

“Sure.” She nods as she listened intently .

“Well there is just something to that feel, it helps individualize the books and gives you that real book feel. So with these you can take them, trade them, or give them to your friends and that gives us a little something back that I feel technology is taking away from us.”

McKenzie gives him the look of astonishment that he was looking for moments ago. “Hmph, I really hadn’t thought of it that way.”

Gibraltar cocks his head slightly. “Is that a sense of approval I am getting?”

McKenzie turns and goes to her purse to retrieve the pink tablet from it. “Well lets not get ahead of ourselves here.” She attempts to put her guard back up. “But I did read The Hatchet here, and it is a pretty good book.” She answers as she goes over to hand him the tablet, holding onto it a bit longer than she intended looking him into the eyes, loosing all the ground she had just gained back to the softness in them.

“See you feel that connection about my book?” He said timidly as his face turned rosy with embarrassment of what he had really just said.

"Yea I did." She honestly answered, then prays ***God please give me strength.***

"It for sure makes the book feel more important. I know that books don't have feelings, however we do have feelings about what we read and this really…well I feel like it allows us to express some of them moreso." He continued to give his philosophy on books and reading.

"These books have feelings." Phathom stepped into the conversation quite confused by it all.

"No…" McKenzie giggles. "But you have feelings about the book dear. You remember when you felt scared he was alone in the wilderness, but then you felt happy when he was able to find food?" She explained to Phathom and gets a understanding nod from her.

"I have another question?" She returns her focus back to Gibraltar who is sitting there eating up her attention. "How are you able to get the tablets to weigh less than my cell phone?"

Gibraltar bobbles his head back and forth, pondering his answer to her question. "I am not the engineer, nor do I have any type of skill sets to building electronics. I'm just…well lets just say I was the one who came up with the idea (I really like to read). There really is nothing to them though, a simple game and a book don't require a lot of computer power, especially with today's technology." He gave her the best explanation he had.

“Wow…this book has almost five hundred pages.” Phathom said with real surprise in the adventure. “I have never read a book this long before. I might be awhile before I need you to trade me again…Captain Gibraltar.”

“That’s fine.” He approves her taking her time. “Take your time Phathom, just make sure you get your school work done first before you do any leisure reading.”

McKenzie shoots Gibraltar a ecstatic gaze, although he fails to catch it. She can’t figure out whether or not she is glad he didn’t.

“Phathom I am so glad you have your new robot’s foot now, hopefully everything will be running properly with it and you’ll be in the classroom soon. Apollo and I really need to get back to the fire station now.” Gibraltar breaks the sad news.

Phathom looks down sadly on Apollo, bulging out her bottom lip. “Well Apollo, I really don’t want you to go, but I know there is other people that need you to save them.” She hugs Apollo as Gibraltar hooks up the leash.

“Good bye Phathom, have a good night.” Gibraltar turned towards McKenzie. “Miss Ross.” He nods to her as he heads to the door.

Before Gibraltar and Apollo make it out the door McKenzie quickly steps over to catch them. “Gibraltar.” She called him by his first name. “Can I have a word with you before you leave?”

Gibraltar glanced over to Phathom with an (oh-no-not-again) look. They both then step outside the door. “So Captain Crichton.”

“Gibraltar!” He quickly responds. “What’s your first name?”

“McKenzie.” She tells him without thought and slightly embarrassed by doing so.

“Ohh! McKenzie, I like that. Is it ok if I call you by it?”

She gives him a frustrated gaze. “It’d probably be best that you didn’t…now I wanted to talk to you because of our last conversation. I wanted to apologize for getting mad at you. I really need to learn to be a little more understanding.” She gives him an earnest, but half hearted apology.

“Oh, so your ok now that I gave her a pirate doll?”

“Ugh!” McKenzie rolls her eyes at him. “Absolutely not, I am just trying really hard to be ok with you being a big kid.” She insults him although neither one of them truly recognized this as an insult.

“O well…Since we’re now on speaking terms and your ok with me being a kid. Does that mean your willing to go out with me now?” Gibraltar asks her out for a second time.

“No Gibraltar, really I cant go out with you.” She semi politely declines this offer. “But I will tell you what. If you wanted to see me aside from the hospital you could come to Ocean Breeze Apostolic Church. We have service at eleven a.m. on Sundays."

He gazed her up and down and for the first time realizes that she has been wearing a very modest dress or skirt every time he has seen her. "Oh, the dress." He points to her skirt. "The hair." He points to her un-cut very long hair. "I should have known you are one of them church people."

This insult she feels, but doesn't understand. "Well its more than just being church people. Its about being Christian and in my case Apostolic Christian. It is true we live by a closer standard to Gods word than some of the others."

Gibraltar nods as though he understood. "Well that's great, but I really cant go to a church. That's just not who I am. I am a really good guy though, I don't have to go to a church to be one of those. So maybe we can go out on just one date and if you still think I am an evil devil we wont do it again. Also I'll only drink wine, that would be ok right? Didn't Jesus drink wine?"

McKenzie looks at him sadly and just now notices that she really does kind of like him and really would like to go out with him. ***Jesus help me.*** She prays. "Look Captain Crichton, I am sure you really are a great man in many different ways, but it has way more to do with a certain set of ethics that we live by, than just the drinking of alcohol of any type. It's not about morals, its about the Apostolic lifestyle. I'm sorry I can not go out with you." She said this looking him straight in the eyes, not knowing how she was able to do so without completely falling apart.

"Ok." He said quietly as he bows his head and he and Apollo walk away leaving McKenzie sadly watching them go.

Nine

Gibraltar walks into the big open bay door to Station Thirteen. There he finds his crew Samuel, Barry, and DeAndre all toweling off the sparkling ladder truck. "Aww...I think I'm gonna cry, all of you working so well together making sure the truck is so clean."

"Oh great!" Barry quickly stands up and attempts to hide the towel behind his back. "You wasn't suppose to be here for another ten minutes. And you definitely wasn't suppose to see this."

“What Sarg. am I suppose to be the only one doing the menial work around here?” DeAndre states being the low man on the totem pole, definitely not wanting to do all the cleaning himself.

“No of course not, you have Bea and Felipe also.” Barry jokes with him.

“You have me too.” Samuel chimed in still shining the chrome knobs with his towel. “I actually find this work therapeutic, plus it makes me feel good to be driving a sparkly truck that shines so well going down the road.”

Beatrice walks around engine number two hearing Samuel say this. “Oh…so it makes your head feel bigger when your behind the wheel of it. Is that what your saying LT?” She laughs at her own punch line.

“Well as long as it don’t feel too big that he tears any more awnings up, we should let him think that.” Gibraltar disses his Lieutenant, not letting him forget about his recent incident.

“Ouch.” Samuel gets up mimicking holding his side as though he has been punched in the gut several times. “Low blows from all around today. What is this beat up the Lieutenant day?”

Beatrice walked up closer to him standing beside the truck. “At least we think your important enough to hit on.” She slapped him hard on the shoulder knocking him slightly forward as though he had just made the play of the game.

"Hey Doc, we're almost out of saline IV bags." Beatrice gets herself back to work making sure all her bases are covered.

"Ok put it on the inventory sheet. They should come in next week." Gibraltar steps around the back of the truck looking over every square inch of the truck making sure he wont be finding any more surprises.

"Yea that's why I am mentioning it. I don't think we have enough to make it till next week." Beatrice follows him around the truck attempting to break the news gently.

"What!!!" He stops and faces her red faced as though his blood pressure just went through the roof. "Why the heck wasn't it on the week before then? If you knew you were going to run out." He curses at her with his frustration.

"Hey!" Beatrice stands her ground not going to let him speak to her this way. "I'm not one hundred percent sure if we used extra this week, or if we just missed it last week. Whether it was a mistake or just a fluke…I don't know. But it don't give you…no right to talk to me in that manner." Now mad she turns and starts to storm off.

"Bea! Wait!" He takes a couple steps to approach her feeling remorse by his actions. "Your right, I'm sorry."

"Your plenty old enough not to know that sorry only gets you so far." Bea holds her hand up stopping him letting him know she wasn't ok with the way he approached her. “Now I’m going to accept your apology this time, but I can’t say that if you ever speak to me like that again I wont be looking to put in for a transfer to another station.” She threatens to leave Station Thirteen.

“No Bea, please don’t do that.” He pleads with her knowing that he would never find another Paramedic half as good as her. “Look, I know I sometimes have a real anger problem, and I know there really is no excuse for this, but I really have been under a lot of pressure with all the extra work Marshall Spector has shoved down my throat. Again I really am sorry, can you please remind me when we get back from visiting Phathom? So that I can make a note to go by another station to get a few of them to get us by until next week.”

Beatrice knows Gibraltar’s intentions are good so she gave him a slight, but forgiving smile. “Ok Doc, thank you for the apology. Were you wanting Felipe and I to come with the ambulance to the hospital? If so I think I’ll have to go wake Felipe up, all his studies has really taken a toll on him.”

“No, that’s ok.” He shakes his head not really wanting the ambulance around anyways. “Leave him be, besides I think its probably better she wait a little longer before she see’s that ambulance again, it might give her some bad flashbacks.”

"Ok well…you all have fun, tell her I said hi." She turns to walk away leaving Gibraltar standing there feeling like a complete dope.

Gibraltar continues his inspection around the truck and gets to the side in between the two trucks where everyone else is congregated. "Ok crew. We ready to ride?" He quizzed them all excitedly about their next excursion. They all give him a 10-4 sharing his excitement of doing something different.

"Hey Doc!" They were all loading up when Barry stopped them all wondering. "Where is Apollo?"

"Oh no." Gibraltar's eyes open big remembering where he left his dog. "He must have fallen asleep before we made it here. He usually whimpers to let me know he is back there."

"Not good Doc. What is up with you lately? That is not like you."

Gibraltar runs out the door without answering the question only to return moments later with Apollo in front of him. They load into the passenger seat of the big ladder truck with the rest of the crew and Samuel pulls them all out of the station.

"Ok Phathom." Doctor Tolbert begins to talk looking up from his tablet putting his focus on her. "Now that first step is going to feel like you are stepping off of a cliff, you need to trust your new foot is there to catch you.

Phathom stands up from her hospital bed and looks up to nurse Marjorie, and gives a nervous smile before she steps out with her prosthesis and pauses before she shifted her weight.

"Its ok Phathom you know how to walk, just walk." The Doctor gave her his gentle command, with confidence in his voice.

"Ok." Phathom takes a deep breath and clumsily swings her right foot in from of the other one, and pauses again.

Excited she took her first step she looks up to the nurse. "You did it Phathom, you made your first step." Marjorie shares her excitement giving Phathom the boost she needed to continue.

Now she takes several more strides to the door with the nurse holding onto her shoulders as a balance. "Ok Phathom, very good." She helps her get turned around. "Now I am going to step out in front of you so now your going to be on your own. We need to see how you do with unassisted steps."

Phathom stands there all wobbly legged telling herself over and over again in her head ***I got this, I got this.*** "Ok Doctor Tolbert, here I go."

Just as Phathom is about to take that first step the door swings open, hitting her in the back throwing her to the floor face first, catching herself with her hands before her face smacked the ground.

"Phathom!" Marjorie steps up and kneels down, then turns her glare back up to Gibraltar coming through the door, giving him an evil eye that looks as though she is really going to hurt him. "Are you ok?" She sympathetically checks on her.

"Oh my gosh! Phathom. I am so sorry, I didn't realize you were standing in front of the door. Are you ok?" Gibraltar now concerned with her and feeling bad for knocking her down.

"Yes!!!Yes!!! I am fine. Its not like it's the first time I have ever fellan before." She shews everybody off with her pride being hurt more than anything else.

"Here let me help you up."

"No!!!" Doctor Tolbert stops the nurse from helping her up. "Phathom? Do you think you can get up on your own?"

"Of course I can." She says with all the confidence in the world.

"Good, it's a good test for us." The Doctor almost sounds happy she was knocked down.

Marjorie stands and steps back giving Phathom some space. Phathom first puts her right foot on the floor then contemplates on how she is going to get the prosthesis on the floor. She makes an awkward move and places her hands out in front of her. With both feet under her she straightens her knees with her palms on the floor out in front of her and holds this pose for a moment thinking about how to stand all the way up. (Almost as though she has forgotten how to stand.)

She then pushes really hard against the floor popping herself up. "I did it!" She yells and jumps with excitement not even thinking about not having a foot there she crashes back to the floor, and starts laughing at herself. "Maybe I should wait before I try to jump." She claims to Marjorie who is already knelt down beside her again. They all chuckle at her for this.

"Ok Phathom, you ready to try this again." She quizzed her as she steps the half step away again.

"Yes ma'am I got this." With more confidence this time she makes the same movements as she did moments ago and slowly rises to her feet." Watch this Captain Gibraltar I was just about to take my first unassisted steps before you rudely knocked me down." She jokes with him still making him feel worse about hitting her with the door.

"I'm sorry." His face turns red with a pouty face.

Phathom walks towards her bed with Marjorie a couple steps ahead of her. "Very, very good Phathom. Thanks to Captain Gibraltar? Is that who you said you are?" Doctor Tolbert asked Gibraltar looking at him.

"Well it's actually Captain Crichton, Miami Dade Fire Department. Gibraltar is my first name is what I preferred Phathom calling me by. My team and I were the ones to get her off the bus and to the hospital." They shake hands.

"Ah, very well. You all did an excellent job. As I was saying though we actually was able to do a little more testing than I was planning on since you knocked her down." Doctor Tolbert chuckles at the incident again.

Man do they all have to keep reminding me about my goof up?

"Ok Phathom, physical therapy is going to start working with you everyday and it will not be too much longer before we can get you out of here." Doctor Tolbert gives his instructions on his way out the door. "Take care now, I will see you in a few days."

Phathom jovially waves him a farewell. "Ok, thank you Doctor Tolbert."

Gibraltar opens the door for the Doctor. "Hey Doc, I have a quick question I'd like to ask." They both step outside the hospital room. "So Phathom really likes pirate stuff, and its kind of a running joke her and I have about her having a peg leg like a pirate."

Doctor Tolbert completely confused by where Gibraltar is taking this conversation. "Yesss…and."

"Well…and I was wondering if you could make her a wooden peg leg prosthetics?"

The Doctor screws up the look on his face pondering Gibraltar's ask. "I am sure I could Captain, but I really don't know if that would be appropriate."

"Oh come on Doc! Its not like she'll be wearing it all the time. Just maybe as a costume occasionally." Gibraltar all but begs the Doctor to see his reasoning.

Doctor Tolbert stands there quiet a moment really thinking this over. "If I were to make one that would connect to her stump, even though it would seem like a cheap piece of wood. It would be far from being cheap." Doctor Tolbert now thinking about the sale.

"Ok, no problem. I'll pay for it whatever it cost."

As Gibraltar and the Doctor finish up their conversation nurse Marjorie walks out of Phathom's room leaving the door open behind her. Gibraltar thanks the Doctor and walks back into Phathom's hospital room.

"Arghrr!!!Captain." Phathom imitates as he enters back into the room.

"No, no Phathom you're the captain today. I'll be the first mate." Gibraltar makes her the honorary Captain for the day.

"Aye…Aye…ye od'er matey." She returns accepting the position.

"Where are your shoes? That's kind of gross walking on the hospital floor bare footed." He makes a comment thinking about how many diseases there must be on these floors.

Phathom looks to him puzzled and confused about why it was so bad to walk around bare footed. "What! No way! Mrs. Sanchez sweeps and mops it everyday…and gives me a lollypop." She points over to the bedside table where there is a pile of suckers.

"Ok yea, but its still a hospital room." Gibraltar continues his argument as though he had a chance to win and cringes at the thought of being without shoes in the hospital room.

"Arghh!!! Whatever der matey if you are to be me matey, you got to stop being a fraidy cat."

"Okie Dokie." Gibraltar laughs. "Cap'n Phathom get your shoes on I'm going to go find us some wheels to get to our ship."

"Whoooaaahhh!!!" Phathom's eyes bulge out as Gibraltar pushes her down the side walk towards their fire truck. "I'm the Captain over that truck?" She claims slightly intimidated by its massive size.

"Yep you sure are and you even have a crew to boss around. Arghh!!!Ye der slacky's, dis ere is ye new Cap'n. Cap'n Phathom reporting to erder ye duty's." Gibraltar brings on a strong pirates expression pushing Phathom up beside the truck.

"All aboard!!!" He helps Phathom into the drivers seat before quickly running around to the passenger seat.

Samuel, Barry, and DeAndre from the back seat go over and show her a lot of things most of which was of no interest to her, while she sit there petting Apollo in her lap. They even showed her how to use the horn and sirens of which they only allowed a very brief test, there in the hospital parking lot.

After their all sitting there for a few minutes all of their alarms on their phones start to sound off. "Umm!!!Doc!!!" Barry spoke with a shaky voice. "We have an Amber Alert." He lowers his phone.

"Umm…Okay???" Gibraltar drawl's out the okay wondering why Barry was acting so funny. "So who is it? Are they close by?"

"Yea…umm…well…you could say that. Here check it out." Barry held up his phone to Gibraltar, showing him the Amber Alert.

McKenzie is almost to the hospital when the alert comes across her phone. She pulled her phone from the cup holder where it normally rides and noticed the Amber Alert. There with a picture of Phathom and all her details, last seen in her hospital room. She takes a deep breath, places her phone back in the cup holder and frantically puts the pedal to the medal.

Moments later McKenzie is flying into the hospital drive opting to skip out on trying to park she heads straight towards the front entrance, to the side of Phathom's ward.

She gets to the front and see's the big fire truck parked out front and instantly feels somewhat relieved. She pulled up behind it in the fire lane parked and jumped out in a hurry.

On the side walk she see's Gibraltar and another fire fighter standing there beside the truck. She rushes over to them. "Good Gibraltar you all are here. I guess you all got the alert? Is there any information to go on?"

"Hi Miss Ross, this is my Lieu..."

"Thank you for trying to help." McKenzie cuts off his introduction. "Do we know anything? Do they think she ran away? I mean it'd be kind of hard for her to run away just now learning how to use her new foot. Surely someone abducted her. Gibraltar you have to find her!" She starts to cry.

Gibraltar takes a reassuring hand and places it on her shoulder. "She is fine, she's in her hospital room resting. I assure you it was all a big misunderstanding." He tries calming her down without making her mad at him.

"HUUHH!!!" She sighs heavily and drops her shoulders. "How is an Amber Alert a misunderstanding?" She sternly questioned.

"Well." Samuel now wants to attempt to defuse her growing frustration. "You see Doc here thought it'd be helpful to her morale to get her out and show her the fire truck, but forgot to mention to the nurse that he was bringing her out."

"What!!!" McKenzie's expression goes from exasperated to fuming mad in an instant.

"We told the nurse at the station on our way out." Gibraltar desperately attempts to defend his actions.

"What!!!This is ridiculous. I should have known it was something you caused. You are such a child! Ugh!!!" She screams at his as she shoves past him knocking him backwards on her way into the hospital, not even thinking about turning around.

Ten

"What the heck are you doing?" JJ questioned as she sit her steaming plastic tray on the table in front of her seat.

"Well…" McKenzie begins to explain as though her actions are normal. "The fire sauce is too hot, and the hot sauce is not quite hot enough." She talks while she takes the end of her double stack taco and shoves it into the glob of sauces and stirs it around.

"Ughh!" Jemma sigh's sticking her tongue out. Not understanding how her bestie eats such. "That's gross, is that a cold soggy taco?"

"Hey its not gross, cold taco's are the best. It has to be a double stack though, the soft shell holds the soggy crunchy one together." She takes a bite of her taco as JJ shakes her head shivering at the thought of such disgust.

"You know that's not how your suppose to use taco sauce, right?"

McKenzie shrugs her shoulders. ***Well that's how I eat it.*** "Ell ah pfer ipping things." She swallows her bite. "So this is how I am going to use it, I'll do the same for my two burrito's also. You know I kinda feel like we have had this conversation before." She said thinking back on the conversations they have had everyday the past two years at lunch.

“Yea probably so, but its still gross, McKenzie!” Jemma shutter’s with a repulsive look on her face.

“How are things with Jonas?” McKenzie asked her friend at the same time wishing she hadn’t.

“Oh…my…” Jemma begins huffing and puffing as she takes too big, and too hot a bite. She hurry’s and opens her water bottle and guzzles down a good drink to cool her mouth off, now mad at herself for burning the film off the roof of her mouth. “So he is really great, we’ve been spending a lot of time together. I really think he might be the one.”

“Oh yeah…really?” McKenzie crunches her brow. “A greasy mechanic?”

“Yea I know…It seems dull, but he has plans. He’s going to open up his own shop when he gets the money saved up, then he would be a garage owner. The boss mechanic, not just some lackey.” JJ shares the dream with her new boyfriend, thinking about how nice it can possibly be.

“Well I wasn’t meaning to imply that being a mechanic is a bad thing.” McKenzie shoves the rest of the double stack taco into her mouth which was really close to half of it.

“Yeah…sure you weren’t.” JJ sarcastically makes her friend feel bad about her discriminatory thoughts. “Miss I can have a Fire Captain, but I’m too good for him. What are you waiting on the President of the United States to ask you out?"

"Ugh!" She sighs with her mouth still really full before taking a drink of her coke to wash it all away with. Thinking about her next approach. ***Is she right, do I think I'm too good for him?*** She wonders herself. "I've been over this. It's not that he's not good enough, or that I'm too good for him…" She pauses in attempt to come up with a better defense to argue her case. "Besides the president is way too old for me." Was the best she had. "Look JJ I really don't want to argue about this. I am sorry to have jumped to conclusions about Jonas, that is really out of character for me and wasn't right. You know that I have just been going through some things and all lately." She apologizes unwrapping one of her eight layer burritos.

"Well you don't have to take it out on me. I have been trying to help you, maybe this Gibraltar is the answer to all your problems. At least if you go out with him…maybe you wouldn't be jealous of Jonas." JJ remarks bitter sweetly giving McKenzie chills at the reality of her true words.

"Oh my gosh…JJ I'm not jealous…maybe a bit envious that you have someone, but I get that that is not right though. Really though I am happy for you." She takes a large bite off the eight layer burrito.

"Ok" JJ nods still upset with her friend but trying to be understanding. "Yea I accept your apology. Sorry for the extra jab, you just kinda made me mad. But really you don't have to envy me, you could have someone who I ninety-nine percent sure is a really good guy/person. They don't just let anyone be a Captain over a fire station." She attempts to encourage her friend with sympathy.

"Yea, yea…I know this is what you think, but I haven't told you his latest venture yet though…have I? He is such a big kid, I can't believe they ever let him become a Captain."

JJ screws the look up on her face wondering why McKenzie is being so defiant with this obviously perfect match. "Come on, it cant be that bad. I mean getting a nine year old a doll should be hardly classified as childish." She comments wryly.

"Oh no, this time he went way over board. Like so much so, I wouldn't be surprised if they canned him for it. He actually abducted Phathom the other day." Jemma gives her a confused look, knowing he didn't actually abduct her. "Well he didn't actually abduct her, per se. He was getting her out of her hospital room showing her the fire truck and forgot to let her nurse know he was taking her, and while he has her in the fire truck the hospital puts out an Amber Alert on her."

JJ's jaw dropped and she almost choked on her food. "Oh my…" She coughs out. "No way…that's probably serious business for them, to cause a fake alert like that. Is he going to loose his job?"

McKenzie shrugs with a smirky grin half hoping they do out of spite. "I don't know, I haven't talked to him, but I'm sure there will be some serious repercussions if they don't fire him. Surely they'll probably demote him or I really don't know what other kind of sanctions there are for them, but I doubt it gets swept under the rug." As she says this she begins to feel bad for him, and sorry that she wished he would get fired.

"I can't imagine it would." JJ just shakes her head at her friends latest news.

McKenzie pulled into her sisters driveway and parked right behind her sisters car that was parked under the car port, leaving room for her brother-in-law to pull up beside her. She grabs her phone and a plastic bag with cookies for her nephew, stepping out of her car.

Walking towards the side entrance under the car port she gazed over at their front stoop that was decked out in an assortment of fall theme items, a couple bales of hay, pumpkins, gourds, even a scarecrow showing a different array of the fall colors.

She continues on through the car port beside her sisters car, admiring (slightly envious) of the baby-on-board sticker on her back glass. Stepping up the two steps that lead directly into her sisters kitchen she looks through the screen door. She opens it saying "Knock...Knock..."

“Mimi!” Her three year old nephew yells as he runs and wraps up McKenzie around her knee’s.

“Hey bubba, how are you?” She bends over and picks him up.

“McKenzieeaaahhh!” Her sister called her out with an exasperated sigh. “I’ve told you not to call him that.” Standing at the stove with a spoon in her right hand stirring a pot, and her eight month old in her left arm, Chloe complains about her sister’s pet name for her son.

“Ok fine, Eziekiallll.” McKenzie exaggerates his name as she smooches at his cheeks while he flails and giggles happily in her arms. She continues over and sits the bag with the cookies in it on the table.

“Just Zeke…plain and simple.” Chloe states (more a demand) as her sister comes over and kisses her on the cheek.

“Ok sis, I love you too.”

“Here take two of them.” Chloe let go of the spoon and stuck the baby out for McKenzie to take in her other arm.

“Aww! Hi there Sydney.” She gladly accepts the baby, kissing her on the cheek. “So what do you think Sydney is going to call him when she begins to babble more?”

“Umm…Zeke, this is why I am telling you this.”

"Yess ma'am." McKenzie takes both children over to the table and sits with them both in her arms. "I really don't see what the big deal is, but ok. So Zeke what have you been up to?" She questioned with a silly face at her nephew.

"Well…the big deal is that's what his father and I want him to be called . The pet name bubba is a childish and I feel like it stunts their maturity. I mean look at Arthur for instance, he still hasn't grown up.

Zeke cheerfully wiggles his way out of McKenzie's arms as she laughs at her sisters latest philosophy. "So you think its because we called him bubba? I always assumed it was the middle child syndrome going on." McKenzie jokes at her brothers expense.

Zeke brings back a coloring page to show his aunt what he has been up to. " 'ook Mimi 'ook at…I olor pitty uh."

She takes the coloring page admiring his work. "Awwww…it sure is bub…I mean ZEKE."

Chloe shoots her sister a glare from the stove. " Nope, its definitely because we called him bubba. I am thoroughly convinced of this."

"Sydney!" McKenzie pinches at her nieces cheeks. "Can you say Mimi?"

"Baba." Sydney burble out.

"Ohh great!!!See what you've already started." Chloe complained about her sisters attempt to teach her daughter to call her brother bubba, as she turns one of the knobs on the stove and opens the oven.

"That was more like a bye…bye…than a bubba."

"Baba." Sydney attempts to mimic her aunt.

"McKenzieeahh!!!" She sighs again.

"Mmm…it smells really good. What are we having?" McKenzie always hungry asked hopefully.

"Roast chicken, with potatoes and carrots, mac-n-cheese. For Zeke of course."

By this time Zeke has come back with a box of crayons and a coloring book holding his arms up for McKenzie to pick him up. She awkwardly pulls him into her lap with Sydney on one leg already. "Mimi olor or me?" He says dumping the colors out onto the table.

"Mmm that sounds delish Chloe, I am starving." She claims excited that her sister is cooking for her.

After closing the oven back Chloe walks over to the counter and leans her back against it. "McKenzie? When are you not starving? You know Dewayne keeps asking me about you. Maybe you should try to go on another date with him."

"Ughhh Chloeee!!!" McKenzie sighs out her name. "I've told you this before, Dewayne is a nice guy and all, but its just not right. I'm just really not attracted to him like that."

Chloe looks at her sister not understanding her at all. "What! How are you not? He is probably the most attractive single in our district. He's definitely more attractive than anyone at Ocean Breeze."

McKenzie helped Zeke scribble onto one of the coloring pages with a green crayon, wishing her sister would drop her cupid act. "Well it goes way beyond looks Chloe. I mean I don't know, I just know he's not right for me."

Chloe steps away from the counter wishing her sister would just try to see reasoning. She walks over to them all at the table and looks down at the coloring book. "Good job bub…Argh…McKenzie see what you've started. So what? You just going to stay single your whole life?"

She shrugs with both children in her lap feeling the pressure. "Sure feels that way…" She pauses her thoughts. "Buttt…" She drawls out the word immediately wishing she hadn't said it. "But never mind, I'm probably going to die alone."

Chloe's eyes get big recognizing the but. "No…who is he? That was definitely there's a someone else but…Who is it McKenzie? Which church does he go to?" She demands answers as she rubs her sons head.

"No, its no one." McKenzie clams up.

“Come on sis…you have to tell me. We tell each other everything.” Chloe lies in attempt to hear her sisters latest love fling.

“Chloe!” McKenzie crunches up her eyebrows at her sisters attempt to get her to talk. “We’ve never told one another anything.” She hits her sister with the truth of the matter.

Chloe tilts her head. “I know, your right, but we still talk. Come on, who is it?” She looks at her sister intently with persistence wanting to hear who her sister is starting to like.

“Ok fine, promise you won’t say anything to Mom or Dad…or Arthur for that matter.”

“Yea…” Chloe nods eagerly about to come out of her skin wishing her sister would just spit it out already. “Yea of course not…lips are sealed.” She makes a zipping motion across her mouth with her fingers.

“Ok, so he doesn’t go to any church.”

“What!” Chloe cuts her off. “No…no…no never mind I don’t want to hear about this. I take it back, your not bringing me down with you when Mom and Dad come questioning this.” Chloe definitely upset at herself now for prodding at her sister so persistently.

“Sis…come on you just told me…wait no you just convinced me to discuss this with you. And I could really use your spiritual help here.” McKenzie now mad that her sister don’t want to listen.

They both stare heavily into one another's eyes for what seemed like a very long moment. "Ok fine, but don't expect me to lie to anyone if I am asked a direct question." Chloe negotiates with her sister, really kinda glad she did.

"Fair enough." McKenzie would never expect anyone to lie for her, so she was ok with this ask. "His name is Gibraltar Crichton. He's the Fire Captain at Miami Dade Fire Department Station Thirteen. Now we are not dating or anything like that. In fact I really find him very childish and annoying and I rejected him when he asked me out. But he is persistent…" She raises a brow to her sister's recent prodding. "And he keeps showing up and I keep telling him NO…I cant date him. I even invited him to church which he politely told me he wasn't a church person, which made my point even stronger." McKenzie picks up a red crayon as her sister takes a seat across the table from them.

"Well McKenzie…" Chloe attempts to speak in a soft and somewhat understanding way. "I'm not going to act as though I understand. I really don't, I married Mike six months after leaving my high school sweetheart, so I really cant imagine being alone. I do think Mom and Dad would be mortified, though I don't believe they would say as much."

McKenzie gives her sister a knowingly glare. "I know Chloe, but its more than just upsetting them. It goes against who we are as God's children and for sure against who we are as Apostolic. Don't worry I'm not going to date him, I just needed to get that off my chest. Thanks for listening."

Chloe stands and puts her right hand on her sisters cheek feeling sorry for her struggles. "Of course, I love you, and I am not worried in the least bit. I know you and you are not one to do anything to jeopardize your faith."

Eleven

Samuel walks through the open door of his Captain's office, in hopes to aggravate. "What's up Doc?" He said walking straight to the mini fridge stocked with water grabbing a bottle.

"You see." Gibraltar already aggravated by him, looking up with his eyes. "You know those water bottles are for my guests who visit here, could you not get your own?"

Samuel shrugs, enjoying his start to their conversation. “Hmph.” He walks over to the couch in the corner of the office a flops down lazily. “Well…I am your guest right now.” He flatly replies as he puts his feet on the coffee table.

“More like a pest that I can’t get rid of.” Gibraltar mummers as he continues his paperwork wishing he would just go away.

“What is it with you these days? It seems as though all you do anymore is paperwork.”

“Yea.” Gibraltar nods with frustration. “Everybody and their mothers want to know every little detail about what we are doing around here, and in order to keep you getting paid I have to get creative and fudge it a little, acting like your doing something other than laying back on my couch with your feet propped up.” Growing more angry talking about it. “On my coffee table!!!”

Samuel nods with a satisfied smile perching his lips out contemplating his next harassment. “Oh, since your making me look better now, you think you could fudge the paper a little more to get me a raise?” He takes a long pull off the water bottle, then sits the half empty bottle down on the coffee table where he fully intends on leaving it.

Gibraltar reaches over to his post it notes on his desk. “Samuel will be satisfied with fudge for his quarterly bonuses.” He says out loud as he makes the note.

“Make sure its peanut butter fudge.” Samuel holds up a finger un-phased and still enjoying this conversation.

“Is there something your needing?” Baffled Gibraltar quizzed his LT.

“Nope, just bored and seeing you get flustered is very gratifying, and really good entertainment.” Samuel claims as he reaches over into the sucker bowl taking one out and popping it into his mouth.

Gibraltar chuckles not wanting him to see any more of his frustration, he gets a thought. ***Ok I bet I can fix this.*** “Oh yeah! So I found your new shift mate. He will be starting with you all on your next on shift.” Gibraltar sits his pen down and lays back in his chair getting ready to return some of his frustration back to Samuel.

“That’s good, how much experience does he have?” He sits up on the couch showing interest.

“You remember Alex?”

“What!” He cuts him off standing up. “That scrawny little guy who couldn’t even connect the hose to the truck?” Gibraltar nods as Samuel walks over and sits across from him at the desk. “No! Absolutely not, we cant use him we need someone who could at least carry a cat out of a burning house."

Gibraltar crunches his brow a little more satisfied that he's not the only flustered one in the room now. "Samuel, he is not that bad. He just needs some extra training, is all. That's something you can do to keep from being so bored, work up some training exercises to go through with him. Start feeding him good and maybe you can get him to put a little muscle on."

"Agh!!! Come on!!!" He whines taking the sucker out of his mouth flailing it around as though it is a wand. "There has to be a better option for us."

"Nope." Gibraltar shakes his head. "Fraid not, all the dang unions have it where all the factory and industrial jobs pay mostly double what it does to be a fire fighter. So why run into a burning building for half as much as you can make to just stand there in one spot? It'll be just fine, give Alex a chance. Barry can teach him how to eat and run, then you and DeAndre can teach him how to build muscle and be a smart..."

"Ugh!!!" Samuel interrupts Gibraltar bobbing his head back and forth not wanting to go with it, but he recognizes his demise. "Haha!" He gave a sarcastic laugh. "Ok, but if he can't hang he may get stuck washing the trucks, and shining our boots." He puts the sucker back in his mouth laying back in the chair.

"How's the wedding planning?" ***Why do I always do this to myself?*** He questions his question as he picked his pen back up returning to his work. "Is Samantha getting just as aggravated with you as I am?" He adds the second question.

"Oh my gosh." Samuel exasperated with the topic. "Is she ever." He claims standing back up. "I will be so…so…glad when this is all over in a couple of weeks." He talks in a daze as he steps up beside the desk gazing out the floor to ceiling windows into the fire station.

"A couple weeks? Huh?" Gibraltar questioned thinking about the date. "Do I need to rent a tux? Cause you know I am going to have to take it out of your raise if so."

"No…no…she has been back and forth."

"Wha…wait…" Gibraltar glanced back over his shoulder. "What do you mean she's been back and forth. Aren't you suppose to be the one making the tux choices for the men?"

"Haha!" Samuel laughs at this thought. "Yea right, everything I say or choose is always wrong." He makes his way back over to the couch and eases himself down onto it. "She keeps telling me that she wants us to wear our dress uniforms. Then she doesn't like how the pants look, so she wants tuxes. Then now she's back on us wearing our dress uniforms."

Gibraltar stops his writing and looks across the office to his friend truly wondering about him. "So who's the one wearing the pants here?" He gives a smart remark. "So do I need to get with her to plan your bachelor party also?"

"No, no, no, no…" Samuel jumps back up off the couch. "Do not say anything to her about that. She has been very adamant about me definitely not having a bachelor party. If you even mention it that's the end of me, you can kiss my…"

"Whoa…whoa, whoa." Gibraltar holds a hand up with the pen in it. "So your telling me, your going to let your fiancé take away my right as the best man to throw you a bachelor party?"

Samuel steps into the middle of the office and cocks his head slightly at the fact that he just knows he can't under any circumstances have a bachelor party. "No, no, its not like that she just…"

"Yea, yea, just like that she is definitely the one wearing the pants here. I'll go with you next week to pick out your dress. What are the color themes of your wedding again?" He makes fun of Samuel very sarcastically.

"Well…I really don't…"

“Gibraltar shakes his head looking back down the papers in front of him. “I don’t give a good God dang what colors they are Samuel. You need to grow a pair and stand up for yourself. I’ll have your party planned this weekend whether you like it or not. If you don’t go with it, I will be having you kidnapped. All I need to know is what color hair would you like the strippers to have?” Gibraltar is very sure he will be throwing his friend a huge bachelor party.

Samuel walks over and plants both hands on Gibraltar’s desk looking straight at him. “No Cap…you can’t, your going to ruin my marriage before I even get started.”

“Yea I know.” Gibraltar looks up at him bug eyed. “What else is a best man suppose to be for?”

“Ugh!” Samuel sighs and stands back up turning around quickly throwing his head back. “No Doc…No bachelor party.” He turns back around facing his Captain. “Period…anyways enough of that talk. So what’s up with you and your teacher stocking. How’s it coming with her umm…Miss…” Samuel makes an attempt to find her name in his memory banks sitting back down at the desk.

“Miss Ross.” Gibraltar reminds. “Her name is actually McKenzie.”

“Ah!” Samuel leans forward. “So you two are on first name based now? Huh?”

“Nah.” Gibraltar smirks slightly thinking about how it came about he got her name. “Not hardly, she did slip up and tell me though, but she also told me that she prefers that I not use it.”

“Hmph.” Samuel really doesn’t understand their relationship. “What have you done to make her hate you so much? Or is she just that tough a cookie?”

“Well.” Gibraltar bobs his head back and forth thinking about how he actually did break some of her barriers down during their last encounter. “I think its probably a little bit of both. It’s hard to say, I certainly did find out one aspect that she seems unwilling to budge on. She seems to be a real strict (goody-two-shoes) Christian, and will only date someone who is like that. I really don’t understand, its not like I am really a bad guy…” He paused contemplating on whether he is or not and on his next choice of words. “Well…I mean I know I have some anger issues from time to time, and I may swear a little too much, but surely she can’t hold all of that against me.” He talks sympathetically to himself forgetting that he was actually talking to Samuel.

“So because you’re a cussing Fire Captain she wont go out with you?” Samuel rhetorically asked. “Nah…that cant be it. You must have done something else.”

Gibraltar sits forward in his chair trying to figure out what it was that he may have or may not have done. “Well Samuel…I really don’t know…I mean I was thinking, maybe its that she finds me childish, but really what guy isn’t? She did invite me to church, so its almost as though she was contemplating some sort of friendship at least, but I really don’t know and I don’t know what to do. I have to figure something out, and fast. Phathom will be out of the hospital soon…very soon.”

Samuel gets up from his seat. “So.” He starts to talk walking back over towards the couches.

“Hey toss me one of them bottles of water!” Gibraltar demands.

“What’s the magic word?” Samuel reaches for another sucker.

“Umm…toss me a dang bottle of water or your fired.”

“No…no…Doc its easy. Samuel…will you please toss me a bottle of water.” He mocks his Captain as he grabs a bottle of water from the fridge. When he tosses it over he misses his mark by a long shot and it bounces off the window behind Gibraltar before rolling up under his feet.

“What the heck did you do that for??? You could have broke the window!” He yells at Samuel. “You idiot.” He mumbles under his breath, thinking about how aggravating he sometimes is.

“You see Doc…I’m just trying to help you here. Maybe you should go to the church. Have you thought about that?”

"No…no…" Gibraltar picked the water bottle up and takes the cap off. "You know I am not going there. That's not me I don't have to go to no church to be a good guy."

Samuel sits back down taking the sucker out of his mouth thinking about how it might do his friend some good to go to a church. "No…maybe not, but that may be your only option if you want to see her anymore when Phathom is discharged from the hospital. That is unless you plan on stocking her at the school that is."

Gibraltar takes a drink, thinking about what his friend had just said, as an idea switches on in his mind. "No…no…I wont be doing that." He lied. "And I definitely wont be going to no church for a date." He sits back in his chair contemplating how his next move should work. "I'll figure something out." He said out loud to himself laid back in his chair gazing at the ceiling.

Gibraltar stands and goes over to the filing cabinet shuffling through the files when the alarm started buzzing and the lights begin to flash. "Station Thirteen!" Barbie from dispatch comes over the radio. "We have a single house fire out at Coral Gables, Seventy Sixty-Nine South Main."

Gibraltar looks over at his Lieutenant. "Coral Gables? That's at least fifteen minutes out, if we fly. Barbie isn't that Station Fifteens territory?" He called back over the radio.

"Yea Doc, that's right, but their all hands on deck right now with a tanker truck off a bridge right now. You all are the best we have at the moment." She responds curtly.

"10-4 Barbie, on our way twenty minutes out." Gibraltar Speaks into his radio, as they scramble to get going. "Ok LT, you all take the smaller engine, I'll take my ride I can get there a lot quicker and asses the situation before you make it there." He gave his orders as they both run out the door.

"You got it Doc, see you down there."

Samuel takes a left out of the office to go slide down the pole while Gibraltar takes the right going down the stairs, two and three at a time.

Gibraltar turns left onto Main Street, and instantly decided there was no need to look for the address on his GPS as he looked into the sky and saw a thick dark black cloud of smoke billowing up, about a mile away.

Once he was close to the house he saw that it was completely engulfed in flames. There were two patrol cars parked in front of the yard to the house. Gibraltar parks his SUV in the neighboring houses yard and swiftly jumps out of his vehicle. Running to the rear of his SUV he grabs his fireman's pants, he no more than gets the suspenders pulled over his shoulders as he looks over to the flaming house and thinks. ***There is no saving anything from this place.***

Over in the front yard of the house that is on fire, there are three police officers and a handful of other spectators gathered around a man on his knee's in the grass. Gibraltar runs over to them all, still only in his fireman's pants, not fully dressed out.

He steps over in front of the small crowd to the seemingly hysterical man on the ground. Sir, my name is Captain Crichton with Miami Dade Fire Department. Are there any pets or animals in the house?"

The guy cries out and leans forward almost blatantly ignoring Gibraltar. "Sir!" Gibraltar raised his voice. "Is there anyone left in the house?"

"Nooo!!!" The man yells back. "But its all gone my whole house, everything I have…its all gone…AHHHH!!!" He cries out with, a way over the top exaggerated scream.

Gibraltar steps back away from the crowd and pushes the button on his radio. "Station Thirteen." He addresses his team, being in the separate district using their frequency. "This is Captain Crichton, we have a total loss fire here. No injuries claimed, but we will need to hose down the neighboring houses to keep the fire from spreading."

"10-4 Doc." Samuel responds immediately. "Five minutes out."

Gibraltar runs over to the police officers. “Hey guys, can you please move your patrol cars so that I can get my truck in closer to the house. The thought of their cars being in the way clearly hadn’t crossed their minds.

Gibraltar walked back over to the man in the yard still on his knee’s except now he was up petting a small dog. “So…sir what happened here?” He interrogated the man wanting to get to the bottom of the situation.

“What do you mean what happened here? Everything is on fire.” The man responds in a highly offensive manner.

“No crap wise…” Gibraltar pauses taking a deep breath. “Your right sir…” He attempts to start over. “But I am just curious if you seen what happened, or do you know how the fire was started?”

As Gibraltar was questioning the guy his team pulls up in the yard with the smaller fire engine. They were all almost out of the truck before Samuel even had it in park. Sam and DeAndre take a hose to the nearest fire hydrant which luckily was right across the street, while Barry connected the other one to the truck.

Barry takes the business end of his hose to the right side of the house. “Let me know when your ready!” Gibraltar yells out running over to the truck to turn the water on for Barry.

Barry sprays down the house and yard to the right side while DeAndre gets the one on the left side. They then let the house that was burning, burn almost all the way down before they attempted to put the fire out.

Afterwards Gibraltar looks back to the crowd that had mostly dispersed, and all that was left was two of the patrol officers. He walks over to them. “Hey officers? Where did the owner to the house go?”

One of the officers looked to him quizzically, then over to his partner as though he was looking for approval to speak. “Umm…I think he said he was going to his sisters…” The officer scratches his head as though he might scratch out a memory. “His aunts maybe…or one of them two. Not real sure.”

Gibraltar’s face begins to turn red and he can feel his temperature starting to rise. “Well, what was his name?”

Same thing, the one that seems to be the lead looks to his partner again. “I think it was Greg.” He’s unsure. “No it was Steve.”

“Steve Bosch.” His partner came to his rescue.

Gibraltar frustrated shakes his head and glanced over at his team finishing up at the fire truck. So I am guessing since you really didn’t even get a name, you probably didn’t get a statement from him either, did you?”

“Umm…no it’s a fire.” The one who seems to be in charge speaks up again. “Isn’t that your job?” He claims offensively as though he shouldn’t have to worry about it.

“Oh my gosh…are you two rookies…or are you just complete morons?” Gibraltar begins to curse at them. “Do they not train you guys anymore? Or are you two just total numbskulls?” He continued to bash them.

“Hey mister, we are the cops and you are the fireman. We deal with the bad guys and you deal with the fires. That’s just how these things work.” The officer stated this, without the duh it should have had.

“Yea except! What if Greg or Steve or whatever the name was is the bad guy who started the fire…Arghh!!!” Gibraltar throws his hands to his side and just walks away before he cursed them anymore.

Gibraltar goes over and checks on his team seeing they are all, almost packed up. He sends them on before he goes into (or on rather) the burnt pile of what used to be a house. He walks into the charred pile and on through the house, looking thoroughly at every piece of charred remains.

Gibraltar makes his way into what appeared to used to have been the master bedroom. Upon further inspection he thought that it looked like this to be where the fire had started with some sort of accelerant.

He takes a plastic bag from his pocket and scoops up some of the ashes placing them in the bag and back into his pocket, then continues walking on through the house.

“Captain Crichton!” He hears some one call on him and he turns around.

“Spector.” Was the last person Gibraltar expected to see at a lone house fire.

“What are you doing here Captain Crichton? This is Fifteen’s territory.” The Marshall demands the question, not at all understanding why this Captain was so far away from home.

“Well.” In attempt to remain civil Gibraltar goes over and shakes the Marshall’s hand. “Fifteen was on another call and we were the next closest, but as you can see we was a little far out to save much. The guy that was here said that there was nobody or any animals left in the house when I arrived, then the two moron police officers couldn’t even get his name much less a statement. So that is what I was trying to do, assess what happened here.”

Spector non-chalantly nods and continues to walk through the house. “The man who owns this house.” Spector speaks as they walk together through the kitchen. “Is Steve Bosch, I was just on the phone with him. He said the fire started in his laundry room.”

“Well Spector…” Gibraltar thinks about what he should be saying to the Marshall. “I think he’s lying. I found what I believe to be an accelerant in the master bedroom." He claims pulling the bag back out from his pocket holding it up to show Spector.

The Marshall's eyes get big seeing the evidence bag, but does not freeze on it long. He turns his attention to the dryer. "Yep it definitely started here. See the cord melted there? Pretty simple case." He stands back up straight. "Thanks for your help Captain Crichton. I can handle it from here. I'll go ahead and get that sent off to the crime lab for Station Fifteen's Captain, so you don't have to worry with it anymore." Spector held out his hand for the evidence bag.

"Nah, I don't mind its not a problem I can take it by there. My team was the one's who worked the fire anyways."

Marshall Spector takes a step forward. "Yes Captain Crichton, you all were and we greatly appreciate it, but I am the Marshall here and I must insist on taking this one in myself and you do not need to worry yourself with it anymore. Your district I am sure has enough issues to deal with all its own." He is very insistent not going to back down from this one.

Gibraltar notices something doesn't feel right but isn't about to further argue with the Marshall. "Yea I do have plenty of work that I need to get to, thanks." He stated as he reluctantly hands over the evidence bag.

"But thank you again Captain Crichton. If there is anything I can ever do for you my door is always open."

They shake hands again. “Okay thank you Spector, I’ll see you around.”

They separate and as Spector goes back towards the back of the house Gibraltar makes his way back to the front. He turns back to see if Spector is watching him leave. He see’s that he is not, so then darts back to what’s left of the master bedroom and fills another evidence bag with the seemingly accelerated burnt ash, and sneaks back out the front.

Twelve

“Ok class!” McKenzie addresses her students just before the bell. “For your homework assignment in math, I would like for you all to do the summary to lesson fifteen in your textbooks on long division.”

The lunch bell sounds as she finished giving out their assignment. All at once the whole class jumps up from their seats, except Santiago.

McKenzie noticed him eagerly watching all of his classmates file out of the room from his desk on the front row.

Young Maria is the last one to walk down the aisle, as she comes by Santiago he sticks his foot out and trips her. “Hahaha!” He laughs at her as she tumbles into the floor and the backpack that she had placed over one shoulder slid across the floor, barely bumping into the front of McKenzie’s desk.

McKenzie quickly jumps out of her seat from behind her desk, but at a much slower pace than Maria jumped out of the floor. At a lightning speed she jumps up from the floor, her pale white face turnt beat red, as she’s fuming mad.

Maria turns around to Santiago who is just getting up from his desk, and quickly approaches him. “You sorry stupid little!!!”

“Ugh, Maria!” McKenzie raises her voice drowning out all her explicit language.

No sooner than Santiago attempts to step back Maria plants her right fist into his left eye. “Maria, Don’t!!!” McKenzie rushes around her desk to get in between the two of them.

“S-s-s-sheee…punched…m-m-mee in the e-e-eyyyee!” Santiago cries as he knelt down in the floor holding his hand over his eye.

“Well you shouldn’t have tripped me, you idiot!”

McKenzie grabs Maria and pulls her away. “You all go to lunch, now!” She yells back to all the students who have stuck around to watch the show.

McKenzie kneels down to meet Maria’s gaze. “You can’t be doing stuff like that Maria…”

“But he tripped me.” Maria cuts McKenzie off. “Miss Ross.”

McKenzie holds her hand up hushing Maria. “I know, I seen that also, which is why he will also be going to the Principal Bright’s office.”

Santiago stands up all teary eyed. “She punched me in the eye.” He cried out again.

“That she did.” McKenzie confirms turning towards him seeing his eye is already begging to swell. “And it looks as though you are going to have quite the shiner from it…Maria!” She turns back to address her, looking her in the eyes. “Where did you learn to talk like that? You know you can’t be saying hateful things like that.”

“Well.” Maria shrugs as though she had done nothing wrong. “That’s what my mom says to my dad all the time when she punches him, when he makes her mad.”

Oh great how am I suppose to get onto a young girl for only doing something her parents have taught her. Oh well at least I am just the teacher, boy do I not envy the principal or counselor right now.

“Ok both of you, grab your things we are all going to take a trip to Mr. Bright’s office so that he can determine your punishments.” McKenzie walks behind her desk keeping a close eye on the two of them as she grabs her purse. “Ok lets go.” She put a hand on Maria’s shoulder pushing herself behind her in between the two of them.

As they walk to the door and exit the classroom, McKenzie see’s JJ standing in the doorway across the hall. “Hey Miss Jackson, I am going to bit late for lunch. We have to make a trip to Mr. Bright’s office first.” JJ gives her friend a surprised, knowing smirk across the hall as they take off in opposite directions.

They are walking down the hall when Santiago starts tapping on McKenzie’s arm. “Miss Ross, I have to go pee.” He says out loud as they all come up on the bathrooms.

“Ok Santiago, make it quick.” He opens the door, snarls his nose and freezes in place. “What’s the matter?” McKenzie questioned him wondering why he froze in place at the door.

“It…” He waves her down to his level to tell her privately and whispers. “It stinks, I can’t go in there.” He whines.

“Santiago do you need to go phh…to the restroom or not?” He dances back and forth holding his nose and rushed through the door into the bathroom.

"Maria." She looks across the hall to the girls restroom. "Do you need to use the restroom while we are here?" She shakes her head no, at the same time Santiago comes running out of the bathroom gasping for air. "Santiago, are you ok?"

He shakes his head no, looking up at her taking quick short breaths. "I had to hold my nose and I couldn't breath." He claims frantically.

The three of them walk into the front part of the offices just outside the principals office. McKenzie directs the two of them to sit in the chairs just outside the door when she hears Mr. Bright. "Ok Captain Crichton." Her heart flutters and skips several beats. "That sounds great, we will be in touch."

McKenzie's mind begins to race. ***What do I do?*** She asked herself as she wanted to run around the corner, had Maria and Santiago not been sitting there she would have. ***Ok no big deal I got this.***

She takes a deep breath and knocks on the door frame as she enters. "Mr. Bright." She called out with a shaky voice.

"Oh excellent timing Miss Ross." ***Or really terrible timing really.*** McKenzie thinks to herself. "This here is Captain Crichton."

Gibraltar holds up a hand. "Would it be alright if I went by Captain Gibraltar? I feel like it would be more personable for all the children."

“Oh sure.” Mr. Bright walks around his desk. “Gibraltar you say? That is an excellent name, sounds really…really strong…I like it, Miss Ross this here is Captain Gibraltar.

Gibraltar reaches his hand out to McKenzie who reluctantly takes his hand. As their hands connect she feels what she thought to be a thousand butterfly’s flapping around in her stomach. “Hey…doc Cri…I mean Captain Gibraltar, pleased to meet you.” She stutters out, not wanting Principal Bright realizing she knew him.

“Like wise.” Gibraltar nods, smiles, and plays along, confident and not nearly as nervous as she was.

“Captain Gibraltar…Gibraltar, hehe.” The principal chuckles at himself. “I really like saying that, Captain Gibraltar here is the one who pulled Phathom off the bus, that first day when it crashed.” He praises him for his heroic work.

“Oh…Oh yeah, I thought he looked familiar.” McKenzie begins to gain her composure, without Mr. Bright ever noticing it gone.

“Anyways he is starting up a Non-Profit Foundation called Save-The-Books. Captain Gibraltar briefly tested his theory with Phathom and has explained to me his vision, which I find to be an incredibly ingenious idea. We are going to give it a full classroom trial. He claimed that Phathom truly enjoyed his books so I have agreed to let him use your classroom. Well that's assuming you are ok with an attempt to get your students to read more, that is."

Jesus help me! McKenzie prays. "Of course." She agreed, not exactly having any other options. "I would love to hear all about it. Do you have any flyers, brochures, or a website?" She questioned hoping he didn't have any of the bases covered.

"Oh yes." Mr. Bright steps in. "He has all of the above, in fact he has given me several of each." He comments as he reached over his desk grabbing the stack handing McKenzie half of what felt like a hundred of each.

"It's all in there, my vision, my purpose, and my goal Miss Ross. I believe you will find it all to your satisfaction." Gibraltar claims with all the confidence in the world.

"Ok great! I'll get with Mr. Bright after I have had a chance to go over it all to be in touch with you, but right this minute I have more urgent business to conduct with the principal about a couple of my students. It was nice to meet you Captain Crichton." She states jabbing her hand out at him shaking his hand, very quickly.

"No problem Miss Ross, thank you principal Bright. I hope to hear from you soon." They shake hands again and Gibraltar swiftly leaves the office.

❖

McKenzie placed her plastic grocery bag on the table across from JJ who was already half finished with her Lean Cuisine. “Did you get your two trouble makers taken care of?” What were they doing anyways? Smooching in the corner?”

McKenzie starts pulling things from her bag, three Tupperware containers, a fork, a spoon, yogurt, and a bottle of water. “Ha, no I wish it would have been something so simple.” McKenzie thinks back onto the incident trying to get Gibraltar out of her mind. “So Santiago trips Maria, (quite intentionally) she jumps up steaming mad and socks him right in the eye after yelling a handful of explicit terms towards him.”

Jemma bursts out in laughter almost hysterically so. “That’s great! At least now maybe he wont be tripping any more girls after that. What do you have in there?” JJ looks over at McKenzie’s lunch inquisitively. “It definitely doesn’t look like fast food.” McKenzie pops the top off the main container. “Oh wow! That looks amazing and it doesn’t even look store bought.” JJ admires her lunch.

“Nope.” McKenzie shakes her head taking a small container and shakes it up vigorously so, before opening it. “Its not, I made it last night. It’s a berry, berry, berry chicken salad.” She pours the very generous amount of dressing over the top of the salad and sits the empty container back in the middle of the table.

“Wow! That’s so colorful.” JJ intent gazed at the salad, almost jealous of her friend lunch. “Is that strawberries?” She grabs the small container running a finger around the edge of it, then licking it off of her finger. “Oh wow!” She blinks her eyes big. “That tastes amazing. Pow! That’s like a party in my mouth, that dressing rocks. What is it?”

McKenzie gives her a smirky grin. “Yea that stuff does rock.” She brags on her ability to make an amazing dressing. “It’s a balsamic honey vinaigrette, and yea there are strawberries, raspberries, and blackberries in here, but the dressing is my favorite.” She comments eagerly stabbing her salad with her fork.

“That’s so amazing, I’m proud of you.” JJ praises. “If you can cook like that I don’t understand why you would ever be eating a cold foot long chili cheese dog. What’s gotten into you?” JJ’s eyes get big with a revelation. “Ooahh! I bet you went out with that Fire Captain.” She claims as though a light went off in her brain.

“Ahem!!!” McKenzie chokes just having removed him from her memory. “Ah…ah…no…” She attempts to defend herself with her mouth full.

“What is it then? You don’t just alleviate from your routine for no reason.”

McKenzie takes a drink of her water. “Ugh! I told you I can’t date him.” She says almost yelling it. “I was talking with my mom the other day, and she simply reminded me that I do at least partially know how to cook.”

“Partially?” Jemma responds enviously. “That’s hardly partially, I know chefs who couldn’t make a vinaigrette half that good.”

McKenzie shrugs thinking about her recent run in with Gibraltar contemplating on saying anything about it. ***No I definitely can not get in to this with her.***

“So what’s in here?” Jemma grabs the mid size container opening it. “Oahh…pineapple my favorite!” She states grabbing a chunk from the container.

Ugh! What the heck, I need someone to complain about his audacity to.

“Get this.” McKenzie said as she reached into her purse pulling out the flyers and brochures. “When I was taking Maria and Santiago to Principal Bright’s office Gibraltar was in there.”

“Gibraltar?” JJ screws up her face and crunches her brow.

“Yea Captain Crichton.”

“Ooahh!” Jemma’s face brightens up with this thought. “So your at least on first name bases with him now? Gibraltar…I like that, it’s a good strong name.”

McKenzie cocks her head giving her friend a frustrated look. “No way…he’s a doush and now he’s going to be aggravating me in my classroom…Ahhh!!!” She complains. “I have done turned him down over and over. I told him I won’t date him, and now he goes to Mr. Bright…Ahh!!!” She huffs out a completely baffled breath. “And gets our principal on his side. So now I’m going to have to deal with him, and all his childish games with all my students.” She briefly glanced at the flyers and brochures before handing them to JJ. “Look what he’s going to be doing, bringing gaming tablets to pass out.”

Jemma takes the brochure and flyers reading off. “Save-the-Books Foundation. Let’s not leave books in the past. Instead let’s take them into the future.” She gazes up at McKenzie who was working on some of her pineapple. “Umm…this doesn’t look like gaming tablets. It looks like reading tablets, and surely Mr. Bright wouldn’t allow him to bring it into the school if it wasn’t something very productive. He is pretty picky about these kind of things.”

“Ughh!” McKenzie gives her friend a bug eyed hard stare. “So your still taking his side. I knew I shouldn’t have brought this up. Hmph!” She pouts out a frustrated breath.

"Oh come on McKenzie. Your acting worse than my students, there is no sides here. Your just mad because your hurt and lonely and God keeps bringing you the perfect guy rubbing him in your face. But because your so stuck up in your family's church crap you can't see it."

McKenzie's jaw drops clear off her face. "Uhh! I can't believe you, you know it isn't just church crap. Its my life, sure my family has set my roots and it is important to all of us, but God still makes us all individuals. And our lifestyles isn't unimportant, we want our family's to all walk closely to God and the Holy Spirit as one for generations to come." She frantically grabs the brochures and flyers out of JJ's hands and shoves them hard back into her purse.

"I'm sorry." JJ recognizes the hurt her words just caused. "That was a low blow, I just whole heartedly feel like you should give him a chance."

McKenzie still pouting although slightly less so makes a change of subject. "So how's things with Jonas going?" She questioned not really wanting to talk about relationships feeling extra lonely.

"Its going really good…in fact." JJ leans over the table and starts to whisper not wanting any gossip material to get out. "I really think he is going to ask me to marry him. In a couple of weeks we're suppose to go up to Orlando for a hot weekend."

McKenzie gulps down choking, and almost swallowing the whole chunk of pineapple she just put in her mouth. "What!" She said louder than she meant to, coughs and takes a drink of water. "You barely know him, you ca…"

"But!" JJ interrupts her. "He is so perfect and ambitious and I just know he is the right one. He's already taking the next step into his life, he's actually suppose to be taking me to look at a shop he is planning to buy today."

McKenzie pushes the container of pineapple across the table. "Here I'm finished with this." JJ gladly accepts it. "I'm sorry, I know I shouldn't say anything about your relationship. God knows I'm not the right one to judge about that. I just worry about you is all."

"I know." JJ smiles and nods to her friend.

Thirteen

McKenzie knocks and enters the hospital room. Startled and caught by surprise, Gibraltar is over at the counter while Phathom is sitting on the edge of her bed petting Apollo.

"Miss Ross! Your just in time, Captain Gibraltar was just about to let me open my going home present." Phathom excited about the gift as well as finally getting to leave the hospital.

"Oh! Well, that was nice of him to get you a going home present." McKenzie dryly remarks unsure of what to think. "I didn't even know you were about to go home." She mummers out the addition somberly.

"Yes she is, in fact Doctor Tolbert is on his way to do a few last minute tests to make sure she is ready to go. How are you Miss Kenzie."

"Uhh!" Phathom's eyes perk up at the sound of her name (shortened). "That is not her name, that is Miss Ross. We was just talking about her Captain Gibraltar."

McKenzie looked over at Gibraltar with one them, (if-looks-could-kill) looks. Quickly snapping back out of it and returning her focus to Phathom. "Yes you are right Phathom, my first name however is McKenzie (Not Kenzie). It is Miss Ross to all my students." She shoots a stern glare over at Gibraltar. "And it is definitely Miss Ross to you also Captain Crichton." She barks at him angry at his calling her his own pet name.

“Why is that?” Phathom curious now as to why the teachers go by their last names.

“That is a very good question Phathom.” McKenzie walks over towards her. Apollo perks his nose up smelling McKenzie’s skirt and try’s to lick her hand.

“Haha.” Phathom giggles at Apollo’s attempt to smell her teacher. “I think Apollo likes you Miss Ross!” She claims cheerfully.

McKenzie reluctantly pets Apollo, her mood quickly softening as she does so. “So Phathom, when we are greeting people, it is a proper formality to say Mr., Misses, or Mrs. and their last name.”

Apollo returns back to Phathom. “Oh.” She comments already bored with the topic. “Guess what Miss Ross?” McKenzie looks to her. “I get to play fetch with Apollo for my go home test. I bet nobody else gets such a awesome test.”

McKenzie looks to her and turns back into stern teacher mode. “Phathom, when we are saying a word that starts with a vowel, we always use the word an before it not a.”

Gibraltar steps up between the two of them with a poorly wrapped box. “Come on Ken…I mean Miss Ross, can we not let her not be in school for just a little while here.”

She shoots Gibraltar another evil eye and starts again to scold him.

“Sorry Phathom.” He cuts in before she has a chance to speak. “My wrapping job is very poor, I’ve never been able to figure out how to keep the wrapping paper tight around a gift.”

“I’m just going to rip it up anyways.” Phathom shrugs as if it is no big deal, and instantly starts ripping away the paper, throwing paper everywhere. McKenzie leans over and watches curiously wondering what is in the box. “You got me shoes!” McKenzie gives Gibraltar an almost approving smile that still says I really wish you would stop being so childish. Phathom’s expression quickly turns into a confused look. “What is this?” She questioned as she pulled the gift out of the box.

“That Phathom, is a real life wood peg leg, so this Halloween you can be a real live pirate.” McKenzie’s ever softening smile turned right around into a deadly frown as her face turns steaming red with anger. “Really?” Phathom questions still unsure about the idea.

“Aiyia ya matey Arghh!” Gibraltar imitates, completely ignoring McKenzie’s gaze. “You really can slide your robot foot off and this peg leg right into its place. I hope you like it, it took a lot of convincing to get Doctor Tolbert to go a long with it.”

Phathom looked down in the box and seen the eye patch to go with it. She smiles and removes the patch placing it over her left eye. “Ayia Cap’n Gibraltar, peg leg Phathom porting for duty sir!” She solutes him with her left hand. All the while McKenzie standing their steadily tapping her foot with a gaze stuck on Gibraltar who simply doesn't even acknowledge it. "At least I bet I'll get the most candy out of all my class." Phathom appreciates Gibraltar taking the patch off and putting it and the peg leg back into the box.

"Phathom, did you have any questions about class or school work today?" McKenzie asked in attempt to get away from her frustration. Phathom simply shakes her head now, and McKenzie does not push the issue knowing everything she must have on her mind right at the moment. "Ok, well if you can think of any questions just ask. This is so exciting!" She attempts to bring zeal to herself. "You going home tomorrow and all, also you don't need to worry about the homework tonight or logging in to class tomorrow. You need to worry about getting settled back in at home with your family."

"Okie dokie, Mom and Dad don't want me to ride the bus anymore, but I told them I am a big girl and I would like to ride the bus again with my friends."

McKenzie steps closer looking in the box at the wooden peg leg before turning her gaze towards Gibraltar in a frown with disapproval written all over her face. Then she turns back to Phathom with the biggest smile she can muster. "That's very brave of you Phathom, and you do not need to be afraid. I am quite sure you will be just fine."

Phathom nods her head putting the lid back on the box and places it on her table taking notice of the bright green neon tablet. “Oh yeah Captain Gibraltar, I finished Amazonia.” She stood, a bit wobbly as she pushes Apollo back out of the way. “It was really…umm…adventurous and sometimes scary. Especially when those piranhas grew legs and chased them. The game was a lot more funner too.” She claims her enjoyment over reading the book.

“See!” Gibraltar looks at McKenzie. “If I would have had her download the book, I would probably never even known if she liked it, or even read it or not.”

McKenzie gives him a skeptical look and snatches the tablet from Phathom as she attempts to hand it to Gibraltar. “Very good then.” She remarks in a snobby manner not wanting him to see her real interest. “I’ll take it and read it now so that Phathom and I can talk about it, plus I am still unsure if I want to allow you to be bringing these into my classroom.”

“Fine.” Gibraltar shrugs with the smirkiest smile she had ever seen.

“Wow! Phathom.” Doctor Tolbert speaks in his normal spunky tone as he walked into the hospital room. “You are very popular today.”

Phathom being in a good mood bobs her head back and forth like a model might. “It comes with the looks.” She arrogantly remarks as she pokes at her hair with a palm.

Doctor Tolbert walks toward the middle of the room causing McKenzie and Gibraltar to bump into one another in attempt to get out of the way and they both nervously apologize as they retreat to separate corners of the room.

“Wrriiittt…Apollo…” Gibraltar whistles for his dog to come over. “Get out of the way.” Apollo obediently walks over under Gibraltar’s feet and laid at his feet, without as much as a whimper.

“Ok Phathom.” Doctor Tolbert walks over to the bed and pushed the table out of the way noticing the peg leg prosthesis. “I see you have received your new pirates gift. What’d you think? Captain Crichton swore to me you’d like it, I wasn’t so sure myself.”

“Enh.” Phathom shrugs still unsure herself. “Maybe at least I’ll get more candy than all the other kids.” She reiterates the only positive side she can find in the gag gift.

“Hehe…” Doctor Tolbert chuckled at her revelation about the gift. “Yea probably so. Now I do not want you to try it on for a while though, we need to get you used to your new foot first. Make sure to bring the wood peg leg to one of your appointments after you have had some time on your robotics prosthesis first. Ok now go ahead and get back into the bed I want to run a few more tests real quick. Lay back in the bed for me, dear.”

Phathom pushed herself up into the bed and lays down flat. Doctor Tolbert lays his tablet beside her feet. “Ok Phathom, I want you to raise up your right foot.” She listens and follows the directions of his calming voice. “Ok, now wiggle your toes.” She does so wiggling the toes to her actual foot. “Very well, you can go ahead and lower your foot. Now raise up your left foot.” She raises up her prosthetic foot. “Now wiggle your toes.” He demands her with almost the same exact whispering intensity as he had with her real foot, but nothing happens as he watches the struggle in her face. “Ok Phathom.” He makes a couple quick swipes on his tablet. “Now don’t let that discourage you.”

“Ughh!” Phathom lazily plops her prosthesis back down on the bed. “I was trying to wiggle my toes.” She whined with grave disappointment.

“I know you were, its ok, not a problem honey. Lets try something different. Now raise your right foot up again.” Frustrated not paying attention she raises her prosthesis back into the air. “No…no…Phathom your right foot.” She listens. “Now close your eyes and take a deep breath. Ok now rotate your ankle.” She spins her foot around in a smooth motion. “Very good, slowly lower your foot back down and raise your left foot back up.” She continues to listen to Doctor Tolbert’s calm soothing voice. “Rotate your left foot just as you just did the right one.” Phathom ends up moving her prosthetics in a jerky back and forth motion. “Ok very good.” He keeps his excitement at bay. “Now take another deep breath.” She takes another slow deep breath. “Now rotate your left foot again.” She rotates it again, this time in a much smoother motion, not perfect by any means, but much better.

“Ok Phathom.” Doctor Tolbert picked up his tablet and quickly goes to work on it. “Very, very good you can go ahead and rest your leg.”

“Whew…good my leg was starting to get tired.” She claimed in an exasperated tone.

McKenzie and Gibraltar both look at each other with surprised faces. “So what does all that mean Doc? Why can she move her ankle but not her toes?”

Doctor Tolbert looks up from his tablet. “Well, I cant be one hundred percent, but honestly that was way better than I was expecting and I am very confident that within a couple of weeks she will be able to move the toes on her prosthesis easier than she can on her real foot.”

“Really?” Phathom’s face brightened up.

“Yes dear really, its just going to take a little time to learn to move your toes with your calves muscles, but I am very optimistic that this AI program will help you be able to do such. I was working on a program that would have been able to connect to your other calve to learn the movements faster, however I ended up hitting too many road blocks and dead ends with that route. We are several years away from that technology (maybe even a generation). This AI program is self learning, and as we all just witnessed it is learning very quickly. Now lets get your shoes on and get you outside."

McKenzie comes over and hands Phathom her socks and shoes as she sits back up on the edge of the hospital bed.

"Captain Crichton would you mind seeing if you could find us a wheelchair? We don't want her to wear the new foot out before we get a chance to try it out."

Gibraltar gladly accepts the mission and exits the room with Apollo to his side.

"So Doc?" McKenzie just thought of something else. "Does this foot being robotic and all, won't it need a battery? Or something like that?"

"Oh yes absolutely, but it really uses very little battery power and the battery we built into it will probably last a full month or more. However because the base I will be giving her to charge it with also will transmit data back to me I have suggested that she plug it in once a week overnight. This will allow us to keep everything updated as well as know if any problems arise." The Doctor proudly explains his invention.

Phathom pulls back a small section of the fake skin at the top of the prosthesis. "See Miss Ross, this is my charging port."

“I see, your already a step ahead of me.” McKenzie zealously admires where she needs to plug in the cable.

Gibraltar and Apollo returned with a wheelchair just as Phathom finished tying up her shoes. “Ok ready Phathom?” Doctor Tolbert asked in his usual, very unusual upbeat tone of voice. “You all can follow me.”

McKenzie slings her purse over her shoulder and begins to push Phathom as Gibraltar puts a leash on Apollo and takes a couple of quick steps to catch up to the Doctor.

Walking down the hallway McKenzie is pushing Phathom about ten yards behind when Phathom starts to giggle.

“Hehe…” McKenzie chuckles at her laugh. “What’s so funny Phathom?”

“Its Doctor Tolbert…look at him walk, he waddles like a duck.” She laughs some more at saying this.

McKenzie takes notice of this waddle Doctor Tolbert seems to have. ***That’s odd, he walks with both feet almost pointed completely sideways…hmm…*** “Now Phathom, that’s not nice. We shouldn’t laugh at people because of how they do something.” McKenzie explains to her gingerly.

“Oh.” Phathom said out loud gaining a bit of understanding as the conversation goes no further.

McKenzie then takes notice of Gibraltar's stride which is almost a perfect heel to toe walk. ***God please help me keep away from this.*** She prays to herself before looking down at her own stride which is a walk with her own feet pointed slightly outward. She takes all of this in as she pushed Phathom onto the elevator.

Outside the hospital Doctor Tolbert is watching Phathom and Apollo play in the grass. McKenzie and Gibraltar somehow get stuck behind with each other. "So the weather is nice." He awkwardly makes an attempt at small talk, unable to come up with anything more to say at the moment.

"Yep." McKenzie states without any emotion in the word, at all. They stand there in an extra long quiet moment. (One of those two minute moments that felt like a lifetime.)

"Why?" McKenzie breaks the silence.

"Why what?" Gibraltar wondered out loud as McKenzie was taking too long trying to figure out how she was going to say, what she really wanted to say.

"Why did you go to Mr. Bright and weasel your way into my classroom? I have told you twice that I cant date you. Why cant you respect that?" She makes her argument.

Gibraltar sadly drops his gaze to the ground in front of him. “Well I wasn’t necessarily trying to get into your class. But you said it earlier Mr. Bright has given you the opportunity to turn me away.”

Her jaw drops and she pushes him hard on the shoulder forcing him to look at her. “Uhh Gibraltar!” She angrily calls him by his first name. “Are you kidding me right now. You know good and well that I cant do that, then I would be the bad guy. You’re the schools hero, just because you happened to be on duty when the busses crashed.”

“Ohh!!!Ughh!!!” Gibraltar slaps his hand over his heart as though she had just stabbed him there. “That’s crazy McKenzie, I know I done everything right and the best job anyone could have done.” He stated as he started to get upset himself.

“Well you didn’t…” McKenzie attempts to find everything wrong with him. “In fact anyone with half a brain could have done what you did, and also you should have splinted her leg before you moved her.” McKenzie hits him even harder with her words.

“Well…” Gibraltar stands there slightly frozen with hurt for a moment. “McKenzie.” He continues in another attempt to defend himself to her. “Yes that would be protocol typically, and I promise I thought about it several times, before I finally decided it was more important to get her to the ambulance quicker. Every situation we deal with is different…and we sometimes have to make fast judgment calls changing our protocol and I felt…" He paused for another unintentional dramatic moment. "And I still feel like I made the proper adjustments for the situation I had at hand. And fine McKenzie you don't want me around, I'll call Principal Bright and tell him that I have had some other things come up and wont be able to start this project right now."

They both stand there for more awkward silence, giving McKenzie time to feel the harshness she had put into her words. "No…" She all but whispers.

"No what???McKenzie I am not asking you out again."

She solemnly shakes her head and gazes straight into his eyes. "No…I know…I am sorry…" She apologizes giving him a forgiving gaze. "I didn't mean to imply that you didn't do a proper job, and no don't call Mr. Bright. Let me look over your flyer and brochure, read the other book maybe, so that I can make a professional, (not emotional) decision, and I will get back with Mr. Bright." She attempts to turn their relationship into the professional one.

Fourteen

"Yes Samantha, I have all the invitations in the mail." Samuel said into his phone not quite arguing with his fiancé. "Yes honey! I double checked the reservations for the venue." He claims in attempt at not sounding frustrated as he looks and see's Alex from his rear view mirror pull into Station Thirteen and park beside him, looking at his clock he notices that it is seven a.m. sharp. "Hey babe my new trainee just pulled in, I need to get in here and show him around. I'll talk to you in a little while." He hangs up his phone after she finally lets him go.

Crawling out of his truck he doesn't even get the door shut before his phone chimes with a new message. "Ugh! Samantha it hasn't even been thirty seconds." He gripes out loud as he pulls his phone right back out of his pocket and reads {Hey honey I love you! Have a good weekend at work, I will see you Monday morning.} He placed his phone back into his pocket, thankful she wasn't asking anything else, at the moment.

"Hey Alex!" He greets his rookie getting out of his car. "Are you ready for it?"

Alex steps out with a bag on his arm. "Good morning sir. I'm sorry I don't remember your name."

Samuel reaches out to shake his hand. “No problem, properly I should be called Lieutenant Brooks, but we are far from proper around here, so LT or just Samuel…either works, whatever is easiest for you.”

“Ok Lieutenant Brooks.” Alex nods.

Oh joy! He’s going to be one of those. Samuel thinks about how squirrelly the guy looks. “Ok, lets get in there and get started. There’s going to be a lot to go over this weekend, its going to feel a bit overwhelming at first, but the first thing on the agenda is that we have to find some breakfast.”

They both head for the front door to Station Thirteen. “Ok, I guess I could eat a little.” Alex remarks.

I hope you can eat a lot. Samuel thinks as they walk through the front doors. Alex follows Samuel up the stairs and into the dining area smelling the sweet aroma of bacon and eggs. “Oh my gosh, it smells amazing in here.” Samuel eagerly stated as they walk in seeing Beatrice place a pan of biscuits on the table. “Hey Bea, looks as though you made an early start.”

She looks up at Samuel and Alex as they walk over to the table. “Yep, you know me always early to rise. I was a little bored sitting at the house, so I thought I would cook some breakfast for everyone to get us ready for our long weekend. You must be Alex.” She walks around the table to introduce herself. “I’m Beatrice, but you can call me Bee.” She pokes her hand out.

Alex chuckles at her. “Bee? Like queen honey bee?”

“Haha…she is not at all like honey, there is nothing sweet about her. Maybe we could call her queen bee though, I like that one hadn’t thought of that one yet.” Felipe mentions as he reaches for a biscuit. He juggles the fresh biscuit in his hand, as its hot out of the oven.

“Hehe…serves you right.” Bea laughs at Felipe burning himself with her biscuits. “That’s Felipe, he and I are the medics.” She points across the table. “That over there is Barry, and DeAndre next to him.” They both give a quick wave and hey as the continue to stuff their faces.

“This looks cool.” Alex admires the morning breakfast set up, thinking they already feel like his family. “Do you always cook breakfast in here?”

Beatrice shrugs pointing Alex to a chair. “Have a seat I’ll fix you a plate.” She begins scooping extra large portions onto a plate for him. “Well…we will all be cooking all of our meals in here for the next three days.” She explains a little of how things work. “Sometimes I do, sometimes Barry does, and sometimes you will.”

“Uh…uh…” Alex’s eyes get big as he stutters out. “I do not know how to cook, I’m sorry that wasn’t in the job description.” He stands up to leave.

“Where you going Alex?” Samuel quizzes almost hoping he would go ahead and walk out.

“Well I didn’t know that I would have to cook. I’m sorry I am not qualified.” Embarrassed he lowers his head.

Beatrice hurry’s over to him. “No Alex that’s non-sense.” She quickly takes him by the shoulders. “I’ll teach you how to cook. In fact I have been needing someone to show some of my new recipes to anyways.”

“Really?” His face perks up with her generous invitation and he smiles at her as he retakes his seat at the table. “You are willing to teach me how to cook?” He starts to get excited.

“Absolutely Alex, we are all a family here. We all work together and teach each other all kinds of things here.”

Alex begins to frown again feeling left out. “But I don’t know anything to teach anybody.” He whimpers lowering his head.

“Whatever.” Barry steps up to the plate. “I bet you know all sorts of things. Like where to buy the best watches, that sure is a nice piece you have there.” Barry desperately wanting to make Alex feel like he belongs.

Alex looks to Barry confused. “Yea but, that’s not me teaching you how to do anything.” He responds as he begins to soften up a little feeling more accepted.

“Sure it is, you can teach me what to look for in a watch.” Barry still trying to fit him in.

Alex thinks on this a moment before he shyly nods his head. “Yea…I suppose I know about watches.” Then he takes a bite of his quiche. “Oh wow!” His face brightened up as his taste buds were tickled with all kinds of goodness, and he turns his gaze back towards Beatrice. “You can teach me how to cook like this?” He asked her as she sits down beside him.

“Yep.” She gives him a proud smile. “I guarantee you within a month you will be twice as good a cook as LT. every time he tries to cook he ends up burning it.”

Alex smiles at her acceptance of him and turns his gaze over to Samuel. “Lieutenant Brooks, aren’t we as fire fighters suppose to be stopping things from burning?” Alex questions literally as everybody at the table laughs at him thinking he is joking. “What!” Alex starts to slightly tremble. “I didn’t mean to make fun of him.” He cries out.

DeAndre takes a drink of his OJ washing his food down. “Haha…” He laughs, not too hysterically though. “No need to worry about that Alex, we all give him a hard time about it.” Alex looks to him not quite understanding, but his mood eased back up as he felt more welcome.

“Yea Alex, it is ok. I really know how to cook, I just choose to burn everything so nobody will expect me to do any of the cooking.” Samuel smartly remarks as though he really did know how to cook.

“Yea Ok!” Beatrice sarcastically calls Samuel out.

“What did you say his name was?” Alex taps Bea on the shoulder and points towards Barry.

“Oh.” Barry gets up to walk around the table to shake Alex’s hand. “Where are my manners, sorry I was focused heavily on my breakfast. I’m technically Sergeant Hill, but everybody just calls me Barry.

“Oh.” Alex looks at him dryly. “Sergeant Hill, like Lieutenant Brooks?” He states as a question pointing at Samuel.

“Yea like Lieutenant Brooks, except we just call him Samuel or LT.” DeAndre puts in his response. “And I am just DeAndre I have no title.” He follows Barry’s lead and goes over to introduce himself.

“De…DeAndre…I like that name.” As Alex turns back to his breakfast Gibraltar comes into the dining area. “Oh! Captain Crichton.” Alex calls out to him as he walks in.

“No Alex, we call him Doc.” Beatrice explains their Captains pet name.

"Good Alex, glad you showed back up. Have you reacquainted with everyone?" Gibraltar curtly responds to Alex's presence.

"Yeah and Bea told me she was going to teach me how to cook." Alex claims eagerly ready to learn.

"Yea…Good for her." Gibraltar rudely responds to Alex, although Alex didn't catch it. "Hey Samuel? Have you spoken with your PI buddy yet?" Samuel clearly doesn't remember what Gibraltar is talking about. "You know the one who we were having test the ashes from the Coral Gables house fire."

"Oh yeah." This jarred his memory. "No I haven't spoken to him yet, I was planning on calling him today."

"Wait a minute…Doc…" Barry now confused and wanting in on the news of the week. "Why didn't you just send the ash to the crime lab like we usually would?" The Sergeant questions his Captain.

"Well Barry…" Gibraltar pauses contemplating on whether or not he really should be discussing this news. "Listen up everybody! What I am about to say we need to keep between ourselves only, until I figure out the extent of the situation. To answer your question Barry I am almost certain that Marshall Spector has some really fishy business going on, and I do not want him to be tipped off by any of the law enforcement agency's. Ok Samuel if you talk to him and its positive for any kind of accelerant, see if we can't get him to come in and chat with us next week. We may need to further use his resources to get to the bottom of this."

"You got it." Samuel shows Gibraltar that he is on his side here.

"Ok Alex." Beatrice gets up from her seat. "I am going to show you the first and most important part about cooking in the kitchen. Doc do you want some breakfast?"

"No." He shakes his head sitting at the table holding up his cup of coffee. "Just coffee for me this morning."

"Ok Alex." He stands with Bea. "Lets get these dishes done."

"Oh." Alex gets excited with the thought of actually knowing how to help. "I know how to do dishes." He claims very zealously. "Hey Bea, why are you wearing a skirt?" Gibraltar takes notice of her skirt for the first time. "Won't it be difficult for you to run into a house fire with a skirt on?"

"Oouahh!!!" Felipe makes a sighing sound at the thought of Alex bashing her skirt, and her ability to do her job properly. "You better watch out Alex, she'll take you on our obstacle course and show you up in that skirt." He makes the challenge for her.

"Since when did you start to wear a skirt to work Bea?" Gibraltar questions not noticing it before Alex pointed it out.

"What! Doc seriously I have always worn one." She's baffled that he hasn't noticed this before.

"Uh no…" He looks to her and shakes his head. "You haven't."

Everybody starts laughing at Gibraltar. "Yea Doc she has wore one everyday since she has been here." DeAndre claims and everyone else concurred with him.

"You mean to tell me that I have worked with you for six months now, and you haven't once noticed that I am always wearing a skirt." Bea trying to figure out how she has squeezed this past him for so long.

Baffled at himself Gibraltar gazes around the table at everyone staring at him waiting on him to talk. "I guess so! Wow, what's wrong with me?" He asked himself, but out loud.

"Well Alex, that is a very good question, and evidently much more observant than others around here." Gibraltar curiously steps to the side attempting to eavesdrop as they walk into the kitchen with the dirty dishes. "So I always wear a skirt to my knee's at least. I do this because I am an Apostolic Christian with the United Pentecostal Church. In fact I always have been and the only person who has ever seen me in pants is my husband." She says proudly glancing out the door catching a small portion of Gibraltar's arm through the doorway.

"What is the United Pennycostal Church?" Alex questions intently wanting to know more.

"Oh." She looks to him very proud that he is showing so much interest. "Well Alex it is a Church organization, I go to Ocean Breeze Apostolic Church."

"Ahem!!!" Gibraltar chokes on his coffee just outside the doorway.

"You ok out there." Bea yells at the doorway at the sound of Gibraltar's choke.

"Anyways, have you ever been to a Church before Alex?" Beatrice quickly returns her focus to his curiosity.

"No…I mean I have heard about them, but I have never went to one."

Now even more excited she barely let Alex finish his statement before she started to speak again. "Well Ocean Breeze is like my family…or one of my family's. Kind of like everybody here is another one of my family's and then I have my husband and our family's, so in total I have four family's and they are all equal to me. I love all my family's the same, anyways that is the best way I can explain it. You should come to church with me sometime." She gives him the invitation.

"That sounds fun." Alex sounds hungry for a new life.

❖

Later that morning Samuel walks through Gibraltar's open office door. "Hey Doc, I just got off the phone with Ja'Maar Enby" He states as he takes a seat, as Gibraltar leans back in his.

Gibraltar crunches his brow. "Is that your Private Investigator buddy?" He states more than questions as he lazily plops both arms onto the rests of his chair, nervously clicking his pen over and over in his right hand.

"Yeah it is, and he said the ash tested positive for…umm…" Samuel puts a hand to his chin in attempt to remember what the accelerant was called. "Anh! Anyways he said it was basically like jet fuel, the stuff burns extremely hot."

Gibraltar swivels around in his chair gazing out the floor to ceiling window over Station Thirteen, contemplating. "Wow! Man oh man!" He says as he spins back around.

"So Ja'Maar said that he will try to make some time to come by next week, he's pretty busy though." Samuel lets him know about the PI's schedule and hope of when he may come in.

Gibraltar nods still in deep thought. "Ok, sounds good. Send him back a message and tell him the sooner the better, maybe even see if it'd be better or quicker that we come by his office."

"Ok will do…Cap…" Samuel solemnly begins to speak. "Are you sure Alex is going to work out??? I mean he seems kind of slow, are we sure we should be sending someone like that into a dangerous situation?" He questioned, legitimately concerned for Alex's well being.

"Yeah Samuel." Gibraltar leans back forward to start back on his paper work. "It'll be ok, I think he is just nervous, give him a chance. Get him out on the obstacle course and see what his reaction time is like. I believe he is going to be much quicker than you are giving him credit for."

"Ok." Samuel stands back up. "But if he can't hang, I will not be sending him into any questionable situations." Samuel upsettingly walks out of Gibraltar's office.

Fifteen

McKenzie hears the muffled sound of a violin, as she makes her way across the back parking lot of Ocean Breeze Apostolic Church. ***Hmm...Arthur must be warming up for service today.*** She thinks as she gets closer and noticed the familiar tune to be What a Beautiful Name, her favorite song. She opened the back door bringing the sweet melody of the chorus to life in her ears and saw exactly what she knew she would, her brother playing the violin warming up in the fellowship hall.

Arthur takes notice of her walking in the back door and cuts the song off short. “Hey sis, how’s it going?” He greets her as they meet in the middle and he gives her a one arm hug with the bow in his right hand careful not to get it twisted in her hair.

“Hey Bubba, wheww!” She let out a sigh in a deep breath. “Quite honestly it has been a really long couple of weeks.” She complains, without really meaning to.

Arthur walks over to the table where his violin case is laid out open and placed the instrument inside. “Oh yeah!” He loosens the horse hair to his bow before putting it back into its perspective place in the case, locking it and his violin all in. “There a guy I need to go beat up?” He jokes with a hap-hazard tone.

“Ugh!” McKenzie puts her purse and Bible on the table. “I wish it were so simple Bubba…I really do.”

“Well it really is, just tell me his name and where to find him.” He makes the threat pounding his right fist into his left hand, wanting to be the hero, little big brother.

“No…no…Arthur, Its not like that.” McKenzie takes another deep breath, sighing as she takes a seat at the table in front of her things.

“What is it then? There is clearly something on your mind. And I want to help.” He takes a seat right across from her looking to his big sister.

“Well there is this guy.”

“I knew it!” He cuts her off excitedly.

“Hold on.” She cuts down his ambitious thoughts. “Now you can’t tell Mom or Dad.” She gazes hard on him for a promise to keep what she has to say a secret.

“No way, of course I won’t tell them. I told you I can take care of it.” He repeats the punching motion eager to protect her.

“No…Bubba its not like that. Its just that he is not Christian…” She pauses looking for her next words. “And…well…he is a bit childish, but honestly other than those, (two big things) he is perfect.” Her gaze goes past her brother in a day dream.

“Oh yeah, how is he perfect, if he is not Apostolic?” He questioned earnestly knowing how they all live and have been taught.

“Well.” She reaches in her purse and takes her phone out, but doesn’t look at it. “So he’s really cute for one.”

"Ugh…sis!!!" Arthur makes an awful face at her. "You know I am sure there are cute Apostolic singles out there also."

"Bubba that is far from the main reason." McKenzie softens her brother back up. "He is the Captain of a fire department, which I really love all of our heroes, (who don't right?) and he's good with people and children, (although mostly one himself) and he in fact he actually saved one of my students the first day of school this year."

"Oh yeah." Arthur nods his head. "I seen something about that on the news a while back, I meant to ask you about it, but I forgot."

McKenzie goes on to re-run her brother through the whole story, then about how Gibraltar showed up, and how he helped out with Phathom. "You see? He is also really good with kids, another perfect trait. Then there is my favorite thing about him, is his ambition." She pulls out the crumpled flyer and brochure of Gibraltar's Save-the-Books Foundation and hands them over to her brother. "He's working on a Non-Profit to get kids more focused on reading. The idea is really ingenious and its really melting my heart, and I am trying really hard to not let it."

"Whew…" He sighs looking through the pamphlet. "Sis, it really looks like your in some kind of situation here."

"Yea." She looks knowingly at her brother. "Tell me about it. So I have one of his books here." She pulls out the bright neon green tablet out of her purse. “I just finished it this morning.” She hands it over to her brother. “For sure do not tell Mom or Dad about this. It’s a crazy Sci-Fi book, they’d really flip out knowing I read something like that.”

“Anh…” He takes the tablet from her, looking it over. “Dad was telling me the other day about watching Star Galaxies. He seems to be lightning up about some of the secular stuff, (keeping his focus of course more towards the church) but as long as its not to violent, sexual, or has a lot of cussing in it, he said it actually had a lot of good value lessons in it.” He states matter-of-factly.

“Really!” McKenzie surprised crunches her brow. “That’s kind of funny, because I read that book and I felt like I found a good Apostolic analogy in it.”

He looks over the table puzzled at his sister as he sits the tablet down on the table in between them. “How so?” He questioned.

“Well…” McKenzie picks up her phone checking the time, and decides she has enough time to give him her insight to the book. “It is a really neat and a very well written book. Its called Amazonia by: James Rollins. In there, there is this species of aunts, (I’m not sure if this is a real species or not, I meant to look it up, but I forgot) but anyways they live in this tree. They have a radius around this tree protecting the tree from all other life around it. The aunts feed the tree and the tree feeds the aunts (without the tree the aunts cant live and visa-versa). Then at the end of the story there is a tribe of people in exactly the same boat. When the tribes people get too far away from the tree that they have always lived off of, they get sick and die. There is something in the fruit of the tree that their bodies are…umm…essentially addicted to. (Now I am ninety-nine percent sure this is not real, it's some of the science fiction behind the book, but I bet the aunts are real.) I was thinking after I read that, it is kinda how I feel at about the church, and I am feeling the closer I get to Gibraltar the further away my spirit gets away from my life source, The United Pentecostal Church is my tree and it has the fruit for my spirit to stay alive." She explains this all to her brother who is very intently listening to her well thought out theory.

"Wow sis, that sounds interesting. I'd like to read it."

"Yea absolutely!" McKenzie pushed the tablet from the center of the table towards him. "I'd love to have your input, anyways I still have to determine and give Principal Bright the okay for Gibraltar to bring his Non-Profit into my classroom. Thank you." She shows her brother gratitude for being there for her.

"Ok, I'll read it and let you know what I think, so…" He wonders what he should say next. "What are you going to do about…Gibraltar? Did I say it right?"

“I’m not sure.” She sadly lowers her gaze at this thought.

“Are you going to go out with him?”

“Oh no.” She quickly shakes her head. “I can’t do that, I can’t allow my spirit to get away from that tree, not even a little. In the book science is able to make a medicine for the tribal peoples physical body, but spiritually Apostolic fruit can not be duplicated. So I think the only thing I can do is continue to let him know that we could be friends at the church if he wishes to come. But otherwise if I decide to let his Non-Profit in the classroom we will have to keep our relationship purely professional.”

Arthur smiles at his big sister. “You see there? I knew I could promise not to tell Mom or Dad, because I knew they raised you right.” He looks at his watch. “Oh crap!”

Well mostly right. McKenzie thought to herself hearing her brother say this.

“I gotta get ready for praise and worship.” Arthur jumps up grabbing his violin case before running off.

Sixteen

With Alex in the passenger seat Gibraltar pulled into the station. “Ok Alex, just cause you have that certificate now might mean you can officially go on calls, but it don’t mean I still won’t can your tail.” He rudely threatened Alex before they get out of the vehicle, while Alex says nothing sitting there looking forward with a stoic expression.

“Station Thirteen!” Static comes over the radio. “Barbie here, we have a frantic lady on the phone who was driving down the interstate behind a SUV that was swerving recklessly. After a couple of miles at a high rate of speed it crashed into the median barrier, bouncing off of it then rolling four or five times into the ditch.”

Gibraltar hearing this slams his door back and throws his vehicle in drive, catching Alex off guard and shutting his door with the momentum. Alex quickly scrambled to get back into his seat belt as Gibraltar spins the tires out of the driveway.

“10-4 Thank you doll.” Barbara from dispatch then gives them the mile marker. “Ok we’re close three minutes out. How about my wagon you two got a copy?” Gibraltar called back to his medic team.

“Yea Doc, copy.” Felipe (Johnny-on-the-spot) calls him back. “Bea and I are loading up now, right behind you.

“We’re right behind them with engine number two.” Samuel the last to respond on the radio, knowing the smaller truck would be the proper choice for a simple car crash.

“10-4 stay aware, see you all down there.” Gibraltar hurry’s down the road just moments away from the interstate and the mile marker where the wreck occurred. “Hey Barbie? Do you have any more information?”

“Negative babe, the lady is so frazzled from the whole situation she really couldn’t give me anything to go on. The way she was talking she narrowly dodged the wreck herself, then couldn’t stop or turn around in the traffic to go help.” Barbara gives him the no-news-bad-news.

Gibraltar listened closely to dispatch, slightly discouraged as he comes up on the mile marker he was given. He slows down checking the ditches until he finally see’s the terribly crumpled SUV laying on its roof.

Gibraltar glanced over to Alex who was shaking and very nervous. “Hey rookie you better snap out of it, its just you and I right now, and I need your full attention on this wreck.” He almost yelled at him in the cab of the vehicle right before he threw it into park.

Gibraltar instantly jumped out of the SUV and ran around to the back where the hatch was already mostly opened. As he grabs his bag he noticed Alex still sitting in the passenger seat frozen. “Get your tail out right now!” Gibraltar cusses at him up through the truck. “We have to get over to the wreck those people in that SUV need us here and now.”

As he continued to yell at Alex he seemed to begin to thaw from his frozen state. Alex jumps out as Gibraltar runs by his side and jogs with him step for step down to the wreckage.

As they approach the SUV Gibraltar notices the baby on board sticker on the shattered back window. ***Dear God please don't let the baby be in there.*** He catches himself praying, and wondering if this is how one does so.

Alex right behind him. “This looks really bad Captain Gibraltar.” He states gazing at the crumpled mess.

The roof over the front seats is completely caved in, looking as though nobody could be upright in the seat still. They get to the drivers side window that is less than half its normal size and Gibraltar gets down on his knee's to further assess the situation. Looking through the driver's side window he immediately gets a whiff of a whiskey smell hitting his old factory senses hard. The driver of the SUV is laying on the roof in a twisted, contorted, bloody mess.

“Whannhh!!!Whannhh!!!” He hears the baby cry out from the back seat. He double checks the rest of the vehicle and noticed that there was just the driver and the baby that was in the back seat, which appeared to be strapped into its seat. ***Dear God, please let this baby be ok.*** He catches himself praying again.

"Alex! Go around to the back passenger side window." Gibraltar makes the quick decision hearing how loudly the baby was crying, that the driver needed his attention more so.

"Ok!" Alex called out, not mere seconds later. "I'm here Captain, now what?"

Wow that was quick. Gibraltar thinks as he is trying to find a pulse on the contorted body in the front. "Ok Alex? Listen carefully." He quickly begins giving direction to his rookie. "Do not unfasten the baby from the car seat. Simply cut the seat belt holding the car seat in, and see if you can maneuver it out of the window." He does not find a pulse.

"Yes Sir!" Alex replied confidently.

Gibraltar stares around to the whole situation in the front seat, really not wanting to move her, he decides that he does not have a choice. He grabs her with blood everywhere, and pulls her out as gently as the situation would allow. He pulls her out from where the front windshield used to be and lays her on the ground flat on her back, and checks for a pulse again.

Felipe and Beatrice roll up with a gurney. “Ok no pulse, we need to get her on the gurney and start CPR.” Gibraltar gives the demand, Felipe helps him get her onto the backboard. “Bea, go check on the baby.”

As he was saying this Alex runs around the SUV with the car seat in his arms. “The baby is right here Captain Crichton.” Alex respond flatly as Beatrice takes the car seat, sits it on the ground and begins to look over the crying baby.

Gibraltar and Felipe get the unresponsive woman onto the gurney. “Oh my gosh, there is so much blood.” Felipe stated looking at the massive gash across the young lady’s chest.

“Ok Felipe lets get her to the ambulance and start CPR.” Gibraltar and Felipe quickly get the gurney onto the ambulance.

Beatrice comes running and jumping into the back of the ambulance with the car seat in her arms. “She appears to be ok, not even a scratch.” Bea states thankfully as she sits the car seat down in the wagon.

Thank you God, did you hear me? Gibraltar prays again.

“Does she have a pulse?” Beatrice questioned buckling the car seat in.

“No!” Gibraltar quickly responds. “Felipe get us to the hospital ASAP.” Gibraltar looks out the back of the ambulance at Alex standing at the back door. “Follow us to the hospital in my ride Alex!” He demands as he see’s the others pulling up in the other fire truck. “Let the rest of the crew know we have everybody, they can stay and help clean up if they don’t have anything more pressing to deal with.”

“Ok.” Alex replied with a stolid expression as he closed the back doors.

Gibraltar starts chest compressions as Beatrice attempted to start an IV. ***“Come on here you can’t die on us.”*** Gibraltar catches himself pleading with God out loud. “One…two…three…four…he counts off the compressions.

“Starting adrenaline now.” Beatrice pushed down the plunger on the syringe.

“Very good, lets get her intubated and bagged. One…two…three…four…” He continues counting down the compressions.

“Ok I’m about to head on.” Felipe yelled back from the drivers seat.

“Gosh dang it Felipe, I told you already get us to the hospital.” Gibraltar cursed at his driver. ***“Come on you can’t die!”*** He pleads again looking up at Beatrice’s eyes, that are beginning to tear up.

A hour after they arrived at the hospital Beatrice walks out very somberly into the waiting room. Felipe Alex and Gibraltar all three sitting there waiting. Gibraltar had went and washed his hands and face, but his clothes remained covered in blood. They all waited patiently on the news.

"Well." Beatrice red eyed from all the crying begins to speak. "She didn't make it. The doctors said that her blood alcohol levels was so high they couldn't even understand how she was even able to function, and it was certainly a miracle that the baby was fastened into the car seat properly. The baby (Thank you Jesus) is perfectly fine not a bruise, scratch, or even whiplash, other than being scared half to death God truly saved that baby."

Gibraltar slowly stood up. "Who are they? Has the family been contacted?" He asked softly.

"Yes…well…" She responds choking up again. "So the mother is twenty-two year old Ashley Jenkins, and the baby's name is Natasha. Figuring all this out is what took so long." She sniffles again. "So there is no listed father and both of Ashley's parents are also deceased. The social worker finally was able to get a hold of a long lost aunt that told us Ashley was nothing but a problem child, drug addict, and she doesn't care what happens to the body or the baby." She begins to cry heavier. "***God excuse my language***…She actually said 'I don't care what happens to that bastard child, she might as well die too'" Beatrice collapses to the floor into a fury of tears.

Gibraltar comes and lays over her sharing her grief. “I’m sorry Bea.” He whispers in her ear. “This job can be a little to much from time to time.”

Beatrice sits back up to her knee’s and looks at Gibraltar who is also sitting on the ground with her, both whipping away the tears. “A little! This job is impossible at times Doc! This really hurts my heart, my husband and I have been trying to have a baby for a year and a half now. So maybe this is a sign from God that there are others out there that need me more so. Natasha is barely three months old with no family at all. I am going to…” She pauses. “Talk to my husband first of course, but I am going to adopt her. The social worker told me it could be possible, it might not be easy she claimed, but she is willing to help me out.”

“Are you sure Bea.” Gibraltar shows concern. “This is a huge step, to go instantly into parent hood. There will be no nine months planning period, you will become instant parents.” He shows her a rare compassionate side of himself.

“Yes.” Bea nods knowing that Natasha needs her right now and nothing else matters. “Of course this is a good point that I would like to discuss with my husband first, but Natasha needs us and if that is God’s will then she will have us.”

Gibraltar catches himself thinking about how it must feel to want to live in God's will, or what does God's will even mean. He begins to question his own existence.

"Hey Alex." DeAndre greets his rookie crew member walking into the waiting room. He quickly noticed all the sad expressions and wanted to run away from all the sadness. "You ready to go?" He quickly adds.

"She died." He told DeAndre, not knowing exactly what to feel, he knows its sad and that he's very upset about it.

"Yea buddy." DeAndre puts an arm around Alex. "This job can be sad, but hey guess what? I heard you was a hero that saved the baby's life today." He attempts to lift his new partner up.

Alex gets a slight glimmer on his face. "Yea I guess I did." He proudly states as he gives everyone else a sad farewell.

"Hold up a minute I need to talk to Cap before we go…Hey Doc you have a minute?" DeAndre asked and they both step over to the side to talk in private.

"Thanks for coming to pick up Alex, I really just need to go home and wash this day off of me.

"Yea of course." DeAndre gives him a reassuring nod. "Here's the card to the escort service I was telling you about." He hands Gibraltar a flashy business card. "We can use this service for Samuel's bachelor party, and my friend down there said that since you are planning it on a Thursday night, it will be no problem at all to get three or four girls for the night."

Gibraltar's conscience instantly goes to McKenzie. ***What would she think about me having strippers at my bachelor party if we were planning a wedding? (God why am I thinking this way.) God? Am I praying to you again?*** He begins to feel the weight of the world take hold of him. "You know DeAndre?" He pockets the business card. "Samuel has told me over and over that he didn't want strippers at a bachelor party. I am thinking maybe we should honor him. This is after all suppose to be about him and Samantha, not us wanting to have a good time."

"Well ok Doc." DeAndre gives him a slightly disappointed look. "You are the best man of course, so this is your call."

Gibraltar gave him a big smile, that really felt good in light of everything that had transpired this day. "Ok cool, we are still definitely having a bachelor party, but probably more of just a dinner and maybe some games of some sort. Either way we are still going to have to kidnap him. He's never going to believe that we really aren't going to have any strippers." (Ding.) Gibraltar's phone chimes with a text.

"Yea…no…" DeAndre fumbles with his words. "He wont, we'll have to figure something out.

Gibraltar nods reading his text form Samuel. {Hey! Ja'maar Enby said that we can come by his office in a hour or so.} He hits the thumbs up reply. "Well speak of the devil, I have to go. Samuel and I are going to go meet his PI buddy in a bit.

"Good luck!" They both nod To one another and walk in opposite directions.

"Samuelle…my friend!" Ja'maar greets with a deep bold tone of voice. He walks around his desk as they enter.

"Ja'Maar its so good to see you." The two of them shake hands, both of them engaging strongly into their introduction. "This here is Captain Gibraltar Crichton." He introduces his Captain and friend.

"Just Gibraltar is fine." Gibraltar claims as he shakes hands with Ja'Maar wondering if he had to grip his hand so tightly.

"Ahh Gibraltar! What a beautiful city, your parents must have great taste. Come…come…have a seat." Ja'Maar points them to two seats in front of his desk. "So how are you gentlemen doing today?" He asked passionately and respectfully making small talk before business.

"Well…" Samuel non-chalantly shrugs his shoulders, looking straight at the PI. "We have had a bit of a rough morning, but we are making it."

Ja'Maar slides his laptop over to the side out of the way to have better view of his guests. "Mmmhmm…" He gives them a knowing frown. "I understand completely, tragedies are de toughest tings for our minds to deal wit and you gentlemen constantly serve our communities tragedies. For dis I give you two de utmost respect for what you do." They both nod appreciatively showing him grace. "So traumatic experience's are someting I am very experienced wit, sadly. However it has brought me into dis business." He leans back comfortably in his chair wanting to give more information about himself. "So Gibraltar, if you have a few minutes I would like to tell a story to you as to why I became a Private Investigator.

"Yea…no of course I have the time, besides you do seem like an interesting kind of guy."

Ja'Maar smiles showing a mouth full of extremely white teeth, shining through his extraordinarily dark complexion . "Samuel here has heard dis story (maybe even more dan once over drinks). He has as well, explained to me some of his. And Sir you have a very humble Lieutenant undah your command."

Samuel looks over and smiles to Gibraltar, thinking that he had just lost a bit of his integrity with Ja'Maar's compliment.

"I was a boy growing up in Somalia…my fader…" Ja'Maar pauses seemingly organizing his thoughts. "My fader was a pirate." He said this slowly allowing his words to carry more weight. “You see in America, when you tink of piracy, you tink about illegally downloading music, media, apps, or hacking into tings. Den if you were to ask someone to describe a pirate, dey ‘d tell you a pirate is a man with a wood peg leg, or a hook as one of his hands wit a patch over his eye.”

Gibraltar chuckled at Ja’Maar’s description in thought about his and Phathom’s recent pirate adventures.

“Well dis description couldn’t be more wrong of what a pirate really is. My fader who would fly in a helicopter and take over huge ships for ransom.”

“What?” Gibraltar’s eyes bulge out as his face turned much more serious. “People really do things like that? I thought that was only in the movies.”

Ja’Maar nods before he continues. “My fader was a ruthless man, he killed many people. De tings I witnessed him do haunts me everyday, dis probably is de worst ting about de whole situation. I watched a man shoot him in de back of de head, execution style seventeen years ago on one of de ships and I have to dis day never shed one tear for da man. So fortunately for dis incident.”

Gibraltar’s and Samuel’s gaze becomes more somber as they intently listen to Ja’Maar’s horrific story.

“I was able to change my life. You see all dese companies was not going to keep paying dem ransom money over and over again. Eventually my fader was out smarted by a security company. I was wit him on de raid, and watched him gunned down. I never wanted to go wit him, but he never left me wit any option. Dat security company dat executed my fader was de best ting dat ever happened to me. I was seventeen at de time and dey offered me asylum to come over here to America, and den gave me a job. It worked out perfectly, no I haven’t been able to completely stop dese mad men like my fader, but I have had some very grateful moments, and helped many people avoid some of dese tragedies people like my fader has caused. Hopefully I have righted some of de wrongs my fader had done. So after fifteen years wit de same company dat killed my fader, I have become able to open up my own company and focus a bit more on helping Miami out. I love Miami, dis is my home. I have a beautiful family and I only have good tings to say about de many blessings I have had here.” Ja’Maar takes a photo from his desk corner and props it up in front of Gibraltar.

“Wow!” He paused looking hard at the picture. “You have a really beautiful family, and wow that is an amazing story, you go man wow…I really don’t know what to say.”

Ja‘Maar takes the picture back up and placed it back in its perspective spot. “Yeah, it was a tough childhood, but it certainly shaped me. I am still de President of a Non-Profit dat I am working wit to help keep de water ways safe from pirates, but dat's a story for a different day. Lets get down to why you are here. Samuel tells me dat you wanted de sample tested for accelerant because you fear de corruption goes high up in de chain of command?"

"Yes Sir." Gibraltar nods eager to get down to his business. "I really believe that the Fire Marshall has some big scamming going on."

Ja'Maar makes a couple quick strikes on his laptop keyboard. "Ok, Harry Spector Miami Dade County Fire Marshall. Is dis him?" He turns his laptop around showing Gibraltar a picture he found online.

"Yes that's him, so I am not really sure what's going on, or where to even start." Gibraltar claims unknowingly so.

"Dat's fine, dat's why you came to me. Dis is my domain, so dat's de first step. Now dis business having to be off de books so de state won't be funding it, and dis work is kind of expensive, but I am sorry I can't run a business witout fee's." Ja'Maar attempts to politely turn them away.

"No…" Gibraltar holds a hand up. "Of course not, I would never expect that. I understand and I will personally pay any fee's and costs out of my own pocket."

"Haha…" Samuel laughs and cuts him off. "Yea Ja'Maar, don't worry about money Doc here is filthy rich."

“Ugh!” Gibraltar sigh’s giving Samuel a harsh glare. “Anyways Ja’Maar, I will gladly cover any cost out of my own pocket. Then if I am right I will sew Spector for reimbursement.” He claims vindictively.

“I’m sorry Captain, but dere is a good chance dat you may never see de money again wit dat in mind.” Ja’Maar speaks matter-of-factly. “Dis business can (and often is) really harsh. Law enforcement does not have proper funds, so people come to us. So often we get sucked into dese sad sob stories dat we end up not able to consciously turn away, dis in turn costs us lots of money. I’m still a small company, only two years into dis and far from turning a profit. I wasn’t wanting to turn you away, but I was going to have to.”

Gibraltar looks respectfully over the desk at Ja’Maar. “Ok, I understand. So what’s the first steps we need to take?”

Ja’Maar picks up his pen. “Sorry I am really not meaning to be rude now, but who do I need to make de bill out to is all you need to worry wit at dis time.”

“Not rude at all Ja’Maar, I am glad we can help one another. Just me Gibraltar Crichton. That’s C-R-I-C-H-T-O-N.” Gibraltar spells out his last name for the detective.

“Very good, I am going to start out wit checking out de insurance agent to be house dat burned over in Coral Gables. I’ll be putting him under heavy surveillance and see what I am able to come up wit. We will go from dere." Ja'Maar stands. "I will keep you apprised on what's happening." He speaks walking around the desk as they all say their farewells and depart.

Seventeen

"Alight class, I truly hope I was able to better explain synonyms to give you all a better understanding. Just remember a synonym is simply a word that has another word that can mean the same thing. Does anyone have any que..." McKenzie turns her gaze towards her opening door. "Arthur...hey bubba, what are you doing here?" She quickly changed her question at his interruption.

"Hey sis." He walks over to her with the bright green tablet in his hand and gives her a quick one arm hug.

“That’s your brother?” Santiago inquisitively questioned from his front row seat. “He’s too big to be a bubba.” He claims thinking about his baby brother back home.

“Haha…” McKenzie chuckled at his perception. “This here class is my baby brother, Arthur.” She gets ewws, and awws from the majority of her class.

“Un…uhh…Misses Ross, he is definitely no baby.” Maria calls out from the back of the classroom.

“Very good observation Maria, he is no longer a baby is he? But he will always be my baby brother. I know several of you have baby brothers or sisters, can each of you that does, raise your hands.” A little better than half of her class raise their hands. “You see all of you one day will be like Arthur and I here, all grown up. You will still be able to call them your baby sibling, just like I do here, because this moment here makes them your baby siblings for life.” McKenzie makes tells her students jovially as she slowly walks back and forth in Front the classroom.

“Hey! That’s not fair…” Arthur whines as though he was a child again. “How many of you have older brothers and sisters?” He questioned getting nearly the same response that McKenzie had out of her class. “Ok , and how many of you are tired of them calling you their baby brother or sister?” He comments getting several exasperated sighs from around the room and he laughs at all their reactions. “Is my big sis, Miss Ross teaching you all anything?” Nearly the whole class all said yes with one big roar. “Ok then, can anyone teach me something that she taught you today?” The whole class grew eerily quiet for an extra long moment.

“What? Really? Nothing?” McKenzie growing frustrated at the lack of her students response.

“Ouah…ouahh…” Little Ashley raised her hand waving it back and forth in attempt to get them to notice that she had it up.

“Ok good, go ahead Ashley.”

“We learned that syn…” She pauses trying to remember how to say the word. “We learned that synomyms…”

“Synonyms.” McKenzie corrects.

“Oh…synonyms…they…they are words with the same meaning.”

McKenzie nods with approval. “Ok now can you give me an ex…” The final bell rings cutting her question short. “Ok class!” She calls out loudly over the ruckus. “Remember homework in spelling and math tonight. Have a good evening at home.”

The class all begin to flow out the door, a couple of them greeting and picking at Arthur, as he greets and pokes back at them, on their way out.

"Ok, now that's over. What's up bubba? Everything ok?" McKenzie quizzes her brother as she sits at her chair behind her desk filtering through all her papers from the day.

"Yea its good. I just finished the book, and I thought I hadn't had a chance to meet your class yet this year, so returning the book gave me a good excuse to do so." He explained his simple reason for stopping by.

Wow, maybe this whole book idea is worth proceeding forward with after all. She thinks to herself as she stands up. "Hold on." She holds her hand up running over to her door and looks across the hall to JJ standing in her doorway with a flow of students steadily moving out in between them. "JJ!" She yells across to her getting her attention. "Suzie B's this evening?"

Jemma hold up a thumb with her right hand. "Sounds good." McKenzie reads her lips.

McKenzie steps back into her classroom where her brother is checking out the work on the white board. "Wow sis, looks like you had a busy day." He said as he admired all of her work.

"Well bubba, everyday teaching fourth graders (well probably any grade) is a busy day, but it is also very rewarding. So what did you think about Amazonia?" McKenzie eager to get his input on Gibraltar's book, and idea.

"Oh! Wow!" He hands over the tablet. "It was a very good book, with plenty of adventure and excitement. I definitely seen and understood your analogy, but can't say that I quite feel as you do though."

"Ugh!" McKenzie torques her head placing the tablet back into her purse. "Of course you don't, you have a fiancé who is smart and beautiful. So you can't possibly feel the same way." She defends her frustration. "So I guess the tablet book thingy might be a good idea after all?" She finishes with a questionable statement not wanting to talk about her loneliness any longer.

"Yea of course…the game was really awesome…"

McKenzie sadly lowered her gaze. ***Ugh! Boys…always wanting to play games.***

"Yea, but I am trying to think more about the practical matter here, because that was the only book on the tablet and you had to bring it here to me, we not only had the chance to talk about the book, but you also had the opportunity to meet my class." She said in a very hopeful way.

"Yea McKenzie, I certainly think that this Captain…"

"Gibraltar!" She corrects him. ***Lord help me why do I keep falling, over and over into this trap.***

“Well…Gibraltar…” He makes a smooching motion with his lips in a lovey dovey manner. “Is onto a clever idea, so if I were you I believe I would continue on with his foundation.”

“Awwe.” She goes over to hug her brother. “Thank you bubba, I really needed some help here. Ok, I have to go now and see if I can catch Mr. Bright before he leaves. I’ll walk you out.” McKenzie grabs her things and they both leave the classroom together.

“Mr. Bright!” McKenzie knocks on the door frame and enters his office.

“Miss Ross, come on in.” He points her to a chair in front of his desk, happy to see her.

“Sorry to come in so late being after school, and all. I am sure you have plenty of work your trying to finish up.”

The principal sits back in his seat relaxing a bit. “None sense Miss Ross, I always have a minute for any one of my teachers. Besides I rarely get away from here before six o’clock anyhow. So what’s up? Your two trouble makers haven’t been at each others throats again? Have they?”

McKenzie sits in the seat he pointed her to, keeping her purse in her lap, otherwise making herself comfortable with his warm welcome. “No Sir…in fact I feel that they both have learned their lesson, the three days of

ISS done them both some good and it was…I feel a proper punishment seeing as they both had fault in the incident. I truly only came by to let you know that I feel like we should move forward with the Save-the-Books Foundation."

He stares over happily giving her a proud vibe. "Ok, very good I will call Captain Gibraltar first thing next week and see if we can't make an appointment to see exactly the next steps we need to take to proceed. So what have you found out about the foundation that made you want to proceed with it?" Principal Bright is curious to his teachers interest.

"Honestly Sir, I have read two of the books thus far, and also seeing Phathom's excitement over them is a big factor. Have you had a chance to read one?"

He looked at her puzzled not ever even seeing one of the tablets. "No, he only left me the flyers and brochures."

"Oh…" ***Typical Gibraltar.*** McKenzie bashes him with her thoughts. She pulls out the tablet that her brother just returned to her. "Here you go, this is Amazonia by: James Rollins. It is actually a really good read and I personally would feel better if you were to read it and play the game before making any final decisions or calling him back."

"Ok, I'll check it out." He agreed with her gladly accepting the bright green tablet.

"So…you see Sir, that is another reason, I do think this is an excellent idea. We now download so much, that so much of our material gets buried in all our gigs of data. Then we rarely talk about what all we've read, not that many people read much more than short meme's, blog's, or simple quotes any more (technology really has started to dumb us down a bit). Which I kinda do feel like this might help get our students get more focused back on reading, and hopefully away from all the short clips learning, something I strongly feel is really destroying the attention spans to our next generation."

"Hmm…" Mr. Bright pauses putting a finger to his chin, emphasizing at how impressed with her philosophy he is. "Wow Miss Ross, that is a very deep philosophy you have there and I am afraid that you might be right. I know we definitely need to put more focus on focus, focused reading, and the attention spans of our children. I'll do as you ask, give this book a whirl, and I will get back to you on Monday. Sound good?"

McKenzie happy she is beginning to see light in this whole situation. She shows the Principal her appreciation, letting him know that she will see him soon, and heads out of the office for the evening.

McKenzie sits in wait in a corner booth when the waitress approached. "Hola como estas?" The waitress greeted her in Spanish.

“Muy bein.” McKenzie returned with the little she knew. The waitress then spits out a whole line in Spanish, which McKenzie didn’t comprehend a word of. “Oh no…I’m sorry me Spanish is no good.” She stated apologetically wishing she knew more Spanish.

“Iz ok me name iz Rose Marie you like drink?” She asked for her drink order, in a not so fluent English.

“Yes, two water’s please. I have someone else who will be joining me in a minute.”

“Ok, two agua be ight back.” She scurries away as McKenzie watches the door for her friend and colleague.

Very quickly Rose Marie returns with the two waters and two straws. “Ou make order now?”

“No thank you…” McKenzie shakes her head. “I’ll wait a few minutes.” Rose Marie nods and does some sort of nervous bow as she steps away from the table.

A few moments later McKenzie see’s JJ walking through the front door with a man in tow, she looked as though she was dragging him in. She noticed that he is clearly a Hispanic wearing a red bandana over his head. She waves towards them as Jemma gazes around the diner and seen her there, then drags the man down the narrow aisle.

"McKenzie!" JJ greets her excitedly as she scooches into the booth on the opposite side, and the man takes the seat beside her. "This is Jonas, you remember the one I have been telling you about?"

McKenzie reaches her hand across the table. "Hi I'm McKenzie, its so nice to finally meet you."

Jonas looks at her, then at her hand, then back at her before he finally shakes it. "So you've been talking about me?" He questions seriously gazing over the table.

Jemma laughs at his response and rubs him on the shoulder, not seeing the realness in him. "Of course we have been talking about you. I talk with McKenzie about everything."

"She does." McKenzie agrees. "Even the things I don't want her to talk about." She attempts to lighten the mood.

"Its all good honey, you don't need to worry. I love you, and you are perfect is the only thing I can tell anyone about you." He seems to ease a little.

McKenzie gets an eerie creeping feeling come up inside of her and quickly pushes it aside, wanting to be happy for her friend. "So, JJ tells me you are looking to buy a garage." She looks straight at Jonas.

"He is, you should see the place. Its awesome!" Jemma answers for him happy about his venture.

"No its not, it's a dump." JJ looks at him, not at all seeing the same agitated face that McKenzie does, she quickly shoves the feelings off again.

"It is not." JJ still excited about the idea. "It needs a little bit of work sure, but that's ok. It's a start honey, and its something for us to work towards." JJ plants a kiss on his left cheek wanting to encourage him.

Rose Marie comes back over to their table. "Hey Rose Marie, sorry I didn't realize there was going to be three of us, we're going to need another drink. What would you like Jonas?" McKenzie questioned Jonas as he gazed up to Rose Marie.

Jonas smiles and gazes at the waitress with devious eyes, then quickly begins speaking in Spanish to her. Rose Marie giggles and stares back on him with a giddy look, before she retreats from their table again.

"So you two have a big weekend planned?" McKenzie attempts to forget about what she just seen between the waitress and JJ's boyfriend wondering what he must have just said. Knowing that JJ (although Hispanic herself) doesn't know Spanish, but did not seem to care in the least bit. "What are you thinking you will be doing?"

JJ shrugs taking a drink of her water staring down at the menu. "Probably mostly hotel time." She smiles at her response, but dares not look up at McKenzie. "Probably go to the beech some, do some swimming, that sort of stuff. We are having to put most of our money towards the new shop, so we can't do much."

McKenzie noticed her say 'our money' and hopes that her friend isn't making a mistake and putting her savings into this business. "Well either way, the beech and swimming always sounds fun." She is trying really hard, to sound excited for her friend.

Eighteen

Both of the shifts that run Station Thirteen are all gathered around the dining table (which also serves as their conference table). Every seat at the table is taken, except for one.

Sylvester the Lieutenant of the other shift begins to talk. "Thank you guys for the food."

"No problem." Bea chimes in. "It is the least we could do since you all are covering for us.

Samuel, Barry, DeAndre, Felipe, Beatrice, and Alex all sit at the table eating in there dress uniforms, anticipating Samuel and Samantha's wedding.

"Wow Alex, this is really good meatloaf. Did you make it?" Barry questioned appreciatively.

"Well…" Alex flatly shrugged his shoulders. "Bea done most of it, I really just helped."

Beatrice quickly shakes her head. "No…" She kids with Alex. "Stop being so modest Alex, you did most of it. Before long your going to be a better cook than I am. You are a very quick study, I admire that." She gives him extra praise for all his willingness to learn and help out.

Alex's face brightened up with joy proudly taking all the compliments. He stands and begins to clear the table. "Don't Alex!" Sylvester calls out at him. "You all go get ready, we'll take care of the dishes. You should never have to cook and do the dishes."

"Pcha!" Beatrice blows out a loud snort. "You should try explaining that to Samuel…Sylvester, you really need to teach him how to be a real Lieutenant." This gets chuckles from the entire room.

Gibraltar walks into the dining area, and everyone greets their Captain as Alex hands him a plate full of food. "Here Captain Crichton, Bea and I fixed lunch for everyone today."

Alex attempts to hand Gibraltar the plate. "I don't want that dang plate, we have to go." Alex lowered his head and sadly returned the full plate to the kitchen area.

"Doc!!!" Beatrice glares with an angry stare at Gibraltar and chases after Alex.

"What!" Gibraltar oblivious to his reaction towards Alex. "Thank you all for covering today for the wedding. The Sam's will be leaving right after the ceremony to get a head start on their honeymoon, so there wont be a reception today. We shouldn't be too long, and will take back over as soon as possible." Gibraltar explained the full situation to them all.

"Well Samuel, you ready to go get hitched?" DeAndre excited for his Lieutenant's big day.

"Now that you say it like that, I think I have butterflies in my stomach." Samuel gets several chuckles from around the room.

"Your just now getting nervous?" Sylvester reiterates.

"Ooo..." Samuel's face goes pale white as he comes to more realization of the situation at hand. "God no, I've been up all night jittery. I'm not sure I should go through with it, my mind has went back and forth, over and over in my head, whether I am making a mistake or not."

"Well Samuel, now's your chance to run. Speak know or forever hold your peace." Gibraltar commented towards his friends skepticism.

"What it is? Is Samantha that bad?" Samuel now has the other Lieutenant curious as to his choice of woman.

Gibraltar, Barry, and DeAndre all look over at Sylvester bug eyed with (if-you-only-knew) expressions across their faces.

"Oh…no…its not that at all, really she's perfect, and I honestly need this. I am sure these are normal, natural, questionable feelings. Honestly I feel like I am about to become the luckiest man alive." Samuel spoke in complete confidence.

"That's good, I'm glad you know your making the right choice, but we better get you there before you become the most beat up newly wed I have ever seen." Gibraltar recalled the conversation in his head, from the day before with Samantha, about not letting Samuel be late.

The lot of them all get speffied up, and head out to the front of the station, all getting into their perspective vehicles.

Samuel and Gibraltar are riding together in Samuel's car. "What in the world?" Gibraltar glanced into the back seat that is no longer there, packed out with so many bags. "Are you two moving away and not telling anyone?"

"Haha!" Samuel sarcastically laughed out at Gibraltar's rhetorical questions. "Not hardly, Samantha just can't live without most of that stuff.

Its ninety percent her stuff, I told her there was no use in her packing all those clothes, that for the next week she wouldn't be wearing that many of them. Then she suggested that maybe she wanted me to take them all off of her, which I will admit that gave me great encouragement to load all the bags into the car."

"I'm sure it did Samuel, I'm sure it did." Gibraltar reaches over and slapped Samuel in the chest with his left hand.

They get just a few minutes away from the venue when the rain kicked in. "Oh…man…please God, it can't start raining."

Gibraltar hears Samuel say this prayer, and wonders what his friends opinion is on prayer, but shy's away from the topic. "Oh…no…" He instead says. "Does the venue have a pavilion? Or an awning on the beach?"

"No way this can be happening." Samuel cries as the rain intensifies. Gibraltar wonders again, whether or not his friend is saying a legitimate prayer. "No…they do have an inside part that stays ready for a situation like this, but Samantha is dead set on a beach front wedding." Samuel said as he was becoming more anxious with each rain drop which was becoming more and more.

"Well…can you cancel or reschedule?" Gibraltar attempts to take some of the worries."

"No way, this is Miami. We knew it was a risk with the outside wedding, so do the venues. They are non-refundable, this is certainly something Samantha and I had discussed, but I have been praying everyday since that discussion."

Did he just say he prayed everyday?

"That this wouldn't happen, not only do I want my wife to have her perfect wedding, she also badly wants to have the beach wedding, and I am afraid this is going to ruin it." Samuel's anxiety continues to increase as they pull into the parking lot and the rain is not just rain anymore. It is a storm that is not going to go anywhere anytime soon. "Well it looks like an inside wedding it will be." Samuel depressively states.

"Hey Samuel, I want you two to have the perfect wedding also. Lets reschedule it, and I'll cover the cost."

"No!!!" Samuel yells looking straight over at Gibraltar. "You can't do that, I can not go through planning another wedding…No way, don't even mention you offered. Please I am begging you, lets get this over with. As much as she may not like it, none of this is truly what this is about. This is really about us, the wedding is just for everybody else. Anyways that is why we decided against having a reception. We'll have our whole lives to party and eat with each others family's and your only giving me seven days for our honeymoon and I plan on taking advantage of every minute of it." As Samuel says this last part his tension eases dramatically with the thoughts.

Gibraltar holds his hands up in mock surrender. "Just trying to be the best, best man!"

"You are the best man…you are…Lets go get me married!"

They both jump quickly out of the vehicle and run to get underneath the awning to the venue. Gibraltar and Samuel stand there in wait under the hotel's busy drive through awning. There are several bellhops gathering bags, and valets in bright yellow ponchos rushing around. They stand there watching the rest of their team run through the parking lot haphazardly attempting to cover their heads, in attempt from getting too wet.

Samuel pulls out his phone to check the time. "Wow Doc!" He exclaims. "We are really early."

"Pcha!" Gibraltar pushes air through perched up lips. "If you'd been there for Samantha's conversation with me about getting you here on time, you'd have pitched a tent here last night."

Samuel grins big at his Best Man's joke, with an understanding gaze, giving himself a momentary relief of stress. "Well all of Station Thirteen are here and all looking sharp." Samuel's voice cracks with nervousness. "Thank you all for being here for me. I can't even begin to explain how much having you all here is the greatest gift you all can give me." His eyes begin to tear up. “We’re a little early.” He quickly re-gathered his composure. “Let’s go make sure they have us all set up, since the rain has definitely changed the plans.”

“Umm…yeah…” Beatrice carefully starts to talk, not wanting to rub Samuel the wrong way. “Wasn’t it suppose to be a beach front wedding?”

“Yea it was Bea.” Not to disappointed with her soft tone of voice, he certainly became less disappointed than he was moments ago. “We have an inside back up plan, this is Miami after all. So we cant be too disappointed about it raining.” He explains to them all as he and Gibraltar take the lead and walk through the front doors.

“Greetings! Welcome to Hotel Miami.” They were all greeted by a man dressed in a Hotel dress uniform from head to toe, which included a round top hat with a short bill on the front of it. They all continue into the front lobby each smiling and nodding to the welcoming face of the greeter.

As they walk further into the hotel the chaos does not stop, it does however feel slightly more controlled than the busy hustle and bustle this Saturday afternoon was bringing outside. Walking into the main lobby area, (which was a huge room) and in the center of this room was a raised platform with several tables all full of people laughing and enjoying a late brunch.

“Which way?” Gibraltar speaks loudly over all the noise of the place, as he looks over at Samuel.

“I dunno.” He mumbles as he shrugs his shoulders. “Lets try this way, I see a sign over there.” He points to the right and slowly begins to walk around the huge platform.

They walk past several huge pillars with a hallway leading off to the bathrooms. The place is eloquently clean and every piece of marble and stone seem to irradiate energy with its glimmering shine. Before they approach the main desk one of the pillars had a sign on it. Gibraltar catches himself thinking about the convenience of the sign being before the main desk.

“Ok look here.” Samuel starts reading the signs. “Conference rooms third floor, pool and spa fourth floor. Ha! Wedding chapel’s fourth floor, there we go…umm…but where are the elevators?” He casually adds lost and nervous about getting the day over with.

“Look there over there.” Alex points across the front desk to the other side of the room.

They all walk together in front of the main desk getting appreciative gazes from the crowds, even a couple of children poke their parents and point out their curiosity to the way they are all dressed in their uniforms.

They all squeeze comfortably into one elevator and ride it to the fourth floor.

As soon as the elevator door opens a sign on the wall directly across from them shows the wedding chapels are to the right. They all continue that way down the huge hallway, admiring the classical art work and sculptures. Coming up onto an open door on the right side there are workers seemingly busy, running in and out of the banquet halls.

Upon walking into the wedding room Samuel begins to tense. “No…no, no, no…This can’t be happening!” Beatrice noticed his frustration and begins to share his uneasy feelings.

“What this is kinda cool!” Barry claimed with his dry enthusiasm, not understanding that there is an issue at all.

“No way!” Samuel throws his hands over his face in total devastation. “This is it, my marriage is completely ruined before it has even started.” Samuel starts to cry, not wanting to be there anymore already.

“What’s wrong?” Alex is confused. “What’s wrong Lieutenant Brooks?”

“What’s wrong!!!Alex is everything, there is nothing right in here. In fact this whole set up couldn’t be more wrong. Who has a black wedding?” Samuel begins to cry again, having to take a seat at one of the tables with his knees growing weak.

"Oh…" Beatrice speaks hopeful. "So the table clothes aren't suppose to be black?"

"Umm…definitely not!" Samuel speaks with a duh tone in his whine.

"And the arch isn't suppose to be decorated with black and pink roses?" Beatrice still kinda shaken by the set up of the wedding hall.

"No…" Samuel shakes his head. "Our colors are suppose to be white first off. It is a wedding, not some goth devil party. Then Fireman red and magenta, three bright simple and happy colors. Not this nightmare of a place out of some vampire movie."

Gibraltar puts a comforting hand on his best friends shoulder. "I'm going to go see if I can get these jerks straightened out."

"Its no use…" Samuel whines and shakes his head some more laying it in his lap. "Its already all ruined."

"Hey You!!!" Gibraltar calls out running over to a young girl setting up tables. "What the heck is wrong with you all? What kind of operation is it that your running here?"

The girl begins to tremble from his anger towards her. "Umm…umm…" She stutters. "I am just doing what I was told to do." She shakily claims, almost starting to cry.

“Well go get me your boss! I need to speak to him right now!” Gibraltar’s voice deep and raspy as she scurries away without another word.

Gibraltar returns back over to the crew gathered around a broken Samuel. “Ok, she is going to go get her boss. We are going to get this straightened out Samuel, I promise you.” Gibraltar arrogantly speaks to them all.

Mere moments later a manager walks in from the hallway. “What seems to be the problem here?”

“I’ll tell you what the problem is!” Gibraltar stepped up into the mans face. The manager is of equal height and build to Gibraltar. He calmly takes half a step back from Gibraltar’s confrontation, not showing the least bit of worry on his face. “The problem is you are running a low down pathetic operation here. I won’t have for it, I need you to bring every dang employee you have here and get this banquet hall fixed right. Right now! You only have a hour until my friend walks down the aisle, and it better all be right.”

Still slightly confused by what Gibraltar is asking the manager begins to talk once Gibraltar finally finished with his rambling complaint. “Ok sir, I am unsure what exactly I am supposed to be fixing here. Can you please be a bit more specific here?”

Frustrated like a child, Gibraltar slings his arms down to his side. "The whole thing is wrong." He waves his right hand around the room. "What kind of moron writes down the color black when it is most definitely suppose to be white?"

"Ooohaa!" The manager chuckles and his already calm face eases even more, not that he was ever worried in the least bit, just a typical day in the business. "Sir I believe you all are in the wrong Chapel. We do have two weddings today, yours is probably across the hall."

Samuel perks his head up at this news and darts out of the room, within thirty seconds he was back before any of them even had a chance to move from where they were when he left. "Oh my God! Its perfect!" Samuel runs up to the manager in a stiff quick hug and kisses him on the cheek. "Absolutely perfect." And in an instant Samuel is back out of the door.

Gibraltar gives the manager an angry gaze. "Well you really should put a sign up." He stated walking by the manager not wanting to admit his wrong doings.

"Knock, knock…Everybody decent?" Gibraltar said as he cracked the door to the brides quarters.

"O'goody, you're here!" Samantha said excitedly quickly ushering Gibraltar through the door, careful not to gaze out afraid she might see Samuel.

"Hey Sam? Have you seen Samuel?" Gibraltar looking slightly worried, not wanting to over play this.

"Uhh!!!" Samantha's mind begins to race. "Ehh…I thought he was suppose to be with you."

Gibraltar's face breaks, and he smiles unable to go with this bad joke as long as he initially intended. "Nah I'm kidding…" He looks her up and down as the color in her face begins to return. "You look great Sam. I like that dress and the place is set up gorgeously."

Samantha smiles and returns back to her seat where a stylist continues to make sure every strand of hair is in exactly the right place. "Yea I really wanted the beach wedding though." She sadly remarked. "But…it will be alright though. Its more for everyone else than us anyways. Hey I wanted to thank you for taking Samuel out for his Bachelor party. I was so relieved when he asked you to be his best man and not DeAndre. No offense to DeAndre, of course. I love him as a brother, but I know he would have had strippers there and who knows what would have happened then. Thank you Gibraltar."

As she is telling him this Gibraltar gets a warm and fuzzy feeling inside of him from her compliment. ***Am I starting to grow up???God was I just praying???***

Nineteen

McKenzie watches as Phathom walks out of her classroom, with barely a limp in her near perfect heel to toe stride. She wonders whether or not this has anything to do with the AI and her prosthesis.

As she glanced across the hall through both doorways, she takes notice of Mr. Martinez busying himself straightening up the desk. ***JJ, where are you? I really hope you are ok.*** She said a quick prayer as she pulled out her phone, knowing that there isn't going to be a text from her friend, whom she hadn't seen or heard from in almost a week. The last time she saw her, was when her and Jonas was suppose to be going away for the weekend.

From Mark, she has a message, she opens the text screen and reads. {McKenzie, hey there this is Mark. JJ is at my place and she would like to see you if you could come by my place after class. She would appreciate it.}

Oh my God! Thank you for responding. She taps the reply button. {Yes…} She pauses remembering she has a meeting. {It will be a little while, I have a meeting I must go to with Principal Bright, so it may be a little later.}

McKenzie sits back in her chair impatiently waiting for the reply, which comes quickly. {Ok, see you when you can get here.} Is the response with his address at the bottom of the message.

What happen to you JJ? Why are you with Mark, Jonas must have done something. She has to push her thoughts away, knowing she has to get to the meeting for Save-the-Books Foundation with Principal Bright and Gibraltar.

McKenzie gets butterflies in her stomach, thinking about the meeting with Gibraltar. These feelings however quickly dissipate with worry for JJ. ***Jesus please help me.*** She simply prays as she took a deep breath and gathers her things to head out the door.

❖

“Hello Mr. Bright!” McKenzie greets the Principal looking down at one of the chairs in his office, occupied with a student who is dressed in all black, with the palest white foundation make up on that she has ever seen. The student has his or her (she cannot tell) fingers crossed together with the nails painted black.

She catches herself guessing he, or she is about twelve years old, wondering how parents can teach such a young child to do these things. “Oh no…sorry I didn’t…” She quickly shoves her thoughts away.

“Its ok Miss Ross, you can have a seat.” Mr. Bright interrupts her. “Lunar here was just leaving, our discussion is over for the day. However Lunar I want you in my office first thing tomorrow morning. Do you understand me?” Mr. Bright lowers his head across his desk in attempt to catch Lunar’s lowered gaze. Lunar sadly nods and exits the office.

“Miss Ross, this job some days can be the most rewarding thing in the world. Then there are these days like today that makes you want to ring the parents necks. I honestly cant understand why a parent, not only allows their child to be so confused, but they encourage them to be confused.”

McKenzie smiles to the Principal emulating his awareness. “I can completely relate, so is Lunar a boy or a girl? I honestly couldn’t tell.” She questioned earnestly.

"Ugh!" Mr. Bright rolls his eyes. "You know that's another thing that's frustrating. This whole gender thing, they don't even really allow us to say what is or what's not. Lunar is definitely a girl and so confused. That is what she was in my office for, her teacher has said that she has approached two female students and one male student and said she wanted to…umm…" He paused a moment contemplating on how he is going to word it. "Well lets just say, the four letter word was not love."

McKenzie's jaw dropped clear off of her face at his statement. "Wow…" She shakes her head and leans back in her seat. "So what are you going to do about it?"

Principal Bright stares past her in deep thought. "Miss Ross, I really don't know what I should do…What would you do?"

This question really hits deep in McKenzie's soul. ***God, why did I ask this?*** "You know Mr. Bright, this is a tough situation…" She pauses thinking a moment. "Do you know the reason we as United Pentecostal ladies wear dresses and don't cut our hair? It is primarily for gender distinction. Where in many ways our society certainly has evened out with our technology. Our men don't have to go out and work the fields as much anymore, and the women have to get jobs to be able to afford to live, so we share more of the house work (or should at least). But man and woman are certainly different, with different rolls and God has made this very clear to us." Mr. Bright is leaned forward completely engaged in every one of McKenzie's words.

"How about this Mr. Bright, maybe this can be a good learning tool God is trying to give me. How about you let me speak with Lunar, maybe I'll take her for ice cream after school one day and see if we can find a root to this issue. I really don't believe this to be a typical situation for typical punishment."

As Mr. Bright's face brightened with zeal, McKenzie thinks about everything else on her plate right now. Felling overwhelmed, Gibraltar's foundation, JJ's situation (whatever that may be), work, the church. ***God I hope you know what you are doing, please give me strength.*** She prays to herself.

"You'd do that for me? Miss Ross that would be amazing, I was really torn about punishing her, for her confusion." McKenzie gives him an (un-noticed) half smile. "Have you heard from Miss Jackson? She has not shown up these past three days and I am beginning to worry about her."

McKenzie sets her purse on the floor wondering how she should play this. "I just received a text from her, I am suppose to go by and see her after our meeting. I honestly do not have a clue to what has happened, I also am very worried. When I talk with her I will acknowledge your concern, and if she is ok with me passing on the information to you I will let you know tomorrow."

The principal does a quirky pucker of his lips with a curt nod of his head. “Ok…I respect that, now on to Save-the-Books Foundation. So are we ready to start this? Do you have some available time to talk with your class about this next week? If Captain Gibraltar is ready?”

“I think so.” As McKenzie answered these questions Gibraltar knocks on the door frame and enters without invite.

“Good afternoon Captain Gibraltar!” Mr. Bright stands and happily greets him, McKenzie follows suit, although a bit less enthusiastically, thinking about all the current struggles she is needing to deal with. “Have a seat…please.”

Mr. Bright returned to his seat behind his desk. “So Miss Ross and I were just discussing Save-the-Books Foundation and she feels like she will be able to make some time next week. Will this work for you?”

“Umm…” Gibraltar quickly gazes at McKenzie, then back to the Principal. “Well I was really hoping to get some of this figured out. I haven’t truly got it all set up yet, I need some board members to have a meeting before I can file for my 501(c)(3). He claims.

“Captain Gibraltar!” The Principal spoke angrily, but very controlled. “I am taking a big risk here letting a Non-Profit into my doors at all. And now your informing me that its not even technically a Non-Profit at all.”

Gibraltar takes a deep breath. “Yes Principal Bright, I’m sorry…I was just really hoping that I could have Miss Ross on my board.

“Ahem…” McKenzie stares really hard on Gibraltar. ***Really…Really…***

“Well.” Mr. Bright said as he sits back and relaxed a bit. “I think that’s an excellent idea.” He thinks about how it will go over easier with the school board with a teacher on the board of the Non-Profit.

McKenzie on the other hand is thinking about how Gibraltar just conned her into more work. “What do you think Miss Ross? You being on the board of this foundation can help stir this, in a more educational direction.”

McKenzie scooches back into her seat more and slumps her shoulders, slightly. “I guess so.” She shrugs them.

“Ok then, good deal its settled. You two can work together and figure out when you will have your first board meeting. Then when you get that over with, your Articles of Incorporation filed with the Secretary of State, and the packet for the 501(c)(3) sent off we can re-have this meeting to determine when we would like to start.”

Gibraltar’s face looked as though he had just won the lottery. “Thank you!”

McKenzie’s face has total exasperation all over it. “Ok Mr. Bright.”

They all stand together. “I will see you tomorrow Miss Ross. Lunar should be here about 7:45 in the morning, maybe you can catch her before classes start.”

“Yes sir.” Is the most McKenzie was able to muster out, without sounding completely out of it.

McKenzie and Gibraltar exit together, as they walk through the reception area to the offices she keeps a step ahead of him. Gibraltar almost has to trot to keep pace with her, neither has said a word.

Out in the hallway and where they appear to be alone McKenzie stops and turns towards him. “What were you thinking?” She doesn’t let him answer before she takes off and leaves him standing there in the deserted hallway.

“Ma…” She hears him “Kenzie…” say her name in a ever fading tone. However she has had enough for one day and she knows the day is far from over, so she does not stop.

“Mark!” McKenzie greets him at the front door to is apartment.

“McKenzie…How are you? It’s been a long time.”

She gives him half a smile. “Yea Mark it has been, how have you been?”

He gives a one arm shrug and tilts his head. “Come on in, JJ is in the kitchen Just a little warning she may have a couple of bruises.”

Ok, a couple of bruises that’s not so bad. She thinks to herself as they walk through the eerily quiet apartment. McKenzie takes notice of this, no sounds of fans, TV’s, or radio’s, just quiet.

Walking through the door to the kitchen/dining area of the apartment she catches sight of JJ sitting at the table with her hands on it. She looks up to her, JJ’s entire face is bruised (which looked to be a couple days old) both eyes black and swollen, her bottom lip appeared to have been busted, and both cheeks a mixture of blues and yellows.

“JJ!” She yells into a sob as she runs over and embraces her friend.

“McKenzie th…” They both begin to cry in each others arm.

Mark stares sadly onto them from the door. “JJ.” He speaks softly. “I am going to give you two some privacy. If you need anything at all I will be in the living room.” He compassionately offers his help.

“What happened Jemma? Where you in an accident?” JJ lowered her gaze, and slightly shakes her head. “Would you like some coffee?” McKenzie asked noticing the sweet fragrance of the fresh brew.

“Sure.” JJ stands.

McKenzie sits quietly at the table as JJ makes each of them a cup of coffee in silence. A few moments later JJ walks both cups over to the table and sits one down in front of her friend. McKenzie looks up to her apologetically, even though she had nothing to do with it. JJ sits down in front of her, their knees almost touching.

McKenzie waits patiently for her friend to be ready to say what she needs to say. "So…Jo…Jonas was the one who gave me this pretty face." McKenzie gasped, instantly she put her hand over her mouth not meaning to sound so surprised at what her friend had just said.

"So…our nice weekend." JJ seemingly begins to gain some strength and composure as she stirs her coffee blankly. "Our weekend away…Ugh!" She sighs. "The one where I was really thinking that I was coming back from engaged." She pauses taking a sip of coffee thinking on her next words. "Instead I came back bruised from head to toe."

McKenzie only seeing her face hadn't thought about the rest of her body, as she is wearing long sleeves and pants. She is still too stunned to talk and allows JJ to continue.

"So Friday after school he ends up taking me to a cabin in the Everglades." She pauses beginning to sob. "I…was…" McKenzie places a comforting hand on JJ's knee causing her to jerk, uncomfortable with even being slightly touched, however she warms quickly to her friends intimacy.

“McKenzie…I was so scared when he took the dirt road. I got this gut feeling that something wasn’t right.”

JJ pauses, taking in a deep breath in attempt to regain composure. “So I am not really ready to go into many details about what Jonas done to me, but long story short he tied me up and beat me…and beat me…” McKenzie gasped again and begin to cry for her friend. “For three days, he had me tied up to that bed. I just knew he was going to kill me the whole time I was there.”

McKenzie starts crying more. “No…JJ…I’m so sorry this has happened to you. He didn’t…” She pauses for a long moment, really not wanting to ask the question, not really knowing how to ask the question.

JJ looks into her eyes knowing exactly what her friend is trying to ask her and simply nods her head and they both begin to cry heavily. McKenzie takes her into her arms and they continue to cry together for what seemed like an eternity.

They both finally stop crying and sit back in their seats, living in each others eyes. “JJ…Principal Bright asked me about you today. I really didn’t know what to tell him.”

JJ wipes the tears away from her cheeks, delicately with her shirt sleeve. “I really don’t know either.” She said. “I cant go in like this.”

McKenzie nods looking down and depressed. “Well…I have to see him first thing in the morning, and if you would be ok with me talking with him, I’ll give him an explanation and explain to him that you will need the rest of the week off.”

“No!” JJ quickly shakes her head. “No McKenzie you cant tell him what happened.

McKenzie unsure the direction she should approach the situation. “Well…JJ I cant lie to him, you know that, but I don’t have to tell him the exact situation. It may keep you from getting any extra dividends, but I think I can probably lighten the situation.” McKenzie’s honest with her friend.

“Ok…Thank you McKenzie, for everything. I don’t know what I could ever do without you.”

Well I think you need to be thanking God. McKenzie prays to herself, not wanting to push the topic at this moment.

“Hey, so you remember Phathom?” McKenzie wants to change the subject to a more positive note.

“Mmhmm…” JJ looks curious.

“Today I was watching her walk, and she’s walking better than the Doctor who built the foot for her.

JJ chuckled at this comment, as she does so she moans grabbing her side. “Really!” She said excitedly, very ok with her friends attempt to distract her.

“Yea really!” McKenzie smiles empathetically.

Mark sticks his head in the door. “Are you two ok in here?”

They both nod and he starts to retreat. “Hey Mark!” McKenzie stops him.

“Yeah.” He turns back around looking puzzled.

“I have had several people from the church ask me about you. You know they all miss you, you did kinda grow up with them all. Are you going somewhere else? Where I can tell them that you are doing ok.”

He crunched up his brows. “So I have to be going to church to be doing ok?” He questioned way more defensively than he meant to.

“No…no…Mark sorry I wasn’t…I did not mean to imp…”

He holds up a quick hand stopping her. “No McKenzie…I’m sorry its been a long couple of days and really I am not ok, but please don’t mention this.”

“No of course not.” McKenzie quickly shakes her head understanding the tough situation at hand.

"Hey I was thinking of ordering pizza, are you two hungry?" Mark asked them wanting a distraction.

McKenzie looks at JJ who ever so slightly nods her head, with eyes asking her to please stay and eat.

Twenty

"So Alex." Barry places a hand on his shoulders and looks him in his worn face. "Now the important part in this obstacle, is that you pace your self on the first part, the mile run. However you will need a lot of pep in your step to make the fifteen minute mark. I want you to finish, not fall out, so worry more about your breathing and not the time. You have been doing good and consistently making progress with me on the cardio machines, so I have confidence in your abilities." Barry slaps him on the back.

With all of Station Thirteen there watching, Samuel begins the countdown. "Ok Alex on the count of three." Samuel calls out with a stop watch in his hand. “one…” He slowly drags each number out. “two…three!” He yells with enthusiasm.

Alex is off with no hesitation, he starts off running really fast, then quickly slows to a pace where he feels he can make the mile. Two laps in (the halfway mark) he begins to feel his legs burn. Being used to the stair master and elliptical he did not realize that running was so much different on the legs.

Alex pushed on and at the end of the fourth lap he runs to the inside towards the obstacles. He zig zags through the twenty-five yards of slalom style cones, before he goes through the over and under part.

He jumps the first wall with ease at its two foot of height making his way climbing and limboing over and under walls and bars, that all vary in height. Once at the final part, Alex out of breath makes his way over to the three story high tower, with six, half flights of stairs. He ran up these with ease, and almost relieved.

At the top of the tower he does a quick pulse check of the carotid artery of their dummy (who name happens to be Buster). With all his strength and might, he lifts the one hundred thirty-five pound Buster onto his one hundred twenty pounds frame, in a fireman’s carry.

Struggling to make his way down the steps he weaves and bobbled his way through the first half flight. When he attempts to make the first step down on the second half flight he misses his step, and tumbled. He and Buster topple and roll over one another down the remaining seven steps.

"Alex!" Beatrice yells as she starts to take off running.

"No Bea!" Gibraltar grabs her shoulder halting her. "He has to do this on his own." He demands.

She shrugs his hand off her shoulder with a quick yank. "He could be hurt!" She huffs out angrily as she turned back towards the tower when she noticed Alex picking himself and Buster back up.

Alex then slowly makes his way down the remaining steps, and carry's Buster the final twenty-five yards before lazily dropping him down with a 'thwop.'

"Time!" Samuel yells. "Seventeen minutes six and a half seconds." He calls the time out.

Gibraltar approaches Alex. "You cant just throw him down like that. If that'd been a live body, he'd be dead now." Gibraltar gripes at Alex, who is now slumped over with his hands on his knees, huffing and puffing. "Run it again…DeAndre take buster back to the top. Alex if you don't do this in fifteen minutes or less, you are fired!" He speaks harshly.

"Gibraltar!!!" Beatrice yells at her Captain using his first name stepping up, and into his face. "Alex needs a rest, stop being so mean…I'll make you a bet. I'll bet you that I can run the course faster than you and if I do you will have to start giving Alex the respect he deserves."

Gibraltar gives Beatrice a grim smile.

"Bea." Alex says timidly, putting his hand on her shoulder while she is still in Gibraltar's face, not daring to back down.

"No Alex." She turns to face him. "He needs to start treating you with more respect, besides I know I can smoke his lazy rear in this obstacle course. He don't do anything but sit around the office all day anyways." Bea challenges Gibraltar, talking through Alex.

"Hahaha." Gibraltar laughs a deep hysterical laugh. "I might just fire you to, when I beat your tale." He claims haphazardly.

"Bea..." Alex whimpers, giving her puppy dog eyes.

"Its ok Alex." Beatrice talks driven by anger. "He is going to have to start treating everyone nicer when I show him up." She spoke with complete confidence in her abilities.

DeAndre comes back over to them having replaced buster at the top of the tower, missing all the drama.

"Ok...Bea, you want to go first?" Gibraltar challenges her.

"No way hosae, lady's first." She accepts his challenge.

"Ok Samuel." Gibraltar shrugs at her snide comment calling him the lady. "On your count." Samuel counts him off.

"Bea." Alex speaks as Gibraltar takes off. "You cant run the course as fast as him, he's way bigger and stronger than you." Alex looks worried for them all. "I don't want you to be fired, because of me."

Beatrice gives Alex a reassuring smile. "It's ok Alex, don't worry. Its not always about size and strength, and he cant fire us. He is just being a pompous prick."

Alex drops his jaw with surprise never having seen her so angry, definitely didn't think he would ever hear her talk like that.

"Sorry Alex, I shouldn't allow myself to live vicariously through him."

"Vi…Vicarious?"

"Yea that's when you act like someone else…in simple terms." He nods with a slight understanding. "But anyways Alex, I didn't really mean to let him make me so angry. However I am not sorry about it, my anger here I feel is completely dignified. Do you know why Jesus got mad in the Bible?"

Alex quickly shakes his head, listening intently as he has come to enjoy her Bible story's. "Jesus got mad at the guards in the temple because they mocked a less fortunate lady, and I feel strongly that this is exactly how Doc is being towards you. Not that your less fortunate at all, in fact I believe you are twice the man he is, but he has been bullying you, non-the-less."

"Really?" Alex's face brightens up, Beatrice enjoys seeing this rare optimism from him and nods with a smile. "Wow, he's good. "Alex admires Gibraltar as he quickly carry's Buster down the steps.

"Oh! Alex you just wait and see, its about to get really good." Beatrice attempts to give him a sneak peak…of what's to come.

"So Alex, you seem really interested in Jesus and the Word of God." He shrugs with a partial grin. "You should come to Ocean Breeze Apostolic Church sometime."

"Time!" Samuel calls out as Gibraltar fly's across the line, just in time to hear Beatrice invite Alex to church sending all kinds of emotions through his mind. Gibraltar gently sits Buster on the grown as he gasps for way more air than he thinks he should be reaching for. "Fourteen minutes fifty-seven seconds." Samuel calls out his course time.

"No way! You are adding to that, I know that was in the twelve minute range." Gibraltar argues.

"Nope Doc, I think maybe all the paperwork you are doing is effecting your workout time. Maybe you should put some dumbbells in your office." Samuel smirks to his Captain.

“Ok Bea, your up.” DeAndre said as he returned from replacing Buster again.

“Yea Bea…I’ll go.” Alex accepts her church offer, anxious to get her approval.

“On three…” Samuel calls out again and counts her off.

Beatrice fly’s around the course. “Wow Cap, she nearly hit a six minute mile.” Samuel remarks watching Bea make her way through the obstacles.

“Hmph.” Gibraltar grumbles.

“Yea…it looks like she is really about to smoke you.” Felipe says proud of his partner.

“Whatever.” Gibraltar lowered his gaze to the gravel under his feet, shuffling it around with his boots. “Better watch it, I’ll can you too.” He mumbled inaudibly, staring at the ground.

“Time!” Samuel calls out, almost afraid to say the time.

“Wow Bea! That was awesome!” Alex said runs over to congratulate her. “And your not that much bigger than me. “He adds.

“Uhh! Alex.” She slaps him on the shoulder, dropping her jaw with a gasp. “Your not suppose to comment on a woman’s size.”

Alex confused at what he did wrong. “Why not Bea? Women comment on our sizes all the time.” He claims, completely unaware.

“Thirteen minutes and twenty-three seconds Bea. You are the winner hands down.” Samuel avoids looking in Gibraltar’s direction while declaring her winner.

Beatrice steps over to Gibraltar. “Good, now I think you owe Alex an apology.” She all but demands.

“Whatever.” He huffs out, turning on his heels as he begin to storm off.

“Hey Doc.” Samuel remembered something and ran over to catch up with Gibraltar. “I forgot to mention, I spoke with Ja’Maar a couple days ago. He has learned quite a bit these past couple weeks.”

With his gaze looking away from his Lieutenant. “Samuel!!!Why the heck do you wait to tell me the important stuff. Am I just going to have to fire the whole dang crew and start a new.” Gibraltar clearly frustrated.

“Sorry…I’ve been busy, I know Doc you think the whole world is suppose to stop, and wait to revolve around you. But it doesn’t and you really need to stop taking all this anger out on all of us.” Samuel snaps back. “I don’t know what has gotten into you lately, but your normal angry self seems to be way angrier these days.”

“Whatever Samuel.” Gibraltar clearly isn’t going to talk about it. “Tell Barry to drive the crew back to the station. We need to go see Ja’Maar, and figure out what he has learned.” Samuel nods, and quickly runs back to do so.

❖

Gibraltar and Samuel pull up into a strip mall parking lot, pulling straight over to a grey sedan with tinted windows. The windows are not so tinted to attract attention, but you cant very well see into them.

“Right there.” Samuel points and Gibraltar parks beside Ja’Maar who waves them to his car.

They both get out of Gibraltar’s SUV and walk over to get into the PI’s car. Gibraltar takes the front passenger seat as Samuel gets into the back.

“Jeeze! If I’d known you two were going to show up in de bright red monster dat screams…Hey-look-at-me…I’d had you two wait and meet me back at de office.”

“Oh…so…” Samuel attempts to apologize, but is interrupted.

“What do you have Mr. Enby? I have things to do.”

“Straight to bizness.” Ja’Maar sarcastic with Gibraltar.

“Oh, someone didn’t have their wheaty’s this morning, and has had stomach pains all day.” Samuel makes a snide remark towards Gibraltar’s attitude.

Gibraltar just turns around and glares at Samuel, but has no response to return.

“So, way over on de other side of de strip mall.” Ja’Maar points to the far side across Gibraltar’s lap. “You see Country Farm Insurance?” He watches as they both nod their heads. “De agent dere is one Sergio McMillan, he is de one who insured de house out at Coral Gables.”

“So it was an insurance scam?” Gibraltar jumps the gun. “I knew it.” He impatiently added.

“Hold on a minute, I don’t have no solid proof and chances are dey…chances are it is going to be incredibly difficult if not impossible to get such.”

Gibraltar glares at Ja’Maar with a crooked face. “So your telling me that son of a gun, Spector is going to get away with this?” He complained irritably.

“No…not at all what I am saying. However it is likely dat dey have covered deir tracks and buried his connections very deeply, but hear me out here. I started out by checking dis Sergio out, his background and everyting. He is really squeaky clean, a dual citizen to here and Russia.

His moder is from Moscow, and his fader is from Philly. I tought I would just dig into his fire claims to see if dere was any utter arsons and what I found was really fishy." Ja'Maar teaches them of what he has learned.

"Ahh…non of his claims came back as arson?" Samuel states quizzically.

"Very good Samuelle, you ever tought about being a private investigator?" Ja'Maar looks back to him with a hopeful grin on his face.

"Come on, lets get back on track here. What would none of his claims not having arson involved be fishy?" Gibraltar's still impatient wanting to pin this guy now.

"Duh Doc…because there is a certain percentage of all fire claims that are arson." Samuel makes his friend feel three inches tall.

"Oh…ok…" Gibraltar duh's himself.

"Right again Samuelle, I didn't know dis before, but I did de research and determined dat somewhere between twenty-five and forty percent of claims are arson. Now I wish'd I could give a more precise percentage, but with our Internet now dat tinks it knows too much, I had to make my determination by combining statistics from several different sites. Anyways not truly relevant, de point is dat it is usually a much higher percentage dan zero." Ja'Maar gives them how he came up with his numbers, giving himself more credibility with the two of them.

"I went to digging a bit more, and home insurance is not de only ting Sergio sales. From everyting I have learned so far arson is one of de most difficult crimes to prosecute for, I'm tinking just maybe dere is anutter route I can take. I haven't had a chance to dig into any of his utter claims yet tough."

Gibraltar turns and looks at him puzzled. "So your thinking that Sergio is involved in other insurance frauds?"

He gently shakes his head as he pulls up his binoculars looking across the vast parking lot towards the Country Farm Insurance office. "Captain Crichton."

"Just Gibraltar is ok." He starts to soften up a bit.

"Ok Gibraltar, if dere's one ting I have learned in de bizness, it is to never assume anyting and prove everyding. Now if he is involved in arson frauds, den he very well could be involved in automotive, boat, or even life insurance frauds. Anyone of dese frauds could be very lucrative."

"Whooaa!" Samuel pokes his head up between the seats with his head mere inches away from Ja'Maar's. "You think he is killing people for their insurance money?"

"No Samuelle!!! I am praying to God dat he wouldn't stoop dat low."

Gibraltar gets a quirky feeling in his stomach, hearing Ja'Maar say he was praying to God.

"However life insurance policy's can easily be worth many millions, and I haven't found any of Sergio's money trails yet, or even know if dere is one. Like I said as of right now everyting is very speculative and if he is up to something, he is extremely cautious wit it dough. We was able to get one utter ting dat caught our eyes, I had one of my men surveil his place over de weekend which is why I am here now. Last Friday night at about ten pm Marshall Spector show'd up at Sergio's private place of residence." Ja'Maar pulls up some photo's of the Marshall going into his house.

"What!!!" All of Gibraltar's anxiety returned ten fold. "I knew it, that's all the proof we need. We can take that to the DA and get warrants, and then the feds can come in and bust him." Gibraltar says this as he wants everything to happen yesterday.

"De DA would look at dat and laugh in our faces and tell us dat we are nuts. Dey are going to want bank statements, text messages, or even a recorded conversation someting of dat nature. And even with all of dose, depending on how dere obtained de prosecution could reject Dem all. Gibraltar dis is big boy stuff, Spector is not only de Fire Marshall he also is running for State Senate."

Gibraltar picks the binoculars up and takes a gander. “So this Sergio is trying to become a Senator?” He questions not all the way paying attention to what the PI said.

“No…Spector…”

Gibraltar drops the binoculars into his lap. “What…no way, we cant let that smug prick into any office.” All his anger has returned with this revelation.

“Well de cost of dis operation has just went way up, and de guarantee of my ability of being able to do anyting about it, way down.” Ja’Maar speaks honestly.

“I don’t care what it cost!” Gibraltar stares straight through Ja’Maar. “You have to take this guy down.”

“Ok…” Ja’maar unsure shakes his head. “I am going to for sure need anutter deposit, and I really don’t know which direction I plan to take. If Spector is only involved in arson and dis Sergio has a whole different underground network, it will definitely be impossible to pin any of it on Spector. Den I don’t have any idea who I can take dis to, if I do find any evidence Secret Service, DOJ, FBI, CIA, NSA de list goes on. Determining who’s jurisdiction it is, itself can be tricky, for if we choose de wrong one it could be swept under de rug, or maybe even someone could tip dem off and dat could be very dangerous for all of us at dis high a level."

Gibraltar takes a deep breath. "Ok, I will try to be patient with this. This needs to be done right so he…or they cant continue to do these things."

Ja'Maar places a serious hand on Gibraltar's shoulders. "Gibraltar." He glances back at Samuel. "Samuelle, both of you are going to have to keep dis ting completely quiet, and do more dan try to be patient. Dis a very sketchy situation dat could get extremely dangerous quickly. If you wish me to continue I am going to need both of your words to let me completely handle dis wit absolute discretion, and if you learn anyting you must let me know immidiately." The two of them give the investigator their word before departing from the vehicle.

Twenty-One

“Hey dad.” McKenzie hugs her father in the parking lot of Suzie B’s Café. “Thank you for coming to eat with me.”

He smiles at his daughter while keeping an arm around her walking towards the entrance. “Of course McKenzie, I can always find a little extra time for any of my children.” He loosens his grip allowing her to open the door for him.

As theY enter the café the fresh aroma of cheeseburgers and French fries are very welcoming. “Mmm…smells fabulous.” Her dad commented as he took a big whiff of the greasy air.

“Well I think it smells like another heart attack to me dadd.” McKenzie snarls her nose to her father as they both walk to the back in the almost deserted place, being late afternoon.

“Ola…mi name Rose Marie, can I get drink?” The waitress McKenzie has become more familiar with asked politely in battered English.

McKenzie gets a queasy feeling in her stomach remembering how Jonas was towards the waitress, several weeks earlier. “I’ll just have a water…please.” She proudly answers.

“I’ll take a coke.” Her father orders, getting a worried look from his daughter, McKenzie however says nothing.

“No problemo, be right back.” She spoke jovially as she drops off the menus and turns back towards the kitchen, before she makes it to far she paused and turned back. “Mi so sorry, the lunch menu no long available. Its after one.” She states as she picks back up the extra lunch menus.

“That’s no biggie, I am sure I can find something fattening in here Rose Marie, thank you.” Mr. Ross smiles to her just before looking down at the menu.

McKenzie waits until the waitress is out of ear shot before she speaks. “Ughh!!!Daddd!!! Shouldn’t you be watching what you eat? And picking something in the healthier category? Didn’t you just have a heart attack?”

“Uhh.” He haphazardly rolled his eyes at his daughter. “McKenzie that was eight months ago, and your mother has my heart under control. I have had nothing but salads, fruit, water, and all these no fat and no greasy foods. Surely you can let me splurge this one time, since she isn’t around.”

McKenzie gives her father a frail look that goes unnoticed as he was studying the menu with great enthusiasm. “I guesss…” She drawls out the word not really wanting to enable him, but also feeling sorry that he even has to worry about it at all.

“Oh my! This all looks so good.” He speaks while McKenzie watches him intently, thinking about what she wants to discuss with him, and how much she might actually say.

Rose Marie returns with their beverages and placed them in front of them before taking two straws out of her apron pocket. “You order now, or need more memento?”

“Umm…yes How big are your burgers?” Mr. Ross asked.

“Scuse me?”

“Your burgers?” He takes his hand making a small and large circles with them.

“Ahh! The burgers, mucho grande.” She holds out her hand showing her estimated size of their burgers.

“Very good.” He nods and smiles mischievously. “Give me the Blue Cheese Burger…” He pauses pointing at the one he wanted on the menu contemplating on how he wanted it. “Go ahead and make it a double…I’m starving, with fries…wait no lets go with the onion rings.”

Rose Marie jots all this down on her pad as McKenzie wonders whether she is writing it in Spanish or not, she quickly shook the thought of. “Do you have a grilled chicken Caesar Salad?”

Rose Marie’s eyes grew big. “Ceaser salad chicken, mi like best.” She responds happily as she jots this down, then takes up the menus before scurrying away.

“So McKenzie? What’s on your mind, to want to eat with your father?”

"Ahh." Offended McKenzie drops her jaw. "Dad, can I not just want to have lunch with you?" She claims defensively.

"Umm…well I guess you could, but lets just say that I have this feeling and I know when something is up with my eldest daughter."

She returned him a roll of her eyes. "Mom…she told you didn't she?"

He shakes his head as he lowered his gaze to the table in between them. "You know mom and I have always shared every detail of our lives together, which I know you have seen for twenty-six years now. Why would this come as a surprise to you?"

She shrugs her shoulders taking a quiet drink of her water. "So do you remember that terrible twang that Arthur used to make with the E-string on his violin just to annoy everybody?"

Her dad chuckled at this memory. "Well…it did not annoy me, because I did not allow it to. But I do remember how pestered you three ladies were by this…yes."

"Hmm…" McKenzie thinks about this as though her father has already analogically answered her question, before she even compiled the analogy. "Well that awful twang sound is kinda how my mind is feeling right now."

"Hmm…" He mimics her. "Why are you letting it?" He said as he shrugged and took a drink of his soda savoring the sweet carbonated goodness as though there is no other care in the world.

"Dadd!" She scolds. "How can you be so calm as though I shouldn't be worried? How can you sit there when your daughter has all these problems, and just calmly shrug and drink your coke?"

He just smiles and takes another sip of his coke. "So…your problems are so great I should be worried with you also? Are you sick or do you have cancer? Or is there something like that I need to know about?"

"No…its nothing like that."

"Okay…is your life in danger? Or is someone trying to kill you?"

"Uhh well…nooahh…" She sighs out with a long breath.

"Then I really don't see your relevance in me worrying also. I do want to hear you out and see if I might can give you some advice, which will most likely start with, leave the worrying to God. Sure we can change things, take different routes, and hopefully ease our struggles, but honestly I have found that worrying about my struggles is more of a struggle than it is worth." Her dad speaks encouraging words that he wonders if she even just heard him at all.

McKenzie sits there watching herself twiddling her thumbs on the table in front of her, wondering how to start the conversation. "Dad, I have many struggles going on right now. All of which I just wish I had someone to talk with about them."

Her dad pooches his lips out making an all too familiar face, which brings is daughter great comfort. "Well McKenzie, last time I checked you do have someone, in fact there are many someone's. I am sitting right in front of you, then there's your mom of course, your sister, your brother, even JJ although I don't always agree with her. I'm so confident in you and the way I raised you that I have faith you can take on the world, Not to sound too cocky." McKenzie's face cringes hearing her father say this word. "But I feel that I followed God's commands while I raised all of you, so I know you'll make all the right choices."

Nope definitely not talking about Gibraltar. The thought comes to her mind.

"But dad." She pauses to arrange her next words more carefully. "Its just not the same, talking with any of you. I mean there's a lot of things I cant talk with you about. I might be able to talk about some of these things with the others, just like there are things I can talk about with you, that I may not be a able to talk about with them. Ahh" She sighs heavily, feeling as though she just rambled on for hours. "But I want someone that I can talk to about anything. Like you was saying about you and mom sharing everything…I want that."

McKenzie's dad nods his head knowingly so. "Well daughter…I wish you would know that you can certainly talk to me about anything…" ***No I cant!*** McKenzie thinks and knows she cant, just as she knows she wont is why her father is comfortable saying these comforting words. "But I do understand, I most assuredly need your mother. She is not just a want, and I believe your want is a need as well McKenzie. Most of us humans need the other, that's why God made Eve. Just because he made Eve to need Adam, does not mean he didn't make Adam to need Eve. I know he did, however there now is only about four billion Adam's that he has created, but he's only created one for you. Some of us have to be a little more patient for God to connect us to the right one. He's out there for you McKenzie, I know he is, your just not quite ready for him yet." He spoke with all the confidence in the world for his daughter.

McKenzie's mind wonders off to Gibraltar thinking that just maybe…maybe God's going to bring him to the church and save him, she dazes out towards the white picket fence.

"Chicken salad de Ceasar." Rose Marie snaps McKenzie out of her day dream, placing the salad in front of her. "And queso Azul buggar for mister, anything more?" She places his burger down in front of him.

"Yes ketchup would be great…please and thank you Ms. Rose Marie." She takes a few steps over to the table next to theirs and grabs a bottle and placed it on the table in front of McKenzie's dad. "Mmm" His mouth waters over the burger.

"Blah." He stares over at his daughter as she mixes the fried chicken into her salad. "This really looks amazing, I've really been enjoying eating more healthier lately. Mom told me to start cooking, therapeutically...well not exactly like that, but that's how I took it and it does seem to be helping."

"Mmm come to papa." Her dad takes a huge bite out of his burger.

"Daddd!!!" McKenzie sighs out with her face turning red with embarrassment, quickly looking around making sure nobody else heard him say that.

They both sit around in silence for a bit enjoying their food and each other's company.

"So JJ got beat up." McKenzie finally blurts out breaking the silence, causing her dad to almost choke on his food. "And I am suppose to be taking this Bi-Sexual twelve year old goth chick for ice cream this week, her names Lunar, sounds out there...Huh?" Surprisingly calm, she takes another bite of her salad.

Her dad finishes chewing the bite slowly before taking a drink, taking all of this in. "Wow McKenzie." Still shocked. "First off is JJ ok?"

"Yea." She mumbles as she nods her head. "Physically anyways, she has a lot of bruising. If she was only beaten it would have been better, but because it was much worse than that she has a lot of mental and emotional damage that's just going to take time to heal."

"Oh my, that's terrible! Let her know we all will be praying for her, and if there is anything we can possibly do we want to help." Her dad shows solid concern and compassion towards her friend.

McKenzie pushes her salad out of her way finished with all of it, all except for a few cherry tomatoes gone. "Ok will do, she's staying with Mark right now. He's been a big help getting her through all this. I really hope she takes notice on how much he really cares now."

Mr. Ross scrapes the last bit of ketchup off his plate with the last onion rings. "Well Mark, there's someone God raised right, but has struggled relationship wise." He talks at the same time still holding onto the onion ring. "I pray often to God about Mark. He is such an amazing young man, I hope he returns to God's will for him. Especially since I feel that my strict following of God's and the Churches guidelines really pushed him away. Do you know why Mark left the church?" He asked his daughter as he bit off the part of the onion ring that had the ketchup on it, then he placed the other half on his plate and pushed it out of his way.

McKenzie simply shakes her head.

"Anyting more?" Rose Marie asked as she removed their plates from the table.

"Yea Rose Marie, I'll take a strawberry milkshake…please."

McKenzie rolls her eyes to her father. "I'll take a cup of coffee." She adds looking up to the waitress.

"So Mark had went to another church, one where I feel they have allowed the world to comfortably move in, and they didn't hold the same standards that we do. Now don't hear me wrong, I know you know my strict policy's and that you know that we invite anyone in doesn't matter how they look. They can be in dirty clothes, wear there hats in our sanctuary, or women can even wear there mini skirts. We never turn anyone away, but our spiritual leaders must show that God has made them different, has renewed their lives. Anyways long story short Mark got on our platform for praise and worship in blue jeans and a T-shirt. I didn't pull him off (you can trust I wanted to). However I did ban him from the praise and worship team until I felt he was spiritually ready to return. He then slowly started missing services until…well you know the rest."

McKenzie laughs at this realization. "So you believe that's the reason he left the church?" She questions thinking that maybe it is something she can use to bring him conviction again.

"Well I know it wasn't the only reason, I'm sure your friend JJ may have had a little something to do with it."

“Haha.” McKenzie started laughing. “I’m sure she probably had everything to do with it. She probably told him he looked good in that T-shirt.” She comments honestly.

Rose Marie returns with the coffee and shake. McKenzie takes the coffee wrapping both hands around the mug feeling the warmth surge into her hands. “Anyting morzz.” Rose Marie reiterates, they both thank her and shake their heads as she placed the check on the table. “Gracias you pay at front.” She returned back to her other work.

“Yea McKenzie, its often funny how quick us men are at taking a bite of that fruit, it can also be very damaging in some instances. So what about this goth girl…umm…Apollo you said her name was?”

McKenzie’s stomach turns a somersault, as she feels her salad making an attempt to go the wrong direction. ***Coincidence? Or does he know something? No he couldn’t know, who would have told him? I didn’t say anything to Arthur about Apollo.***

“No dad…Lunar.”

He chuckled. “Wow, how did I get Apollo out of that? Guess I was just thinking of space.”

McKenzie relaxes noticing his sincerity. “Well…Lunar.” She takes a gulp of her coffee feeling more relaxed as the warmth travels to her stomach. “Is a twelve year old that is really struggling. She was in the principals office one day when I went in to visit with Mr. Bright. He really didn't know what to do with her, he really didn't feel right about punishing her sexual confusion at such an early age, or at least not right off the bat. So I offered to talk with her."

Her dad listens very carefully as he drinks his milkshake.

"I talked with her the next morning and asked her if she wanted to go get some ice cream next week sometime, If her parents would be ok with it. Then she really broke my heart." McKenzie starts to tear up. "She said yea, with the brightest smile from the darkest place I have ever seen, dad." McKenzie started crying unable to continue saying what she wanted to say.

"This is a blessing McKenzie." Her father spoke to her as calmly and casually as anyone could ever speak. "You will be able to learn and maybe teach me some things. It is so difficult as a Pastor, as we get older our world changes less, while the younger generations change more. Often at times it is very difficult for us to keep up with this. This is what has caused many churches to fall victim to the world, feeling they have to change with the times. Which we do, but we have to be careful to change according to God's word and will. We have to keep our churches as places of prayer, worship, and praise, not looking like some rave or party with fancy flashing lights and smoke machines. We want to always point towards God and his changes."

McKenzie takes all this in whipping her tears away with a napkin. “Yea…I’ve never thought about it that way.”

He smiles brightly at his daughter. “Nor did I McKenzie, until I had this guy just last week come to me and say he appreciated our worship service more than I could imagine. He had been to multiple other churches that their worship services reminded him of the raves and parties he used to go to taking all kinds of drugs and partaking of all kinds of other mischievous party acts. You see McKenzie, it is very important that we change the world, and not let the world change us.”

She glares with appreciation to her fathers pure insight. “Lunar…” She gets back on subject. “Tells me that her parents wont care, they never notice her coming or leaving as she wants. ‘I always try to let them know where I’m going though.’ She tells me wanting to be responsible. But your absolutely right dad, this is a true blessing from God. A distraction I needed, and hopefully I will be able to change Lunar’s life during the process.”

McKenzie I don’t think you will ever realize how proud I am of the yo…” He pauses taking the young out of his mouth. “Woman you have become.”

Twenty-Two

"Whoaah." Samuel walked into the office and noticed dumbbells sitting beside Gibraltar's desk. "So I see someone decided that I had a good idea after all. Huh?"

Gibraltar looks up from his paper. "I suppose a blind squirrel gets a nut now and again." He postulates. "What do you want?"

Samuel shrugs as he walked over and took a seat. "I dunno Doc, can I not just come in to talk?" He spoke with concern towards his friend.

"Its just that usually you come at me to be annoying, or only when you need something." Gibraltar claims with total aberration.

"Yea." Samuel nods his head understandingly so. "I'm sorry that it does tend to be that way, more often than not. I did choose you as my best man because you are my best friend, and I am really starting to get concerned about you. You have been a real prick lately, and its rubbing off on the rest of here at Station Thirteen."

“Whatever…” Gibraltar mumbles out a sigh, sitting back in his chair crossing his arms in a teenage pouty gesture. “Its just…I don’t really want to talk about it.”

“Ok fine.” Samuel stands up. “Just in case you are wondering…Do you want a water?” Gibraltar shakes his head with his arms still crossed as Samuel gets himself a bottle of water. “Samantha and I are doing really good…” He paused and took a big pull from the water bottle. “ Actually better than really good, its been amazing since we got the wedding over with. Its almost like the act of getting married was the biggest struggle of my life. Since I was able to make it through all the wedding planning and such, she and I will be able to handle anything life throws our way.”

Gibraltar’s posture softens up a bit as he relaxes and begins to gently rock back and forth. “That’s good Samuel, I pray…” Gibraltar caught himself using the word pray instead of hope. He paused a minute to see if Samuel noticed, if he did so he did not react to it in any way. “That that is the most difficult struggle that you two have to endure.” He said sincerely.

“Thanks Cap.” Samuel sits back down across from Gibraltar with a new shine on his face, finally seeing a bit of light from his friend. “But life is full of struggles and we will have plenty more. I just hope to God that Sam and I are completely ready to stand together through them all.” He speaks realistically.

Gibraltar's focus hones in on the hoping to God, he catches himself wondering if there is something more to all of this.

"So what is it Doc? Did that teacher turn you down again? Are you still stuck on her?" He attempts to sympathize with his Captain.

"No." Gibraltar stiffens back up and pretends to go back to his work, putting the barrier straight back up.

"Doc...come on you cant keep doing this. Your going to have to talk or something. Your going to end up pushing everyone away." Samuel puts his hands on the desk opposing Gibraltar and leans forward, trying to get through his defenses. "Maybe you should try going out with someone else. I mean there are plenty of other women out there, surely there is another one out there that catches your attention, to distract you from McKenzie."

McKenzie...McKenzie... The name echoes through Gibraltar's mind. He takes a deep breath, then sits up looking big eyed at Samuel. "You know what?" Surprised. "Your right." He takes his wallet out of his pocket and pulls out a business card. "I need a distraction."

"What's that?" Samuel is curious as Gibraltar laid the card on his desk.

"This here." He picks the card back up holding it up. "Is the escort service I was going to use for your bachelor party, before I let my conscience get the best of me."

"Haha..." Samuel laughs and sits back in his chair. "Well...that's not exactly what I had..."

"Station Thirteen!" Barbie comes over their radios as the alarms begin to sound. She gives a brief description and the address to where the emergency at hand was.

"10-4 Barbie, on our way." Samuel calls back to her. "Gotta go Doc, we'll continue this conversation later." Samuel runs out the door leaving Gibraltar staring at the cards on his desk.

McKenzie...McKenzie...McKenzie...The echo in his mind intensifying the longer he looked at the card. He swivels around in his chair and looks down at his crew all climbing into engine number one. "AHHH!!!" He screams way over the alarms. "Get out of my head!"
McKenzie...McKenzie...McKenzie...The scream did no good at subsiding the echoes.

He then gets up and picks up the two biggest dumbbells in the set on the floor and just before he decides to throw one of them through the window...he stops himself and begins curling them, over and over he lifts them burning out his frustration through his muscles. When he cant lift them anymore he sits them down on his desk and grabbed the card from it. Then he takes his phone from his pocket and dials the escort service.

❖

Gibraltar and the escort walk into the kitchen of Fire Station Thirteen carrying several bags of groceries. “Starry.” He gazed over at the very attractive young woman in a tank top, and a very mini skirt. “So what’s your real name?” ***Yea McKenzie, I’m sure she will get rid of yours.***

“Hehe…” She giggles looking around the whole place taken aback. “I’m not suppose to give out my real name. Wow! Are you really the Captain of this place?” She nudges into him flirtatiously.

“Yep, sure am.” He sits his bags down on the counter top, then takes the two lighter ones from her hands. He looks her up and down in attempt to be attracted to her. “Come on Starry.” ***McKenzie…McKenzie…***His head still rings. “Ok, why do they call you Starry then?”

“Oh...” She grabs Gibraltar by the shoulders and turns him towards her, blinking and smiling dumbly at him looking straight into his eyes. “That’s easy, I chose the name cause my daddy always told me my eyes sparkled like a starry night sky.”

“Hahaha…” He laughed at her comment, quickly he broke her gaze and started busying himself with the groceries. “Have you ever made homemade lasagna before?”

She shakes her head no, not that Gibraltar could see it. “Oh no!” She steps next to him pushing herself up against him as she helps him remove the items out of the sacks. “I never cook anything, I mostly have Mickey D’s do my cooking for meee…" She pokes an elbow at him drawling out he me. "Your so hot, and you're a fire fighter, and you cook."

McKenzie…McKenzie…Ahhh get out of my head.

Gibraltar looks back to Starry and put his hands on her shoulders, trying his hardest to be distracted by her, but there really is only one thing on his mind, and this escort cant even come close to pulling his mind away. ***Ahh…Why am I doing this?*** He tells himself. "Well your going to learn to cook today Starry." ***Surely she'll grow on me, she is very pretty after all.*** "Here you go, open this. We're going to start making the pasta noodles it takes the longest having to roll it all out flat, and its probably going to get messy."

"Mmm…" She smiles opening up the bag of flour. "I bet I can dirty up a kitchen." She reiterates.

Gibraltar's stomach cringes, not because he enjoyed what she said, but because what she said totally appalled him. "So we are cooking for the rest of the crew. They should be back from their call shortly, hopefully we'll be most of the way done by then.

As Gibraltar and Starry set the table a couple hours later the big garage door begins to whirl. "What's that noise?" She questioned bending over the table setting plates out attempting to get Gibraltar's attention.

The harder she tries the less and less interested he becomes. “That is the crew, and they are back which is good timing the lasagna is almost done. In fact lets go ahead and go check on it.”

“Ok.” She bobs her head back and forth as she skips over to him, rubbing shoulders with him as they walk through the kitchen doors.

A few minutes later they walk back out of the kitchen, Gibraltar has the lasagna in his hands and Starry has her hands wrapped around his elbow. Barry and Samuel are standing there in the dining area as they both came in with dinner.

Barry and Samuel look at one another then back over to Gibraltar and Starry as though they were deer stuck in headlights, frozen stiff. “Oh, hey guys.” Both of them still unsure of what to think, they give him a dull hey. “We made lasagna.”

“Mmm…” DeAndre walked into the dining area. “It smells amazing in here…Oh…Hey Starry.” He casually spoke as he sees her holding onto Gibraltar’s elbow. “What are you doing here?” He questioned her as he grabbed his glass from his place sitting to fill it with tea.

“Ohhah…your Captain and I…” She starts to talk playfully as she circles around Gibraltar. “We just made you all lasagna.”

Barry and Samuel still speechless take their seats at the table.

“Well that’s cool.” DeAndre un-phased at all by the situation grabs a piece of garlic bread. “I’m starving…” He adds.

“Hehehe…” Starry giggles at DeAndre. “Ohh! Big A your always starving…hehehe.”

Gibraltar’s skin begins to crawl, feeling more and more dengy by the moment.

“Did she…” Barry slaps Samuel on the shoulder and starts whispering to him. “Did she just call DeAndre…” Samuel looks at him with a nodding grin.

Beatrice and Alex walk into the dining area, Alex heads straight for his seat at the table, not at all taking notice of Starry hovering around Gibraltar. Beatrice’s jaw all but hits the floor as she makes an attempt to stop it.

“Oh hey Bea…Alex, this is Starry.” Gibraltar introduces. “Where’s Felipe?”

Beatrice still staring uncomfortably so at Starry, who is completely oblivious at the un-comfort. “Felipe…oh...” She quickly shakes her head and blinks a couple of times. “He went to lay down, he has a headache.”

Samuel jumps up in an instance. “I’ll go get him, he’s not going to want to miss this lasagna.” He runs out the door very enthusiastically.

"Hey Starry, that's a pretty name." Alex claims in his normal flat tone. "Are you a hooker?"

"Hehehe…" Starry giggles.

"Alex Uhh!" Bea slaps him on the shoulder. "That's another thing your not suppose to say to women."

"No…no…" Starry replies. "Its ok, I'm just an escort. We only go out on dates with our clients." She looks at Gibraltar and gives him a seductive wink, almost causing him to gag.

"What Bea, my mom was a hooker and that's how she dressed." Alex said this as though his mom was just another normal professional woman.

"Ohh…Alex…" Bea states as though he just gave her the biggest revelation of her life. "I see…" She solemnly adds.

Twenty-Three

"Hey Lunar." McKenzie said as she walked up to the young lady all dressed in black. ***Jesus help me to vanquish all of my negative stereotypical thoughts today.*** She prays silently as she looks at this young pre-teen who was dressed like a punk rocker. Lunar is only twelve years of age, however with her short cropped hair, pale make up, and worn green eyes she carries the soul of someone twice her age.

"Hi Mrs. Ross." Lunar responds apathetically.

"Oh! No its just Miss Ross, I am not married." Lunar glares to McKenzie with a quaint shrug. "You ready to go?" Lunar nods and quietly walked around to the passenger side of McKenzie's car.

"All set?" McKenzie attempted to lighten her mood with her voice, as she fastened her seat belt. "Do you have a specific place you like to get ice cream, Lunar?" She questioned before driving off.

"No." Lunar shakes her head curtly. "All the other kids go to the mall, but they don't really like me much anyways. They make fun of the way that I dress, I presume most of the teachers do to…well except you. You look at me differently, you look at me like your sad…like me."

Lord help me, I'm supposed to be strong for Lunar. McKenzie prays as tears begin to swell up into her eyes, as Lunar talks of her loneliness and not fitting in. "Ok Lunar, how about this. Do you like flowers?"

Lunar's eyes light up at this question. ***There is a twelve year old girl in there.*** McKenzie breaths a sigh of relief. "Well I know this beautiful garden spot, with a bunch of gorgeous, and colorful flowers. We can go to Suzie B's, get our ice cream and take to their garden." McKenzie gives her a forced smile.

"Ok Miss Ross, why ain't you married? You seem like your old enough and your very pretty, you shouldn't have to be lonely like me."

McKenzie begins to choke up at Lunar's words, quickly she started her car trying to push her emotions back into check. "Well Lunar…I am…" She begins to gain her composure as she pulls into traffic. "So why don't we be lonely today…together."

"But I'm not alone today Miss Ross, I have you." Lunar claims so zealously that she gave McKenzie some strength.

"Hymph!!!" McKenzie chuckled and quickly glanced over at her. "We have each other…Hey Lunar why don't you call me McKenzie."

"Really?" Lunar stares over at McKenzie with some brightness showing through. "McKenzie? That's such a beautiful name."

McKenzie laughs thinking about this. "Well it don't rock nearly as much as Lunar, but thank you. So what's your favorite ice cream?"

“Umm…” Lunar shrugs, McKenzie doesn’t take notice trying to pay attention to the wild traffic. “I guess chocolate, that’s the only kind I have ever had.”

McKenzie shocked by this, but does not show it, not wanting to disappoint her new young friend. “Oh…well cool, maybe will get to try something different today. Suzie B’s has a dozen different flavor to choose from. And they are…well in my opinion very delectable.” Her love for ice cream shows through her voice.

“Really???Twelve different flavors of ice cream? I didn’t know they made that many.” Delight shows through Lunar’s voice.

“Yep!” McKenzie surprised at the thought of a twelve year old not knowing that there are hundreds of different ice cream flavors. “They always keep twelve different flavors out, they’ll change one every now and again. They of course keep your normal ones vanilla, chocolate, neapolitan, cookies and cream…umm…I think peppermint.”

Lunar looks to McKenzie who is smiling talking about all the different ice cream while she pays attention to the road. “Peppermint?” She snarls her nose. “That sounds gross.”

“Haha” McKenzie laughs and glanced momentarily over at Lunar. “I know right…I always thought the same thing, and everybody always called me weird. Oh…looky here, we’re here.” She claimed as they pull into the parking lot. “Come on lets see if we can find something better than peppermint ice cream.”

They both get out of the car together and walk up to the café. ‘Ding…ding.’ The bell on the door rings as they enter Suzie B’s. “Ola coma estas.” Rose Marie greets them from behind the counter. “Just two you today?” She questioned as she picked up the menus.

“Si Rose Marie, we’re just here for ice cream though.” McKenzie lets the waitress know as she pulled Lunar over towards the ice cream freezers.

“Uoahh goody!!!” Rose Marie spoke enthusiastically stepping over behind the ices cream. “Which flavor choose?”

Lunar’s eyes get big bouncing back and forth at all the different choices. “Oh my God Miss…I mean McKenzie, I don’t know which one to pick.” She speaks hectically getting confused by all the choices.

“Its ok Lunar, take your time.” Lunar scratches her head, while McKenzie places a comforting hand on her shoulder. “You don’t have to choose just one either, I sometimes like mixing my flavors.”

“Really?” Lunar responds quizzically.

“Do you wont bowl or cons?” Rose Marie asked forcing Lunar to gaze up to McKenzie.

“Its up to you.” McKenzie shrugs. “I like the waffle cones.” She added optimistically.

“Ok…” Lunar’s mind finally settling down makes her choice. “I want the waffle cone with chocolate and peppermint.” She ordered excitedly.

“Make that two!” McKenzzie reiterates.

They both get their ice cream cones and McKenzie pays at the counter. Then they both happily walk out of the front door.

From the sidewalk out front McKenzie points to their left. “They have a very pretty flower garden here, want to walk through it?”

Lunar eagerly licks at her ice cream as they walk towards the flower garden. “Mmm…this actually isn’t too bad.”

“Hehe…” McKenzie giggles as she licked her peppermint ice cream. “No…perhaps its not, maybe we’re not nearly as weird as we were thinking…Huh?”

They walk underneath an arch entry way that has decorative vines growing all around it. Walking into the garden that has many different colors and types of flowers McKenzie looks over at Lunar’s face and saw a very bright face, one that she wouldn’t expect to see on someone dressed so darkly.

“Wow…Miss McKenzie, these flowers are all so beautiful. What kinds are they?”

Why did she have to ask me that? “Well…Lunar.” McKenzie licks up the side of her cone that was about to drip onto her hand. “I am a fourth grade teacher, not a botanist. So I am sorry I cannot answer your question, however I will tell you that none of them have anything on your beauty. You are such a pretty young lady, did you know that?”

“Pcha!” Lunar rolls her eyes to McKenzie’s compliments, blowing out a sigh with a (yea-right) look. “What is a…botist? Am I saying that right?”

McKenzie smiles at Lunar as they approach a bench. “Well not quite, its botanist…b-o-t-a-n-i-s-t…botanist.” She spells out the word to help her better understand. “Its really the scientific name for a gardener, or more so an educated gardener. A botanist goes to college to study different plants.”

“Oh…that’s really cool.” Lunar bends over holding her ice cream in her left hand, she delicately cups her right hand around a magenta colored flower bring it to her nose, and takes a big whiff. “I like science.” She stands back up, and flops down on the bench next to McKenzie. “That flower really didn’t have a smell, maybe I can become a botanist. Then I can figure out why some of them smell and some of them don’t.”

“That sounds like an excellent goal Lunar, your certainly smart enough. You just have to study and work hard, and you will have no problem." She encourages her as she takes a bite off the sweet waffle cone.

"Well…that'll never happen then…I'm not a good worker. My mom is always telling me how lazy I am, no matter how hard I try or how much cleaning I do I am just a 'lazy slob' she always says so. I'm thinking its just who I am."

Oh!!!No Lord help me. McKenzie prays not understanding at all how so many parents lack compassion for their children. ***God I really needed your strength here to not go strangle this woman.*** She continues to pray hard to herself, struggling with all her mite to fight back all the hurt, anger, and sadness. ***Jesus what am I suppose to say? I cant bash her mother.*** McKenzie struggling with what to say takes another bite of her cone.

"You know what I am in science terms?" Lunar spoke first giving McKenzie slight relief of not having to speak just yet, but worry that the conversation isn't about to get any easier. She gently shakes her head as she slowly chews the waffle cone with Lunar staring intently on her. "I am what scientist would call an ecological anomaly."

"What's that?" McKenzie twerks her face.

"Well McKenzie…ecology is the science concerned with the interactions of organisms and their environments, and an anomaly is something unusual or abnormal."

McKenzie chokes at her intellectual philosophy, still too shocked to speak. She listens on as Lunar continues with her philosophical views. “All the other kids don’t like me in their environment, the teachers wont hardly look at me, even none of the dogs I see wont even let me pet them. In fact I think its because you’re an ecological anomaly also that we get along well. The flowers don’t have legs to run from us, this is the first time I have ever felt like I fit in anywhere. Maybe I am suppose to be one of them bomist.”

“Its bot-a-nist.” McKenzie says it again this time breaking up the syllables in hopes that she wont say it like that again. “Wow…Lunar, you are a really smart girl and you’ll find your…” She pauses re-ordering her words. “We’ll find our way in God’s environment, I promise.”

Lunar looks to McKenzie confused as she shoves the last bit of the waffle cone into her mouth. “Gods environment?” She mumbles out.

“Yea Lunar, this is Gods world and I promise you neither one of us are ecological anomalies. Although I do often feel this way also, God does have a place for us all though.

Lunar looks all around the garden, not even coming close to understanding what McKenzie just said to her. She turns and glares directly at McKenzie. “Have you ever thought about killing yourself?” She boldly asked this question.

Oh God! I can not possibly do this without your help. Please give me the right words to say. McKenzie sincerely looks to her creator for the right words to say. "Lunar…honey, I cant say that I understand that feeling." She claims honestly hoping that she needs honesty and not relation. "But I know its not the right answer, no matter how tough life gets, we have to keep going."

Lunar starts to cry leaning over to McKenzie. "But it just seems like the world would be better off without me, like I am just in the way."

McKenzie wraps her tightly into her arms. "No way Lunar, I need a friend." She somehow manages to sob out. "And you're the perfect one." McKenzie attempts to dry up her tears and be strong for Lunar. "You got me to try peppermint ice cream. There has never (in my twenty-six years) been anyone that has ever been such a good friend to me."

They separate and Lunar looks McKenzie into the eyes both of them still glazed over from the tears. "Really?"

"Absolutely." McKenzie wipes the tears away from Lunar's face smearing the pale foundation everywhere. "Oops, we're getting your make up all messy, here I have some wipes somewhere." She digs through her purse taking out some wet wipes and begins to wash all the make up off of her face. "Lunar? Why do you wear so much of this make up? You have such a gorgeous face, there really isn't a need for you to cover it up."

Lunar shrugs. “I dunno, I guess cause my mom showed me how she used to dress when she was my age. Maybe I can do like you and start to not wear any make up. You sure are alot prettier than all the other teachers who wear lots of make up.”

McKenzie gives Lunar the most genuine smile she had ever seen. “That is completely up to you Lunar, you do what makes you comfortable.” She placed her hand over Lunar’s face gently stroking her cheek with her thumb. “You ever go to church?”

“What’s a church?”

“Now that’s a good question.” McKenzie so glad to be away from the tough stuff. “It is a place where we worship God, our Creator and its like my second family. Without them I would most definitely feel like one of those ecological anomalies you have been talking about. Their actually having a pizza party tonight with the youth group, think your parents would be ok with you staying out a little bit later?”

“Yes…I mean no…” Lunar shakes her head quickly and excitedly. “They don’t care what I do, as long as I leave them alone.”

McKenzie just grins not wanting to show how much this actually frustrates her. “Ok sounds good, how about we call them and I’ll let them know that I have you and you’ll be home by eight thirty.” Lunar begins bouncing on the bench unable to sit still as McKenzie's invite has her more excited than she had ever been.

Later that night McKenzie lays in her bed and begins to pray. ***Dear God, thank you for letting our youth group be so accepting of Lunar and taking her in like she was one of them. Thank you Lord, and God I want to apologize for being so impatient and stubborn, and thank you for using my struggles to save a life. Lord thank you for showing me that I needed to feel what it was like to be an ecological anomaly, if for nothing else but to save Lunar's life. God I am sorry I haven't always been appreciative to all your lessons, in fact I know that I have always cursed you for keeping me alone, but now I am thanking you that you have kept me alone so that I am able to show Lunar that you don't create ecological anomalies. Thank you Jesus, Amen.*** McKenzie then cries herself to sleep from the emotionally overwhelming day.

Twenty-Four

Alex Parks is car in front of a sign that reads [Guest Parking.] ***I guess I would count as a guest.*** He thought to himself. He then admires in 'Awe' the modest but elegant church building with big bold letters across the top [Ocean Breeze Apostolic Church]. Reading this he immediately remembered Beatrice telling him the name of the church.

He steps out of his car with his blue jeans and t-shirt on, puts on his (The U) baseball cap, and begins to make his way to the front doors. Walking up underneath the large drive through awning, he takes notice of several groups all chatting and enjoying the nice weather, some of them gaze in his direction with welcoming smiles.

He continues towards the glass doors, and just before he made it up to them one swings open wide. "Alex!" The familiar voice with a familiar smile welcomes him.

"Bea!" They embrace in a quick hug.

"I'm so glad you could make it, come in." Beatrice leads him into the front foyer.

Entering in the foyer there is a much larger crowd all gathered into separate groups talking amongst themselves. Alex begins to feel a bit uneasy and out of place. “Was I suppose to wear a suit and tie?” He questioned Bea, as he noticed that almost all of the men wore one.

“No…Alex, its ok you look great. Nobody will care what you are wearing here, they will just be glad you came, I promise.” Alex’s tension eases slightly with Beatrice’s welcoming compassion.

“What about the cap?”

Bea shakes her head. “Alex, if the cap makes you more comfortable, by all means wear it. Now stop worrying about how you look and lets go meet some people.” She grabs Alex by the hand and pulls him over to the welcome counter.

“Hey McKenzie, this is Alex. He’s the one who saved Natasha from the wrecked car a couple weeks ago.” Beatrice claims this as proudly as any mother could.

“Oh wow! Alex, thank you so much for your heroic services.” McKenzie shakes the heroes hand.

“Thank you.” He nods shyly towards her homely smile, not really knowing what else to say.

“Hey McKenzie can you, or do you have someone that could watch the front door for me. I want to go show off our local hero.” Beatrice proudly asked, so that she could take Alex to introduce him to some of the church family.

“Sure.” McKenzie grabs a gift bag for Alex. “Here Alex, this is for all of our first time guest. There’s a card in there you can fill out and get all the updates on what is going on here at Ocean Breeze Apostolic Church. There is a pen in there you can use to fill out the card, and you can just drop it off in the offering pale when it comes by during service, keep the pen though its yours.”

Alex gladly accepted the gift before having to make a couple quick steps to catch up to Beatrice, who was on a mission. Alex was a few minutes early because Bea explained to him that she would like to introduce him to some people if he came in early. Otherwise he is always right on time wherever he goes.

They walk into the expansive sanctuary. “Whoa!” Alex freezes as he stares at the five sections of seats, one slightly larger in the middle with two sections on either side of it. “This place is huge.” He exclaims as he looks around the place seeing more and more groups of people congregated all over the place. He does take notice of a few other guys (not many) dressed as casually as he was, but no baseball caps.

“Come on Alex.” Beatrice called him already a couple steps ahead of him again, he pulls his cap off and double times it to catch back up to her. “Yea, honestly it’s a little too big, but it works. We have some really good smaller connect groups, where we can get closer to each other. They all run most Sunday nights, now don’t tell the Pastor this.” Bea pauses and leans over to whisper in his ear. "My husband and I usually put the football game on after our Bible study." She gives him a devious grin.

"Now come on, I want you to meet my husband. You can sit down here with us." She walks quickly down the right center row towards a guy who has several of the young girls all gathered around a car seat about four rows deep, out of the ten there is. "Hey Joel, this is Alex…Alex this is Joel, my husband." She zealously introduces them.

"Alex! Oh my gosh…It is so nice to finally meet you." Joel held out a welcoming hand. When Alex grabbed his hand Joel pulls him in for a big hug, that made Alex feel awkward, but welcomed the warm fuzzy feeling it left in him.

"Hello Amanda, Stephanie, and Stacy, how are you all?" They are all making googly faces with Natasha in her car seat, barely acknowledging Beatrice and Alex. "And you, I'm sorry if we have, but I don't believe we have met yet." She talks softly to the very short haired young lady all dressed out in black.

"I'm Lunar." She quickly sticks her hand out learning their inviting gesture already.

"Well Lunar, I'm Beatrice (you can call me Bea). Its so nice to meet you, that is such a cool name, with a pretty smile behind it."

Maybe I am pretty without my makeup. Lunar enjoying the feelings she is getting from everyone at Ocean Breeze. "Thank you." She said with rosy cheeks in a bashful manner.

"Hey girls, did you all know Alex is the one who saved Natasha from the crashed car?" Joel now praises Alex heroic actions.

Alex dropped his jaw. "That's her?" He looks at baby Natasha for the first time since that day. Joel nods placing a hand on Alex's back pushing and guiding him up to the car seat. "She looks so much bigger."

Beatrice started pulling her out of the car seat. "Well Alex, baby's grow fast. Do you want to hold her?" She asked a reluctant Alex, not that she was really giving him a choice.

"No…no…I cant." He holds out his palms in attempt to reject this offer.

"Oh come on Alex, you saved her life, you can at least hold her for a minute."

Stacy throws her arms to her side. "Uh! No fair, I have been trying to hold her all morning." She pouts righteously.

"She's been asleep Stacy, be patient I told you that you will get a chance to hold her." Joel easily reprimands her.

“Here you go Alex, just be sure to support her head. She is really probably strong enough now, but we don’t want to take any chances.”

Alex cradles baby Natasha in his arms, gently swaying back and forth, gazing intently at the cooing baby. “I’ve never held a baby before.” He claims this flatly, but with slightly more empathy than he normally would have.

“Your kinda a whippersnapper of a guy aren’t you.” Lunar said without recognizing this to be an insult, nor did Alex. He glanced at her with a puzzled look trying to determine what she just said, Lunar honestly just thinking she was politely telling him how skinny he was.

“Ugh! Lunar!” McKenzie walked up as she called Alex this. “Have you been reading the dictionary again?” Lunar nods as McKenzie grabbed her by the shoulders and pulled her to the side, a bit more forcefully and motherly than she had intended. “Lunar, that’s not a nice word.”

Lunar twerks her face confused at what she had done wrong. “What I was just telling him how skinny he is.”

McKenzie nods slightly. “Well…he may be so, but just like its not polite to tell someone how fat they are, the same holds true for telling someone how skinny they are. Most fat people want to be skinny, and most skinny people want to be fat. So it hurts their feelings to tell them they are so.” McKenzie softly explains this to her as the worship team to begin with their first song. “Ok Lunar, go get in your seat. Do you have someone your going to sit with?”

“Stephanie.” Lunar points a finger over a couple rows in front of them. “Said that I can sit next to her.”

“Very good, now we need to pay attention. See you after service.”

Alex sitting next to Beatrice clapped his hands off beat and sang the words off the screen, (well mumbled more so) with the rest of the church. Looking over occasionally at Beatrice and Joel where he see’s complete joy and serenity on their faces, which is contagiously growing on him.

“Praise the Lord church!” The pastor called out over the fading praise and worship music as he stepped up to the podium. “Please remain standing for the reading of The Word, I promise not to continue to ramble on and make you stand there too much longer.”

The worship team all but Arthur quietly exit the platform, while he continued to play soft notes on the violin.

“So if you will turn in your Bibles to the very familiar versus of Proverbs 3:5-6. Many of you can probably quote these by heart, if you cant you should be able to. It will make a difference in your walk with God for sure.” The pastor paused and took a drink of water giving everyone a chance to get their Bibles turned to the page.

“Proverbs three, five, and six.” He reads from his Bible, although he most assuredly could quote these two scriptures. “Trust in the Lord with all thine heart, and lean not unto thine own understanding. In all the ways acknowledge him, and he shall direct thy paths.”

He steps back off the podium to pray. “Dear heavenly Father.” He takes a deep breath and looks up towards the sky. “Please allow us to take in the words you have spoken to us, and apply them to our lives to hold all our trust in you with every step we make. In Jesus name I pray, Amen.”

After his short and sweet prayer the Pastor stepped back up to the podium and vaguely glances at his notes. “Thank you all, you may be seated now. I want to speak to you for a few minutes this morning on trust. Trust-in-God-in-all-your-ways.” The words pop up on the overhead screens with the picture of a Bible in the background.

“Trusting in God is something incredibly difficult for us to do, it is unnatural and does not always come easily.” He walks to the right side of the platform. “But we must trust in God, are you having marital issues???Put God first and he can find you compromises…Financial struggles???Put God first.” The pastor real careful here not to mention tithes not wanting to loose anyone’s attention, there is a place and time for those talks. “Is there a new job or promotion your looking at? Trust him he will provide. Now I don’t want to get too far off topic here but I have to mention.”

The pastor walks over to the other side of the platform focusing on the whole crowd he had there this day. Looking over towards Alex, Joel, Beatrice, and baby Natasha he begins to speak again. “Are you wanting a child? Trust in God.” He holds out a welcoming hand towards them all. “We have this morning with us a very special guest, Alex. He is the hero that saved sweet little Natasha from a wrecked vehicle.”

Alex’s face turns beat red as he gets a really nervous feeling Beatrice pats him on the shoulder. “Thank you Alex, for your service.” The pastor shows his appreciation as the crowds applause begins to dwindle.

“This is a prime example of trusting God. Joel and Beatrice have been trusting in God all of their lives, and have been praying for a child for several years now. But God’s timing is more proper, he knew that if Joel and Bea had already had a child that sweet little Natasha would not have had such a beautiful place to go to.” Pastor nods and smiles to them all before stepping back to look to his notes.

He continues to preach on trusting God for the next thirty minutes, weaving and wobbling back and forth across the platform. Often times sternly raising his voice, but not ever to the (face-turning-red-point) that many United Pentecostals preach with.

“In closing.” The pastor steps down off the platform and walks to the front of the middle aisle, getting on the same level as the whole congregation. "I want to say to us all (myself included). We rally here each week, not to talk about the bad things we did this past week, we rally here to talk about the good things we're going to do, this next week. So when we think about the golden rule, do unto others as we would have them do unto us. Lets not think about the bad things we didn't do, lets think on all the good things we can do for the next person, and God will bless you."

As the worship team begin to softly play worship music again the Pastor returns back to the platform. "Now I know we have several new faces in the crowd today, so I feel totally compelled to make this altar call. Acts two, thirty-eight." He begins to quote. "Then Peter said unto them, repent, and be baptized everyone of you in the name of Jesus Christ for the remission of sins, and ye shall receive the gift of the Holy Ghost. This being said I would like to invite anyone who would come forward, to do so, and welcome Jesus into your hearts, lay it all at his feet."

As the pastor continues to encourage people to come forward Alex begins to poke Beatrice. "Bea." He whispers in her ear. "What's it means to be saved?" He questioned her earnestly.

"Well Alex, it is when you ask God to forgive you for the things that you have done wrong, and invite Jesus into your heart." Beatrice explains to him as the praise team softly sings Come to the Altar.

"What if I haven't done anything wrong?" He asked her seriously.

“If your conscience is clean that is good Alex, but you can still invite Jesus into your heart. Would you like to go up there? I’ll go with you.” He nods to her and she takes him by the hand and leads him to the front.

Beatrice walks Alex through the motions and prayer to salvation. Moments later Lunar walked up behind them and tapped Alex on the shoulder. “Mr. Alex.” She spoke softly. “I asked God to forgive me for calling you a whippersnapper.” She begins to sob.

“Its ok Lunar, you didn’t have to do that.” He placed his right hand on her shoulder showing growth and comfort.

“Alex.” The pastor strolled over towards them reaching out a hand and embracing Alex in a warm greeting. “Thank you so much for everything.” He spoke with plenty of zeal. “So did Beatrice help lead you into being a part of God’s Army with us?” Alex glares at the Pastor quizzically. “Did she help you become saved, and invite Jesus into your heart?” He reiterates.

“Yes.” Alex nods shyly, understanding his question the second time. “Can I be baptized now?” He asked hopefully.

“Ooh!!!Me too…” Lunar starts jumping up and down grabbing the Pastor by the coat sleeve. “Me too…Pastor Ross, I asked God to forgive me for calling Mr. Alex a whippersnapper, can I be baptized to?” She said so, so enthusiastically she looked as though she was about to jump out of her clothes.

"Haha..." Pastor Ross chuckles. "Well of course you can Lunar...Now I'm sure Alex will be unavailable next weekend for work, so how about two weeks from today? We'll have the two of you a baptizing service."

"Yayy!!!" Lunar grabs Him tightly around the mid section squeezing him really tightly.

"Ok Lunar, McKenzie will help you get prepared for it, and Alex Joel and Bea will help you out. Now if you all will excuse me, I must get out front to greet those leaving."

Twenty-Five

Gibraltar sits at his desk, staring at his computer screen, with his email pulled up. He has refreshed his email screen half a dozen times, hoping that McKenzie would check hers and respond, on this Monday morning. He had emailed stating that he had the tablet books ready to go and had planned the first board meeting for Thursday evening, to go ahead and get started. He had sent the email Friday evening, and she has still failed to respond.

"Ahh!!! I'll just call her later today!" Frustrated he slammed his laptop closed as he muttered this out.

He swivels around in his chair and gazes down into the station watching his crew hard at work. ***He really has turned out to be a good fireman.*** He thought as he watched Alex shine the knobs on engine number two. ***Maybe I should start being nicer to him.*** He thinks honestly, maybe wanting to change something in himself.

Every since the past week when he took Starry back to the escort service he has been even more frustrated with himself. Even though all he did with her was cook a meal, he still has this gut feeling that he was wrong for doing this, laying heavy on his heart. For the life of him he can not even begin to understand why McKenzie is so stuck on him, he doesn't even know the first thing about her. Just the thoughts of her are so overwhelmingly right on his mind.

"Knock, knock." Gibraltar shakes the thoughts as he spins around in his chair.

“Ja’Maar!” He stands and meets the PI in the middle of his office, with a stout hand shake.

“Gibraltar, so nice to see you again. How are tings going my friend?”

Gibraltar shrugs, and tries really hard not to show his frustration. “Come have a seat. How are you?” He curtly attempts small talk, even though deep down inside he’s boiling with inpatients to discover what he has learned.

“I’m well…doing well. Now listen, I know how you prefer getting straight to business.”

Gibraltar awkwardly waves his hand embarrassed by their previous encounter now. “No…no, its ok bruhder. Maybe one day we will have time to go out and have a friendly dinner, but now I have to tell you I have learned a great deal more.”

“Really?” Gibraltar sits back in his chair crossing his hands over his stomach with interlaced fingers. “What have you found out?”

“To be blatantly honest wit you, it is not looking good.” Ja’Maar sits back in his chair to arrange himself into a more comfortable position. “I looked more into dis Sergio McMillan, digging deeper into his auto claims, and life insurance claims. Its almost scary what I have found out.”

“Oh! Good we can take this to the law enforcement?” He eagerly wants these men to pay for their wrong doings.

“No…” Ja’Maar held up a hand indicating for Gibraltar to listen for a minute. “We cant, dis guy is very careful. Our problem now is not so much as busting him, as it is Spector. Spector is using dis guy, and dat I am almost certain of, but de problem is dere is really no way for me to prove It. Dey have completely ghosted de money trail.” Ja’Maar coughs trying to talk.

“There is a bottle of water over there in the mini fridge.” Gibraltar points to the corner of his office at the fridge, so Ja’Maar gets up to go retrieve himself a bottle. Gibraltar waits patiently for him to return and get situated to continue his findings.

“We’ve had twenty-four hours surveillance on dis Sergio, and I am telling you it is looking more and more impossible each day. We followed him to a yacht, (Money Talks) what kind of arrogant man names dere boat dis? Anyways I did figure out dat he is using an alias, John Dear…D-E-A-R. (Couldn’t be more obvious if he’d used John Doe, right?) I cannot find de money dis ting was bought wit, where it came from, or anyting about it. None of de numbers on it match anyting, in any databases. I know he is pushing all his money through an offshore account, and I know typically how dese work.”

Gibraltar screws the look up on his face. “I cant say that I am super familiar, Is there not some way you can trace it online?”

Ja'Maar stares intently into Gibraltar's eyes. "I'm afraid not, now I'm not saying dat we have reached a complete dead end, but dis expensive job just turned into an extraordinarily expensive job. I did catch him mentioning Nassau, I believe he is using a bank dere, out of de Bahama's. Now dese banks are super discreet, dey wont use online transactions at all. Even sometimes wit dere sketchy clients dey will use crypto currency (which dere are too many of dese now to keep up with) and in simple terms launder dese internet currencies into hard currency for deir criminal clients, such as cash, gold, silver, diamonds, or sometimes bonds."

Gibraltar weaves back and forth listening with a keen ear to the PI, in total shock of these revelations. "Wow! Sound like there are a lot more criminals out there than what anyone realizes."

Ja'Maar chuckles at his not knowing. "You have no idea, but it gets worse, my friend." Gibraltar sighs as he listens. "I tink dese hard untraceable currencies are how Spector is funding his Senate Campaign, and his lead is so far ahead of de utter two dat he will inevitably have one of de Senate seats when dis election is all said and done."

"What!" Gibraltar slammed both of his fist onto his desk making several pens and a paper weight slightly bounce into the air. "There is no way, we cant let this jerk into the Senate."

Ja'Maar tilts his head to the side. "Well Gibraltar, I am going to be honest wit you, dis is a long shot and we are now talking about taking our investigation off US soil, who knows how far I'll have to go to collect proof. If it is only to de Bahama's you can easily add two more zero's behind de deposit I am going to require, and if its even further (which is likely) such as a Swiss bank we are looking at a million dollars just to get started. And dis could possibly be all for nuting."

"Whoah!" Gibraltar lets out an exasperated sigh taking in all the information he was just given. "Ja'Maar, you have done amazing work."

The PI holds up both hands in mock surrender. "I get it Gibraltar, I understand. I am sorry I couldn't be of anymore help."

"No…" Gibraltar quickly dismisses his feelings shaking his head. "Ja'Maar that's not exactly what I am getting at. Its just that I have liked your work and honesty, but do you feel like this is something another company would be more suited for? I mean maybe you can point me in the right direction here."

Ja'Maar takes a deep breath looking for his next words. "My resources are no where near enough to accomplish a task of this magnitude. If you wanted to continue I would be sub-contracting parts of dis job out, and you can trust dat I will be giving you de best work for your money. But I must admit, a million dollars or more is a bit steep for some vindictive feelings."

Gibraltar understandingly nods. "Well Ja'Maar, you let me worry about my feelings. I often times feel that I need to be doing more good with some of my money anyways, and taking down a crooked politician surely counts towards that."

Ja'Maar stands. "Ok Gibraltar, let me make a few phone calls and see if what I have in mind is even remotely possible, and if so I will be wit you shortly for de deposit. I'll certainly have a lot of pockets to pad."

"Gibraltar stands with him. "Ok, sounds good. Here I'll walk you out.

The two men walk outside together shooting the breeze, taking all the tension off of their previous conversation.

Gibraltar walks back into the station through the middle open garage door where Alex is just finishing up with the detail on engine number two. "Hey Captain Crichton." Alex jumps off the fire truck.

"Hey." Gibraltar mumbles as he walked past him with his head down.

Alex follows closely behind him. "I went to church with Beatrice yesterday and got saved!"

"Yea, yea." Gibraltar turns and attempts to wave him off.

Alex persistently follows his Captain. “I get to get baptized in two weeks.” Alex claims zealously.

“Good for you Alex!” Gibraltar turns around to him. “What! You want a high five???Or no you probably want a dang cookie.” Gibraltar’s ruthless attack really hits Alex hard, it takes everything he has to keep from crying. “Where’s Samuel? I need to talk to him.” Gibraltar added rudely.

Alex to upset and hurt to speak just points into the station, towards the last place he saw his Lieutenant. Gibraltar storms off in the direction he just pointed.

Standing in the gym talking with Samuel as he finishes up his curls, Gibraltar gets him up to speed on Ja’Maar’s investigation.

“Gibraltar Crichton!!!” A loud angry voice bellows out. “What the heck are you thinking!” Beatrice grabs Gibraltar by the shoulders forcing him to turn around and face her. “Alex has done nothing but everything anyone of us ask of him!” She pokes him in the chest pushing him back against the wall, taking an extra step ensuring that she is still in his face. “Just because your mad at the world!!!” She yells in his face. “And you want to be the most pathetic excuse of a man, with the most reckless behavior you can come up with…don’t mean…” She pauses taking a breath. “Does not mean you have the right to treat us like the trash you are becoming. If you say one more cross word…” She pokes him hard on the shoulder again showing her seriousness. “One more cross word and I will be quitting, and taking your reckless behavior up the chain of command on my way out the door. Captious?” She says sternly taking a single step back, still holding her ground.

Nearly shaking in his boots Gibraltar curtly nods in agreement. Beatrice turns on her heels and walks away. Alex still unsure of what just happened looks at her. “Come on Alex, lets go shoot some hoops.” They both walk out of the gym area together.

“Boy! She sure told you.” Samuel laughs.

“Shut up…” Gibraltar storms out of the gym, without finishing his conversation with Samuel.

Twenty-Six

McKenzie starts writing on her white board. “Ok class, here are the words to define for today.” She stated as she wrote out the first word.

Her classroom door then opens and she quickly glanced over, in that direction. “Principal Bright!” She calls out to him as she continued writing.

"Ou…Ou…Principal Bright." Several of the kids called out to him raising their hands and bouncing in their seats in attempt to get him to notice them, while others whispered about to themselves.

"Misses Ross…Ah… Jubilant, that word brings me great joy every time I read it." The principal chuckled at himself with plenty of zeal.

"So, what brings us the honor of having the Principal join us in the classroom today?" McKenzie wonders.

"Nothing special, just making rounds. Thought I would stop in and say Hi."

Several of the kids still frantically flailing their arms through the air above them, wishing the Principal would call them out. "Well class, you remember all of your problems and issues, you all have been bringing to me? This is the man you should be telling, so who would like to be first to tell your problems to Mr. Bright." All the hands that was up quickly vanished, and the classroom went solemnly quiet. "Hmph…" She glares over to Principal Bright. "Guess you should have came in ten minutes ago."

He gives her a curt smile before turning his attention to the classroom. "Ok class, pop quiz." He addresses getting uuh's, aww's, and aww man's from the majority. He takes the page of definitions from McKenzie's hands and looks over them. "Ok who knows the definition to splendid?" Several hands pop into the air. "Santiago." The Principal points him out.

"Umm…" Santiago freezes once he was called upon. "Umm…does…it mean…good?"

"Well that was a splendid try, but I am looking for a bit more detail…Ashley…I believe you had your hand up." He calls upon another student.

"Yep, it means your really smart." She quickly answers.

"Wow, very good Ashley. Or it can also be very pretty here according to the definition Ms. Ross has here. Ok…hmm, lets see here the next word is, remorse." Several more hands pop back up, including Santiago's again, who has hand his hand in the air more than not since Principal Bright entered the room. "Ok Celeste." He points her out in the back left corner of the classroom.

"It is a feeling we have when we are sad." Celeste claims in total confidence.

"Very good Celeste, that is close but it is more specifically the guilt or sadness someone feels when they have done something wrong." Not wanting to dive any deeper into this conversation Principal Bright quickly moves on. "Ok what about harvest?"

Maria jabs her hand into air. “That’s when you pick your garden.” She yells out before being called upon.

“Or when you pick your nose.” Santiago picks at Maria.

“Shut up Santiago, he didn’t ask you.”

“Maria!” McKenzie shouts over her. “He didn’t ask you either, now there will be no talking like that in my classroom, and for your punishment you are going to have to wright sentences today on how you can be more polite.”

“Ugh!” Maria huffs and crosses her arms over her chest. “What about Santiago? He started it.”

“Maria!” Principal Bright steps in. “Would you like to come to my office?” She quickly shakes her head no. “Then you worry about Maria, not Santiago.”

“Uhh!” She huffs out another big breath, slumping forward in her desk with her head down and her lips pooched out.

“Ok now…where were we? Oh yeah, harvest.” No sooner than he gets the word out the lunch bell rings.

The entire class jumps up in unison. “Ok class we will finish writing the definitions after lunch. Have a good break.”

Principal Bright hangs around while the class leaves for lunch. ***Oh great!*** McKenzie thinks to herself. ***I should have known better than him just popping in.***

“Everything going good Miss Ross?” He questioned with concern.

“Yea.” She crunches her brow as though she herself was in trouble. “Why wouldn’t it be?” She quizzed curtly.

“No reason, just checking.” He replaces her sheet of definitions on her desk.

“That’s pretty impressive, How you know every student by name.”

“Well Miss Ross, it takes a lot of reading their names over and over, and looking at their pictures as I am doing so. I really wish I had time to know them better, but I find it more important that I know every one of them before I know one of their favorite colors.” The Principal tells of the passion he has for each and every one of his students.

McKenzie glares at her desk in deep thought of what he had just said, taking in completely his interesting view. “I like that Mr. Bright.”

JJ sticks her head in the door. “You com…oh…Principal Bright, I’m sorry.” He gives her a quick wave, that its no big deal.

“Yea JJ, I’ll be there in a few minutes. Let me finish speaking with Mr. Bright.” McKenzie answers.

"Ok." JJ nods and dips back out of the classroom before she gets sucked into any conversations.

"How's she doing?" He asked, concerned with his teacher. The question makes McKenzie's stomach churn at the lie she had told him about the situation. "I'm still in aww, that was some accident she had."

McKenzie had fabricated a story about JJ falling off of a cliff side. ***God why did I have to go so elaborate.*** She prayed.

The story went where JJ was stuck for three days all broken up. ***It was to protect my friends integrity.*** She justifies. It has been frustrating for her to keep up with the lie, and now that JJ is back, she also is going to have to use McKenzie's fabricated story. All of this bothers McKenzie in a single thought.

"She's good, she was excited to come back to work." McKenzie musters out the statement, with what felt like fully churned butter in her stomach.

"Oh yeah Miss Ross, I had one more thing I wanted to discuss before you go to lunch. Have you and Gibraltar had a chance to have your first board meeting yet? I really would like to try this thing out in the next couple of weeks in your class to see if we want to pursue it throughout other classrooms next semester." The Principal really is pushing the Save-the-Books Foundation on her.

“Yea…I just received an email from him.” She lies once more to him, the email is now five days old and she had ignored it, plus his call Monday afternoon. “Our first board meeting is set for tomorrow evening, maybe we can start next week.”

God please forgive me. She prays as she fabricated another lie. ***Please let Gibraltar to have not canceled it.*** She adds to her prayer immediately feeling remorse for asking God to help her cover up the lie.

“Very well, just keep me posted. I would like to be part of that first hand out and see how it is going to go.”

“Yes sir.” She curtly responds as he departed her classroom leaving her there, feeling the guilt.

McKenzie sits her Mickey D’s bag down and digs out the cold sandwich and fries before flattening the bag on the table, across from JJ who was already working on one of her Lean Cuisines.

“I should have known your love for disgusting cold fast food would overwhelm you and make you return.” JJ said as she made a clicking noise with her tongue shaking her head.

“What, I’ve been busy with the church and Lunar.” McKenzie stated as she squirted a healthy blob of mustard onto the flattened bag.

'Lunar?" JJ crunches her brow with her mouthful.

"Yea, she's the twelve year old that I have been helping out. Did I now tell you about her?" She looks as equally surprised. "Hymph…oh well…Hellooo! Big Smack, oh how I have missed you." McKenzie full of desire dips the burger into the mustard, takes the sandwich by both hands and takes a large bite, getting mustard all over the sides of her cheeks.

"So who is this Lunar? She's twelve, but why are you helping her? Is she from your church?"

McKenzie once she washed the bite down tells her bestie no and gives her a quick rundown of who Lunar is. "So she has been coming to church with me this past couple weeks, and she has made good friends with Stephanie there. Its almost as though she has moved in with them, can you believe her parents don't care about her so much as to allow her to always be gone?" McKenzie takes a deep breath in attempt to mellow out her frustration. "Anyways, they seem to be helping her out mentally a lot, so maybe its for the best her parents don't get back in her way."

JJ pushes her empty plastic tray forward with her plastic fork in it. "Yea I just want to slap some of these parents sometimes, I cant figure out what they are thinking…or well if their even thinking at all." JJ shares her frustration.

McKenzie nods taking a drink of her flat coke. “Yea, I definitely think many of them don’t think.” She dips some of her cold fries in the mustard.

“So Mark has been telling me some of the stories about when you were all younger and in the church. It sounds like you all had a lot of fun there.”

McKenzie chews and swallows the fries. “Yea we did…we still do have a lot of fun there. You should get Mark to come back sometime. I think you’d really enjoy it.”

JJ chuckles at this thought, quickly shaking her head. “No way I would fit in there, I’m not the dress type.”

“Well Jemma…there isn’t anyone there going to make you wear a dress, nor would they say anything about you wearing pants there.” McKenzie speaks to her friend honestly.

JJ gives her a shrewd look. “You mean they wouldn’t condemn me to hell for wearing pants or makeup? There’s no way I can go anywhere without that, my face is still fairly bruised.”

McKenzie shrugged her shoulders and finished chewing her food. “Look JJ, we teach women that we wear modest skirts and dresses to distinguish ourselves from our male counterparts. It is certainly not a requirement to come to our church. When we get saved we want to be different, and we want people to see that God is working in us. So this is a very good way for us to let our light shine, but honestly anyone could wear anything to our church. We're confident and trusting in God's Spirit, that people will see what we have, following his word that they will want to become saved, and learn how to follow him in their own path." McKenzie walks into the slowly opening door, that her long time friend is finally opening for her.

"You mean to tell me your people aren't going to scold me if I were to walk into your church wearing a pair of tight Yoga pants?" JJ now curious pushing the issue a bit deeper.

"JJ look, I cant guarantee that someone there might not talk about you, but that's everywhere, and we would never condone it, nor do I think you'd hear it. Our few snakes we have in our church typically stay well hidden, which is definitely a good and bad situation. We're all still human though, so there's always going to be imperfections everywhere you go." JJ listens to McKenzie more intently than she ever has before. "So JJ, why don't you and Mark come to Lunar's baptism, its going to be a lot of fun. I think you will enjoy it, its not until the Sunday after next." McKenzie looks at her friend compassionately as she makes this invitation.

"Well..." Jemma reluctant. "I don't know...well its just that...I don't know. Mark has been so helpful these past couple weeks, (he really always has been there for me) but I really just don't know. I just feel like I shouldn't go and get his hopes up, in case I get bored with I'm again and I get to feeling as though I need more."

McKenzie takes a deep breath and pushes more than half of her meal to the middle of the table. "Look JJ, you and Mark both need to put God first and I know you can make it work. We do live in some amazing times, and I know Mark cares deeply for you, and he really only wants to totally jibe with you. Even if that means you need him to act like an eleven or twelve year old so that you wont get bored with him again. You know what you should do? Take him to Toys-Aint-Us and get him the biggest super soaker they sale so that you can have water gun fights all day long. Surely you wouldn't get bored and feeling unfulfilled then."

JJ bursts out into a hysterical laugh, gaining the attention of all the other teachers in the break room, she did not however care. "Well McKenzie that's good, maybe your onto something here. I think I might be happy with him to just grow up a little and act like he's at least seven or eight maybe, definitely not the five or six he typically acts like though."

McKenzie gently shakes her head with a strange grin on her face.

Twenty-Seven

Dear Lord, please help me, give me your strength to get through this. I am so not prepared to go into this, in Jesus name. McKenzie prayed as she crosses the parking lot at Station Thirteen, worried about going into this board meeting with a bunch of strange men.

Just as she is about to open the door it swings open as Beatrice is backing out of it with a car seat and Natasha in hand. “Beatrice! Oh wow, I didn’t realize you were working at this station.” McKenzie states as she coo’s and pinches baby Natasha on the cheeks.

They both step out of from the doorway to talk. “Yea but I don’t know for how much longer though. I’m suppose to be off today, but I ended up having to bring in some extra saline. We’ve ran out twice now in the past several weeks.” Beatrice complains. “What are you doing here?” She added the question.

“Well…your Captain, Captain Gibraltar is trying to start this Save-the-Books Foundation, and he wants to use my class as the guinea pig classroom. My Principal…well I was kinda strong armed into being on the Board of Directors to it.” McKenzie shares some frustrations of her own.

"Oh, I think I've heard some of them vaguely speak on this." Beatrice commented.

McKenzie stands there in deep thought staring straight at Natasha with her right index finger in the babies hand. "Bea, you're the answer to my prayer!" Beatrice looks puzzled at her. "You can be on the board with me, I really could probably use a female with me. I'm sure its an all male board aside from myself and the fact that your Apostolic even better."

"Oh No!!!" Bea looks hard onto her. "No way McKenzie, I cant possibly…"

"Come on Bea…" McKenzie cuts her off. "I really need you, I was just saying a prayer and you walked out the door. This is definitely God's timing at its best."

"No…" Beatrice still standing firm. "McKenzie, I am sorry its just a strange coincidence, besides I doubt if Doc would even remotely entertain the idea of me being on the Board of Directors with you…not that I want to be on it with that man." She adds in her frustration with Gibraltar.

"What do you mean? That man? Do I not need to be here?" McKenzie reaches for insight becoming more unnerved herself.

"No…No…that's not what I mean at all. In fact I am quite sure that this Non-Profit is a great thing. Doc is not a bad guy, and he is quite intelligent, its just…" Bea pauses looking for the right description. "Its just that he has been very quarrelsome around here lately."

McKenzie steps back gazing out across the parking lot, wondering if her stern rejection that she made with him is possibly the case to his quarrel mindset. "Look Bea." She looks back at Beatrice with a sad puppy dog face. "Please, I really need you. Besides it could be a lot of fun. This Foundation really is a brilliant idea, but it certainly wouldn't hurt to have more of a Godly woman influence in it."

Beatrice sits the car seat down on the sidewalk. "Ah…" She blows out a sigh. "McKenzie I don't know, Doc and I aren't exactly on good terms at this moment."

McKenzie's eyes brighten up. "Oh! That's perfect, I'm not exactly happy with the way he forced me into this anyways. So maybe he needs both of us to help hold some of his childish antics more accountable…" She pooches out her bottom lip. "Pleaseee…I really don't want to beg you."

Beatrice pulls her phone from her skirt pocket. "Well if he'll let me, which I am almost sure he wont go for it."

McKenzie grabs Bea's shoulders almost giddy, bouncing back and forth. "Oh I'm sure I can make sure he does." McKenzie confidently knows.

"Ok, I have to call Joel and let him know what I am doing. This will probably actually make him happy, he's been at me to find something extra for myself."

McKenzie bounces up and down unable to hold her excitement at bay. "Ok you call him, I'll watch sweet little Natasha while you do." McKenzie squats down beside Natasha and begins talking with her, careful to use no baby goo, goo, gaa, gaa like many people would. Instead she speaks softly and gently using simple words and phrases.

"Welcome everyone." Gibraltar begins to speak from the head of the table. "Bea!" He takes notice of her sitting beside McKenzie at the table. "What are you doing here?" He abruptly said.

"I thought she would be a very beneficial addition to the Board of Directors, so I invited her in." McKenzie speaks for Beatrice.

"Well I only had room for six board members." Gibraltar argues.

"Oh." McKenzie opens the binder in front of her. "Is that so, Is that what you have in the By-Laws?" She quickly flips through the pages knowing exactly what she is looking for, being familiar with the documents from her church experiences. "It says here that the number of Board Members is to be no fewer than four, and to not exceed fifteen. Does anyone other than Mr. Crichton have any objections to Mrs. Faulkner being part of The Board of Directors to this Save-the-Books Foundation?" She questions the room, who all sit perfectly still not wanting to become part of the growing tension. "Sorry for the interruption, but I guess that settles it, you may continue Mr. Crichton." McKenzie states with a satisfied grin.

"Ok…fine…but I only have six binders made up, so you'll have to wait on yours Bea." Gibraltar said this clearly frustrated.

"No problem, I can share with McKenzie for now." Beatrice smirks.

"Ok fine." Gibraltar reiterates somberly. "Welcome Mrs. Faulkner to Save-the-Books Foundation's first board meeting. Now before we get to the voting or business side of things I would like to introduce everyone here." Gibraltar takes a sip of the coffee he has in front of him. "Everyone here knows me, so I'll skip me and start with Samuel Brooks, my Lieutenant, then we have Barry Hill who is my Sargent here, and I guess now we have a fourth here from Station Thirteen, Beatrice Faulkner our paramedic. I am sure you all will have very contributory attributes to bring to our foundation. Then we have Adam Day, my CPA."

"Nice to meet you all." The older gentleman with balding gray hair greets the group, barely looking up from his phone, not seemingly paying any attention at all.

“Then we have Steve Elon.” Gibraltar points to his right where a man in his early forty’s sits with two tablets in front of him, occasionally working his way between the two separate tablets.

“Ditto.” Steve remarks.

“Mr. Elon here is the tech genius behind our tablets. He has three separate patents on them (two software and one hardware). He has donated these patents to Save-the-Books Foundation, which is a very generous contribution, thank you Steve.”

“Its no big deal.” Steve non-chalantly waves a hand. “Glad I could help.” He stated as he leaned back in his chair.

“Ok.” Gibraltar continues. “In front of you all is a binder with our Conflict of Interest Policy, Articles of Incorporation, and our By-Laws. There are many things throughout these all that we will need to vote in, but first off is going to be the office positions. I’ll be the president, since it kinda is my company, then…”

“Ahem…” McKenzie waves a hand interrupting Gibraltar. “I’d like to make a nomination, I would like to nominate Beatrice for president.” Beatrice tilts her head bug eyed at McKenzie.

“Haha…” Gibraltar laughs not so hysterically. “Yea that’s not going to happen, its my money, my company, I’m president and that’s that.”

McKenzie slams her binder shut, stands up scooting her chair out loudly causing Natasha to begin to wail from the abrupt noise. “Well fine then, I am out of here.” She said as she grabbed her purse and headed for the door, leaving Beatrice there trying to calm Natasha down.

“Wait!” Gibraltar halts her at the door.

“No way.” McKenzie takes a step back inside. “I came on to be part of a Non-Profit Foundation, not some company that is ran by some dictator. I thought I was going to come and be part of a team starting a Non-Profit, not part of some company ran by some frivolous madman who has to be in control of every situation.” She turns to leave again.

“Wait…” Gibraltar jumps up. “Uh…uh…” He stutters looking for his rescue words, as McKenzie paused at the door she didn’t turn around. “I need you and your classroom.”

Fuming mad McKenzie turns around and approaches Gibraltar. “No you don’t! You have your money! You don’t need me at all!” She exclaims with gritted teeth.

He takes a small step backwards in attempt to deescalate the tension. “Fine.” He begins to speak, thinking that he will win the vote anyways. “If we vote, and I win fair and square, will you stay on and be ok with it?”

“Ok, if your going to be fair.” McKenzie still not happy nods and frugally returns to her seat. “And as long as you run this Foundation as it should be I will stay, but if you make any attempts to dictate, anything again…I’m out…no ifs, ands, or buts.” She swivels her chair to look at Beatrice who now has Natasha calm rocking her back and forth.

“Ok then…no dictating, I promise…Lets vote, Samuel?” Gibraltar started the voting with his best friend.

Samuel sits back in his chair contemplating and afraid to cast his vote. “Well Doc, I’m sorry, but I am going to have to vote for Bea.”

“What!” Gibraltar chokes at his best friends vote.

“Well Cap, I’ve been telling you, you have been flying around here like a chicken with its head cut off lately, and you’re a loose handle. I feel like Bea is better suited to be President of the Foundation.”

Mad at this statement Gibraltar lazily flops down into his seat and slightly slumps over. “Ok Barry?”

“That’s easy Doc, I couldn’t go against my Captain, its of course you.” Barry didn’t hesitate his support.

“Ok good.” This gave Gibraltar a bit of confidence back. “Alright Steve?”

“I vote you Gibraltar.” Steve states casually as he makes a couple quick taps on one of his tablets.

“Well…I don’t think I need to ask you Miss Ross.”

She gives him a smirk. “Nope, I did nominate Mrs. Faulkner so my vote should be a given.”

Gibraltar sullenly sits back in his chair. “Ok Mr. Day, you’re the deciding factor. Your vote?” Gibraltar sits back up straight in his chair knowing his accountant hasn’t really been paying attention and surely wants him to be president.

“Well…” Adam puts his phone down on the table in front of him and sits back in his seat rubbing his hand on his chin in deep thought. “Gibraltar I’m sorry, but for the purpose of Save-the-Books Foundation I will have to vote Mrs. Faulkner to be President. She has to be better with money than you are…well she at least cant get no worse, that’s for sure.”

Gibraltar sits back and bows his head to his chest in defeat. “Ok Bea.” He solemnly raises his head. “You are the President of Save-the-Books Foundation. Its your floor, you can run the show now.” He continued to pout.

“I nominate you VP.” Samuel speaks with way too much zeal in his voice.

"I second that." Beatrice stands with the baby in her arms. "Any opposition?" Everyone at the table shakes their heads as she gazed around. "Ok then, wow…I'm sorry everyone, this definitely came as a surprise to me. McKenzie did not even run this by me and I certainly did not want this." Gibraltar slightly perks up at her humbleness. "I don't know how I, the only one who don't know anything at all about this Foundation just became President of it, but you all have spoken and I intend to give it my best and full attention. However Gibraltar I am going to need my Vice President to step up and chair this first board meeting to get us started. Then sometime soon, you and I can sit down where you can get me up to speed. As President I do not want you or anyone else looking at me as such. I want us all to listen and work with one another as a team, exactly how Non-Profit businesses are meant to be ran. Thank you all and now I would like to return the floor back to you, Doc."

"Ok…" Gibraltar reluctantly begins to speak again in a low barely audible tone. "I have Adam as treasure, and Steve as secretary. He's good at keeping documents and online things in order. Anyone oppose these two positions?" No one does. ***Of course not.***

Gibraltar guides them all through the binder getting the process all voted in, keeping his funk throughout the entire meeting. Once he dismisses everyone quickly leaves, except for Beatrice and McKenzie.

Beatrice begins to change Natasha's dirty diaper. McKenzie!" She called her out startling her and Natasha. "I don't know how to be president of a Non-Profit Foundation. What were you thinking?"

McKenzie shrugs. "I dunno, I just knew that I didn't want that man who doesn't act any older than any of my students to be bringing a program into my classroom."

Beatrice finishes fastening Natasha's diaper and starts putting her in her car seat. "Well he's still bringing this program into your classroom, except now I'm the responsible leader of it." She's upset at herself that she allowed herself to take the position.

"You didn't have to accept it Bea." McKenzie claims.

Beatrice picks up the car seat with Natasha in it. "Are you kidding me, after what I went through with him this week, I couldn't not have accepted it."

Twenty-Eight

Alex shuffles his way into Station Thirteen's dining area, at seven a.m. on the dot. He is red hot, sweating and burning up with fever.

"Whoa Alex, you look like walking death." Felipe comments as he see's Alex walk in. "Are you ok?"

"Yea…" Alex coughs a couple of times, barely able to speak. "I think I have allergies." He mumbles this commonality.

"Oh my gosh Alex! You look like your burning up with fever." Beatrice sits the pan of biscuits on the edge of the table, quickly running over to Alex and placing the back of her hand on his forehead. "Oh my Alex, you are scorching, here sit." She pulls out the chair directing him to it. "Felipe can you please set the rest of the breakfast on the table?"

"Ugh!" He sighs out, and gives her a (yes mom) smile and scurries off to the kitchen.

"Alex hold on right here, I'm going to go get my med bag. I'll be right back." He nods, clearly ill while Beatrice goes to retrieve her bag.

The other three crew members walk through the door. "Boy we sure are glad to see you all, we'll meet again on Monday morning." Sylvester from the other shift comments. "I hope you get to feeling better Alex." He shows his concern as they all avoid getting too close to him as they walk through and out of the dining area.

“Dang Alex, you look like your about to croak!” DeAndre gives his two cents.

“It’s just allergies.” Alex reiterates in attempt to not have anyone treat him like he is a leper, or he has COVID.

Beatrice returns and sets her bag on the table, at the same time everyone else sets up at the other end.

“Umm…Alex, do you really think you should be here?” Samuel speaks what Barry and DeAndre are also thinking.

“Yes he should, we are service workers you shouldn’t let a little bug stop your service. You jerk!” Bea defends Alex as she checks his temperature.

“Maybe their right, I don’t want to get you or anyone else sick.” Alex attempts to stand, but Beatrice pushes him back down in the chair, she does so very easily do to his weakened state.

“One hundred-one point two, wow Alex you have a high fever. Non-sense, you are going to stay right here where I can keep an eye on you.” Beatrice caringly said as she pulled out a stethoscope and blood pressure cuff then checked the rest of his vitals. “Well your heart rate is slightly elevated, and your oxygen is ninety-four, but I can tell you are congested so this is to be expected.” Beatrice places the stethoscope on his chest and instructs him to take a couple of deep breaths, she then moves it around to several other spots and has him do the same there. “Ok Alex I don’t believe the congestion is in your lungs or bronchial system, so its not pneumonia or bronchitis. You probably just have an upper respiratory infection. Come on, I’ll set you up in the ladies dorm to isolate you from all these fraidy cats.” She shoots all the other crew members a snarl.

Beatrice gets Alex laid into one of the beds and walks over to a medicine cabinet. “Bea, I should go home. I don’t want to take your room from you.” Alex worried she wont have her space.

She pulls out a couple different bottles of over the counter medications. “Non-sense Alex, I can sleep on the couch…besides I rarely spend much time in here anyways. I really just use the bathroom occasionally and it has a door. You are going to stay right here, unless your fever gets any worse. If that happens you will be going to the hospital. Otherwise you are going to spend this weekend right here in this room, we have to get you well for your baptism next week.” Beatrice made an attempt to make him feel better.

“I’ll be right back. I’m going to get you some water. Are you hungry?” Alex shakes his head and tells her that he didn’t feel well enough to eat.

Alex lays there while Beatrice is gone, hating himself for becoming a burden, but very happy she is so willing to be of help. “Bea.” He has a coughing spell while he tried to speak. “I really should go.” He fails at his attempt to raise up out of the bed, his head too dizzy after the coughing spell.

"Your not Alex, now here sit up so you can take some medicine."

"What about when there is an emergency?" He questions, not at all wanting to hinder the team.

"You are going to stay right here Alex, now that's final. The guys can handle it and its rare for us to be out too long, so just know that I will be back to help. Now take this, its some cold medicine. It is nighttime so it will help your rest, and hopefully break up some of the congestion. Then here is six hundred milligrams of ibuprofen, that should break your fever, and here is two thousand milligrams of vitamin C. I want you to take the vitamin C twice a day for three days, then keep taking it once a day for the next week at least. I have found that high doses of vitamin C can actually be much more effective than antibiotics in many cold and upper respiratory situations." She hands Alex her cocktail of medications for him to take. "Just don't tell big Pharma I said so, they may cut my brake lines." Alex does not catch her sarcastic pun, but she chuckles at herself anyways.

"I don't want to be a bother." He slightly tears up, truly not wanting to be a burden on her.

"Stop it Alex..." She pats him compassionately on the shoulder. "Now go ahead and lay back down. I'll be coming back in to recheck your vitals in about thirty minutes or so, and see if you might need anything. I'll fix you some soup for lunch, do you like chicken noodle?"

Alex nods to her question as she pulled the blanket up to his chin. "Hey Bea…" She paused in the doorway with her hand on the light switch.

"Yea Alex?" She gazes empathetically at him.

"Thank you…for everything."

Beatrice flips the light switch off. "Its really no problem Alex, we all need someone every now and then. See you in a little while." She exits the room leaving the door slightly cracked.

An hour or so later Beatrice quietly walks into the room to check on Alex, he's sound asleep laying where she had left him. She gently puts the back of her hand to his damp forehead, and notices that he has a slight spastic twitch from the breaking fever. She decides to let him rest and slowly backs back out of the room.

She steps out into the hallway and trots down to Gibraltar's office. Knocking on the door frame she enters. "Well hello there Apollo." She greats the Dalmatian at the door giving him a quick rub down.

"Hey Bea." Gibraltar mutters as he glanced up at her from his paperwork.

"Good morning Doc." She greets him flat leveled, and open heartedly in hopes to alleviate some of the soreness from the previous nights meeting. "So Alex is sick." She takes a seat across from him.

"So and!" He continues writing.

"Gibraltar!" Beatrice raised her voice perking his ears up, reminding him of his mother trying to get his attention when he was a kid. "What is wrong with you? Can you not show the least bit of sympathy anymore? It seems as though this last month you have become this heartless evil man, not at all like the hard working, smart, mostly caring Captain I started working with six months ago." Bea makes a legitimate attempt to counsel through his defenses.

"I don't want to talk about it." He defiantly spoke as he attempted to go back to writing, but he cant because he is becoming too frustrated.

"Well Doc, had I known you were this reckless pain in the rear who brings hookers to work with him, I would have never came to work here." She sits back slightly relaxing her posture.

"Starry is an escort, not a hooker." He tries to minimize his action. "And that was the first, last, and only time I will ever do that, and all we did was cook lasagna, then I took her back." He makes light of the situation, more for himself than Beatrice's sake.

“Well that don’t really matter to me Doc…well sort of, it does please me that you didn’t hire her for certain needs you men feel you have, but that’s besides the point. The point is that if I would have known that is who you are I would not have come to work here.”

Gibraltar leans back in his chair thinking heavily. “Bea.” He begins to soften up. “That is not who I am, that’s what I am trying to tell you. None of it ever felt right, I thought that’s what I wanted…or needed, but quickly realized it wasn’t.” He paused for a long moment, while Beatrice waits him out. “Look Bea, I’m definitely no saint, but I’m not a bad guy, especially when it comes to women. I’m thirty-three and could have any number of women I want, but really have only ever had one real girlfriend and a couple very short lived flings. I’ve never even really thought about marriage, or children. I have always been so emerged in my work and studies, then McKenzie comes along.”

Bam! A shocking revelation hits Beatrice hard in the chest, while Apollo comes over and sniffs her skirt smelling baby Natasha on her. Beatrice pats Apollo on the head. “McKenzie huh?” She passes picking her jaw up off the floor, trying to figure out the scenario she needs to be focused on, out of the thousands that are running through her mind. “Let me guess, then you asked her out and she said no because your not Apostolic?”

"Ugh!" He sighs laying his head back on his chair. "Why am I talking to you about this? You are just like her. And no I don't think its cause I am not a Christian, I think its because she thinks I'm too childish."

Beatrice shakes her head clicking her tongue. "No…no…Doc you have much to learn. It is precisely why she wont date you. You cant be just Christian either, you have to be one hundred percent saved through Jesus Christ and baptized in his name. This choice has to be made by you, not her. It is definitely not because you are childish, all men are this and need us to help them grow out of this."

"That's just it, she makes me want to grow up and I cant stop thinking about her. She's always on my mind…from my waking thoughts to my going to bed dreams, I cant shake her out no matter how hard I try. That's why I thought I needed the distraction and went to the escort service. I picked Starry up thinking that she could get McKenzie out of my mind, but it only made it worse."

Beatrice leans forward crossing her arms onto his desk looking him directly in the eyes. "Gibraltar I really don't know what to tell you, other than McKenzie is an amazing woman of God and she will not at all alleviate from her beliefs, not for you, not for anyone or anything. Now on a greater note." She sits back in her chair. "If this is the reason you have become so reckless, you may need to re-think your steps. So what…a girl rejected you…boo…hoo…get over it, we have bigger fish to fry. So get a hold of yourself!" She barks at him. "If you don't, you are going to end up pushing everyone away. You really do have an amazing team around you, so you better straighten up if you don't want to be left out in the cold (so-to-speak)."

"Your right Bea." He said softly as he leaned over to pick up a box from beside his desk. "Here you go Prez, I put this box together for you last night after our meeting. It has the seven different tablets we are going to start with, quite a few of our flyers and brochures, plus I have already emailed you a file with all the information you will need. I really do want this to work like a partnership."

Beatrice nods, interrupting him with a thank you.

"Steve is suppose to file the Articles of Incorporation today, and I'm working with an IRS agent, so hopefully we will be able to get the 501(c) (3) expedited to be able to accept tax deductible contributions. I'll connect him with Adam today, so everything should be set and rolling soon."

They continue to talk and discuss Save-the-Books Foundation for the next hour and a half, Gibraltar bringing Beatrice fully up to speed.

"Doc, you really are a genius. This is an amazing Foundation you have built here. Keep your wits and you are going to make some very grand accomplishments."

Gibraltar bows his head humbly with an embarrassed smile. Bea takes the box and gets up to leave. “Oh Bea!” He calls her back as she had just stepped through the doorway.

“Yea Doc?”

He closes the binder on his desk. “Here, this is the Presidents binder. I have the Vice Presidents in my desk.” He tells her with a surprisingly acceptable tone and she places the binder in the box and exits the office, followed by Apollo.

Twenty-Nine

McKenzie walks into the teachers lounge, nodding at a couple of the other teachers in passing without a word, they return the same welcome. She strolls through to her normal, back table where JJ sits mixing together a large salad.

“Hey JJ, Wow that looks really good.” She places her bottle of water on the table and takes her seat.

“Where’s your lunch?” JJ questions as she shoves the first fork full of goodness into her mouth.

“I’m fasting today.” She answered, jealously looking over at JJ’s perfectly made salad with fresh crisp romaine lettuce, baby spinach leaves, perfectly grilled chicken breast, croutons, parmesan, and coated with a beautiful layer of Caesar dressing, McKenzie’s favorite creamy dressing.

“Here I brought plenty, in fact there’s no way I can eat all of this.” JJ said as she raked some out of her bowl on to the lid of her Tupperware container.

“Really JJ, I cant.” McKenzie shakes her head. “I really need to fast at least one day, and of course you would choose the one day I chose to, to bring that awesome salad. Which this is more of a reason to tell me that I am doing the right thing. I grew up in a church that preaches and teaches fasting regularly, and I have never even attempted it. So I’ve decided that I am going to enhance my walk with God and the fact that out of two plus years you bringing those disgusting T.V. dinners, and yet you decide to bring on this day…that, that is enough proof to me that this will certainly strengthen my walk with God.”

JJ shrugs as she rakes the salad back into her container, and doesn’t push the issue any further. “Ok…whatever…it is really good though, Mark and I made it up last night.”

“Oh…” McKenzie takes a drink of water and pulls out a piece of gum as her stomach growls at her. “Your staying at Marks still?”

“Yea.” JJ mumbles with her mouth full.

“Interesting…How’s that going?” She quizzes as she vigorously chomps on the gum, in attempt to get her hunger pains to subside.

“Well.” JJ bobs her head in a back and forth motion pondering the question. “Honestly it started out that I just didn’t want to stay at my place in case Jonas decided to show up.” She pokes around through her salad stabbing a chunk of chicken for her next bite. “But you know?” She skeptically started to talk again. “I took your advice, and took him to the Toys-Aint-Us store. We went to the ages eight and up section, and picked out a game that didn’t make him feel so immature. We ended up getting a new Monopoly edition, it was the perfect long board game we found to play. And boy McKenzie, you should have seen his face when he was finally able to get me to go bankrupt, it was pure joy. We had a lot of fun with it, and I believe it has taken our relationship to a whole new level.” She shoves the fork full of salad with the chunk of chicken on it into her mouth.

McKenzie chuckles at her friends childishness. “Well I am glad I could be of service.” She claims, giggling more shaking her head back and forth as she lowered her gaze. “So you haven’t heard anything from Jonas?”

JJ gulps her food down almost choking on it, almost going down the wrong pipe. “No…I blocked his number. What about your fire captain? I haven’t heard you speak of him in awhile.”

McKenzie nervously fidgets the bottle of water in circles on the table, as she thought about how to answer her friends question. “He’s not mine, I thought I’ve made that quite clear that I wont be dating him. I am a little nervous though.” She gazes at her watch. “In fact I’m about to have to leave, we’re suppose to start Save-the-Books Foundation today. I have to use half of my lunch to help get it all set up, so that we can explain it to my class right after lunch.”

JJ’s face brightens up at this revelation. “Oh yea? So your nervous that your not lover boy is going to be handing out tablets in your classroom? Mmm…hmm…” She teases her bestie.

“JJ please stop, you know my convictions and he isn’t making this easier forcing himself into my classroom like this.”

JJ looks as though a light just came on in her mind. “Why don’t you try dating him? Then he probably wont want to be around you so much. Then I’m sure he would come to the church and you can convert him then.”

McKenzie accidently toppled her water bottle over on the table (with the lid on, so it did not spill). “Jemma…” She speaks softly. “It cant work that way, he has to come to God for himself. He cant do this for me, it would never work this way. I cant force the Holy Spirit to guide him the way I want him to go. God has to direct our paths for them to be his right and proper will. I am having faith that God is guiding one to me right now, I just need to be patient. And if not, then maybe God wants me to spend my life alone. I certainly wouldn't be the first woman he has called this upon. I gotta go…Tell Mark I said Hi…"

"I will…" JJ mumbles with a mouthful as McKenzie leaves the teachers lounge.

Phathom stands at McKenzie's desk looking at a globe, slowly she spins the sphere around. Then the thought comes across her mind. ***I wonder how fast I can spin it?*** She places her full hand on the globe in attempt to spin it faster, when she does so she shoves the globe into the floor, busting it into several pieces.

"No, no, no…" She starts crying as she frantically tries to puzzle it all back together sitting on the floor.

Phathom is sitting in the floor crying with a couple of the pieces of the globe in each hand when McKenzie walks into the classroom. "Phathom…" She seen her there crying. "What's the matter?" She kneels down to help her pick the shattered globe.

“I didn’t mean to, I was just trying to spin it Miss Ross.” She starts balling, wishing she would have just left the globe alone.

“Phathom…its ok, I was tired of looking at that thing anyways. Now we can put in a better one.” She pats Phathom on the shoulder, then they pick all the pieces up and carry over to the trash can.

“Why are you not eating lunch or outside playing with the other kids?”

“Hymph…” Phathom flops back down in the floor sulking with her gaze straight at the ground.

“Phathom? What’s the matter?”

“Lunch sucked.” Phathom still pouting, complained.

McKenzie sits down in the floor beside her, flailing her skirt out around her legs as she did so. “Phathom.” She talks stern, but softly. “We shouldn’t use language like that. Lunch was pizza, do you not like pizza?”

“Ugh!” Phathom looks up at her teacher tilting her head. “That is not pizza, its some square glob they throw on our trays and tell us its pizza. Its gross, I give mine to Santiago…he eats anything.”

McKenzie chuckles at her and thinks about how she is probably right and the fact that Santiago probably didn’t need the extra piece. “Well…why aren’t you outside then?”

"Hmph…" Phathom crosses her arms and sulks again. "My leg hurts, or well my nub. My robots foot is making it sore."

McKenzie ponders this for a moment. "Is it happening everyday, or is it something that just started happening?" She questioned soothingly so.

"Just today, I had it plugged in last night, and I put it back on this morning when I woke up, and its been bothering me all day." Phathom pouts, clearly irritated.

"Well come on Phathom, I'm not sure I know much about this, but maybe there's something obviously wrong, and we can fix it." McKenzie stands and holds out a hand to help Phathom off the floor.

She helps her over to a chair beside her desk, and rolled her pant leg up. "Knock, knock…" Beatrice calls out as she walked through the open door carrying a box. "Oh, hey Phathom." She said as she looked over at McKenzie knelt down in front of her, gazing at her leg.

Phathom stared at Beatrice with a puzzled (do-I-know-you) look.

"You don't remember me?"

Then it dawn on Phathom when she recognized the medic emblem on her shirt. "You're the one who road to the hospital with me in the ambulance, ain't you?"

"That's me! I'm Beatrice, but my friends call me Bea."

Phathom smiles at her soft personality. “Bee? Like the honey bee?” She giggles.

“Yea exactly, only I’m much sweeter. I wont sting you if you try to steal my honey, actually I would probably just give it to you.” Beatrice speaks zealously. “Is everything ok?”

McKenzie stands up glad to see Beatrice. “Well…I’m glad you’re here, this is more your line of work. Her prosthesis is bothering her today.” She takes the box out of Beatrice’s hands and sits it on the floor beside them.

Phathom looked inside the box and seen the lot of neon tablets. “Yay! Is Captain Gibraltar and Apollo coming today?” She asked over joyously.

Beatrice already knelt down looking over her prosthetics. “No Phathom, I’m sorry I don’t think they are going to make it today.” Beatrice claims sounding almost as sad about it as Phathom does.

“Uh!” Phathom huffs and crosses her arms again then looks up at McKenzie, who is just as shocked at this revelation. “This is because of you Miss Ross, why do you hate him so much? You know he is a really nice guy.”

McKenzie stunned into silence. “Well…” Still shocked at how Phathom came up with this. “Phathom…I don’t hate Gibraltar.” She speaks softly trying to come up with the proper words. “Its just that he and I don’t always see eye to eye. I know he is nice, and he was really good to you, and I thought he was coming today. I actually invited him."

Phathom's expression softens up. "You did?"

Beatrice runs her finger around the top of the prosthesis. "Yes Phathom, she did I was there." Bea lies for McKenzie. "So I really don't know too much about these things, but can you show me how you take it off Phathom? And maybe we can see something obvious here."

Phathom nods and pulls it off with ease, then hands the prosthesis to Beatrice. She stares at it for a moment. "Ha…I think this here is probably not suppose to be folded in like this." She states as she quickly seen the problem.

"Wow Bea! I never noticed how diligent you are before." McKenzie praises her as she replaced Phathom's prosthesis. She stands and takes a couple test steps. "Better?" Bea asked.

"Perfect." Phathom said chipperly.

"You want to help us set up Phathom? I have a couple of signs to put up, and I would like to put one of these tablets on everyone's desk." Beatrice informs the both of them.

"Can I?" Phathom excitedly looked up to McKenzie.

“Of course you can Phathom, that would be great.” McKenzie glad she is so eager to be of assistance.

Beatrice picked the box up off the floor and placed it in the chair that Phathom had just vacated. She hands McKenzie a couple of binders that was on the top and retrieved two signs out. “Ok Phathom, I think we can set one of these up on the desk.” She looks around for a place to put the other one. “And how about the other one over there by the windows.”

Phathom nods and takes the simple sign over to the shelf underneath the windows, and puts it up and reads. [Save-the-Books Foundation. Bringing books to the future with us.]

“Is this where you want it…Bee?”

“Umm…” Bea looks over at her. “Yea, but can you turn it a little? Where the whole class can read it better?”

As Phathom and Beatrice are placing tablets on the desk’s Principal Bright walks into the classroom. “Good afternoon.” He said happily as he walked up to the desk where McKenzie sit looking through one of the binders.

“Oh! Hey Principal Bright…” McKenzie quickly gets up from her seat. “Hey Bea, this is our Principal.” She introduces as Beatrice comes down one of the rows of desk’s to accept his welcome. “She is our President to Save-the-Books Foundation.” She informs Mr. Bright.

“Nice to meet you.” He said as he shook her hand with a puzzled look on his face. “What happened to Captain Crichton?” He questioned with confusion.

“Misses Ross don’t like him, so he and Apollo cant come.” Phathom comes over and butts in, speaking her feelings.

“Hahaha…” Principal Bright laughs knowingly and pats Phathom on the head as he does so. “I doubt it is that Miss Ross don’t like him Phathom.” He said as he continued to chuckle looking down on Phathom. He shifted his eyes to McKenzie without turning his head, catching her nervous head bow and rosy red embarrassed cheeks.

“Umm…Phathom…” Beatrice tries to shift the focus. “Did we make sure all the tablets work?”

Phathom looks up to Bea. “Oh!” She’s easily distracted and quickly goes to start turning all of the tablets on.

“So you’re the President?” He stares at Beatrice’s fire department shirt. “Let me guess? You work for him, and he conned you into running his Non-Profit?”

McKenzie and Beatrice look to one another with great laughter in their eyes. “Yea something like that.”

Beatrice turns her focus back on the Principal. “Ok Beatrice, so what’s your game plan here?” He asked her curiously wanting to know how this is going to go down.

“Well Principal Bright.” She speaks slowly trying to remember exactly how she had planned to do this. “We are going to introduce Save-the-Books Foundation, and attempt to get the students excited about reading. This really is a good Foundation, with great goals, and purposes addressing some of the issues technology has created. Our younger generations are reading less and less, and humanity is loosing our focus. So I plan to explain the books to them and get them excited about the game they get to play (that seems to be all kids want to do these days is watch T.V. and play games). So if we can get them focused on the game that they have to read and pay attention to their reading to play, the game better. Than maybe we can excite them into reading more.”

Principal Bright perched his lips out awkwardly as he listened intently on Beatrice’s game plan. “Ok very good, I am going to sit over here out of your way. Don’t even act as though I am here.”

Thirty

"Push…Push…seventeen…" Samuel all but yells at Alex, standing over him pushing up the barbells at the bench press. "Three more…come on Alex, you got this…two…one…" He helps Alex replace the weights on the rack.

"What! Hu…Hu…Hu…" Alex breaths heavily. "Wa…Wa…I need water." He finally manages to get out.

Samuel gives him a hand sitting up and hands him a bottle of water. "Alright Alex, good work, look at those guns." He squeezes Alex's bicep complimenting his exuberant work. "Seventy pounds, twenty times, four reps. That's sure a long ways from where you started last month."

Alex drains the whole bottle of water still out of breath. "Ta…thanks"

"Come on Alex, I still have twenty minutes left, you can finish the last bit out with me." Barry calls him from one of the two stair masters in their gym.

"Aghh…" Alex rolled his eyes, threw his head back, and sighed from exhaustion, but none the less went over and stepped up to the other stair master next to Barry.

[Beep…beep…beep…] The stair master starts up and Alex turns the speed up and starts running the stairs.

"Whoa Alex…" Barry reaches over and turns his machine down for him. "You have to pace yourself Alex, you wouldn't make it thirty seconds at that speed." Alex already breathing heavily almost falls off the machine from the adjustment Barry made. "There you go, you should have no problem making it twenty minutes at that speed."

"Ugh…" Alex complains. "This isn't even half as fast as your going."

Barry shakes his head as he's jogging up the stairs. "No Alex, but its twice as fast as I started out many years ago. So just trust me, I have been doing this a while."

Almost bored with the speed of his machine Alex lets out another sigh of complaints. "Cant I just go a little faster Sargent Hill?"

Barry glares over to Alex. "No Alex, I'd rather we work on your endurance rather than your speed. Don't worry, your young enough that in six months (if you stick with it) you'll be able to out do me."

Alex looks over to his Sargent zealously. "Really? You'll make it to where I can climb steps for an hour straight?" He claims with excitement in his voice, ready for that day to be today.

"Yes Alex, just listen to me, and stick with it. It wont come over night, just be patient."

They continue on the stair masters as Samuel and DeAndre continue to lift weights behind them. For the rest of the twenty minutes they run the stairs in total silence, when Barry stopped so did Alex.

“Hu…huu…” Alex breathes heavy bent over with his hands on his knees. “Wow Barry!” He stands up straight and puts his arms over his head opening his lungs up. “That ended up being way tougher than I expected.”

Barry pats him on the back. “Good work Alex, I told you so, just listen to us and we’ll all have you whipped into shape before you know it.”

Alex bobs his head up and down still fairly worn out. “Thank you all for helping me.” He shows his appreciation, almost emotionally so. “I’m hungry.” He adds.

“Well come on.” Barry grabs a couple of hand towels, tossing one to Alex, and they both sop up the sweat that is pouring off of them. “Let’s go see if we cant find you something to eat.” He states as they both walk towards the door.

“Whoa Alex…” Samuel steps in between him and Barry cutting Alex off. “You do not need to follow him to the kitchen. You need something better than a dozen doughnuts to grow muscle.”

DeAndre checks his watch. “Yep its brunch time anyways, I could probably eat a doughnut or two.”

The four of them all walk out of the gym and start to head up stairs. "Your always hungry DeAndre." Alex makes an awkward attempt at joking with him, same as they are always doing to one another.

"Your right Alex." DeAndre stops right out of the door waiting on Alex to come through. "I can always eat, in fact I wake up every morning ready to eat, and I go to bed every night eating."

"Really?" Alex looks to him puzzled. "You eat in your bed? Wouldn't that be messy? Do you get crumbs everywhere?"

"Alex..." DeAndre puts a hand on his back pushing him forward (more so guiding him) to the stairs. "It is extremely messy, so much so that I end up having to wash my sheets and blankets every day. Its always as though a chip bag exploded leaving crumbs all over the bed."

DeAndre's statement gets a good laugh out of Samuel and Barry as they all trot up the stairs. They walk into the dining area where Felipe sits at one end of the table with doughnuts and coffee, while his partner is at the other end with binders and papers scattered all over the table.

"Mmm...That coffee smells good." Samuel walks over and pour himself a cup from the carafe.

"Good workout?" Felipe questioned looking at them all sweaty.

DeAndre and Barry go to grab doughnuts, and Alex attempts to follow suit. “Nope Alex…” Samuel slaps his hand. “Your coming to the kitchen with me.”

Felipe looks over to Barry and DeAndre stuffing their faces with the fresh doughnuts he just picked up. “Oh come on LT, he’s a scrawny guy a doughnut or two wont hurt him.” He complains.

“No probably not.” He grabs Alex by the elbow to lead him. “But it doesn’t quite accomplish the growth we are trying to get out of him.”

They walk into the kitchen, Samuel jumps, startled not realizing Gibraltar was in there. Gibraltar stood there in front of the fridge, staring hopelessly into it. “Oh! Hey Doc, what’s happening?”

Gibraltar closes the fridge, undecided. “I want something to eat, but I’m not hungry and I don’t know what I want to eat.” He rambles out as he steps over to the counter and leans his back up against it, in deep contemplation. “Good workout?” He glares at them with a flat expression on his face.

Samuel goes over and opens the fridge, quickly grabbing the exact ingredients he knew he was going after. “Alex is really pushing hard, he’s doing really good. Now its time to get him some muscle growing fuel. Here Alex, sit this stuff on the island.” Alex steps over towards the fridge, still hungry wondering what Samuel has in mind. “Eggs, spinach, mushrooms.”

Samuel calls out the ingredients as he places each in Alex's arms. "Hmm..." He stares in the fridge a moment longer. "Ahha...onion and bell pepper." He turns back around grabbing a knife and a cutting board as he does so. "You want an omelet Doc?"

Gibraltar stands there hearing Samuel's question, but not really hearing it. "No..." He said curtly.

"Ok Alex, we're going to make us some omelets with olive oil and spinach, so that we can make you like the sailor man." Alex confused does not understand Samuels pun.

"Haha..." Gibraltar laughs dryly. "That scrawny of a guy could never be like the pipe smoking sailor cartoon man, no matter how much spinach you eat, don't let the LT fool you."

"Spinach?" Alex gives Samuel leery look. "Don't sailors cuss a lot?"

Samuel works diligently chopping up the peppers, onions, and mushrooms. "Yea they typically do, but don't listen to Cap. He only thinks he knows what he's talking about."

"Well...I don't think God wants me to cuss. I'm suppose to get baptized in three days and I don't want to mess it up." Alex worried about offending, stands there watching Samuel work.

"Haha..." Gibraltar now fully engaged into their conversation. "Baptized huh? So what some guy is going to dunk your head under water and make you a good guy? Sounds like some foolish way to trick you into coming to give them your money." Gibraltar mocks…

"Gibraltar! Come on man! You shouldn't be bashing someone for their beliefs." Samuel pauses what he was doing to defuse Gibraltar's mockery.

"No…I want to hear it from the him, pip squeak." Gibraltar walks around the bar facing Alex, he doesn't step into his face, but he certainly intimidates him. "So your going to take a bath at church Sunday, and its going to clean you right up? Huh?" Alex is confused and really unsure of how to deal with the confrontation. "Well I take a bath at my house every morning, and it cleans me up just fine." Gibraltar's anger continues to grow.

"Back off!!!" Samuel steps in front of Gibraltar putting his hand on his chest. "Your not right Gibraltar! Now back off!!!"

"Gibraltar angrily shoves Samuel's arm away from him. "NO!!!" He yells. "I want him to tell me what's so freaking special about this water that makes them so much better than us?"

[Beep…beep…beep…] The alarms start going off, then their radios begin to static. "Come in Station Thirteen." Dispatch calls them.

Gibraltar turns around. "Station Thirteen here, what we got?" He calls back.

Samuel quickly turns the stove off. "Come on Alex." He takes Alex by the arm and they both flea the hot kitchen.

❖

Gibraltar rides in the passenger seat of engine number one (their big ladder truck). Sirens roaring they slowly push their way through the traffic getting downtown. Samuel repeatedly blares the horn to get vehicles to slid over out of their way.

"Wow…What a mess." Barry stated as he leaned up in between the seats looking out the windshield. "Umm…Doc? You didn't happen to download an app to tell us how we need to take the pile of pick em up sticks out, without collapsing the rest on us? Did You?" He wondered looking out at the huge pile of what used to be a scaffolding, crashed down in a huge pile of steel, wood, and concrete.

"No Sarg. I'm afraid we might just have to pray that we are pulling the right pole first." Gibraltar answered, wondering if praying can actually help. "Sarg, can you hand me the mega phone from back there. We're going to have to get this crowd to move back."

Samuel honks the horn again, parting the crowd to get the fire truck up as close as he possibly can.

Gibraltar steps out onto the step of his now open door, holding the mega phone between the door and the cab. "Ok everybody, this is Miami Dade Fire Department! We are going to need everyone to back away from the wreckage." He looks over to men who are frantically pulling and moving the debris. “And gentlemen, please stop attempting to move the materials. Let us handle the situation, please.” He throws the mega phone in the front passenger seat. “Alright guys, lets do this.” He tells his crew as they all pile out of the truck.

Most of the crowd slightly backed off at least, giving them a little bit of breathing room. A couple of the men were still attempting to move pieces of the torn down scaffolding. “Hey guys!” Gibraltar yells out as they run up onto the scene. “Please stop trying to move anything.” He added in a loud stern voice.

“But there’s a man hurt and trapped in there, we have to get him out.” The man argues.

“Yea, but I don’t want to have to rescue you to because you’re an idiot pulling on the wrong piece and causing the whole thing to further crash down.” Gibraltar grabs the guy by the shoulder yanking him away from the pole he was attempting to pull out.

“Stop!” The man flails out of Gibraltar’s grasp. “The guy is seriously hurt.” The man yells just inches away from Gibraltar’s face.

Samuel jumps in between them pushing Gibraltar back out of the way. “Let us do our job, please.” He turns back around convincing the guy to back away from the wreckage.

Looking into the piled up mess they see the wounded man. The man in a bright yellow vest and hard hat grunting, clearly in a lot of pain. Barry and Samuel walk around looking for the best route to get to this guy.

"Oh wow Doc." Samuel said. "The guy has a piece of rebar through his midsection."

Gibraltar steps over to Samuel's viewpoint to assess the situation further. He see's the man on his back with about two feet of rebar through his gut, and no direct route to get him out. "Alex! Get your tail over here." Alex runs over to where Gibraltar is standing. "You're the small one here, I need you to crawl in there and see what we need to do to get him out of there."

Alex looks to his Captain in a panicky, frozen state. "Wha…wha…what, am I suppose to do when I get in there?" He questioned nervously afraid of the situation.

"That's what I need you to tell me when you get in there. Now Go!" Gibraltar pushes him in the back causing him to slightly stumble forward. "Be careful not to move any of the wrong pieces." Gibraltar added increasing Alex's nervousness.

Alex carefully and slowly shimmy's his way into the middle of the crashed scaffolding, and he makes it to the man. "Hey are you ok?" He questioned the guy who was in so much pain that he could not respond. “Oh Sorry!” He realized he might have asked a silly question.

“Well Alex!” He hears Gibraltar yell at him.

“Umm…” Alex takes a deep breath in attempt to turn his frantic reactions into more diligent ones. “Umm…he’s got this piece of metal through his belly.” Alex called back.

“No crap, like I cant see that. Is it vital?” Gibraltar cusses at him.

“Umm…” Alex really unsure not really knowing what to do.

“Is he bleeding a lot Alex?” Gibraltar growing more and more frustrated with the whole situation.

“Some.” Alex looks around the guy and on the ground. “Not a lot though.” He adds not seeing as much blood as he thought would be around with metal through someone’s belly.

“Ok Alex, that’s good. Seems like the rebar missed all his arteries.” Gibraltar responds thinking that the guy probably would no longer be grunting had it punctured one.

“Cap!” Barry speaks up. “This will take several hours to cut through, then there’s no guarantee we wont make it crash down further, just to get to him.”

“Ok Alex, this guy don’t have the time to wait on us to cut him out.” Gibraltar looks back over to Barry. “If you and LT can get those two poles out with the Jaws of Life, I think Alex can drag him out through there.” Barry instantly responds to Gibraltar’s direction and takes back off to the truck. “Your going to have to drag him out.” He turned back his voice to Alex explaining what he would need to do.

“No way! I cant!” Alex now scared to death.

“Yea you can Alex, now your going to have to lift the man straight up. Try not to move him from side to side in any direction, you got this Alex.”

Alex takes another deep breath. “Ok!” He responds with as much confidence that he can muster.

Thirty-One

McKenzie and Lunar walk into the back fellow ship hall of Ocean Breeze Apostolic Church. Alex, Beatrice, Joel, and little Natasha are all gathered around a table.

"Awwe...Hey baby Natasha." Lunar gazed into the car seat and pinched Natasha's rosy red cheeks. "Oh! Hey Mr. Alex." She shoves her hand out in introduction. "I am quite honored that I am able to get baptized at the same time as a hero!"

Alex screws his face into a puzzled look, wondering what she is talking about. "What do you mean Lunar?"

The rest look on also intently curious.

"You are a hero Alex, you saved that mans life the other day, and you made the front page of the news paper." Lunar pulls her phone out, quickly pulling up the article. "I have been bragging to Stephanie that I get to get baptized next to a hero." She held her phone up for him to see.

"Oh..." He bashfully said, unable to come up with any other words.

"You didn't see it Mr. Alex, they even wrote a nice story with a picture of you dragging the man out."

McKenzie gazes at the picture over Lunar's shoulder. "Wow! That's really awesome Alex. Thank you for your service." She shows great gratitude, forcing Alex's face to become more red.

“Yea listen to this. ‘Rookie Fire Fighter Alex rescues man from a crashed scaffolding, and we at the newspaper would love to show him our gratitude for Alex’s heroic service as an amazing fireman. We here at the paper no longer consider you a rookie for your brave actions. The man pulled out from the wreckage is expected to make a full recovery, thanks to you Alex and your quick response.’ See Alex you’re a hero and all of Miami knows it.” Lunar excitedly read of his heroics, giving him great praise.

“Well thank you, but I really only did what Captain Crichton asked me to do. And Bea put the Band-Aid on him, so really they are the heroes here, not me.” Alex spoke humbly, not really wanting all the recognition himself.

“No Alex, you were definitely the hero. I truly appreciate your modesty, but you can take credit where credit is due.” Beatrice compliments Alex’s work thinking about how far he has came, in such a short timeframe.

“That was really cool of you Alex, I really wish more people were like you.” Joel gives his appreciation, patting him on the back causing him to tear up, as he starts feeling as though he has finally found his home.

For the first time in his life Alex feels as though he is exactly where he belongs. “Thank you all.” He manages to choke out. “But I think I just realized that I was only able to be a hero because of God’s Gift, of my Hoy

Ghost. I really don't remember much about pulling the guy out of there." He said this with the slightest hint of skepticism in his voice.

"I know it was God's gift to you, because you have a purely beautiful soul Alex. He wants to work many more good things through you." Beatrice chimed in still hyped from the event. "Now are you two ready to be baptized and show the world that you are allowing God to change your lives in the name of Jesus."

They both nod nervously so, shaking in their shoes and ready to start their new lives.

"Ok Joel will take you over to the other side and show you the process Alex, and Lunar I will take you over here." McKenzie now gives them their directions.

"And Natasha and I will go out front, so we can get you both on video." Beatrice claims enthusiastically as they all depart.

As McKenzie starts to take Lunar out front she caught sight of JJ and Mark entering the back door. "Hey Lunar, go ahead and go to the sanctuary. I'll be right out."

McKenzie meets JJ and Mark halfway into the fellowship hall. When she walked up to them she had the biggest smile she had worn in years. "JJ…Mark!" She calls out all but running over to them.

“See I told you we should have used the front entrance.” JJ said as she slapped Mark on the arm, paranoid about walking into the fellowship hall.

“Oh no, its fine.” McKenzie claims. “Sorry I am just so excited you two showed up.

“Well to be totally honest.” Mark speaks up. “I have been trying to get her to come for years, and when she told me you invited her to a baptism, I was in there.”

McKenzie giggled at his response like she was once again a giddy school girl. “That is so awesome.” She talks dreamy of having her bestie here with her at all the church events, prayer meetings, and worship services to come. “How’s it going with you JJ?” She stares her up and down noticing that she went with a pair of modest blue jeans, and not the tight yoga pants.

“Its going really good McKenzie…I’m a bit nervous about being here, with the pants and make up and all, but I still have some funky bruising underneath this foundation.” Jemma speaks the truth about her uneasy feelings.

“I told her not to worry about it, that nobody would say anything about her because she is with me.” Mark attempts to comfort JJ.

“Haha…” McKenzie laughs at Marks comment. “Actually…Mark will probably be the only reason anyone says anything about you.” She kids with them, but actually meant it.

“Ha…Ha…” Mark responds very dryly.

JJ wraps her arms around him in a passionate hug. “Well its ok, they can say whatever. I know that I have Mark, and he will be there for me. Really McKenzie things have been way more than great every since you suggested that I take him to Toys-Aint-Us. We have actually been talking about making our relationship official.”

McKenzie giggles and shakes her head at them. “That’s great, I’m glad I could be of help.”

“Yea it has been great!” Mark kissed JJ on the forehead holding onto her. “I will admit I was a bit skeptical at first, especially when we first pulled into the parking lot of Toys-Aint-Us and seen exactly how massive the place was, but when I got in there…I was in heaven and ran all through that place as though I was a big kid. Thanks for the suggestions, who’d thought that we just needed to act like kids again to make each other happy!”

McKenzie laughs at the two love bird comics, totally envious of their fresh found love for one another. “God told us that we need to have child like faith. I am really glad you two are happy.” She smiled at them, with a true glow across her face.

❖

"Alright church!" Pastor Ross spoke as Lunar and Alex walked out onto the platform, dressed in heavy robes to be baptized in. "Today is a very special day, these two beautiful souls have made a bold step in their walk with Christ. Lunar and Alex here have both decided to be Baptized in the name of Jesus." He pauses looking towards them for more emphasis. "Its not everyday the church here at Ocean Breeze Apostolic gets to baptize a true hero, but today…but today we get to baptize Miami's most heroic man. Alex here has done a very brave service for our city and I would like us all to show our gratitude."

The entire church gives a standing ovation with loud claps and vibrant shouts, warming not only Alex's heart, but the whole church feels his compassion.

"So…" The noise dwindles out. "So church honestly though we are baptizing two hero's today. Miss Lunar here also has a hero's heart, I know she will go on and do great things for the Lord and Church." He gazed down on Lunar, who had equal to the biggest and brightest smile he'd ever remembered seeing. "Now church…God spoke to us through one of our great prophet's in Ezekiel eighteen, verse twenty-one. He said 'If we would turn away from all of our sins, keep his statues and do what is lawful, than we will surely live, we shall not die.' Being Baptized in Jesus name is our way of showing the physical world that our Holy Spirit has connected to us…as one, and will help guide us towards a less sinful and more lawful life. Are these two going to become perfect today? And do everything exactly right?” The Pastor asked this rhetorical question, waving a flat palm over them. “No…probably not…for if they do they are certainly much better than I myself. Even through all my hard work, prayer, and dedication, I still stumble. But as we connect, as one with God’s Holy Spirit through the name of his son Jesus Christ, we begin to want to do better, we begin to want to do what is right. This is not some metaphor for the church to idolize and show off to the world. Jesus was God manifested in flesh to allow us to become one with God and our Holy Spirit. When Peter spoke in Acts two and thirty-eight he told us. ‘Repent and be baptized everyone of us in the name of Jesus.’ He did not tell us to be baptized in the father and son, he said be baptized in the name of God and Jesus. They are not separate entity’s, they are one in the same, and when we receive his gift of the Holy Spirit we in turn become one with God through our Lord and Savior Jesus Christ. Ok you two, now lets get started. Did you flip a coin to see who is going to be first?” Lunar and Alex both look at one another totally confused, clearly the thought of who was going to be first never crossed their minds. “Just kidding, ladies always go first in my opinion.”

Pastor Ross gently places a hand on Lunar’s back and guides her towards a set of stairs that are connected to the baptismal. He then walks around to the backside as McKenzie guides Lunar up the stairs and instructs her to exit on the other side that leads to a back door, away from the stage.

McKenzie waited on the other side for Lunar to come out of the baptismal, to help guide her out. "Hey Lunar." She gave her a hand to help her down the steps. "How do you feel?"

"Umm…wet and cold." Lunar answered honestly, giving McKenzie a giggle.

"How do you feel with your feelings?" McKenzie simplifies the question.

"Really…I don't feel no different. Am I not important enough for God to give his gift of the Holy Ghost, whatever that's suppose to mean." Lunar almost depressed now.

"No…no…" McKenzie puts caring hands on both of Lunar's shoulders. "Dear that's not at all the case, God has already given you this gift. You were just baptized to show the world that he has done so. Have you not been feeling different? And are things not going better at school?" McKenzie careful not to mention her home life, looking her squarely in her eyes.

"Yea." Lunar gently nods. "It has been way better every since the first time I came to the church with you, and made my new bestie Stephanie. I haven't thought about wanting to die at all actually…I enjoy looking forward to coming to church to see…" She pauses unsure if she can say it. "To see my new family. Is it ok that I call the church my new family?"

McKenzie begins to cry and embraces Lunar in a compassionate hug, oblivious to getting her dress wet. "Yes of course you can, now do you know what family's do together?" McKenzie pushes her arms straight, keeping her hands on her shoulders.

"Mm…watch T.V.?" Probably Lunar's most optimistic thought about her family.

"Umm…" McKenzie bobs her head back and forth. "I suppose sometimes, but I was thinking more like going shopping. What do you think about you, Stephanie, and me going shopping next Saturday?"

Lunar gets all giddy, completely forgetting about being wet or cold. "Really?" She bounces up and down jovially so.

"Yea we'll make it a girls day out, go out to eat a nice meal, buy some new clothes, and just have a fun day."

Lunar wraps McKenzie up and squeezes her harder than she had ever hugged anyone before. "Thank you! Thank you! Thank you!!!"

Thirty-Two

Alex awkwardly dances around in the kitchen, listening to praise and worship music, humming along to the best of his abilities, not too familiar with all the songs…yet.

“What the heck are you listening to?” Gibraltar walked in complaining, going straight for the fridge.

“Oh! Sorry Captain Crichton, I’ll turn it off.”

Gibraltar grabs the gallon of milk and filled his cup to the brim. “What’s for breakfast?” He rudely adds the question.

“Oatmeal banana pancakes.” Alex smiles happy about his creation one that he found when he typed in healthy pancakes in his search engine.

“That sounds terrible!” Gibraltar turns and walks towards the exit. “I’ll take the syrup in there.” He claimed as he walked out the door.

“You don’t…” Alex stops mid sentence noticing that Gibraltar is no longer in there.

Alex looks down and sees Apollo happily awaiting a treat, he quickly pats him on the head before giving him half a banana, which he gobbled up.

He puts the finishing touches on all the plates, then grabs an extra small plate. “Come on Apollo.” Apollo gladly follows Alex to the dining room.

The rest of his colleagues are sitting around the table patiently waiting for breakfast when Alex placed the small plate on the floor for Apollo. “What your going to feed the dog, but not us.” Gibraltar griped, instantly feeling remorse for calling Apollo a dog, however his pride would never let it show.

“Ughh!” Beatrice sighs. “Sorry Alex, that I did not help you. We have had a huge response to these tablets and I’m trying to get a game plan on what to do next. Out of the twenty-eight kids we sent home with a tablet, eighteen of their parents have emailed us back, some making book requests, some complementing the idea or books, and of course one complaint that we sent their child home with a game.”

Alex listens to Bea as he patted Apollo on the head who had already devoured the small pancake. “That’s ok Bea, it is just pancakes. It was pretty simple, I’ll be right back with everyone’s.”

“Here I’ll help you Alex!” DeAndre jumped up and scurried after him towards the kitchen.

“Wow Bea, you’ve really had that kind of response?” Gibraltar questioned rhetorically with surprise in his tone.

“Yea Doc, I’m really surprised also. I really think we should try two other grades in January, and see what happens. I have been talking with your accountant Mr. Day also about setting up a fundraiser to see if we cant get some funds built up.” Beatrice spoke with plenty of enthusiasm getting everyone’s full attention at the table.

“Well I have plenty of money, how much do you need?” Gibraltar responds, always wanting to fix everything himself.

“Ugh!” Beatrice sighed out a heavy disappointing breath. “Gibraltar! You cant just throw money at everything and think it will be better.”

“You can throw some money my way though, and it will surely make me better.” Samuel chimed in, frustrating Bea a bit more.

“Ugh…you men are all so hard headed, all you can think about is blowing your money. Gibraltar, this Foundation needs your attention, not your money. It’s a great idea that I believe can stand on its own. We just need to put the ground work in and get it out there.”

Alex and DeAndre return to the table carrying plates. Alex sits the first plate in front of Gibraltar, who immediately pops the top on the bottle of syrup he had brought in with him. “These pancakes don’t need syrup Captain Crichton, the cup there is eggnog that you dip them into.

“Whatever…” Gibraltar said rudely as he dumped a copious amount of syrup all over the two pancakes. “Pancakes have to have syrup.”

Alex then takes and sits the other plate he was carrying down beside all of Beatrice’s paperwork. “Well I think it looks amazing, and don’t listen to Doc. He’s just being a jerk.” She tears off a piece of her pancake. “Oahh! Thank you Jesus for this food.” She quickly adds the prayer. “I bout forgot, I’m so hungry.” She dipped the pancake as Alex instructed placing her hand underneath it as she brought it to her mouth, keeping it from dripping on her paperwork. “Mmm!!!” Her eyes widen as she chews and nods her head with approval.

Alex gives a proud smile and retreats to the kitchen to get the last of the breakfast. Moments later he returned with his plate and a bowl of fruit that he placed in the middle of the table, while everyone quietly enjoys his preparation.

“Man! Mi amigo, this is really amazing. Even though dipping pancakes is a bit unconventional Alex, this is really good.” Felipe compliments the chef.

Alex bows his head and says a quick silent prayer. “Well really I got the idea from Lieutenant Brooks.”

Samuel looks confused with a screwed up look on his face. "Umm…no you didn't, omelets is literally the only thing I know how to cook."

Alex chews happily on his bite. "But you keep telling me that too much sugar makes it more difficult for my muscles to get the proper nutrients to grow."

Samuel nods in agreement, recalling the many times he nutritiously instructed Alex.

"Well eggnog has a bunch of sugar in it also." Gibraltar interrupts them defensively. "And these really aren't that good." He added as he pushed his plate forward, simply out of spite.

"Well he's wrong." Barry now comes to Alex's defense. "Maybe Doc, if you would have listened to the chef, and ate it as he instructed…you would have realized this also."

Everyone around the table agrees as Gibraltar slumps down low in his chair and sulks.

"So Alex, I'm super proud of you. You are a rare individual and we are lucky to have you here, and at Ocean Breeze Apostolic Church. You are not like most men who God saves and baptizes, you were already a good guy who God is making better. Most guys God saves are a lot rougher around the edges, they party, and drink all the time, or run around sleeping with any woman that will have them." Beatrice added this last part loud and proud, projecting her voice towards Gibraltar. "Now I'll tell you what Alex, since your now hero status and you were baptized at the church, rumor has it with all the ladies at the church that you are now the most available Bachelor there."

"What do you mean that I'm the most available Bachelor?" He didn't quite comprehend what Beatrice was saying.

Bea giggles at his not understanding. "I mean there are several ladies there that would like to be your girlfriend." She super simplifies her statement.

"Really?" Alex bashfully respond with a beat red face, unsure of how he should approach this situation.

Gibraltar's now more jealous than ever and slumps even lower in his seat and crosses his arms as though he's a teenager again. All the guys noticed this and wanted to make jabs at him, but were all too afraid of the explosion one jab might create, to make any jabs.

"I've never had a girlfriend before, how do I get one?"

DeAndre starts laughing. "Alex don't worry buddy, I'll help you out. We'll turn you into a love machine before you can count to five." He stated matter-of-factly.

“No!!!” Beatrice shoots DeAndre the (I’ll kill you eye) if he so much as makes another suggestion about Alex’s love life. “Alex I will help you, and whatever you do, do not listen to any of these men when they give you advice about women, nothing period. They can teach you the work, working out, and dieting even, but I have got you on the dating and finding you a girlfriend.”

They all sit around quietly finishing their breakfast, after the stare DeAndre received from Beatrice everyone else was to afraid to say anything more on this topic.

After everyone cleared the table and went to there own thing, Gibraltar and Samuel stand drinking coffee by the railing that looks down into the shop area of Station Thirteen . They watch everyone running around the vehicles, doing various chores.

“You know?” Samuel started talking looking down at Alex who had just started shining the wheels on engine number one. “Alex really has become quite the fireman, it looks like I was wrong about him after all.” Samuel wants to add in how wrong Gibraltar has been, and scold him for the way he has been treating Alex, but he holds his tongue hoping that his compliment softly works on his conscience.

“Yea, I’m proud of him.” Gibraltar reiterates, without much conviction in his voice at all.

“Than why are you so hard on him?” Samuel questions his friend with concern.

Gibraltar turns around and leans his back against the railing. “Maybe its because I think he’s got potential, but he needs a tough drill Sargent to make him mentally stronger.” He makes this statement in attempt to convince himself more so than Samuel, but his conscience is hard at work on him. He knows that he hasn’t been fair to Alex, and honestly feels that Alex has become his scape goat for his anger.

“What the heck is he doing here?” Gibraltar said when he turned back around seeing Marshall Spector walk into the far side of the station, carefully inspecting every square inch as he makes his way through the doors. “Oh!!!That son of a…Argh…I’m gonna kill him.”

Gibraltar starts to storm off, but Samuel stops him by grabbing a hold of his shoulder. “Gibraltar stop! You have to be careful, you cant let him know that we are onto him. This is more about Ja’Maar’s safety than anything, please don’t tip him off.”

Gibraltar pauses taking a deep breath. “Ok…your right, but I have to go see what he is doing here.” Samuel nods, staring him straight in the eyes to give him strength.

Gibraltar walking towards the stairs has to make a conscious effort, two or three times to slow his pace, to keep his temper in check. By the time Gibraltar makes it down into the station the Marshall hadn't even made it all the way down the first side of engine number one, as he is slowly scrutinizing every little detail of the truck and shop.

"Marshall Spector! To what do we owe the pleasure." Gibraltar attempts the painstakingly feat of sounding civil.

"Oh, not much." Spector didn't pay Gibraltar too much mind as he continued his inspection. "I'm behind on my annual inspections, so I thought I would come down and get yours out of the way. I know you run a tight ship and expect it to be quick and simple." Spector speaks earnestly to Gibraltar.

Walking around the ends of the trucks both men are quite as Spector continues to gaze up and down them.

"Your trucks are nice and clean, that's good. Its important we present ourselves good to the community. Our reputation is the most important part about running fire departments."

Gibraltar smirks and almost gags at his smug charismatic comment. Then he catches him thanking ***(or praying?)*** to God that Spector did not notice this discontent.

They continue to slowly walk together zig zagging between all the vehicles in the now deserted shop, which moments earlier was full of all the crew members who all seemingly disappeared when the Marshall showed up.

"So you know? Captain Crichton, out of all my other Captains I must say that your work with the capacity checks has been the most detailed, and your work on them exceeds all the other Captains by far. I have half a mind to make you another job offer to take on the entire counties capacity checks."

Oh great! He thinks he's going to take my least favorite part of the job and turn it into a full time position.

"Well Marshall Spector." Gibraltar surprised at how civil he sounds. "I do not do this job for the money." Spector stops and looks to him, and gives a knowing nod. "And honestly, I would have to decline any such offer."

The Marshall gives Gibraltar a politically charismatic smile and continues his walk through. "So you have probably heard that I am in the top running and will probably becoming one of our State Senators next month."

Gibraltar's mind begins to steam at his saying so, making it more real that he probably cant stop this. ***Why is it the higher people get into politics, the more they can do and get away with.*** He starts battling in his mind.

"And with all your hard work, I was really thinking about throwing your name out there to be my replacement."

This statement sends Gibraltar's mind on an unexpected roller coaster ride. He hates himself for thinking about how much good he could do from the position, but more so he hates the thought of being the predecessor of so evil a man.

“Well that's a thought.” Gibraltar said with an abundance of honesty. “Yea I heard you were going out for Senate.” He added with a solemn tone.

They walk up stairs together Spector briefly sticks his head in the kitchen, not really caring too much about details in these quarters. They walk over to the edge of the railing, where moments earlier Samuel and Gibraltar stood chatting.

“So you should really think on the Marshall offer, I know you would be a good choice.”

Gibraltar's skin gets a tingling cringe at the offer of the job that he has actually dreamed about in the past. The offer just doesn't seem nearly so appealing coming from Spector. “Thank you, I will think about it.”

“What the heck is that?” Spector spoke the question with anger in his voice as he gazed out over the tops of the vehicles. “Why is there damage on engine number two?”

Gibraltar more annoyed with his anger than intimidated by it. “Its just a little cosmetic damage, that isn't even visible from the ground.” Gibraltar defends his LT.

“Well cosmetic or not, remember what I was just telling you about appearance? There’s plenty of high places and second stories in this district, so I assure you people take notice to that. We don’t want them saying that we cant take care of our trucks, so I want that fixed A-S-A-P!” Spector made his demand as though Gibraltar should already be on the phone to get it fixed.

Gibraltar now way more annoyed with Spector after this complaint. He so badly wants to deck him in the nose, or at the very least threaten him into admitting all the crimes he is constantly committing, but somehow he is able to hold his temper. “Will it not make our insurance more expensive?” He questioned instead.

“Yea maybe so, take it to a body shop and see what the cost is, and use your better judgement on whether or not to claim it on insurance. Come on Captain Crichton, your not an idiot.”

Gibraltar’s face turned beat red, and he would not be surprised one bit if he had steam boiling out of his ears. “Yes sir…” He bites his tongue so hard he literally begins to taste blood.

Thirty-Three

Ja'Maar, late at night glances over at the GPS on his phone, watching the red dot move, about a mile ahead of him. "Finally I think he's going somewhere he doesn't want me to know about." He whispers to himself even though there is nobody around to hear him. "Are you going to give me de break we need tonight Spector?" He continues talking to himself thinking about how much easier technology has made it to spy on people (or well money and technology).

It cost him a one hundred thousand dollar deposit with a big security firm to get the AI spy bot. The spyware not only connects to Spector's phone calls, camera's, messages, email, it also counts every step he makes, all without him having a clue anyone is watching.

One thing Ja'Maar has been disappointed about is that the spyware is suppose to be able to connect to another phone if the person has one. Which he is almost certain Spector does so, he just hasn't been able to connect with it yet.

He glanced back to the screen. "Alright another evasive maneuver, I have you now!" He continues to follow, completely out of sight.

The car finally stops at one of Miami's big hotels. Ja'Maar steps on the gas to get to him before he disappears into one of the rooms.

He gets to the parking garage and the spyware picks up a phone call Spector is making. "I'm here…" He listens to his conversation through his Bluetooth earpiece. The other end was a female voice that simply said she would see him in a minute.

As he watches Spector get out of his SUV he haggles in his mind, whether he should follow him in or not. "Yea." He decides. "I have to keep some eyes on him." He states to himself as he reaches to his tie with both hands to straighten it up. He quickly jumps out of his car, and begins to follow Spector at a casual pace.

Spector was so paranoid on the road that he knew he was clear, so he's comfortable now that he lost any tail he may have had driving around in so many different circles for the hour or so, that he doesn't even look behind him as he enters the hotel. (Not that it would matter Ja'Maar is completely inconspicuous, and Spector does not have a clue to who he is.)

Ja'Maar steps up quicker to get a bit closer so that he wont loose Spector. He follows him into a bank of elevators, where one opened instantly, and Spector stepped straight onto it. ***Here goes nothing…***Ja'Maar thinks as he takes a couple of quick steps to catch the elevator before it closes.

Spector pays the encounter no attention as he studies his phone. “Oh, we must be going to the same place.” Ja’Maar mentioned as he reached for the elevator panel to see the first floor already lit up. Spector’s focus is elsewhere and didn’t even say a word, which pleased Ja’Maar just fine.

When the elevator doors opened Spector quickly took off, as Ja’Maar casually follows him several paces behind him. They walk into the hotels restaurant, to the right there’s a nice shiny bar with bottles and glasses elegantly placed. There are tables in the center of the restaurant and booths lining the two back walls.

It’s around eleven p.m. so the place is completely deserted, aside from a lone person sitting at the bar. Spector goes back to a booth in the back corner as though he had been there, done that before. Ja’Maar takes a booth along the same wall, sitting the same direction as Spector so they cant see one another, he can how ever see the door from this location.

The bartender who also serves as a server goes to Spector’s table first and takes his order. Ja’Maar hears him easily from several tables behind him.

“Good evening sir, can I start you off with a drink?” The bartender asked for his order as Ja’Maar studies the menu.

“Yea I’ll take a water, and how about a spinach artichoke dip…I could use a snack.” He casually orders thinking about how he missed dinner.

“I’ll get that put right in, and I’ll be right back with your water.” The bartender said as he walked away from the table.

At the same time a very attractive young woman, decked out in expensive and way to revealing of clothes comes into the restaurant. “Hey babe.” She greets the bartender as she walked by him, the greeting definitely showing they knew one another, Ja’Maar takes note.

The young woman goes back to Spector’s corner booth and joins him. Ja’Maar cant see them but can hear them well through the Bluetooth. “Hey Darla, hows things been going?” Spector starting their conversation off with the question.

“Enh…you know another day at the Black Widow Escort Service, the wonderful life of paradise.” She commented as though she was already bored with their conversation.

The waiter in a hurriedly fashion places Ja’Maar’s water on his table and walks off with a tray full of other drinks to the other table. He picks up his phone and searches for Black Widow Escort Service and quickly finds their website. He searches through the website for a few moments, seeing nothing unusual as he kinda figured they wouldn’t leave much in the open.

Ja'Maar then uses his spyware to bounce from Spector's phone over to Darla's to download her information for later research. "Did you meet with Mr. Johnson yet?" He hears Spector question.

"No, we're suppose to have lunch tomorrow though." Darla responds as though she had no care in the world.

Ja'Maar looks through her contacts to see if he could find this Johnson, but with a quick look he is unable to do so. He has other avenues to search for this Johnson when the time permits, so he jots down the name.

"Ok Darla very good, are all the other girls behaving?"

Ja'Maar takes a drink of his water listening in. "Well Sasha stole a couple of credit cards from one of our clients the other day, then there was another one of our girls who left a back window unlocked for one of her boyfriends to later get in there. I fired her on the spot, she was caught by the client." Ja'Maar writes all this stuff down.

"You didn't fire Sasha?" He heard Spector upsettingly ask.

"Nope, I don't think her client caught her, or he's to shy to say so."

The waiter comes back with Ja'Maar's appetizer. "Are you ready to order anything else?" He asked in a sluggish tone.

“Nah, dis will do for now…tank you.” Ja’Maar dips one of the chips as the bar keep walks back to his perch behind the bar.

“You have to fire her, immediately! We have a zero tolerance for this.” Ja’Maar hears Spector say this, which slightly confuses him.

“But…” Darla starts to argue with Spector. “She’s one of our best, and with everything else you have us do, what’s the problem if she can get away with stealing a credit card or two?” Ja’Maar feels as curious as she does.

“Shh…” He hears the loud shush. “We don’t discuss any of that in the open, ever! And fire her now, no tolerance period. We have an image to up hold here, do you understand?”

Ja’Maar is actually impressed with Spector’s charisma and business ethics, but he knows he’s still missing the bigger picture with the escort service.

“Ok Mr. Spector…” He hears her bow to him.

“Call me Senator Spector.” Ja’Maar almost chokes on his chip with Spector’s smugness as she toys with him a little. “Ok you can go now, and send in the other two. I have had a long week.” He demands Darla and the very attractive blonde punctually obeys.

Moments later two more, equally attractive females come into the restaurant, one with short brunette hair, and the other with long thick lushes red hair. Both go straight back to Spector's table and join him. Ja'Maar connects and downloads both of their phones, finishes up his spinach artichoke dip, and pays his tab before deciding he probably got the best he was going to get for the night, and calls it.

The following morning Ja'Maar walks into Gibraltar's office. "Good morning bruhder." He greets as he takes the seat across from the desk from him.

"Good morning Ja'Maar, please tell me you have good news."

Ja'Maar slumps slightly in his chair. "Sorry, I don't tink dere ever any good news when it comes to dis guy."

Gibraltar gets a understanding look across his face. "Yea I think I have come to the same conclusion. He actually came by here a couple days ago."

"Really?" This surprises and worries Ja'Maar at the same time. "You don't tink he is onto us? Do you?"

Gibraltar puts an at ease hand up. "Oh no, it was just his routine inspection. And I seriously doubt he is onto us, in fact he was offering me his job as the Marshall when he takes the Senate Seat."

Ja'Maar sits back in his chair a little easier, and puts his arms on the rest getting more comfortable. "Very good, you don't tink you or Samuelle have possibly tipped him off in anyway? Maybe dat's why he's offering you de job. Even evil people have heard de saying keep your enemy's closer."

Gibraltar takes a casual drink of his coffee pondering the question. "I'm sorry, where were my manners. Can I get you some coffee, water, or anything else?" Ja'Maar waves a hand in gratitude, shaking his head no. "Well…I really don't believe so, but I tell you I don't know how spies do this stuff. Very often I wanted to just beat the tar out of the smug prick, and he was only here a few minutes."

Ja'Maar gives a short chuckle. "Yea…holding your emotions togeter is probably de most important part to spying, and I assure you it has gotten de better part of me on more den one occasion. Dis however is one of dem cases, dat if we let dem get de better of us we wont be coming back from. So I cant stress enough, how important it is dat we hold it togeter."

Gibraltar feels this vicariously as he replaced his coffee back on his desk. "So what have you learned? I'm guessing this early of a visit isn't just social."

Ja'Maar shakes his head. "No bruhder, unfortunately it is not." He pauses in contemplation on where to start. "The deposit you made has certainly helped, I was able to pardner wit a large security firm who has loaned me some spyware dat has been very beneficial. I was up all night deciphering truough files."

Ja'Maar gives Gibraltar a quick rundown of the night he had before, explaining the Black Widow Escort Service, and the conversation Spector had with Darla.

"So can we not take this to the fed's? And get them to start an investigation?"

"No Gibraltar, I'm afraid not…because all de law makers work for all dese top politicians. Wit all de money dey can get away wit just about anyting deir not caught in de act of doing. Unfortunately our country is honestly no different den de communist dey just hide behind utter political party names. Don't hear me wrong, it is much better dan Somalia by far, but dere are for sure de major downfalls and de fact dat de higher up politics are able to get away wit so much is one of dese. I really wasn't able to get much, Darla's phone was a brand new burner phone dat didn't have any information on it. I wasn't even able to find dis Johnson fellow, unless she put his name under a cover name it wasn't in dere, but if I can track dis event down I tink we might be onto someting. Den dis Sasha, since deir about to fire her, she may be a useful asset. I do however really hate using assets, its de most dangerous part of de bizness."

Gibraltar interrupts him with an idea. “Can we not just have her write an affidavit and put her on the witness stand?”

Ja’Maar stands up stretching his back and legs a bit. “Well if Spector was some shade tree mechanic dis could work, but not someone wit so many people on de payroll. It would never get to a DA, de prosecutor isn’t going to take any kind of allegations from an escort on a Senator to a judge. Dey just wont do it, but maybe, just maybe she does have an idea of what’s going on wit Spector and de Black Widow Escort Service, and she can help us build a case to catch him in de act or attempting to act on a crime. Dis is I’m sure witout being able to trace any of de money trail, de only way we will be able to stop him.”

Gibraltar swivels around in his chair, looking down into the station making an attempt to sort through all of the commotion in his mind. “Ok…” He begins to say turning back around when the alarms start buzzing.

“Station Thirteen on deck…” He hears Barbie call over the radio static. “We have alarms going off at the University Hospital. It’s multiple alarms going off on different wings, so its probably another glitch, I’m on the phone right now with their maintenance staff and so far no reported flames.”

The garage doors start opening for engine one to head out. “10-4 Barb…Station Thirteen on our way.” Sylvester calls back on the radio as

Ja'Maar watches the crew from above, diligently load up into the big ladder truck.

"Umm…Do you need to go?" Ja'Maar wonders aloud.

"Nah, these hospitals are always having glitches in there systems, but its protocol that we dispatch a couple of trucks. My team can handle the walkthrough on this one." Gibraltar explains the typical situation.

Ja'Maar retakes his seat, and the alarms fade out. "What is it Ja'Maar? That you need me to do? I really want to help you here, this pig needs to be held accountable for his criminal acts."

Ja'Maar sits back in his chair taking in Gibraltar's question. "Honestly bruhder, dis here is a very dangerous and sketchy situation. Your money has been de biggest help to it all, and I am going to have to only use highly trained individuals moving forward to ensure everyone's safety. Especially if I begin using assets, but let me be tinking on dis, dere may be somting come up once I get in contact wit dis Sasha. Den I will know better how we need to proceed, but as of right now I need you to just do as you have been…Oh…" Ja'Maar pauses coming up with a thought. "Are you sure dat he isn't onto us?" Ja'Maar makes the question, if Spector might know he's been had.

"Well…I mean he didn't seem as though he was and it all seemed as usual business." Gibraltar reassures his words.

“Well he certainly wouldn’t act any different…Dis guy has tons of charisma, and he is a highly skilled pathological liar, sadly most of our politics best virtues…Ok I really hate doing dis, but dis may be a better angle den Sasha.”

Gibraltar leans forward anxiously so. “What do I need to do?”

“First of all, dat emotion you just showed me dere, even tuough it was slight, you need to regcognize it, don’t get antzy ever. All I want you to do right now is call him up and be very interested in de Marshall gig, and let me work up a better profile here. Now if your going to do dis, which it could be a very good angle, but it wont happen over night, and unfortunately we are going to have to let him take de Senate Seat. But if we can maybe get him to feel like you are more like him dan he initially tought, which wont be easy because you have a conscience and are de opposite, but maybe, just maybe we can take him down from his side.”

Thirty-Four

"So Lunar." McKenzie looks into her rearview mirror, staring back at Stephanie and Lunar sitting in her backseat. "Have you ever been to any yard sales?"

Stephanie begins prancing around in the back seat shaking her bestie very jovially.

"No…we…or my mom usually gets all of our clothes from the mall"

"Well we're going o have so much fun…Yard sales always have the bestest stuff, and its always dirt cheap. Which is important, cause my mom only gave me twenty dollars and that's suppose to be for food to. Are we going somewhere cheap, Sister McKenzie?"

Lunar has a depressed look come across her face. "Oh…I forgot to ask my mom for any money." She lies not wanting to talk about her family's financial struggles.

"Its ok Lunar." McKenzie was expecting this. "I invited you two today, so I think I can loan you twenty bucks to spend, and if we hit the mother load and your able to get more clothes for your wardrobe, we can probably spend a little more."

Lunar's face and mood stays somber. "I wouldn't want you to spend all your money on me." She humbly pouts out, honestly not having thought about the money part to shopping.

"Its ok Lunar, a few yard sale clothes isn't going to break me..." McKenzie attempts to cheer her up. "Oh..." And idea sparks. "There are a few things around the house that I could use your help with, if you think you might be willing to help me out?"

"Really!!!" McKenzie sees the light in Lunar's eyes begin to shine again. "Well...I don't know if I will know how to help or not, but I want to try." Lunar answers honestly thinking back on all of her moms criticism.

McKenzie gives her a great big smile in the mirror. "I'm sure you will be a big help, I can show you...its pretty simple stuff around the house. Also Beatrice asked me the other day if I knew anyone that could watch baby Natasha a couple hours, a day for a couple days a week, you could get paid for that."

"No..." Lunar quickly shakes her head. "I don't know how to take care of a baby, I cant change diapers." She snarls her nose. "Or how to make a baby bottle." She adds, not ever remembering a time that she has ever even been around a baby for more than a few minutes in passing.

"That's not a problem, I can teach you." Stephanie speaks enthusiastically, already dreaming of the fun it's going to be. "Its easy, maybe we can both watch Natasha together."

McKenzie contemplates this momentarily. "That actually sounds like a good idea Stephanie. We'll have to talk with sister Bea, she probably wont be able to pay two wages though, so you two will have to split the money." Both girls shrill with excitement all but busting McKenzie's eardrums as they bounce around in their seatbelts.

"You know one of you could have rode up her with me." McKenzie complains looking at her empty passenger seat.

"But its like we have a shofar and we're riding in a limo." Stephanie said as she waved her head back and forth in a conceited motion.

"Ha…ha…I don't think I like that idea very much, maybe we should take your twenty bucks so we can hire a real shofar, and I can join you two back there." Stephanie's jaw drops as Lunar bursts out laughing historically at McKenzie's joke.

"Ouah!!! I really like this song." McKenzie turns the radio up and begins singing along. Then within moments they are all singing praise and worship music bouncing around going down the road.

"Here we are!!!" McKenzie yells over the loud radio as she turns it down.

"Wow…I didn't realize we were coming here." Stephanie gazes out the window. "We've came to youth groups to this church before." She claims as she is unbuckling the seat belt before the car gets stopped.

"Really? That's cool, y'all go to different churches for youth groups?" Lunar anxious to know more.

“Yea…and this place is really cool with a lot of nice people. I know they’re going to have a lot of good stuff. Sometimes the other youth groups come to our church also. Its kinda like our long distance family, my mom always told me. We can go almost anywhere in this country and find an Apostolic Church family that would feel like home when we walked through their doors. She said it’s a beautiful gift God has given us to always be able to find family to worship him with.” Stephanie explains the vastness of God’s order with the church to Lunar.

McKenzie puts the car in park as they all stare out the window at tables full of stuff, boxes of shoes lined up along the outside wall of the church and several racks of clothes hanging at the far end of the parking lot. “Wow Stephanie, that’s a really good way of looking at it. I’ve never heard it put that way before.”

They all get out of the car and gather in front of it. “Lunar, that’s a really pretty dress.” McKenzie compliments her looking up and down at the gorgeous deep blue silky Asian style dress. She gazes all the way down to her shoes and noticed the flat bottom skater shoes she normally wore with her goth outfits. ***Wow that’s so tacky.*** She thought to herself, quickly asking God for forgiveness of her stereotyping.

“Yea its Stephanie’s.” Lunar excited McKenzie liked the dress.

Stephanie wraps her arms around Lunar. "Yea its cool, being the same size we can shop together today. We can share all the clothes we get."

McKenzie laughs at the two of them as she puts a light hand on their backs to guide them towards the yard sale. The three of them meander around and through all the tables with tons of junk and several cheerful shoppers, all shocked at the deals they are finding.

"Wow…that's pretty!" Lunar picks up a picture beautifully printed with various shades of bright blues, pink, and greys that read [Trust in the Lord with all Your Heart.]

McKenzie gazes over at it and seen the one dollar price tag on it. "Yea Lunar, that is gorgeous. You should get it."

"Really!!!" Lunar's eyes shine super bright, making McKenzie wonder how her room must look, so dark and deserted that this might actually be the flicker of light it needs to liven her life up. "Thank you! Thank you!" She puts the picture down momentarily to wrap McKenzie up in a very warm hug.

They continue shopping through the tables looking at various knick knacks that is laid out. "What's that?" Stephanie questioned as she pointed at a large Styrofoam box.

"Hmm???" McKenzie walks around it gazing at it confused herself, yet very intrigued. "You know, I'm not too sure."

"Haha…" They all hear a man chuckle.

"Brother Poole." McKenzie said in a warm greeting.

Brother Poole takes a double glance at McKenzie. "Oh wow! Its been awhile, I almost didn't recognize the great brother Ross' eldest daughter." He spoke with joy. "You surely can tell all of you are dem city slicker Apostolic's. This here ladies is an incubator."

"What's a incubator?" Lunar impatiently interrupts him.

"Hahaha…well it's a really neat contraption, really, you put eggs in here, turn on the warming light in it and it makes ideal conditions for baby chicks to be born." He explains to them what it is and does still slightly shocked that McKenzie didn't know this.

"Baby Chicks?" Stephanie still confused crunches her eyebrows and torques her face thinking he was talking about baby girls.

Brother Poole smiles at her. "Yea, baby chickens. When the mother lays the eggs we take them and become the mother and father raising them in the ideal conditions to make beautiful, healthy baby chickens."

"Oh…" Stephanie shrugs, still not really understanding how works, but quickly her mind went to something else of interest.

“Hmm…That’s really cool Brother Poole, I’ve really never seen one of those. Guess I am one of dem city slickers.” McKenzie giggles at herself.

McKenzie and Brother Poole continue to talk while Lunar and Stephanie browse through the other items. After their all caught up on each other churches latest gossip, McKenzie goes and catches up with the girls.

Lunar is looking at the high heels. “I’ve never worn any of these before, are they hard to walk in?”

Stephanie laughs almost historically at her. “Are you kidding? They make you have to learn how to walk all over again. Look here these are your size, try them on.”

Lunar slides her skater shoes off and puts the high heels on, and takes several shaky steps. “Wow, they hurt my feet and make me walk funny.” She complains.

“Yea the pains and struggles us women have to go through to look and walk pretty.” McKenzie makes the statement excited with all the lady shopping.

Lunar looks up at McKenzie confused by what she just said. “I thought that y’all didn’t wear make up and jewelry because God made us pretty like we are. Why do y’all wear high heels to look pretty?”

McKenzie looks at Lunar intently for her legitimate question that she really doesn’t have an answer for. “Well…” But she’s going to give her one.

“Lunar some people may feel that same way about the heels, I however feel that they make us walk prettier, and God teaches us to walk with him. So this is more about women walking prettier with God, than about changing our appearance to look prettier.”

Lunar walks around a bit more in a very awkward fashion. “Well there not so bad, after all.” She said trying to ignore the pains the heels are giving her feet.

“See I told you.” Stephanie takes her hands flailing both of there arms around. “They are super cute on you, I think they may even have a dress here to match them.”

They all continue shopping for another hour or so at the massive yard sale, and all end up leaving with several bags in each of their hands.

“Wow girls! You two are cheap dates, I cant believe all this stuff only cost us fifty bucks, that’s amazing. All this shopping has made me work up an appetite.” McKenzie proud of all there good finds as her stomach begins to growl.

“Mee too…” Both of the girls said as they rubbed their bellies in the same fashion, then couldn’t stop laughing at their mimicking behavior.

They all sit on three sides of the square table. “Wow this place is fanceee!” Lunar compliments her surroundings.

Their table is set with a pure white table cloth, a vase with a dozen fresh red roses, two candles on either side of the roses, a napkin with silverware rolled up in it, and wine glasses at each sitting.

“Yea this is way nicer than I ever get to eat.” Stephanie adds to Lunar’s comment.

“Well girls, this is way nicer than I get to eat as well. It’s a girls date though, so I thought we should make it extravagant.”

The waiter walks up to their table. “Hello ladies, My name is Antonio.” He introduces himself as he lights the candles. “Welcome to Fazzio’s, can I start you all off with an appetizer?” The dark haired Italian looks towards the two girls and winks one of his bright green eyes, then begins filling their glasses with water.

“Umm…” McKenzie looking over the appetizers in the menu, trying to make a decision. “Yea why don’t we do the mozzarella sticks.” She said to Antonio, while both of the girls are to stunned over his handsome features to speak.

“Ouah! Excellent choice, I’ll go put those in and be right back to take your orders for the entrée’s.” He excitedly scurries away.

Once the waiter is out of earshot Stephanie looks at Lunar still starry eyed with chills running through her spine. “He’s sooo cute.” Lunar nods in agreement with her best friend.

“Uh…now girls, you need to focus on school, not boys. They’ll get you into trouble.” McKenzie trying to be the bigger role model.

“Ugh!” Stephanie drops her jaw. “That’s not fair, everyone else has a boyfriend.” She complains. “And all the older women are married, well except you. But just cause you like not having a boyfriend, doesn’t mean we shouldn’t have one.” She continued to argue hitting McKenzie hard and deep. Stephanie’s words keep her too shocked to say anything. “Besides, didn’t God make us to get married.” She adds to her point.

“Yes Stephanie, he did, but not till God decides for us to have someone. If we rush it we will end up with some jerk that makes us miserable. So what looks good?” McKenzie quickly changes the topic looking over the menu.

“Look here Steph, we can build our own pizza.” Lunar points to the place in the menu for her bestie to see.

“Really?” She gazes over to where Lunar’s finger is in the menu.

“Yea really, look at all these toppings.”

“Yummy...” Stephanie flips her menu over to the page. “I want…” She begins to pick out all her toppings out loud. “Green olives, black olives, pepperoni, and fresh mozzarella.”

“Olives? Really?” Lunar snarls her nose. “Ewwe anchovies!” Lunar squishes her face even more as she continues reading over all the other toppings. “I think I want to just stick with the fresh mozzarella.”

“Mmm…girls, that sounds really good. You are making me hungry.” McKenzie’s stomach begins to growl listening to them talk of pizza.

Antonio returned just as she said this. “Well I guess it’s a good thing that I come baring gifts then.” He states as he sits the fresh mozzarella sticks on the table, and pulls out his note pad. “Did you all decide on what you would like to eat?” He said with a pen in his hand looking at Stephanie who is too stunned by his beauty to speak.

“I’ll have just the cheese pizza.” Lunar speaks up, snapping Stephanie out of her trance.

“Perfect choice, that’s my favorite.” Antonio jots on his note pad.

“Really?” Stephanie excited by his voice. “Then I’ll have the same thing.” She ordered looking up at Antonio with googly eyes.

“Steph, I thought you wanted olives and pepperoni’s?” McKenzie challenges her in attempt to break the connection she feels she has.

She glares at McKenzie almost wickedly so. “But if cheese is your favorite, that’s what I want.” She looked back at Antonio and smiles.

McKenzie's thoughts begin to roll. ***Oh boy! This girl is going to be a handful.***

"Yea but I like olives and pepperoni's also." He shrugs, oblivious to the emotions he is sending through Stephanie.

"You do really??? But is it your favorite?" Stephanie clearly only wanting to go with his favorite.

"Umm..." He looks into the air dumbly so. "Well no the cheese would be my favorite."

"Then I'll have the cheese."

He shrugged again as he made the mark.

McKenzie shakes her head and lowers her gaze. "I'll have the ricotta and spinach ravioli."

Antonio makes a quick scratch on his pad and collects the menu's. As he walks away Stephanie stares him down with a way over exuberant smile on her face.

"McKenzie? Can I ask you a question?" Lunar asked as she pulled a cheese stick from the plate stretching the stringy mozzarella way over the table.

"You just did." McKenzie shrugged with a teasing look on her face.

"Haha..." Lunar said duhly so. "How did you pay for college?"

McKenzie sways her head back and forth as she chews the chewy bite, impressed with her early interest in college preparation.

“She’s Pastor Ross’ daughter and their rich, that’s what my daddy always says when my mom gets on the app to pay our tithes at church.”

McKenzie coughs and almost chokes on her bite. “Well actually Lunar.” She speaks with her mouth partially full to keep Stephanie from talking anymore. “I was able to get a scholarship.”

Lunar’s expression fades. “Oh…so your really smart?” She spoke with a depressed tone.

“No Lunar, actually I am not, but you are. I’m sure you will get an academic scholarship, mine however was athletics, I played soccer.” McKenzie speaks and thinks back how she was able to go to college.

“Really?” Lunar’s expressions brightens back up at this revelation. “Don’t they wear short shorts to play that?”

McKenzie nods remembering back to the struggle she had when she first started, wearing a skirt to all the games. “They do, but I did not. I wore one of my sport skirts with tight capris underneath it. But I really wasn’t that good, I didn’t actually play but a couple of times at The U. I sit on the bench mostly, but they paid for my college, so I did so gladly.”

“Ohhh!!!” Stephanie mumbles with her mouthful. “That’s really cool, I didn’t know you played soccer.”

“I did all through high school, I even made a couple of goals.” McKenzie proud of this achievement and glad for the distraction from boys and relationships.

They chatted away as they ate the appetizer and it was only a few minutes until Antonio showed back up. He first places the pizza’s down in front of the girls. Stephanie now googly eyed towards her pizza, ready to devour it.

McKenzie’s eyes bulge out as he sits her plate down in front of her staring at the one single ravioli on the plate. “Oh…My gosh!” She gasps. “That is one gigantic ravioli.” She states as she stares at the enormity of it, wondering how it all fit on the plate.

Thirty-Five

"Good morning Alex, how are you all doing this morning?" Gibraltar walked into the dining area where the crew all sit around the table drinking coffee and chatting.

"Uhh…Doc are you ok?" Beatrice more than surprised by his mood, especially so towards Alex.

"Yea? Why has it not been a good morning around here?" Gibraltar directed his attention to Beatrice, who is working diligently with an organized mess of paper, binders, tablets, and her laptop on the table in front of her.

"Good morning Captain Crichton. Are you hungry? There is still some breakfast leftover, I made oatmeal, eggs, and fresh fruit." Alex offers to get Gibraltar some breakfast.

"No thank you Alex, I appreciate it though. Hey Samuel, you haven't heard from Ja'Maar lately? Have you? I haven't seen or heard from him in almost a week now." Gibraltar walks over and takes a seat at the table, asking this with concern for the PI.

"No sorry, I haven't talked with him in a couple of weeks, at least."

Gibraltar nods as he pours himself a cup of coffee from the carafe on the table in front of him. "Ok." He takes a generous sip of the not to hot brew, wondering his next moves. "Well…I'll swing by his office after while.

So do you all have big plans today?" He asked his crew showing genuine compassion.

"If you consider Alex benching ninety pounds? Big plans? Then I'd say yes." DeAndre gets into the conversation hyping his colleague up. "He's not been able to push the ninety yet, but we have confidence that he's going to bench it soon. Are you ready Alex?" He pushes to get Alex going.

"Umm…do I have to try ninety today, my chest still hurts from the eighty I did a couple days ago. I really don't think I can take ninety on yet." Alex complains of his sore muscles, rubbing on his chest, dreading the extra weight.

"Yes Alex, you have to press ninety today, one full press. Then if you do that I'll cook breakfast the rest of the week." DeAndre makes Alex a deal.

"Please Alex, don't even attempt it. I'd hate for you to tear a muscle, plus DeAndre sucks at cooking breakfast." Beatrice pleads with Alex to not even attempt it, even though she knows she is wasting her breath.

DeAndre takes Alex by the arm, then he and Samuel lead him off to the weight room to get started on their workouts.

"Oh yea Doc!" Beatrice shuffles some of the papers around and makes a couple of key strokes on her laptop. "So Save-the-Books

Foundation is doing way better than I could have ever imagined. We've had over seven thousand in donations since we introduced a couple weeks ago in McKenzie's class, and we haven't even thought about fundraising yet."

Gibraltar gives her a curt nod with perched out lips, thinking about all the money he had already sunk into this thing, and it's a nice thought to have others sharing his interest with him. "Do you have any ideas for some fundraisers?" He asked.

She stops typing and leans back in her chair. "Yes." She pauses to think about what she wants to say. "I have one or two ideas, but I haven't came up with any solid plans yet. I'll let you know as soon as I do though, or if you have any I would be open for suggestions. I was really kinda thinking about a barb-a-que here with a couple of games, or them bouncy houses…You know…something simple, I don't want to get too elaborate with it. Really its going to have to wait until after the first of the year anyways."

"Hmm." Gibraltar stands and grabs his cup of coffee off of the table. "I like that…simple…I was thinking more along the lines of renting a ball room, paying a orchestra, catering a hundred dollar plate for about a thousand kids, and give them each a tablet to read, but a barb-a-que and bouncy houses sounds more fun."

Beatrice shuts down the tablets and begins to work on further organizing her mess. “Doc this isn’t politics, this is for our kids, and they don’t care about all that fancy expensive stuff. If you wanted to pad the pockets to the crooks in DC you should have thought up a different Non-Profit.”

This stops Gibraltar at the door, hitting a soft spot knowing that the most evil man he has ever met is about to take a very high position in the state. “Hey that’s not right, our political leaders are suppose to be helping our country. We’re suppose to vote them in because they are trying to help us, not because they have the most money to impress people with…Ahh!!!” He all but cusses back at her, the thought of political agenda’s makes him so mad talking about it.

“Whoa!!!Doc, sorry I didn’t mean to hit a soft spot, but seriously if your that worried about it, and it makes you that mad, then why don’t you get into the politics?”

“Thank you Bea…” Gibraltar’s anger eases with her questionable statement. “For all of your hard work, and telling me the things I may not want to hear, but need to hear.” He bows to her showing his sincerity as he exits the dining area.

Walking down the hall Gibraltar thinks hard about her last comment, that maybe he should get into politics, that maybe it would be easier to stop all the hateful, belligerent jerks from selfishly doing whatever they can to help themselves, not at all thinking about others or our future in a whole.

He walks through the wide open door to his office, and no sooner than he gets sit down behind his desk the alarms start blaring. “Ugh!” He sighs at the timing.

“Station Thirteen.” He hears Barbie call with static over the radio. “We have a news five helicopter crash landed on top of a three story house.” She calls this emergency over the radio, then gives the address to where it is at.

Gibraltar jumps out of his chair at lightning speed, runs back out of the door, and runs into Beatrice in the hallway, neither say anything as they both run to slide down the pole.

Once they get to the garage Beatrice goes over to the ambulance, while Gibraltar ran over to engine one, where the team are all sweaty and putting on their fire man attire over their gym clothes. “I’m with you guys, lets go!” He yells out rushing them into the truck as he jumps up into the passenger seat to the large ladder truck.

Gibraltar makes a couple quick taps on his phone, getting garage doors one, and three to open simultaneously. “Hey Barbie…Doc here, are we going to need our other crew for this one?” He calls back to his dispatch over his radio. “They’ll probably take thirty minutes or more.” He adds.

"Yea Doc, call them. I even have two other stations dispatched, they'll probably be that long also. This is an all hands on deck situation." Barbie lets him know to get as much help as he can involved.

Samuel gets in the drivers seat and fires up the engine, waiting on the air pressure to build before he disengaged the brakes.

"Barbie give us some more information, what we got we're a little less than ten minutes out." Gibraltar attempts to find out everything he can before they get there.

Samuel pulls the truck out of the bay and turns on the lights and sirens. The street light already has the traffic stopped so they are able to pull straight out onto the highway.

"Unsure if there are any casualty's yet, there are two patrol cars there. They are sitting up a perimeter to keep the crowd back. From what I have gathered the helicopter is dangling on the edge of the house as though it is about to come crashing down, nose first." Barbie explains the best she can of the situation at hand.

Gibraltar looks at his crew behind him, all sitting there quiet with worried faces. "Ok thanks Barbie." He turns back around in his seat. "Ok team…this sounds like it is going to be a tricky situation, keep your focus, stay aware, and be safe." He gives them all a short motivational speech in attempt to encourage them…and himself.

They round the corner and turned onto the street that dispatch had given them. They immediately see smoke billowing a few blocks down. On the street there are two patrol cars with their officers taping off a huge area to keep people out.

Gibraltar leans over, looking out of the window and grateful that the smoke doesn't seem to have any flames to it, but does not like the rest of what he see's. "Hey Barbie? How big is the crew on the helicopter?" He questioned dispatch as he looked at the wreckage that was just as she had explained it. He was really expecting a wrecked mess, but the helicopter appeared to be in tact.

"There are only two on board, I'm guessing one is a co-pilot/cameraman." She gives him the information.

"10—4 Barbie." Gibraltar continues assessing the wreck through the windshield. "Pull the truck up over in the yard there." He points out the direction for his Lieutenant. "I don't see any movement in there, they could be knocked out, it looks like they had a pretty hard landing. LT, you and DeAndre get the ladder up to the top of the house towards the middle. First thing we need to do is get that thing secured, it looks as though it could come crashing down any moment."

They all give a panicked 'ok' as Samuel parks the fire truck in the yard. Swiftly they all jump out, Gibraltar walks around the front of the truck, looking up the whole time making calculations in his mind, at the same time as making sure he cant see any movement.

Barry starts to work on the controls to the ladder while Samuel and DeAndre get ropes and harnesses out, to hopefully get the helicopter secured.

"Alex!" Gibraltar yells. "Grab me the bull horn." He finally see's movement from the cab of the aircraft. Thankful, but also worried they might rock it off the house.

"Ye sir!" Alex quickly scurries off to the truck.

Gibraltar makes his way a little closer, careful not to get completely underneath the potential crashing point, but close enough to see exactly what he is working with.

Alex comes rushing back with the loud speaker in his arms. "Ok Alex, you stay with me in case I need something else. And under no circumstances do you get any closer to this side of the house." Gibraltar demands this.

"Captain!" Gibraltar Speaks into the bull horn. "This is Miami Dade Fire Department, we are currently working to get you and your co-pilot out of there. I am sure you are probably hurting, but I need you two to keep as still as possible to keep the aircraft from crashing down."

No sooner than Gibraltar finished announcing this flames burst out in the engine underneath the rotors. “Crap Alex, lets get a hose out.” He calls over to Alex as they run quickly back to the truck. “Hurry up guys, you have to get that thing secured. We have to hose it down, and I’m afraid the water pressure will be too much.” He calls over the radio watching Samuel and DeAndre make their way up the ladder.

As Gibraltar is pulling out the fire hose he glances back at the pilot, who is now relentlessly moving with the flames getting closer. He lifts the bull horn back up. “Captain! I need you to please remain calm, you are causing the aircraft to shimmy, and its about to crash down from its perch.”

“Ruff…Ruff…” A Chihuahua barks and runs in front of the truck towards the house, right under the helicopter and continues to furiously bark at the now engulfed aircraft.

Alex takes off running towards the house to go and retrieve the dog. Just as soon as Alex picked up the riling dog the helicopter comes tumbling down on top of them bursting into a huge ball of flames.

“Nooooo!!!!!! ALEXXXXX!!!!!” Gibraltar throws the hose down, unhinges the bull horn tossing it aside, and runs towards the flaming wreckage with his out-cry!

Epilogue

The next day Gibraltar sits at his desk in his office sulking, depressed, and unable to think, concentrate, or do any of the work he had set out before him. Then he hears a knock on his closed door, a door he has never closed. “Uhh…” He sighs out not really wanting any company, but also unable to leave his team hanging, he quickly gets up to go answer it.

When he opens the door he was expecting to see one of his crew members, who are all just as tore up about things as he is. But to his surprise before him stands a large built man, dressed in a suit and tie. “Captain Crichton.” The man reaches out a hand. “I’m Pastor Ross.” He said this as solemnly as one could.

As they shook hands Gibraltar’s mind goes immediately to McKenzie. ***Oh my God, this is her father. He’s a Pastor?*** He questions himself. “Umm…What can I do for you?” He questioned very nervously with a crackle in his voice.

“Can we have a seat?” The Pastor pushes himself into the office without an answer.

“Yea of course.” Gibraltar steps back when he realized it wasn’t really a question.

He walks around his desk to take his seat at the same time Pastor Ross takes an opposing one. “Can I get you a water, coffee, or anything else maybe?”

“No.” The Pastor waves him off and begins to talk. “No thank you, I’m ok. So I am Alex’s Pastor.” He pauses momentarily to collect his own emotions.

Gibraltar can tell he has been doing this a while, and it is almost as though he is numb from it, yet he certainly wasn’t an emotionless man, it still hurts.

“He was such a an amazing young man, and we all really loved him deeply at Ocean Breeze Apostolic Church.”

Gibraltar’s conscious works hard on him as he hears the Pastor talk about Alex and the church. “Yes sir.” He mumbled as he sadly gazes at his desk. “He was loved here…also.” Gibraltar begins to sob, thinking about all the horrid times where he failed to show Alex care and respect. “I just wish I wouldn’t have screwed up and let this happen.” He continued to cry as he blamed himself for this horrible accident.

“Captain Crichton, this was an accident which is an unfortunate circumstance of the job, and God doesn’t do anything for no reason. So we need to remember this, no matter how sad this situation may be God has a purpose here. Alex died not only saved and washed in the blood, but a hero. I truly believe that God is going to use his legacy to help raise the awareness and importance of all of our service workers, so that they will be more recognized and noticed." Pastor Ross spoke humbly of his intentions to make Alex live on.

Gibraltar listens to him intently so, understanding it in many ways. It does not make the pain any easier to deal with, but giving him some sort of awareness, that maybe God does have some sort of existence, and plans in place. He quickly dismisses the thoughts to get back to their conversation. "Yes sir, maybe your right. I sure hope this can teach us all some things, but I was still in charge and he died on my watch, it was my fault!"

Pastor Ross looks Gibraltar dead in the eyes. "Well Captain, if that's how you feel, I know I cant change this. I am here to ask you if you could read Alex's eulogy. You was his Captain and he always spoke highly of you. He greatly appreciated you, and looked up to you."

These words stabbed Gibraltar hard in the heart and he is unable to keep his composure and begins to ball. "I'm…I'm…" He stutters having a difficult time speaking.

"No its ok, there is nothing to apologize for here Captain." Pastor Ross speaks soothingly with a very experienced voice.

Gibraltar grabs a tissue from the box he just recently added to his desk, then slowly nods. “Yes…I’ll give Alex’s eulogy…” He cried out very somberly.

Acknowledgements/Apologies

I would like to thank a great many of people that have been there throughout my life. I wont be thanking any of you individually, but all of you my family and friends, (know who you are) and certainly do have my appreciation, although I have not always shown it so.

I would like to also throw out a big thanks to the Solomon's Porch Ministry for giving me a safe and welcoming place to finish writing, editing, and publishing this work. You all have been a big help and so generous, this was something I was more desperate for than I realized.

Last but not least, I would like to thank the United Pentecostal Church International for showing and branding these core values into my soul.

I have offend a great many of people (especially you ladies) and for all of these actions I am truly sorrowful. I do and continue to make mistakes everyday, just hopefully from here on out I can mostly keep these on paper with fictitious characters. If I have offended any of you in any way, I do honestly seek your forgiveness, because I do honestly want to be a better person, and will always want to be a better person, for I know this is the closest thing to perfection any of us can ever have.

Author's Notes

While I was writing this book I had a lot of fun, I laughed a little, got mad from time to time, and I cried a lot (still do every time I read certain parts). Even though these are made up characters, I truly have felt all of their emotions. This can be a difficult thing while writing.

Now I would like you all to know, that I have never actually even been to Miami, so I am sure I didn't get much right there, sorry. Especially when it came to Station Thirteen, I'm sure I didn't get much right there. Sorry that I picked on you all so much, you were just the lucky number my mind came up with.

Lastly I am really sorry about such a heartbreaker of an ending. I promise you this was not something I chose to do lightly. I quickly grew to love Alex, and even more so throughout the entirety of my writings. So it definitely wasn't an easy decision.

If you have any questions, concerns, comments, or complaints you are welcome to email me directly at brantyarbrough7@gmail.com or find and like me on Facebook or LinkedIn. Thank you all for your support!

Made in the USA
Columbia, SC
13 May 2025

57861261R10237